# Krondor the Assassins

## Also by Raymond E. Feist

*Magician*
*Silverthorn*
*A Darkness at Sethanon*

*Faerie Tale*

*Prince of the Blood*
*The King's Buccaneer*

*Shadow of a Dark Queen*
*Rise of a Merchant Prince*
*Rage of a Demon King*
*Shards of a Broken Crown*

*Krondor: The Betrayal*


## With Janny Wurts

*Daughter of the Empire*
*Servant of the Empire*
*Mistress of the Empire*

# Krondor the Assassins

## BOOK TWO OF THE RIFTWAR LEGACY

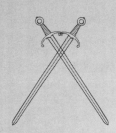

# RAYMOND E. FEIST

AVON BOOKS, INC.
1350 Avenue of the Americas
New York, New York 10019

www.avonbooks.com/eos

This book is dedicated to all the editors who have put up with, inspired, corrected, and aided me, to the ends of improving the work and making me look good: Adrian Zackheim, Nick Austin, Pat LoBrutto, Janna Silverstein, Malcolm Edwards, and my current guides, Jennifer Brehl and Jane Johnson.

Also, to Peter Schneider, who has done far more on my behalf than he realizes.

My deepest thanks to them all.

Raymond E. Feist
Rancho Santa Fe, CA
May 1999

# ACKNOWLEDGMENTS

This book is the outgrowth of a lot of imaginations besides my own. I am indebted to the following people:

John Cutter, Neal Halford, Bill Maxwell, Andy Ashcraft, Josh Kulp, Craig Bollan, and Erik Wycheck at Dynamix, 7th Level, and Pyrotechnix, for creating interesting characters and situations for the games, Betrayal at Krondor and Return to Krondor, which provided characters, situations, and ideas that coalesced into this novel.

Also, and as usual, I stand in debt to the imagination and creative support given me by the usual suspects, also known as the Friday Nighters. Without them, Midkemia wouldn't exist and I would have had to find another job.

# CONTENTS

PROLOGUE

# DEPARTURES

INES of soldiers marched along the ridge.

The baggage train had been broken into two segments, the first of which was now departing with the wounded and the dead who would be cremated with honors back in Krondor. Clouds of dust rose from the trail as wheels rolled and boots tramped toward home, the fine powder mixing with the acrid smoke from campfires as they were extinguished. The rising sun streamed through the haze, orange and pale gold, lances of color in an otherwise gray morning. In the distance birds sang, ignoring the aftermath of battle.

Arutha, Prince of Krondor and ruler of the Western Realm of the Kingdom of the Isles, sat on his horse, taking a moment to enjoy the majesty of the sunrise and the serenade of the birds as he watched his men heading home. The fighting had been blessedly short but bloody, and while casualties were lighter than anticipated, he still hated to lose even one soldier under his command. He let the beauty of the vista before him soothe his frustration and regret for a few moments.

Arutha still resembled the youthful man who had come to

the throne of Krondor ten years before, though lines around his eyes and a small scattering of gray through his otherwise black hair revealed the toll rulership had taken on him. For those who knew him well, he was still much the same man, a competent administrator, military genius, and fiercely duty-bound man who would surrender his own life without question to save the lowest soldier under his command.

His gaze went from wagon to wagon, as if somehow willing himself to see the wounded men inside, as if he could communicate to them his sense of gratitude for a job well done. Those closest to Arutha knew he paid a silent price, pain kept within, for each injury done a man who served Krondor and the Kingdom.

Arutha pushed aside his regrets and considered the victory. The enemy had been in full retreat for two days, a relatively small force of dark elves. A much larger force had been prevented from reaching the Dimwood when a rift machine had been destroyed by Arutha's two squires, James and Locklear. It had cost the life of a magician named Patrus, but his sacrifice had allowed the invaders to fall prey to their own internal conflicts. Delekhan, the would-be conqueror, had died beside Gorath, a moredhel chieftain who had proven as honorable and worthy a being as Arutha had ever met, while they struggled to seize control of the Lifestone. Arutha cursed the existence of that mysterious and ancient artifact under the abandoned city of Sethanon, and wondered if its mystery would ever be understood, its danger removed, in his lifetime.

Delekhan's son Moraeulf had died from a dagger thrust home by Narab, once an ally of Delekhan. As agreed to by Narab, the retreating moredhel weren't being harassed by Kingdom forces as long as they were heading straight north. Orders had been dispatched to allow the moredhel safe passage home as long as they kept moving.

The Kingdom forces in the Dimwood were now dispersing to their various garrisons, the majority returning to the west, and some heading back north to the border baronies. They would start moving later in the morning. The previously secret garrison north of Sethanon would be moved to another location and reprovisioned.

Sunlight began to bathe Arutha as the morning mist burned off, leaving only the smoke and dust to cloud the air. The day was already growing hot, and the cold of the previous winter was fading from memory. Arutha kept his distress deep inside as he considered the latest assault upon the tranquillity of his Kingdom.

Arutha had taken the Tsurani magicians at face value after the end of the Riftwar. For nearly ten years they had been free to come and go between worlds, via several magic rifts. And now he felt a profound sense of betrayal. He fully understood the rationale that had driven Makala, a Tsurani Great One, to attempt to seize the Lifestone at Sethanon, the belief that the Kingdom possessed a great weapon of destruction, some engine of power that would give predominance in war to whoever held it. Had he been in Makala's place, with the same suspicions, he might have acted in the same way. But even so, he could not trust the Tsurani to be loose in the Kingdom, and that meant an end to almost a decade of trade and exchange. Arutha pushed aside worry as to how he would effect the changes he must make, but he knew that eventually he would have to sit down with his advisors and fashion a plan that would ensure future security for the Kingdom. And he knew almost no one would be pleased at the changes he would make.

Arutha glanced to his right and saw two very fatigued young men sitting astride their horses. He permitted himself one of his infrequent smiles, a bare upturning of the sides of his mouth, which served to soften the often somber expression on his still-youthful face. "Tired, gentlemen?" he asked.

James, senior squire to the Prince, returned his ruler's gaze from eyes surrounded by dark circles. James, and his companion Squire Locklear, had ridden a punishing ride, abetted by magic herbs which had kept them awake and alert for days in the saddle. The after-effects of the prolonged use of the draught was to unleash all the pent-up fatigue and body-ache on the young men at once. Both had slept through the night, upon cushions in Arutha's tent, but had awakened tired and bone-weary. Summoning up his usual brazen wit, James said, "No, sire, we always look like this when we wake. Usually you don't see us until after our morning coffee."

Arutha laughed. "I see none of your charms have faded, squire."

A short man with dark hair and beard walked over to where the Prince and his companions sat astride their horses.

"Good morning, Highness," said Pug, as he bowed.

Arutha returned a polite nod and said, "Pug, do you return to Krondor with us?"

Pug's expression revealed concern. "Not straightaway, Highness. There are matters I must investigate at Stardock. The activities of the Tsurani Great Ones involved with this last attempt at Sethanon cause me great concern. I need to ensure that they were the only magicians involved, and that those who still reside at my Academy are free of any guilt."

Arutha looked at the retreating wagons again as he said,

"We do need to talk about the role played by the Tsurani in your Academy, Pug. But not here."

Pug nodded agreement. Even though everyone within earshot was privy to the secret of the Lifestone which sat beneath the city of Sethanon, it was wise to talk only in private. And Pug also knew that Arutha had grave concerns about the betrayal by the Tsurani magician Makala which had led to this last battle between the Prince's army and an invading army of moredhel warriors. He expected that Arutha would insist on far more stringent controls over who and what came through the rift—the magic gateway—between Midkemia and the Tsurani homeworld of Kelewan.

"We will, Highness. First, I must see to the safety of Katala and Gamina."

"I understand your concerns," said the Prince. Pug's daughter Gamina had been abducted and transported by magic to a distant world in order to lure him away from Midkemia while the Tsurani magician attempted to seize the Lifestone.

Pug said, "I must make sure that I am never again made vulnerable because of a family member." He looked knowingly at the Prince. "There's nothing I can do about William, but I can ensure that Gamina and Katala are safe at Stardock."

"William is a soldier, so by the nature of his craft he is at risk." Then Arutha smiled at Pug. "But he's as safe as a soldier can be, surrounded by six companies of the Royal Krondorian Household Guard. Anyone attempting to blackmail you through William will find him difficult to reach."

Pug's expression showed he didn't approve. "He could have been so much more." His look silently implored Arutha to do something. "He still can. It's not too late for him to return to Stardock with me."

Arutha regarded the magician. He understood Pug's frustration and his parental desire to see his son back with his family. But his tone left no confusion as to his willingness to intercede on Pug's behalf. "I know you two have had your differences about his choice, Pug, but I'll leave it for you to work out at your own leisure. As I told you when you first objected to William coming into my service, he's a royal cousin by adoption and a free man of age, so there was no reason for me to refuse his request." Before Pug could voice another objection, he raised his hand. "Not even as a favor to you." His tone softened. "Besides, he's got the makings of a better than average soldier. Quite a knack, actually, according to my swordmaster." Arutha changed the subject. "Did Owyn return home?" Owyn Belefote, youngest son of the Baron of Timons, had proven a valuable ally to James and Locklear in the recent struggle.

"At first light. He said he must mend fences with his father."

Arutha motioned toward Locklear, though he kept his eyes on Pug. "I have something for you." When Locklear failed to respond to the gesture, Arutha shifted his gaze to Locklear. "*Squire*, the document?"

Locklear had been on the verge of falling asleep in the saddle but he snapped to attention as the Prince's voice penetrated his muzzy thoughts. He moved his horse to where Pug stood and handed a parchment down to him.

Arutha said, "Over my signature and seal, this names you the final authority over all issues of magic as they affect the Western Realm." He smiled slightly. "I should have no trouble convincing His Majesty to ratify this for the entire Kingdom. You've had our ear in this area for years, Pug, but this gives you authority if you ever find yourself having to deal with another noble or King's officer without me at your shoulder. It names you official magician of the court of Krondor."

"My thanks, Highness," said Pug. He seemed about to speak, but hesitated.

Arutha cocked his head to one side. "There's a but here, isn't there?"

"But I need remain at Stardock with my family. There's much work to be done and my attention there precludes me from serving in Krondor, Arutha."

Arutha sighed slightly. "Understood. But that still leaves me without a magician in court, if you're unwilling to take residency in the palace."

"I could send Kulgan back to nag at you," said Pug with a smile.

"No, my former teacher is too quick to forget rank and scold me in front of my court. It's bad for morale."

"Whose?" asked Jimmy under his breath.

Arutha didn't look at the squire, but said, "Mine, of course." To Pug he said, "Seriously, the betrayal of Makala shows me the wisdom my father employed by having an advisor on matters of magic close to hand. Kulgan's earned his retirement. So, if not you or young Owyn, who then?"

Pug thought for a moment and said, "I have one student who might be just the person to advise you in the future. There is one problem."

"What would that be?" asked Arutha.

"She's Keshian."

Arutha said, "That's two problems."

Put smiled. "Knowing your sister and wife, I would have thought a woman's advice wouldn't be alien to His Highness."

Arutha nodded. "It's not. But many in my court would find it . . . difficult."

Pug said, "I've never noticed you to be overly concerned with the opinions of others when your mind was set, Arutha."

The Prince said, "Times change, Pug. And men get older." He was silent for a minute as he watched another contingent of his army break camp and start to move out. Then he turned to face Pug, one eyebrow raised in question. "But Keshian?"

"No one will accuse her of allying herself with this or that faction in court," said Pug.

Arutha chuckled. "I hope you're joking."

"No, I'm not. She's unusually gifted despite her youth; she's cultured and educated, reads and writes several languages, and has a remarkable grasp of magic, which is exactly what you need in an advisor. Most importantly, she's the only one among my students who can understand the consequences of magic in a political context, as she's had court training in Kesh. She's from the Jal-Pur and understands how things stand in the west, as well."

Arutha seemed to consider this for a long moment, then said, "Come to Krondor when you can and tell me more. I'm not saying I will not finally agree to your choice, but I need more convincing before I do." Arutha smiled his half-smile and turned his horse around. "Still, the expression on the faces of the nobles in court when a woman from Kesh walks in might be worth whatever risk she brings."

"I will vouch for her; I give my word on it," said Pug.

Arutha looked back over his shoulder. "You're very serious about this, aren't you?"

"Very. Jazhara is someone I would entrust my family's lives to. She is only a few years older than William and has been with us at Stardock for almost seven years, so I've known her a third of her life. She can be trusted."

Arutha said, "That counts for much. A great deal actually. So, come to Krondor when you will, and we will discuss this at length." He bade Pug good-bye, then turned to James and Locklear. "Gentlemen, we have a long ride ahead."

Locklear could barely conceal his pain at the thought of more time in the saddle, albeit at a less furious pace than a few days earlier.

"A moment, if Your Highness permits. I would speak to Duke Pug," said James.

Arutha waved his permission as he and Locklear rode forward.

When the Prince was out of earshot, Pug said, "What is it, Jimmy?"

"When are you going to tell him?"

"What?" asked Pug.

Despite his crushing fatigue, James managed one of his familiar grins. "That the girl you're sending is the great-niece of Lord Hazara-Khan of the Jal-Pur."

Pug suppressed a chuckle. "I thought I'd save that for a more propitious moment." Then his expression changed to one of curiosity. "How did you know that?"

"I have my own sources. Arutha suspects that Lord Hazara-Khan is involved with Keshian intelligence in the west—which he almost certainly is, from what I can find out. Anyway, Arutha is considering how to counter Keshian intelligence with an organization of his own—but you didn't hear that from me."

Pug nodded. "Understood."

"And as I have ambitions, I count it a wise thing to keep current on these matters."

10

"So you were snooping?"

"Something like that," said James with a shrug. "And there just can't be that many noble-born Keshian women from the Jal-Pur named Jazhara."

Pug laughed. "You will go far, Jimmy, if someone doesn't hang you first."

James seemed to shed his fatigue as he returned the laugh. "You're not the first to say that, Pug."

"I will get around to mentioning the relationship, in the future." Waving to Arutha and Locklear, Pug said, "You'd better catch up."

Nodding as he turned his horse, James said, "You're right. Good day, my lord duke."

"Good day, squire."

James put heels to his horse's sides and the animal cantered after Arutha and Locklear. He overtook Locklear as Arutha moved to confer with Knight-Marshal Gardan about the ongoing dispersal of the army.

As James rode up next to him, Locklear asked, "What was that about?"

"Just a question for Duke Pug."

Locklear yawned and said, "I could sleep for a week."

Arutha overheard the remark as he rejoined them and said, "You can rest for a full night in Krondor when we get back, squire. Then you leave for the north."

"North, sire?"

"You came back from Tyr-Sog without leave, although I grand your reasons were good ones. Now the risk has subsided, you must return to Baron Moyiet's court and fulfill the terms of your service there."

Locklear closed his eyes as if in pain. Then he opened them and said, "I thought . . ."

". . . you'd wormed your way out of that banishment," supplied James under his breath.

Arutha, taking pity on the exhausted youth, said, "Serve Moyiet well, and I may order you back to Krondor early. *If* you stay out of trouble."

Locklear nodded without comment, as Arutha put heels to his horse and rode ahead.

James said, "Well, you can sleep in a warm bed in the palace for a night before you leave."

"What about you?" asked Locklear. "Don't you have some unfinished business in Krondor?"

James closed his eyes for a moment as if thinking made him tired, then said, "Yes, there's a bit of trouble with the Guild of Thieves. But nothing for you to be bothered with. Nothing I can't handle myself."

Locklear snorted and said nothing. He was too tired to think of a jibe.

James said, "Yes, after this nasty business with the Tsurani and moredhel, my business with the thieves in Krondor will seem dull by comparison."

Locklear looked at his friend and saw that James's mind was already turning to whatever problems were caused by the Mockers—the Guild of Thieves. And with a chilling certainty, Locklear knew that his friend was making light of something serious, for James had the death mark on him for leaving the Guild to serve the Prince.

And, he sensed, there was something more. Then Locklear realized, with James, there was always something more.

# ONE

## ESCAPE

$\mathcal{T}$HE sounds of pursuit echoed through the dark tunnels.

Limm was nearly out of breath from attempting to evade those determined to kill him. The young thief prayed to Ban-ath, God of Thieves, that those who followed were not as knowledgeable about the sewers of Krondor as he was. He knew he could not outrun them or fight them; his only hope was to outwit them.

The boy knew that panic was the enemy, and he struggled against the terrible fear that threatened to reduce him to a frightened child, clinging to anything that might provide warm comfort while he huddled in the shadows, waiting for the men who would kill him. He paused for a moment at an intersection of two large channels and then took off to the left, feeling his way through the gloom of the deep sewers, his only illumination a small, shuttered lantern. He kept the sliding window closed to the narrowest setting, for he needed only the slightest light to know which way to go. There were sections of the sewer in which light filtered down from above, through culverts, gratings, broken street stones, and other interstices. A little

14

light went a long way to guide him through the stinking byways under the city. But there were also areas of total darkness, where he would be as blind as one born without eyes.

He reached a narrowing of the sewer, where the circumference of the circular tunnel grew smaller, serving to slow the flow of sewage through this area. Limm thought of it as a "dam," of sorts. He ducked to avoid hitting his head on the smaller opening, his bare feet splashing through the filthy water which collected at the end of the larger sewer until the level rose up enough to funnel down the rough and rusty narrow pipe.

Spreading his legs, Limm moved in a rocking motion, his feet high up on the side of the circular passage, for he knew that in less than ten feet a nasty outfall sent waste to a huge channel twenty feet below. Hard calluses kept the jagged build-up of sediment on the stonework from slicing open his soles. The boy shuttered the lantern as he intersected a tunnel with long lines of sight; he knew exactly where he was and was fearful of even the smallest light being seen by his pursuers. He moved by touch around a corner and entered the next passage. It was hundreds of feet long, and even the faintest spark would be visible from one end to the other.

Hurrying as best he could in this awkward fashion, he felt the tug of air as the water fell below him from a hole in the pipe he was in, splashing noisily. Several other nearby outfalls also emptied in this area, known as "the Well" to the local thieves. The sound of all the splashing water echoed in the small pipe, making its exact source difficult to locate, so he proceeded slowly. This was a place in which a six-inch misjudgment could send him falling to his death.

Reaching a point another ten feet further, Limm encountered a grate, almost bumping into it, so focused was he on the sound of those who came behind. He crouched, making himself as small a target as possible, in case a mirrored light was shone into the tunnel.

Within moments he heard voices, at first only the sound of indistinguishable words. Then he heard a man say, "—can't have gone too far. He's just a kid."

"He's seen us," said the leader, and the boy knew full well who the speaker was. He had the image of that man and those who served him etched in his memory, though he had only glimpsed them for a few seconds before turning and fleeing. He didn't know the man's name, but he knew his nature. The boy had lived among such men all his life, though he had known only a few who might be this dangerous.

Limm had no illusions about his own abilities; he knew he could never confront such men. He was often full of bravado, but it was a false courage designed to convince those who were stronger that he was just a little more trouble to dispose of than he was in actuality. His willingness to look death in the eye had saved the boy's neck on more than one occasion; but he was also nobody's fool: Limm knew that these men wouldn't give him the time to even try a bluff. They would kill him without hesitation, because he could link them to a horrible crime.

Looking around, the young fugitive saw a trickle of water coming from above. Risking detection, he briefly shone the barest light he could manage above him. The top of the grating didn't reach the roof of the tunnel, and just the other side of the grate was a passageway running upward.

Without hesitation the youth climbed up on the grate and pushed his free arm through, experience showing him how likely it was that he might pass through such a tiny passage. Praying to Ban-ath that he hadn't grown too much since the last time he had tried such a stunt, Limm pushed upward and turned. His head went first. Twisting it slightly, he thrust his face forward between the top bar and the stones above. Practice had taught him that his ears would suffer less if not bent backwards as he tried to pull his head through. A rising sense of urgency battled the pain he felt, as he sensed his pursuers closing in. Yet the pain from his cheeks as he slowly pressed through the gap grew more intense. He tasted the salty, iron tang of blood and sweat and he continued to wiggle his head through the gap. Tears flowed freely, yet he held his silence as he cruelly scraped both ears, one against stone and the other against filthy iron. For an instant panic threatened to rise up and overwhelm him as images of him hanging helpless in the grate while his pursuers raced to seize him played vividly in his imagination.

Then his head was past the top bar. He easily snaked his arm through, and he moved his shoulder. Hoping he wouldn't have to dislocate his joints to get through, the young thief continued. He got his shoulders through and, by exhaling, his chest followed. He held the lantern in his trailing arm and realized it wouldn't fit through the gap.

Taking a deep breath, the boy let it fall as he twisted the rest of his body through. He was now on the other side of the grate, clinging to it like a ladder as the lantern clattered onto the stones.

"He's in there!" came a shout from close by and a light shone into the tunnel.

Limm held himself poised for a moment, and looked up. The hole above him was barely visible in the faint light hurrying toward him. He shoved upward, slapping his palms against the tunnel walls, keeping his feet firmly on the grate. He pressed hard with both hands on the sides of the vertical shaft. He needed solid hand-holds before he pushed off the grate. He felt around and got his fingers into a deep seam between two stones on one side and had just found another when he felt something touch his bare foot.

Instantly he pushed off with his feet, and heard a voice cursing. "Damn all sewer rats!"

Another voice said, "We can't get through there!"

"But my blade can!"

Summoning all his strength the young thief pulled himself up into the shaft, and in a dangerous move, released his hold on the top of the grate, dropped his hands to his side, and pushed upward. He slapped his palms backwards and braced his back against the wall of the chimney, and pulled his feet up, jamming them acrobatically against the far wall. He heard the scrape of steel on iron as someone shoved a sword through the grating. Limm knew that had he hesitated, he would have been impaled on the point of that long blade.

A voice swore and said, "He vanished up that chimney!"

Another voice said, "He's got to come out somewhere on the level above!"

For an instant Limm could feel the shirt on his back move as the material slipped against the wall and his bare feet skidded on the slimy stones. He pressed harder with his feet and prayed he could hold his position. After an instant of downward movement, he stopped.

"He's gone!" shouted one of the men who had been chasing him. "If he was going to fall, he'd have been out of there by now!"

The boy recognized the voice of the leader. "Head back up to the next level and spread out! There's a bonus for whoever kills him! I want that rat dead before morning!"

Limm moved upward, one hand, one foot, another hand, another foot, by inches, slipping down an inch for every two he gained. It was slow going and his muscles cried out for a pause, but he pressed on. A cool whiff of air from above told him he was close to the next level of the sewers. He prayed it was a large enough pipe to navigate, as he had no desire to attempt another passage downward and back through that grate.

Reaching the lip of the shaft, he paused, took a deep breath and turned, snatching at the edge. One hand slipped on something thick and sticky, but the other hand held firm. Never one for bathing, nevertheless he looked forward to scrubbing this muck off and finding clean clothing.

Hanging in the silence, the boy waited. He knew it was possible that the men who had pursued him might appear in a few moments. He listened.

Impulsive by nature, the boy had come to learn the dangers of acting rashly in dangerous situations. Seven boys had come to Mother's, the Mockers' safe haven, at roughly the same time, within a few weeks of one another. The other six were now dead. Two had died by accident: falling from the rooftops. Three had been hanged as common thieves during crack-downs by the Prince's magistrates. The last boy had died the previous night, at the hands of the men who now sought Limm, and it was his murder the young thief had witnessed.

The boy let his racing heart calm and his straining lungs recover. He pulled himself up and into the large pipe, and moved off in the darkness, a hand on the right wall. He knew he could negotiate most of the tunnels hereabout blindfolded, but he also knew it only took one wrong turn or missing a side tunnel in passing to become completely lost. There was a central cistern in this quarter of the city, and knowing where he was in relationship to it provided Limm with a navigational aid as good as any map, but only if he kept his wits about him and concentrated.

He inched along, listening to the distant sound of gurgling water, turning his head this way and that to ensure he was hearing the sound coming down the sewer and not a false echo bouncing off nearby stones. While he moved blindly, he thought about the madness that had come to the city in recent weeks.

At first it had seemed like a minor problem: a new rival gang, like others that had shown up from time to time. Usually a visit from the Mockers' bashers, or a tip to the sheriff's men, and the problem went away.

This time, it had been different.

A new gang showed up on the docks, a large number of Keshian thugs among them. That alone wasn't worth notice; Krondor was a major port of trade with Kesh. What made this group unusual was their indifference to the threat posed by the Mockers. They acted in a provocative fashion, openly moving cargo into and out of the city, bribing officials and daring the Mockers to interfere with them. They seemed to be inviting a confrontation.

At last the Mockers had acted, and it had been a disaster. Eleven of the most feared bashers—the enforcers among the Guild of Thieves—had been lured into a warehouse at the end of a semi-deserted dock. They had been trapped inside and the building set afire, killing all eleven. From that moment on, warfare had erupted deep in Krondor's underworld.

The Mockers had been driven to ground, and the invaders, working for someone known only as the Crawler, had also suffered, as the Prince of Krondor had acted to restore order to his city.

Rumor had it some men dressed as Nighthawks—members of the Guild of Assassins—had been seen weeks before in the sewer, bait to bring the Prince's army in after them, with the final destruction of the Mockers as the apparent goal. It was a foregone conclusion that had the Prince's guard entered the sewers in sufficient numbers, everyone found down below the streets—assassins, false Nighthawks, or Mockers—all would be routed out or captured. It was a clever plan, but it had come to naught.

Squire James, once Jimmy the Hand of the Mockers, had foiled that ruse, before vanishing into the night on a mission for the Prince. Then the Prince had mustered his army and moved out—and again the Crawler had struck.

Since then, the two sides had stayed holed up, the Mockers at Mother's, their well-disguised headquarters, and the Crawler's men at an unknown hideout in the north docks area. Those sent to pinpoint the exact location of the Crawler's headquarters failed to return.

The sewers had become a no-man's land, with few daring to come and go unless driven by the greatest need. Limm would now be lying low, safe at Mother's, save for two things: a terrible rumor, and a message from an old friend. Either the rumor or the message alone would have made Limm huddle in a corner at the Mockers' hideout, but the combination of the two had forced him to act.

Mockers had few friends; the loyalty between thieves was rarely engendered by affection or comity, but from a greater distrust of those outside the Guild and fear of one another. Strength or wit earned one a place in the Brotherhood of Thieves.

But occasionally a friendship was struck, a bond deeper than common need, and those few friends were worth a bit more risk. Limm counted fewer than a handful of people for whom he would take any risk, let alone at such a high price should he be caught, but two of them were in need now, and had to be told of the rumor.

Something moved in the darkness ahead and Limm froze. He waited, listening for anything out of the ordinary. The sewer was far from silent, with a constant background noise made up of the distant rumble of water rushing through the large culvert below that took the city's refuse out past the harbor mouth, a thousand drips, the scrabble of rats and other vermin and their squeaky challenges.

Wishing he had a light of any sort, Limm waited. Patience in one his age was rare outside the Mockers, but a rash thief was a dead thief. Limm earned his keep in the Mockers by being among the most adroit pickpockets in Krondor, and his ability to calmly move among the throng in the market or down the busy streets without attracting attention had set him high in the leadership's estimation. Most boys his age were still working the streets in packs, urchins who provided distraction while other Mockers lifted goods from carts, or deflected attention from a fleeing thief.

Limm's patience was rewarded, as the faint echo of a boot moving on stone reached him. A short distance ahead, two large culverts joined in a wade. He would have to cross through the slowly-flowing sewage to reach the other side.

It was a good place to wait, thought the boy thief. The

sound of him moving through the water would alert anyone nearby and they'd be on him like hounds on a hare.

Limm considered his options. There was no way around that intersection. He could return the way he came, but that would cost him hours of moving through the dangerous sewers under the city. He could avoid crossing the transverse sewer by skirting around the corner, hugging the wall to avoid being seen, and moving down that passage to his right. He would have to trust that darkness would shelter him and he could remain silent enough to avoid detection. Once away from the intersection, he could be safely on his way.

Limm crept along, gingerly placing one foot ahead of the other, so as to not dislodge anything or step on an object that might betray his whereabouts. Fighting the impulse to hurry, he kept his breathing under control and willed himself to keep moving.

Step by step he approached the intersection of the two passages, and as he reached the corner at which he would turn, he heard another sound. A small scrape of metal against stone, as if a scabbard or sword blade had ever-so-lightly touched a wall. He froze.

Even in the dark, Limm kept his eyes closed. He didn't know why, but shutting his eyes helped his other senses. He had wondered at this in the past, and finally stopped trying to figure out why it was so. He just knew that if he spent any energy trying to see, even in the pitch black, his hearing and sense of touch suffered.

After a long, silent, motionless period, Limm heard a rush of water heading toward him. Someone, a shopkeeper or city worker, must have purged a cistern or opened one of the smaller sluices that fed the sewer. The slight noise was the only mask he needed to resume moving, and he was quickly around the corner.

Limm hurried, still cautious but now feeling the need to put some distance between himself and whoever guarded the intersection behind him. He silently counted his steps and when one hundred had passed he opened his eyes.

As he expected, ahead was a faint dot of light, which he knew was a reflection coming down from an open grating in the West Market Square. There wasn't enough light by which to see well, but it was a point of reference and confirmed what he already knew about his whereabouts.

He moved quickly and reached the crossway that ran parallel to the one he had been travelling before encountering the silent guard. He eased into the foul sewage and crossed the now-moving stream of refuse, reaching the opposite walkway without making much sound.

Limm was quickly up and on his way again. He knew where his friends were holed up and knew that it was a relatively safe place, but given the time and circumstances, nothing was truly safe any more. What had once been called the other Thieves' Highway, the rooftops of Krondor, was now as much an open war zone as the sewers. The citizens of the city of Krondor might be blissfully ignorant of this silent warfare above their heads and below their feet, but Limm knew that if he didn't encounter the Crawler's men along the way, he risked the Prince's soldiers, or murderers posing as Nighthawks. No man unknown to him was trustworthy, and a few whom he knew by name could be trusted only so far these days.

Limm stopped and felt the wall to his left. Despite moving by his own silent count, he discovered with satisfaction that he had been less than a foot off estimating the whereabouts of the iron rungs in the wall. He started to climb. Still blind, he felt himself enter a stone chimney, and quickly knew he was at the floor of a cellar. He reached up and felt the latch. An experimental tug showed it to be bolted from the other side.

He knocked: twice rapidly, then a pause, then twice again, another pause and a final, single knock. He waited, counting to ten, then repeated the pattern in reverse order, one knock, pause, two knocks, pause, and two again. The bolt slid open.

The trap swung upward, but the room above was as dark as the sewer below. Whoever was waiting preferred to wait unseen.

As Limm cleared the floor of the room, rough hands hauled him through, the trap shutting quickly behind him. A feminine voice whispered, "What are you doing here?"

Limm sat down heavily upon the stone floor, fatigue sweeping over him. "Running for my life," he said softly. Catching his breath, he continued. "I saw Sweet Jackie killed last night. Ugly basher working for the Crawler." He snapped his fingers. "Cracked his neck like you'd break a chicken's, while his mates stood watching. Didn't even give Jackie a chance to beg or say a prayer, nothing. Just put him out of the way like a cockroach." He was close to weeping as he told them—and as relief at being relatively safe for the first time in hours washed over him. "But that's not the worst of it."

A lantern was lit by a large man with a gray beard. His narrow gaze communicated volumes: Limm had better have compelling reasons for violating a trust and coming to this hideout. "What else?" he asked.

"The Upright Man is dead."

Ethan Graves, one-time leader of the Mockers' bashers, for a time a brother of the Order of Ishap, and now fugitive from every court of justice in the Kingdom, took a moment to accept the news.

The woman, named Kat, was half her companion's age, and an old friend to Limm. She asked, "How?"

"Murdered, is the rumor," said Limm. "No one is saying for certain, but it's held without doubt he's dead."

Graves sat down at a small table, testing the construction of the small wooden chair with his large frame. "How would anyone know?" he asked rhetorically. "No one knows who he is . . . was."

Limm said, "Here's what I know. The Daymaster was still working when I came to Mother's last night, and he was holed up in the back with Mick Giffen, Reg deVrise, and Phil the Fingers."

Graves and Kat exchanged glances. Those named were the most senior thieves in the Mockers. Giffen had succeeded Graves as leader of the bashers, deVrise oversaw those who burgled and fenced goods, and Phil was in charge of pickpockets, smash-and-grab gangs, and the urchins who ran the streets of Krondor.

Limm continued. "The Nightmaster never showed. Word went out and we started looking for him. Just before dawn, we heard they found the Nightmaster floating in the sewers near the dock. His head was all bashed in."

Kat almost gasped. "No one would dare touch him."

Graves said, "No one in the know. But someone who didn't care about the Mockers' wrath would."

"Here's the dicey part," said Limm. "The Daymaster says the Nightmaster was supposed to meet with the Upright Man. Now, as I understand things, if the Upright Man is supposed to meet with you, and you don't show, he's got ways of sending word to the Daymaster or Nightmaster. Well, no word was heard. So the Daymaster sends one of the boys, Timmy Bascolm, if you remember him—" they nodded "—and Timmy turns up dead an hour later.

"So the Daymaster heads out with a bunch of bashers and an hour later they come running back to Mother's and hole up. Nobody's saying anything, but word spreads: the Upright Man's gone."

Graves was silent for a minute, then said, "He must be dead. There's no other explanation for this."

"And there are bully boys to make a strong man faint chasing through the sewers, last night, so Jackie and I figure the hunt is on and our best bet is to lie low somewhere. We got run to ground last night near Five Points—" both Kat and Graves knew the region of the city sewers by that name "—so after they killed Jackie, I figured my best bet was to get here, with you."

Graves said, "You want to leave Krondor?"

The boy said, "If you'll take me. There's a war on, for truth, and I'm the last of my band alive. If the Upright Man is dead, all bets are off. You know the rules. If the Upright Man isn't here, it's every man for himself and make what deal you can."

Graves nodded. "I know the rules." His voice lacked the rough, commanding edge Limm had come to know as a boy in the Mockers, when Graves was first among the bashers. Still, Graves had saved Limm several times, from freebooting thugs and the Prince's men alike. Limm would do whatever Graves said.

After a moment of reflection, Graves spoke. "You stay here, boy. No one in the Guild knows you've helped Kat and me, and the truth is, I'm fond of you. You were always a good lad, as far as that goes. Too full of yourself, but what boy isn't at times?" He shook his head in regret. "Out there it'll be every hand against us—Mockers, Prince's men, or the Crawler's. I've got a few friends left, but if the blood is running in the sewers, who knows how long I can count on them?"

"But everyone else thinks you've escaped!" objected Limm. "Just me and Jackie knew, 'cause you told us so we could fetch you food. Those notes you sent out, to the Temple, and some of your friends, to that magician you traveled with . . ." He waved his hand as if trying to recall the name.

"Owyn," Graves supplied.

"Owyn," repeated Limm. "Word spread through the city you'd fled to Kesh. I know at least a dozen bashers were sent outside the walls to track you down."

Graves nodded. "And an equal number of monks from the Temple, too, I warrant." He sighed. "That was the plan. Lie low here while they looked for us out there."

Kat, who had remained silent throughout, said, "It was a good plan, Graves."

Limm nodded.

Graves said, "I figured another week or ten days, and they'd come back, each thinking some other had just missed sight of us, then we'd walk down to the docks one night, get on a ship, and sail off to Durbin, just another merchant and his daughter."

"Wife!" said Kat, angrily.

Limm grinned.

Graves shrugged and spread his hands in a sign of surrender. "Young wife," he said.

She put her arms around his neck and said, "Wife," softly.

Limm said, "Well, you play the parts well enough, but right now getting to the docks is no small order." He glanced around the cellar. "What about just going out the door, up there?" He pointed to the ceiling.

Graves said, "Sealed off. That's why I built this place as a hideout. The building upstairs is abandoned, roof beams collapsed. The man who owned it died, so it belongs to the Prince for back taxes. Fixing up old buildings is not very high on the Prince's list of things to do, it seems."

Limm nodded in approval of the scheme. "Well, how long do you think we should stay?"

"You," said Graves, rising, "are staying in the Kingdom. You're young enough to make something of yourself, boy. Get off the dodgy path and find a master. Apprentice in a craft or become a serving man."

"Honest work?" said Limm, as he jumped to his feet. "When did a Mocker seek honest work?"

Graves pointed a finger at him. "Jimmy did."

"Jimmy the Hand," agreed Kat. "He found honest work."

"He saved the Prince's life!" objected Limm. "He was made a member of the court. And there's a death mark on his head! He couldn't return to the Mockers if he begged."

Graves said, "If the Upright Man is dead, that mark is erased."

Softly Limm asked, "What should I do?"

Graves said, "Lie low for a while, until things get quiet, then leave the city. There's a man named Tuscobar, once a trader from Rodez. He has a shop in a town called Biscart, two days' fast walk up the coast. He owes me a favor. He also has no sons, so there is no one to apprentice for him. Go there and ask him to take you to service. If he objects, just tell him 'Graves clears all debts if you do this.' He'll understand what it means."

29

"What does he do?" asked Limm.

"He sells cloth. He makes a good living, as he sells to nobles for their daughters."

Limm's expression showed he was less than taken with the notion. "I'd rather go to Durbin and take my chances with you. What are you going to do there?"

"Turn honest," said Graves. "I have some gold. Kat and I are going to open an inn."

"An inn," said Limm, his eyes alight. "I like inns." He got down on his knees in an overly dramatic pleading. "Let me come! Please! I can do many things in an inn. I can tend fires, and show customers to their rooms. I can haul water and I can mark the best purses for cutting."

"An honest inn," said Graves.

Some of the enthusiasm left Limm's expression. "In Durbin? Well, if you say so."

Kat said, "We're going to have a baby. We want him to grow up honest."

Limm was speechless. He sat in wide-eyed astonishment. Finally, he said, "A baby? Are you daft?"

Graves exhibited a wry smile and Kat's brown eyes narrowed as she said, "What's daft about a baby?"

Limm said, "Nothing, I guess, if you're a farmer or a baker or someone who can expect a fair chance at living to old age. But for a Mocker . . ." He let the thought go unfinished.

Graves said, "What's the clock? We've been cut off from sunlight so long I have no sense of it."

"It's nearly midnight," said Limm. "Why?"

"With the Upright Man dead, or even just the rumor of it, things will be happening. Ships that would otherwise have stayed in Krondor will be leaving the docks before the morning tide."

Limm fixed Graves with a questioning look. "You know something?"

Graves stood up from the small chair and said, "I know lots of things, boy."

Limm jumped to his feet. "Please take me with you. You're the only friends I've got, and if the Upright Man's dead, who knows who'll come to rule in his place. If it's that Crawler, most of us are dead anyway, and even if it's one of our own, who's to say what my life is worth?"

Graves and Kat understood. The peace within the Mockers was imposed from the top down, and it would never be mistaken for friendship. Old grudges would surface and old scores would be settled. More than one Mocker would die not knowing for which past transgression he was paying the ultimate penalty. Graves sighed in resignation. "Very well. Not much for you here, I'll grant, and another pair of eyes and nimble fingers might prove worthwhile." He glanced at Kat, who nodded silently.

"What's the plan?"

"We need to be at the docks before the dawn. There's a ship there, a Quegan trader, the *Stella Maris*. The captain is an old business acquaintance of mine. He was lying low, claiming a refit was needed, against the time when we could smuggle ourselves out of here. He'll sail for Durbin as soon as we board."

Kat said, "Lots of ships will be leaving on the morning tide, so another won't cause too much notice."

Limm look excited. "When do we head to the docks?"

"An hour before dawn. It'll still be dark enough for us to

stay in shadows, but enough of the town will be awake and about so we won't attract much attention."

Kat smiled. "We'll be a family."

Limm's narrow young face took on a sour expression. "Mother?"

Kat was barely ten years older than Limm, so she said, "Big sister."

Limm said, "We have one problem, though."

Graves nodded. "Getting to the street."

Limm sat back, for he knew that there could be no plan, ruse, or providential miracle that would get them safely to the docks. They would simply have to leave this hideout and risk a short walk through a dark tunnel which might house a dozen murderers or sewer rats. And they wouldn't know which until they left. Limm was suddenly tired and said, "I think I'll sleep for a bit."

"Good idea," agreed Graves. "There's a pallet over there you can use. We'll wake you when it's time to go."

Limm moved to the indicated corner and lay down. Kat whispered, "What are the odds?"

"Bad," admitted her lover. "We've got to get the boy some clothing. Dirty boys are nothing unusual at the dock. But not *that* dirty." Trying to muster some optimism, he said, "Still, if the Upright Man is dead, there may be enough chaos in the city that we can slip out without attracting notice."

"Any other choice?"

"Only one," admitted Graves, "but I won't use it unless we're caught."

"What is it?"

Graves looked at the young girl for whom he had thrown away everything and said, "I have one friend left, who gains nothing from my fall. If I must, I'll send Limm to him begging for help."

"Who?" whispered Kat.

Graves closed his eyes as if admitting he might seek help was hard for one as self-reliant as himself. "The only thief who can beg the Prince of Krondor for my life."

"Jimmy?"

Graves nodded. "Jimmy the Hand."

# TWO

# KRONDOR

T HE column rode toward the city.

Krondor was backlit by a late afternoon sun, dark towers rising against a lemon-yellow sky. In the east, distant clouds turned rose and orange against a blue that seemed to shimmer. The column behind the Prince's vanguard tightened up as they entered the southernmost city gate, the one closest to the palace and barracks. Traffic in the area was normal for this time of day: a few traders drove wagons into the city, while farmers who'd visited the city for the day were leaving, starting their homeward journey.

James pointed. "Not much of a welcome, is it?"

Locklear saw that a few curious onlookers were turning to watch the approaching company that was escorting Arutha through the palace district. Otherwise they were ignored by the citizenry, as they had been since entering the outer reaches of Krondor. "I guess Arutha didn't send word we would arrive today."

"No, there's something else," said James, his days of fatigue washing away as curiosity took hold of him.

Locklear looked at the faces of those on the street who

stood aside to let the Prince's company ride past, and saw anxiety. "You're right, James."

The capital city of the Western Realm of the Kingdom of the Isles was never silent. Even at the darkest hours before sunrise, sounds could be heard from all quarters. There was a pulse to any city, and Krondor had one that was as well known to James as his own heartbeat. He could listen to its rhythm and understand what it was saying: *Something's wrong.* It was less than an hour before sundown, yet the city was far more subdued than it should be.

Locklear listened and knew what it was James was hearing, a muted quality, as if everyone was speaking a little more softly than usual. A shout from a teamster to his mules was cut slightly short, lest it hang too long in the air and attract notice. A mother's command for a child to come home was short and sharp, followed by a low threatening warning rather than a top-of-the-voice shriek.

"What do you think is going on?" asked Locklear.

Just ahead, Arutha spoke quietly to the two squires without looking back. "We should find out in a moment."

The young men looked past their ruler and saw a committee waiting for them at the palace gate. In the forefront was Princess Anita, her smile edged with relief at seeing her husband unharmed before her. Still youthful despite ten years of marriage and motherhood, her red hair was gathered up under a wide white hat, looking more like a sailing ship set atop her head, thought James, than anything else. But it was the current fashion, and one did not make jests at the expense of the Princess, especially not when her second smile was directed at you.

James returned the Princess's welcoming smile and basked

for a moment in its warmth. His boyhood infatuation with Anita had matured into a deep, abiding affection, and while she was too young to be viewed as his surrogate mother, she served as surrogate older sister with ease and humor. And it was clear to all who knew them that she viewed James as the younger brother she never had. It went so far as the Princess's children calling James "Uncle Jimmy."

At Anita's right stood twin boys, the Princes Borric and Erland, jostling with one another, as if it were impossible for the two nine-year-olds to remain at rest even for a moment. The red-headed lads were intelligent, James knew, and undisciplined. Some day they would number among the most powerful nobles in the Kingdom, but at present they were simply fractious boys bored with having to act the part of Princes and anxious to be off about whatever mischief they could find. Directly before her mother stood the Princess Elena, four years younger than the boys. Her features were as fine as her mother's, but her coloring was her father's, dark and intense. She beamed at the sight of her father riding at the head of his Household Guard. Succumbing to impulse, she pointed and said, "There's Daddy!"

Arutha held up his hand and ordered a halt. Without waiting for official greetings from the Master of Ceremonies, he jumped from his mount and hurried to his family. Embracing his wife, he then turned his attention to his sons and daughter.

James motioned with this chin toward the welcoming guards and whispered to Locklear, "Willie's on duty."

William, Pug's son, was a cadet, a young soon-to-be officer who presently was learning his trade. He exchanged glances with James, giving the squire a tiny nod.

The order was given for the company to fall out, and James

and Locklear dismounted. Grooms hurried over and took away the tired mounts.

Their duty required the squires to wait upon their Prince's need, so they moved to stand at Arutha's right hand.

Anita gifted the young men with a warm greeting, then turned her attention to Arutha. "I know I shouldn't worry. I know you'll always come back to me."

Arutha's smile was both happy and tired. "Always."

A small knot of court officials stood silently behind the royal family, and Arutha nodded greetings. He saw by their expressions that he would be needed in council before he would be permitted the pleasure of a long visit with his family. He noticed the Sheriff of Krondor in attendance, and sighed. That could only mean grave problems in Krondor, for the sheriff, while an important officer in the city, wasn't properly a member of Arutha's court. Glancing at Gardan, he said, "Marshal, see what the sheriff and the others want, and meet me in my private council chamber in a half hour. I will have this road-dirt off before I sit down to another meeting." He smiled at Anita. "And I'll steal a few minutes to speak with my wife and children." He leaned over and kissed Anita on the cheek and said, "Take the children to our apartment. I'll be along in a minute, dearest."

Anita herded the children away, and Arutha motioned to James and Locklear. "No rest for the wicked, boys." Looking over at the palace guard, he added, "Young William looks as if he's going to pop with news to share, so go find out what's on his mind. I'm sure I'll be hearing a different version of the same tale from my officers in council. If something warrants some snooping around in the city, do it, and be back no later than the end of the evening meal." Then he looked James in the eyes and said, "You know what you must do."

James nodded. As he led Locklear away, Locklear said, "What does that mean?"

"What?"

" 'You know what you must do?' "

"Just something Arutha and I have been working on since you were sent north to Tyr-Sog for . . ."

"I know why I was banished to Tyr-Sog," Locklear said in a tired voice. "Too well," he added, considering his imminent return to that cold and lonely town on the northern frontier.

James signaled to the guardsman in charge of the trainees, who stood to attention as he shouted, "Members of the court!"

The cadets were already at attention, but they seemed to stiffen a bit more as the two squires approached.

James nodded greeting to Swordmaster McWirth. "How are the cadets this afternoon, swordmaster?"

"A worthless lot, squire, but one or two of them may survive to actually be allowed to serve as an officer *in my army!*"

James smiled wryly at the pointed remark, given that he and the swordmaster had little affection for one another. As a member of Arutha's court, the young man was not technically part of the army, and trained with weapons with the Prince; in fact, James was Arutha's favorite dueling partner as he was one of the few in the city as fast as Arutha with a blade. As a squire, he also carried some rank, which meant that often he was put in charge of soldiers who had trained under the sword-master, and it galled the old soldier.

Still, thought James, McWirth was thorough in his job and the officers he turned out, especially those who were chosen for the élite Royal Household Guards, were fine soldiers, to a man. In his travels, James had seen the worst of the army as well as the best, and he had no doubt these were the among the best in the Western Realm.

"I need to speak to the Prince's cousin when you're done with him, swordmaster."

The dour old soldier fixed James with a baleful gaze for an instant, and one more time James was thankful he never had to endure the swordmaster's supervision. McWirth turned and shouted, "Dismissed! Cadet William, over here!"

William came to stand before the swordmaster, while the other cadets headed back toward their quarters, and said, "Sir!"

"Member of the court desires your company, it seems." He smiled at James and Locklear and said, "Good day to you, squires."

The other cadets hurried off to their duties and McWirth said, "And when you're done, I expect you to catch up with the rest of the cadets, else you'll be tending your equipment during mess, is that clear?"

"Sir!" replied William with a salute. The old swordmaster stalked off and William approached Locklear and James.

James asked, "What's the news?"

"Lots," said William. He was a short man, though taller than his father, with dark brown hair and eyes. The boyish cast to his features had faded in the months since he had come to serve in the Prince's army and his shoulders had broadened. He was lethally effective with the two-handed sword, a difficult weapon for most soldiers to master, and his horsemanship was considered exceptional. "I'm to be commissioned next week!"

"Congratulations," said Locklear. "I'm to be exiled."

William's eyes narrowed. "Again?"

James laughed. "*Still.* Arutha appreciated his reasons for returning without leave, but decided it didn't warrant an early reprieve from the icy north."

Frowning, Locklear said, "I depart for Tyr-Sog again, tomorrow."

James said, "Something's funny in the city. What do you hear, Willie?"

Only Arutha's family, James, and Locklear called William by that nickname, a familiarity he allowed no one else. William said, "Odd things. They keep us cadets busy and we don't get to mix much with the others in the garrison when we're not training, but you do hear this and that. Seems like an unusually high number of people in the city have been turning up dead this last week."

James nodded. "That would explain the sheriff waiting for the Prince."

Locklear said, "He doesn't usually do that sort of thing, now that you mention it."

James was lost in thought a moment. He had crossed paths with Sheriff Wilfred Means on more than one occasion when James had plied his trade as a thief. A few times he had come close to being the sheriff's guest in the Old Town Jail. The sheriff acknowledged James as the Prince's squire and treated him with the respect due his office; their relationship was a cold one at best. James suddenly was visited with the image of a younger Wilfred Means glaring up at James as he bolted over the rooftops of the city, the then constable's ginger-colored mustache almost quivering with rage at the boy's escape.

But the sheriff was stalwart in his duty, and tried to keep crime in Krondor as much under control as possible. The city was an orderly one by most any measure James could imagine, and unlike others who held the office before him, Wilfred Means was not a man to take a bribe or barter a favor.

For him to be waiting in person to speak to Arutha as soon as he returned meant something grave had occurred, something the sheriff judged required the Prince's immediate attention.

"You get back to your duties," said James absently to William. "Locky and I had better catch up with Arutha."

William said, "Well, Locky, I will bid you farewell, again, if you're off for the north in the morning."

Locklear rolled his eyes theatrically, but took the proffered hand and shook it. "Take care of this rascal, William. I would hate to see him get killed when I wasn't around to watch."

"Sorry you're going to miss the commissioning," said William.

James grinned. "Don't worry, Willie. I'll find you a celebration, and even without this knave's vaunted reputation as a lodestone for the girls, we'll find us some pretty faces to look upon you in awe as you sport your new badge of rank."

William couldn't help blushing at that. "Take care, Locky," he said.

Locklear bid him farewell, and as William ran off to his duties Locklear said, "Did you see that blush? I warrant the lad's never been with a woman."

James elbowed his friend in the side. "Not everyone is as precocious as you were, Locky."

"But he's nearly twenty!" said Locklear in mock astonishment.

"He's a bright lad and fair to look at. I suspect things will have changed by the time you return," said James.

"You think?"

"Certainly," said James as they entered the palace. "I'm sure I can find him an agreeable girl to bed him in the next five years."

Locklear's grin vanished. "Five years!" With wide eyes he said, "You don't think Arutha's going to keep me up there for five years, do you?"

James laughed at his friend's distress. As the two young men hurried along to their Prince's chambers, Locklear threw an elbow at James—which James adroitly dodged—and for an instant they were boys again.

James and Locklear reached Arutha's private council room just as the Prince was approaching after his brief visit with his wife and children. He moved purposefully down the small hallway that connected his family's private apartments with the council chamber and the formal court. James hurried to fall in behind his liege lord, with Locklear one step after. A pair of court pages flanked the council chamber door, and one quickly opened it so that Arutha might enter.

Arutha arrived to greetings from Master of Ceremonies Brian de Lacy. Standing at his right hand was his assistant, Housecarl Jerome. Jerome and his supervisor bowed as one to the Prince; the housecarl gave a fleeting nod of greeting to the two squires. Jerome had been a member of the company of squires with James and Locklear as boys, and James had been the first one to stand up to the older boy, who had been the resident bully. Now Jerome was studying to succeed de Lacy as the man in charge of the daily business of the court, and serving as the chief administrator of the palace while doing so, and James was forced to admit his fussy attention to detail made him ideally suited for the job.

Arutha said, "I am very tired and would like to join my

family for an early supper; let's save as much as we may for formal court tomorrow. What can't wait?"

De Lacy nodded and then looked up. He noticed who was in the room and said, "Shall we wait for the Knight-Marshal?"

Just then Gardan entered. "Apologies, Highness. I wanted to make sure the men were taking care of their mounts and weapons before I joined you."

Arutha's brow furrowed and his mouth turned up in a familiar half-smile. "You're not a sergeant any more, Gardan. You're the Knight-Marshal of Krondor. You have others to ensure that the men and animals are properly billeted."

Gardan nodded in reply, then said, "That's something I wish to discuss with you." He glanced at the nobles in the Prince's private offices and added, "But it will wait until after this evening's business. Highness?" Arutha indicated his agreement.

De Lacy said, "Two communiqués from Great Kesh via courier arrived during your absence, Highness, informing the crown of matters of small urgency, yet they do require a formal response."

Arutha waved them over to James. "Leave them. I'll read them tonight and compose a reply first thing in the morning."

De Lacy handed them to James who tucked them under his arm without looking at them.

The Master of Ceremonies looked at the sheriff, who stepped forward and bowed. "Highness, I fear I must report a rash of black murders have been done in your city during the time you've been away."

The Prince was silent for a moment as he considered these words, then he said, "You speak then of something warranting my personal attention? Murder is not uncommon in our city."

"I do, Highness. Several men of prominence have been slain

in their beds at night, throats cut while their wives slept undis-
turbed beside them."

Arutha glanced at James and nodded slightly. James knew
what the Prince was thinking: Nighthawks.

For nearly ten years the city had been untroubled by the
Guild of Death. The assassins who had been employed by Murmandamus's agents had vanished at the end of the Riftwar. A
few months ago rumors about their return had begun to circu-
late. Then they had suddenly reappeared in the Kingdom. James
himself had killed their current leader, but was under no illusion
that the Nighthawks would just go away. If there was another
cell of them here in Krondor, they already knew of the death
of one called Navon du Sandau, an erstwhile merchant from
Kenting Rush. Exposing his true identity had almost gotten
James killed in a duel, and it was only by dint of hours spent
practicing the sword with Arutha that James had prevailed.

Looking troubled, Arutha asked the sheriff, "What have your
men uncovered?"

"Nothing, Highness. Of some of the victims, what you'd
expect: men with enemies due to their prominence in their
trade. But others were men of little significance except to their
families. There is nothing of sense about these murders. They
seem . . . random."

Arutha sat back and weighed what he had been told. His
mind turned furiously as he considered, then discarded options.
Finally he said, "Random? It may be we simply do not understand what is behind the selection of victims. Have your men
return in the morning and question the families of the victims,
those who worked with them, their neighbors and anyone who
may have seen them prior to their deaths. There may be some
vital bit of information we are not seeing because we do not

know it is important. Send a scribe with your men to record the conversations. In all of this we may discover some connection between those murdered." He sighed, fatigue evident in his features. "Return to your post, sheriff. Join me after morning court tomorrow and we'll discuss this business at length. I'll want your men's reports by tomorrow evening." The sheriff bowed and withdrew.

Arutha turned to de Lacy. "What else?"

"Nothing that cannot wait, Highness."

Arutha rose. "Court is dismissed until the tenth hour of the day tomorrow." De Lacy and Jerome left the chamber, and Arutha turned to Gardan and the squires. "Now, Gardan, what is it you wished to speak with me about?"

"Highness, I've served your house since I was a boy. I've been a soldier and sergeant to your father, and a captain and marshal to you. It's time I returned home to Crydee. I wish to retire."

Arutha nodded. "I see. Can we speak of this over supper?"

The Knight-Marshal said, "If you wish."

"I do." Turning to the squires, Arutha said, "Locklear, you'd best be getting ready for your journey tomorrow morning. I'll have travel warrants and orders sent to your quarters. Leave with the dawn patrol to Sarth. If I fail to see you before then, have a safe journey to Tyr-Sog."

Locklear tried to keep his expression neutral as he answered, "Thank you, Your Highness."

Arutha turned to James and said again, "You know what to do."

Arutha and Gardan turned toward the royal apartments as the two squires moved in the other direction. When they were out of hearing distance, Locklear mimicked the Prince: " 'You know what to do.' All right: what is this all about?'

James sighed and said, "It means I don't get any sleep tonight."

Locklear said, "Is this your way of telling me it's none of my business?"

"Yes," James answered. He said nothing more as they moved to the wing of the palace which housed their quarters. Reaching the door to Locklear's room, James said, "I probably won't see you before you leave, also, so take care not to get yourself killed."

Locklear shook hands, then embraced his best friend. "I'll try not to."

James grinned. "Good, then with luck we'll see you at Midsummer's Festival, assuming you don't do anything to cause Arutha to keep you up there longer than that."

Locklear said, "I'll be good."

"See that you are," instructed James.

He left his friend and hurried to his own quarters. Being a member of the Prince's court merited James a room of his own, but since he was only a squire, it was a modest one; a bed, a table for writing or eating a solitary meal, and a double door wooden wardrobe. James closed the door to his room, locking it behind him, and undressed. He was wearing travel clothing, but it was still too conspicuous for what he needed to do. Opening his wardrobe, he moved aside a bundle of shirts in need of laundry, and beneath those he found what he was looking for. A dark gray tunic and dark blue trousers, patched and mended and looking far dirtier than they actually were. He dressed in those, pulled on his oldest boots and slipped a well-made but plain-looking dagger into his boot-sheath. Then once again looking like a creature of the streets, he slipped out through the door of his quarters, avoiding servants and guards as he made his way down into the palace cellar.

Soon he was moving through a secret passage that connected the palace with the city sewers, and as night fell on Krondor Jimmy the Hand once more moved along the Thieves' Highway.

The sun had set by the time James reached the transition point between the sewer under the palace and the city sewer system. The sky above might still be light for a while, but beneath the streets it was as dark as night. During the day there were places in the sewer where illumination filtered down from above, tunnels close to the surface where culverts had broken through, others below streets where missing stones or open drains admitted daylight.

But after sundown, the entire system was pitch-black, save for a few locations with light sources of their own, and only an expert could move through the maze of passages safely. From the moment he left the palace, James knew exactly where he was.

While a member of the Guild of Thieves, the Mockers, James had learned every trick of survival that harsh circumstance, opportunity, and keen native intelligence had presented to him. He moved silently to a stash he had prepared and moved a false stone. It was fashioned from cloth, wood, and paint, and in light far brighter than any likely to ever be present here, it would withstand inspection. He set the false stone down and retrieved a shuttered lantern from the stash. The hidey-hole held an extra set of picks, as well as a number of items unlikely to be welcome inside the palace proper: some caustic agents, climbing equipment, and a few non-standard weapons. Old habits died hard.

James lit the lantern. He had never considered keeping a lantern in the palace, for fear someone might observe him making the transition between the palace sewer and the one under the city. Guarding the secret of how the palace could be reached through the sewers was paramount. Every drawing on file in the palace, from the original keep through the latest expansion, showed the two systems as entirely separate, just as the city's sewer was divided from the one outside the city walls. But smugglers and thieves had quickly rendered royal plans inaccurate, by creating passages in and out of the city.

James trimmed the wick, lit it, and closed the shutters until only a tiny sliver of light shone, but it was enough for him to navigate his way safely through the sewer. He could do it with no light, he knew, but it would slow him down to a painful near-crawl to have to feel his way along the walls the entire way, and he had a good distance to travel this night.

James did a quick check to insure he had left nothing exposed for anyone to chance across. He considered the never-ending need for security which created this odd paradox: the Royal Engineers spent a lot of time and gold repairing the city's sewers—and just as quickly the Mockers and others damaged them to have a furtive passage free of royal oversight. James often was the one responsible for identifying a new breach. Occasionally he was guilty of hiding one, if it suited his purposes more than it compromised the palace's security.

Thinking that there was a great deal more to being a responsible member of the Prince's court than he had imagined when he had first been put in the company of squires, the former thief hurried on toward his first appointment.

*   *   *

It was almost dawn when James started looking for his last contact. The squire was having trouble keeping his concerns in check. The first three informants he had sought were missing. The docks were unnaturally silent, devoid of even the boisterous noise usually marking the area's inns and taverns. The poor quarter was clearly a no man's land, with many of the Mockers' usual bolt-holes and accesses blocked off and sealed.

Of the Mockers, James had seen nothing. That alone was not completely unusual. He wasn't the only one adroit at traveling through the sewers and streets unnoticed. But there was something different about this night. There were others who used the sewers. Beggars who weren't Mockers had places where they could sleep unmolested. Smugglers moved cargo short distances from secret landings built into the larger outflows into the harbor to basements farther in the city. With such activities came noises: small, unnoticed unless one was trained to recognize them for what they were, but usually they were there. Tonight everything was silent. Only the murmur of water, the scurrying of rats and the occasional rattle of distant machinery, waterwheels, pumps, and sluice gates echoed through the tunnels.

Anyone in the sewers was lying low, James knew. And that meant trouble. Historically, in times of trouble, the Mockers would seal off sections of the sewers, especially near the poor quarter, barring the passages to Mockers' Rest, the place called "Mother's" by members of the Guild of Thieves. Armed bashers would take up station and wait for the crisis to pass. Others not belonging to the guild would also hole up until the trouble passed. Outside those enclaves and safe areas, anyone in the tunnels was fair game. The last time James had remembered

51

such a condition had been during the year following the end of the Riftwar, when Princess Anita had been injured and Arutha had declared martial law.

The more he had traveled through the sewers below and the streets above, the more James was convinced something equally dire had occurred while he had been out of the city on the Prince's business. James looked around to see that he was unwatched and moved to the rear of the alley.

A pair of old wooden crates had been turned toward a brick wall to offer some shelter against the elements. Inside that crate lay a still form. A swarm of flies took off as James moved the crate slightly. Before he touched the man's leg, James knew he wasn't sleeping. Gingerly he turned over the still form of Old Edwin, a one-time sailor whose love of drink had cost him his livelihood, family, and any shred of dignity. But, James thought, even a gutter-rat like Edwin deserved better than having his throat cut like a calf at slaughter.

The thick, nearly-dried blood told James he had been murdered earlier, probably around dawn the day before. He was certain that his other missing contacts had met a similar fate. Either whoever was behind the troubles in the city was killing indiscriminately—and James's informants had been exceedingly unfortunate—or someone was methodically murdering off James's agents in Krondor. Logic dictated the latter as the most likely explanation.

James stood and looked skyward. The night was fading, as a gray light from the east heralded the dawn's approach. There was only one place left he might find answers without risking confronting the Mockers.

James knew that some agreement between the Prince and Mockers had been reached years before when he had joined

Arutha's service, but he never knew the details. An understanding of sorts had arisen between James and the Mockers. He stayed out of their way and they avoided him. He came and went as he pleased in the sewers and across the roofs of the city when he needed, and they looked the other way. But at no time had he any illusion that he would be warmly welcomed should he attempt to return to Mockers' Rest. You were either a Mocker or you weren't, he knew, and for nearly fourteen years he had not been a Mocker.

James put aside concerns about braving a visit to Mother's and turned toward the one other place he might find some news.

James returned to the sewer and made his way quickly to a spot below a particular inn. It sat on the border between the poorest quarter of the city and a slightly more respectable district, one inhabited by workmen and their families. A rank covering of slime hid a secret release, and once it was tripped, James felt a slight grinding as a section of stone swung aside.

The "stone" was made of plaster over heavy canvas, covering a narrow entryway to a short tunnel. Once inside the tunnel, with the secret door closed behind him, James opened the shutters of the lantern. He was almost certain he knew of every trap along the short passage, but as the key word was "almost" he took great caution as he traversed the tunnel.

At the far end he found a thick oaken door, on the other side of which he knew rose a short flight of stairs leading to a cellar below an inn. He inspected the lock and when he was satisfied nothing had changed, he picked it adroitly. When it clicked open, he pushed it gingerly aside against the possibility

53

of a new trap on the other side of the door. Nothing happened and he quickly mounted the stairs.

At the top of the stairs, he entered the dark cellar, thick with barrels and sacks. He moved through the maze of stores and climbed the wooden steps up to the main floor of the building, opening into a pantry, behind the kitchen. He opened the door.

A young woman's scream split the air and a moment later a crossbow bolt flew through the space James had occupied the instant before. The young man rolled on the floor as the bolt splintered the wooden door and James came to his feet with his hands held palm out as he said, "Easy, Lucas! It's me!"

The innkeeper, a former soldier in his youth, was halfway around the kitchen, the crossbow set aside as he was drawing his sword. He had grabbed the crossbow and fired through the door, across the kitchen, upon hearing the scream. He hesitated a moment, then returned his sword to its scabbard as he continued moving toward James.

He circled around a butcher's block. "You idiot!" he hissed, as if afraid to raise his voice. "You trying to get yourself killed?"

"Honestly, no," said James as he stood up.

"Dressed like that, sneaking at my cellar door, how'd I know it was you? You should have sent word you were coming that way, or waited an hour and come in the front door like an honest man."

"Well, I am an honest man," said James, moving from the kitchen, past the bar and into the empty common room. He glanced around, then sat down in a chair. "More or less."

Lucas gave him a half-smile. "More than some. What brings you crawling around like a cat in the gutter?"

James glanced over at the young girl who had followed him

and Lucas into the commons. She had regained her composure as the intruder was revealed to be a friend of the innkeeper. "Sorry to startle you."

She took a breath and said, "Well, you did a good job of it." She stood upright, and her high color from the fright put her fair complexion in contrast to her dark hair. She appeared to be in her late teens or early twenties.

James asked, "The new barmaid?"

"My daughter, Talia."

James sat back. "Lucas, you don't have a daughter."

The proprietor of The Rainbow Parrot sat down opposite James and said, "Run to the kitchen and see nothing's burning, Talia."

"Yes, father," she said, leaving.

"I have a daughter," Lucas said to James. "When her mother died I sent her to live with my brother on his farm near Tannerbrook."

James smiled. "Didn't want her to grow up in this place?"

Lucas sighed. "No. It gets rough in here."

Feigning innocence, James said, "Why, Lucas. I never noticed."

Pointing an accusatory finger in his direction, Lucas said, "Far less savory characters than you have graced that chair, Jimmy the Hand."

James held up his hands as if surrendering. "I'll concede as much." He glanced toward the kitchen door as if somehow seeing through it. "But she doesn't sound like any farm girl I've heard before, Lucas."

Lucas sat back, ran his bony hand through his gray-shot hair. His angular face showed irritation at having to explain. "She studied with a sisterhood in a nearby abbey for more hours than she milked cows. She can read, write, and do sums. She's a smart lass."

James nodded in appreciation. "Laudable. Though I doubt your average customer will appreciate those qualities as much as . . . the more obvious ones."

Lucas's expression darkened. "She's a good girl, James. She's going to marry a proper man, not some scruffy . . . well, you know the type. I'll have a dowry set by and . . ." He dropped his voice so as not to be heard in the kitchen. "James, you're the only one I know who knows some proper lads, being in the palace and all. At least since Laurie ran off and got himself named duke in Salador. Can you arrange for my girl to meet the right kind of boy? She's been back in the city only a few days and already I feel as green as a raw recruit on his first day of training. With her brothers dead in the war, she's all I've got." He glanced around the well-tended but rough common room and said, "I want her to have more than this."

James grinned. "I know. I'll see what I can do. I'll bring a couple of the more likely fellows down for a drink and let nature take its course."

"But not Locklear!" said Lucas. "You keep him away."

James laughed. "No worries. He's probably riding out the gate this very minute, heading for a long tour of duty in Tyr-Sog."

Talia came back into the room and said, "Everything is ready, father."

"That's a good lass," he replied. "Open the door, then, and let anyone in who's waiting for breakfast."

As she moved off, Lucas said to James, "All right then. You didn't get yourself almost killed sneaking in from the sewers to gossip about my girl and the boys in court. What brings you here before sunrise?"

James's face lost any hint of humor. "There's a war underway in the sewers, Lucas. And someone's killed some friends of mine. What's going on?"

Lucas sat back and nodded. "I knew you'd come asking one of these days. I thought it would be sooner."

"I just got back into the city last night. I was off with the Prince . . . doing some things."

Lucas said, "Well, Arutha would do well to look closer to home for trouble, for he has heaps of it here free for the asking. I don't know the truth of it, but according to the rumors men are killing freely in the sewers and along the waterfront. Citizens and Mockers alike are dying. I hear of Keshians setting up shops in buildings once owned by Kingdom merchants, and new bully gangs working along the docks. No one knows what's going on, save the Mockers who have gone to ground and are hiding out. I've not seen one in a week. Most of my regulars come later and leave earlier, wanting to be home safe before dark."

"Who's behind it, Lucas?" asked James.

Lucas looked around, as if afraid some invisible agency might overhear him. Softly he said, "Someone calling himself the Crawler."

James sat back. "Why am I not surprised?" he muttered.

THREE

# RECEPTION

J AMES waited.

A court page knocked upon the door, his youthful expression neutral as befitted a lad of twelve stationed just outside the royal apartments. An answering voice bid James enter, and he waited as two pages pushed open the ornate wooden doors. Inside, the Prince took breakfast with his family, the fractious twins poking at one another while attempting to avoid parental notice. A scolding look from their mother indicated their failure and they went back to a pretense of model behavior. The little Princess was happily singing a song of her own making while she purposefully put spoon to a bowl of hot breakfast mush.

Princess Anita smiled at James as he presented himself to the family and bowed. "Our squire finally appears," said Arutha dryly. "I trust we're not inconveniencing you this morning?"

James smiled back at the Princess as he straightened, then turned to the Prince and said, "I was dressed in a quite inappropriate fashion for a meal with the royal family, Highness. I am sorry to be so tardy."

Arutha indicated for James to stand at his right hand, where he was expected to wait on his ruler's pleasure unless out on some errand or another. James did so and took a moment to rest in the glow of the only thing in his life that felt like family to him.

The Prince of Krondor and his squire enjoyed a relationship that was eccentric and unique. At times they were comrades as much as master and servant, while at other times their bond was almost brotherly. Yet there was always this one thing between them: James never forgot that Arutha was his Prince and he was Arutha's loyal servant.

"You look tired," observed the Prince.

"It's been a long time since I enjoyed the comfort of a warm bed and a good night's sleep, sir," James replied. "Last night included."

"Well, was it worth it?"

James said, "In one way, very much. In another, no."

Glancing at his wife and children, Arutha looked at James and softly said, "Do we need to speak in private?"

James said, "I judge it inappropriate table conversation, if that's the answer you seek, Highness."

Arutha said, "Retire to my private office and wait. I will join you in a few minutes."

James did as he was told and walked the short distance to Arutha's private office. Inside he found it as it always was, ordered and clean. He eased his fatigued body into a chair near the Prince's writing desk and sat back.

James lurched awake as Arutha entered a short while later. "Sleeping?" asked the Prince with amusement as James came to his feet.

"It was a *very* long and tiring ride home, Highness, followed by another night without sleep."

Arutha waved James back into his chair and said, "Relax a bit while you talk, but don't nod off again."

"Sire," said James as he sat. "Three of my informants have gone missing."

Arutha nodded. "From what the good sheriff tells me, we have a rash of killings here in Krondor again, and this time it looks as if there's no pattern. But the disappearance of your informants tells us someone knows more about us than we do about him, and doesn't want us improving our knowledge."

James said, "I don't see any pattern either."

"Not yet," said the Prince. There was a knock at the door, and Arutha called out, "A moment." To James he said, "That would be Gardan with his retirement documents."

"He is leaving, then?" asked James.

Arutha nodded. "I'm sorry to see him go, but he's earned his rest. He'll go home to Crydee and spend his last years with his grandchildren, and I can't think of a better fate for any man. And I suspect he's correct in his accusation that I don't leave him much to do, really. He suggests I appoint someone with administrative talents to the post rather than a military man as long as I insist on personally supervising the army. And this conversation stays in this room."

James nodded silently.

Pointing to the door, Arutha said, "Let Gardan in on your way out. Then go to your room and get some sleep. You're excused from court duty this morning. You have a busy evening ahead of you."

"More scouting the city?" asked James.

Arutha said, "No, my wife's arranged a homecoming ball, and you must attend."

James rolled his eyes heavenward. "Couldn't I go crawl around in the sewers some more?"

Arutha laughed. "No. You'll stand and look interested as rich merchants impress you with tales of their fiscal heroics, and their vapid daughters try to entice you with their marginal charms. That's a royal command." He fingered a document upon his desk. "And we have word of an eastern noble headed our way for an unexpected visit. So we must be ready to entertain as well. And murder in the streets does so take the joy out of things, don't you agree?" he added dryly.

"Yes, Highness."

James opened the door and admitted Gardan, who nodded a greeting. After Gardan entered the room, James left, closing the door behind him.

The court was nearly empty. In a few moments, de Lacy and Jerome would admit nobles, merchants, and other petitioners to the great hall. With a nod of courtesy to the two men, James hurried out of another side door and started back toward his quarters. He might not look forward to another of Princess Anita's galas, but he did hear his bed singing a siren call to him right now. The last few weeks in the north, especially almost a week-long horseback ride abetted by mystical herbs to ward off fatigue, had taken its toll.

As he reached the corner of two halls, he found a page and instructed the youth to awaken him one hour before the supper bell rang. James reached his room, went inside, and within minutes was fast asleep.

The musicians struck up a tune and Arutha turned to his wife and bowed. Less formal than the royal court in Rillanon, the Prince's court in Krondor was no less bound by traditions. One such was that no one began dancing before the Prince and Princess.

Arutha was an adept dancer. That didn't surprise James. No one could be as nimble when wheeling a sword as the Prince of Krondor and not have a superb sense of balance and exquisite timing. And the dances were simple. James had heard that the court dances in Rillanon were complex, very formal things, while here in the far more rustic west the court dances were similar to those performed by farmers and townspeople throughout the Western Realm, just executed with a bit more restraint and less noise.

James watched Arutha and Anita nod as one to the music master. He held up his bow and nodded to his musicians, a collection of stringed instruments, a pair of percussionists, and three men playing flutes of various sizes. A sprightly tune was struck up and Anita stepped away from Arutha, while holding his hand, and executed a twirling turn, which caused her ornate gown to flare out. She ducked skillfully under his arm, and James thought it was a good thing those silly large white hats the ladies wore this season were considered daywear only. He considered it improbable she could have got under Arutha's arm without knocking it off.

The thought struck him as amusing and he smiled. Jerome, standing nearby said, "Something funny, James?"

James's smile vanished. He had never liked Jerome, that distaste going back to their first encounter when James had arrived in court. After Jerome's first—and last—attempt to bully him, James had knocked down the older boy, informing him pointedly that he was Prince Arutha's personal squire and not about to be bullied by anyone. James had emphasized the message with the point of a dagger—Jerome's own—deftly picked off his belt without Jerome noticing, and the message had never needed to be repeated.

Jerome had remained wary of James from that day on, though he had occasionally tried to bully the younger squires. Since becoming de Lacy's apprentice, and in all likelihood the next Master of Ceremonies, Jerome had outgrown his bullying behavior, and a polite truce had arisen between himself and James. James still considered him a fussy prig, but judged him far less obnoxious than he had been as a boy. And at times he was even useful.

James said, "Just an odd thought about fashion."

Jerome let a slight smile show itself before turning somber once more. He did not pursue the remark, but his slight change of expression indicated he appreciated James's observation.

The court was at its lavish best, with every guest adorned in the height of Krondorian fashion. James found these annual shifts in taste odd and occasionally ridiculous, but bore up under them stoically. This year the guards' uniforms had been changed, at the Princess's request, as the old gray tabards were now considered too dull.

The honor guard along the walls wore light brown tunics— somewhere between copper and gold—marked with a black eagle soaring over the peak of a mountain. James wasn't sure he liked the break with tradition, but noticed the Prince's scarlet mantle of office still bore the old crest.

Another group of guests arrived and filtered into the ballroom. Leaning toward Jerome, James quietly asked, "The usual guests?"

Jerome nodded. "Local nobles, rich merchants, a few soldiers of rank who have earned our Prince's favor."

"Any Keshians?" asked James.

"A few," said Jerome. "Traders." He glanced over at James and asked, "Or did you have some particular Keshians in mind?"

James shook his head a little as the dance came to a close. "No, but I wish I did."

If Jerome was curious about the remark, he didn't show it. James had come to admire his reticence, as a great deal of a Master of Ceremony's time was spent dealing with idiots, many of them powerful and rich. The ability *not* to hear things convincingly was a skill James felt he lacked and needed to cultivate.

A bit of a bustle at the far end of the hall began as the first dance ended. Arutha bowed to Anita and offered his hand, which she took, to escort her back to the dais.

From the opposite end of the hall came the booming crack of de Lacy's staff of office striking the floor heralding the arrival of someone of note. De Lacy's old, but still strong, voice carried the hall, as he intoned, "Your Highnesses, Lord Radswil, Duke of Olasko!"

James said, "Radswil of Olasko?"

Jerome whispered, "Pronounced *Rads-vil*, you ignoramus. One of the Eastern Kingdoms—a duchy, actually." Looking with mock disdain at James he said, "Study the map, my friend. The man's the younger brother of the Grand Duke Vaclav, and uncle to the Prince of Aranor." Dropping his voice even lower, Jerome said, "Which means he's a cousin to the King of Roldem."

A stir spread through the room as those who had occupied the dance floor parted to allow a large man and his retinue to cross to where Arutha and Anita were just sitting down. James studied the man and didn't like what he saw.

The duke was a bruiser, James could tell, despite his fine raiment. A large velvet hat of dark maroon, looking like an oversized beret, dropped off to one shoulder, a large silver brooch with a long white feather sweeping back from it. His black jacket was tailored to fit snugly, and James could see the massive shoulders were not padded, but merely reinforced his impression that Lord Radswil could easily hold his own in the rougher inns of the city. Black leggings and stockings finished the ensemble, all of the finest make. The sword at his side was a rapier, much like the one Arutha wore, often used and a serious weapon. The only difference was that Radswil's had a silver-and-gold-decorated bellguard.

At his left hand walked a young girl, perhaps fifteen or sixteen, wearing a dress to rival the Princess's, though cut as daringly low as modesty permitted. James studied her face. She was pretty in a predatory way, with the eyes of a hunter. For a brief moment he gave thanks that Locklear was gone from the court. Since they were boys, James had joked that girls would get Locklear killed some day, and this one looked about as dangerous as any James had seen, despite her youth.

Then James felt eyes upon him and glanced across. At Radswil's right hand walked two young men, about James's own age from what he could tell. The one closest to the duke looked like a younger version of Radswil, heavy set, powerful of stature and full of confidence. The one farthest from the duke bore enough of a resemblance to be a younger brother, but he was leaner and his eyes had a menacing cast as he fixed them upon James. He was studying James as James had been studying the party, and intuitively James knew what that young man was doing; he was picking out potential enemies in court. James felt a chill run down his back as the duke bowed before Arutha.

Jerome, now acting the part of his office as assistant to the Master of Ceremonies, stepped forward and said, "Your Highnesses, may I present Radswil, Lord Steznichia, Duke of Olasko."

Arutha said, "Welcome to our court, my lord. Your arrival

catches us somewhat unprepared. We thought you would arrive later in the week."

The duke bowed. "Apologies, Your Highness," he said in a deep voice, his speech only slightly accented. "We caught favorable winds from Opardum and arrived in Salador a week before we were scheduled. Rather than linger, we pressed on. I trust we have caused Your Highnesses no undue inconvenience?"

Arutha shook his head. "Not at all. We just lack a fitting welcome, that is all."

The duke smiled and James felt no warmth from that expression. The man was polished and his education was obvious, but at heart there was that brawler James had recognized at once. "I'm sorry, Highness, I assumed the gala tonight was to welcome us."

Anita's face froze for a moment, then the duke turned to her and said, "Highness, I jest. The matter is one of scant importance. We call only out of courtesy to your office and your husband's. We are bound for the Keshian port of Durbin. From there we will venture into the Trollhome Mountains, where we understand the hunting is both plentiful and exotic. Any small gesture of hospitality on your part is a boon beyond our expectation."

James saw Jerome go slightly rigid. The fussy ex-squire was a stickler for protocol and the duke had managed to brush aside an apology from Arutha and return an insult, without making it obvious. This man obviously felt no timorousness being in the presence of a Prince.

Anita had been court bred and knew the intricacies of court manners. She knew that anything she said in response to the slight would only worsen her situation socially. She merely inclined her head and said, "I suspect the subtleties of the east are lost upon us here in the west. Would you present your companions?"

The duke bowed and turned to the younger of the two men. "Your Highness, may I present my nephew, His Highness, Vladic, son of my brother the Archduke, heir to the throne and Crown Prince of Olasko, Prince of the House of Roldem by blood." On cue the young man stepped forward and bowed in greeting to the Prince and Princess of Krondor. Then the duke said, "And this is Kazamir, my son and heir to my house, also Prince of the House of Roldem by blood." The other son bowed effortlessly, with exactly the proper deference for one of his rank before Prince Arutha. Smoothly, the duke turned and said, "And this is my daughter, Paulina, Princess of the House of Roldem by blood."

Arutha nodded greeting. "You are all welcome in Krondor." He made a small gesture to Jerome, who hurried off to ready guest apartments for the duke and his entourage. James was again forced to concede that Jerome was good at what he did. He had no doubt the rooms would be aired, with wine and other refreshments on hand, and a squad of pages ready to do the duke's bidding.

Arutha said, "We are celebrating a safe return from troubles to the north. You are most welcome to remain for the gala."

The duke smiled. "My thanks. From the reports and gossip we heard along the way from Salador to Krondor, I suspect the troubles were not trivial. A gala is most appropriate to celebrate a Prince's safe return.

"I am tired from the journey, however, and will beg your forgiveness and retire. The children, perhaps, might enjoy some music and revelry after our long journey."

James realized this was not an option, but an instruction. The two youngsters turned to their father and bowed, while the Crown Prince merely looked on for a moment, then inclined his head. Radswil bowed to the Prince and withdrew before Arutha had time to do more than wave agreement. Master de Lacy intercepted the duke and his retainers at the door and escorted them to the guest quarters.

Arutha turned to James and said, "Squire James, would you please see that our guests are refreshed?"

James bowed and stepped down the dais and presented himself to the duke's children with a courtly bow. Keenly aware the introduction of the three youngsters revealed the Olaskans' formality in matters of rank, James said, "Prince Vladic, Princess, Prince, may I offer you refreshments?"

Vladic studied James a moment, his dark eyes narrowing slightly, then he nodded.

With as deft a movement as James had seen, he found himself with the Princess Paulina's arm through his, before he had even had the chance to offer his hand, a far more courteous gesture. The familiarity almost caught him off guard. "Tell me, squire," said Paulina, as they moved toward the large table where refreshments were offered, "how do you come to serve the Prince, personally?"

James was struck by two things at once. There was something about her, a scent, perhaps an exotic perfume, that caused his blood to race. He suddenly experienced a fierce desire. And that in turn caused what James had long called his "bump of trouble" to start bothering him. Paulina was a pretty enough girl—many would even say beautiful—and easily one of the most attractive at the gala, but James was long used to the wiles of women and she was not so extraordinarily attractive that he should find himself being so irresistibly drawn to her.

He glared at the two young men, saw what he took to be

a slight sense of amusement in Kazamir's expression, and a mask of neutrality in Vladic.

Forcing his attention back to her question, he replied, "I was granted my office for service to the crown."

Ever so slightly she drew away. "Oh?" she said. If a single word could convey volumes of meaning, hers did.

James smiled his most charming smile and said, "Yes. You wouldn't know, of course, being from so distant a land. Before coming to the Prince's service, I was a thief."

It took a massive application of will power on the Princess's part not to push herself away from James. Her frozen smile looked almost painful as she said, "Really?" while behind her, Kazamir suppressed a laugh. Even Vladic betrayed a slight upturn of his mouth, the hint of a smile.

Just then James spied William, who had been stationed by the table of refreshments, and said, "Allow me to introduce someone to you, Highnesses." He signaled for the young cadet to approach and when William did, James said, "Highnesses, I have the honor of presenting William conDoin, son of the duke of Stardock and cousin to our Prince. He's about to be commissioned Knight-Lieutenant in the Prince's army." He quickly named his companions in order of rank.

Instantly the Princess's manner changed once more and again she was the vivacious charmer. William's color rose and now James was convinced there was something more to this Princess than her more obvious physical gifts. "Perhaps the cadet could show me some of the palace, while you entertain my brother and cousin, Squire James?"

James glanced at Swordmaster McWirth, who stood near the dais, and with a nod of his head communicated the need for William to act as host to the visiting nobility. The old swordmaster's expression turned slightly sour, but he nodded and James said, "William, I'm sure the Princess would love to see the tapestry gallery and Princess Anita's gardens."

As smoothly as an eel slipping through water, the Princess disengaged herself from James's arm and attached herself to William. "And what shall I call you, young knight?" asked the Princess.

"Will, Your Highness. My friends call me Will."

As William led the Princess off toward the tapestry hall, James indicated the food and wine to Prince Vladic, then Prince Kazamir. The Crown Prince took a goblet of wine and sipped it. "Very good," he said. "Darkmoor?"

James nodded. "I believe so. Most of our best wines come from there."

"You're not having any?"

James smiled. "I'm on duty."

Kazamir nodded. "I understand. By the way, you handled that very deftly. Not many young men would give up my sister's company so easily."

"I can well believe it," said James. "There's something about her . . ."

Vladic studied James a moment, again appraising him, and James could not help but feel again that he was being sized up as a possible opponent. Vladic said, "You're perceptive, squire. My cousin has a need to be admired by a great many men. She employs additional supplements to augment her natural appeal."

"Ah," said James. "Magic. A charm or a potion?"

"Her left hand. A ring purchased from a woman who dabbles in such trinkets in our homeland. I fear this need for male attention that drives Paulina will eventually create difficulties for her future husband."

"Then she should either marry a man with great skills as a swordsman, or one with great patience."

Vladic nodded, as he sipped his wine. He then took a small slice of melon from a platter and nibbled at it, his expression every so slightly indicating satisfaction with the fruit. "The court here in the west is a refreshing change from some of the environments we've discovered east of Salador."

James nodded. "I have no doubt. West of Malac's Cross things are very different. I've not spent much time in the east, but it is . . ."

"More civilized?" provided Kazamir.

James smiled. "I was about to say older, but if you prefer civilized, I'll concede the point."

Vladic smiled, and for the first time since they met James sensed the young man was letting his guard down a tiny bit. "Well, it's a function of perspective, I warrant. Our nations are very old, while this Western Realm is relatively young. In Olasko, we haven't seen an elf or goblin in centuries. There are six other states of some size between the far northern lands and Olasko."

"Elves are interesting," replied James. "And I've seen enough goblins to last me a lifetime."

"I hear they're not terribly bright, but that they make good hunting," ventured Kazamir.

"Well, if you're interested in hunting something that carries a sword or bow, I guess." James shrugged. "I'm city bred and have little experience with hunting. I don't understand the appeal of the sport."

"It livens up an otherwise dull life," said Vladic.

James grinned. "I've never found life to be dull, so I suppose that's why."

"You're a lucky man, then," said Kazamir. "We have our

wars, often enough, but other than that, there's little to occupy a man who craves excitement."

Vladic said, "My cousin is like most of our nobles, and seeks glory in overt fashion. But the skills of arms, the sword and bow, the challenge of the hunt, those are secondary in importance to that." He pointed to where Arutha was listening to something being whispered into his ear by one of the local nobles. "He seeks office, or a suitable husband for a daughter or an ally against an enemy, or something from your monarch. Intrigue is a way of life in my father's court."

James laughed. "That's Squire Randolph of Silverstown. I think he's trying to convince the Prince to get one of his pesky neighbors to move his cattle off Silverstown's meadows."

Kazamir barked a rough sounding laugh. "A very small intrigue, then, cousin."

Vladic looked slightly nettled to be mocked so, but said nothing.

"Are you staying long in Krondor?" asked James.

Kazamir shrugged. "Father has planned this as a tour of the west, so I expect we'll stay a few days before moving on. He wishes to hunt the Trollhomes, where it is rumored great boars reside, as well as wild trolls and even, if true, dragons."

James could barely contain his amusement. "Having spied a dragon myself, may I suggest that only a madman would go looking for one?"

Kazamir's expression darkened. "A madman?"

James quickly spread his hands in an apologetic gesture. "A jest, and obviously a poor one. It is just that dragons are everything you've heard of and more. If you hunt one, take an army with you."

Kazamir's expression softened slightly, but James couldn't

be certain the offense had been mitigated. He continued, "Even trolls are to be avoided unless you absolutely must face one. The lowland trolls may be barely more than wild animals, but they are more dangerous than any lion or bear you might hunt, for they are more cunning, and they hunt in groups of two or more. Their mountain kin have language and use weapons. You go hunting them, be assured they'll be hunting you right back."

"Interesting," was all that Vladic said. Then he added, "How is the hunting in this region?"

"Yes," said Kazamir with sudden interest. "Lions, perhaps?"

James shrugged. "If you go north, up into the foothills of the Calastius Mountains, you'll find a good population of game. Closer to the King's Highway it's scarce, but once you get high into the hills there's ample deer, elk, bear, and big leopards. Occasionally a wyvern comes down from the northern mountains and that's as much dragon as I'd be willing to face."

"If we stay for more than a few days, would you be able to arrange a trip into those mountains?" asked Vladic.

James nodded. "I'll speak to the housecarl; he can arrange with the huntmaster and swordmaster to provide guides and men-at-arms. You could travel out for a day and reach some very rough terrain, where game is still plentiful."

Vladic looked pleased, as did his cousin. "Good. I will speak with my uncle tomorrow and, depending on his plans, perhaps I will prevail upon him to depart the day after on such a journey."

Kazamir's smile broadened a bit. "I suspect, however, you'd better also contrive some distraction for my sister while we're gone."

James's frown brought forth a laugh from Kazamir. The squire said, "I think I will prevail upon Princess Anita to fashion that distraction. I suspect most of the young men in the court might be faced with some difficulties given the duty to attend your sister."

"Yet you felt no difficulty in turning her over to that young cadet," observed Kazamir in a guarded tone.

James leaned over and lowered his voice in a conspiratorial fashion. "Young Will lacks . . . experience. No matter how attractive your sister, she would have to initiate anything . . . beyond an awkward flirtation, I think. And if I'm any judge of such things, I doubt she will."

Kazamir slapped James on the shoulder and laughed. "You may be rural, James, but your grasp of certain subtleties is not. Yes, my sister is out seeking a well-connected husband. She will not lessen her chances of such by any idle dalliance. Her husband will expect her unsullied on their wedding night, and she will be. But she will make some young men very unhappy until that time comes."

Given James's background, his view of such issues was far less critical; he had known too many women while a boy, and as a man who enjoyed the pleasures of the bed, to think much of the notion that men had different standards from women. Still, he had met enough men, noble and common, who felt differently that he appreciated the prevalence of that attitude.

"Given her use of . . . enhancements to her charms, doesn't this make things difficult back home?"

"Most men in Olasko are terrified of her father," said Vladic, putting down his now empty goblet of wine and refusing a refill by one of the servants. "In my homeland few would dare his wrath."

James shrugged and nodded his head in agreement. "Seems a wise course were I a citizen of your nation; the duke appears a most formidable man."

Kazamir's smile vanished. "As all would do well to note, James." James was certain that remark was more directed at Vladic than at himself. Then Kazamir's smile returned. "Still, it is tempting for men of my nation to pursue a prize like my sister."

James blinked in confusion. "Prize?"

"As I've mentioned, we are adventuresome, in Olasko. Hunting women ranks as high as hunting cave bears."

"An interesting way to put it," said James as neutrally as possible. "I think my friend Locklear would fit right in."

"He pursues women?"

"Incessantly," said James.

"Then I would suggest he be a well-practiced swordsman," offered Vladic.

"That he is, but why?"

Kazamir answered. "Because in my homeland a young man is expected to have as many women as he might, while it is also his duty to defend the honor of his sister with his blade should another man offend her."

James grinned. "So you have a lot of duels in Olasko."

Vladic returned the grin with a nod. "Constantly."

James said, "Fortunately, my friend Locklear is on his way north to serve along the border for quite some time. We will be spared the spectacle of you having to skewer him early one chilly morning. I prefer to sleep in, given the chance."

"As do I," said the Crown Prince. "Given the length of the journey—" he glanced around the room "—and the unlikelihood that I have time until the end of the gala to meet a receptive woman of rank, I think I shall retire."

Kazamir glanced around the room, and then said, "I concur.

I think a warm bed is more welcome than drink and dalliance tonight."

Instantly James motioned for a page and when the youth approached, he instructed him to escort Princes Vladic and Kazamir to the guest apartments. He bid them both good night and then returned to the dais.

The musicians played on. As soon as he was again at Arutha's side, James heard the Prince's voice under the music. "What do you think about this visit?"

James spoke in tones just loud enough for the Prince to hear. "I think it's odd. On the surface, it appears that the duke is looking for a suitable marriage of state for his daughter while indulging himself in some local hunting."

"On the surface," repeated Arutha, his gaze still on the dancers.

"As there are few sons of suitable rank in this part of the Kingdom—well, none over the age of ten, anyway—that reason barely holds up under scrutiny."

"What other reason do you imagine?"

"Well, the son says they want to hunt dragons and trolls out in the Trollhome, but I find that a bit difficult to fathom. We fought trolls near Romney just a few weeks ago, and I'm sure we left enough of them behind to entertain the duke and his companions for a lifetime. As for hunting dragons, even the dwarves don't go looking for them. They wait until they show up, then turn the entire community out to fight them. No, the duke may be crazy enough to really want to hunt dragons and trolls, but that's not his reason for coming west. I suspect the real reason for this journey will be found in Durbin."

"What could he want in Durbin? There are twenty major Keshian ports he could reach in the east."

James shrugged. "If we knew what it was he was seeking in Durbin, we would know why he's lying."

Arutha glanced over at James. "You suspect something." He turned his attention back toward the dance floor.

James nodded. "But nothing I can give voice to. Just a vague sense that this all ties together, these murders, the disappearance of citizens, the arrival of this outland noble."

"If you discover the whole of the parts, let me know."

James said, "You'll be the first."

"Did you sleep?"

"Earlier? Yes," said James, knowing what was coming next.

Arutha said, "Good, then you know what to do."

James nodded, bowed to the Prince, crossed to bow to the Princess, then removed himself from the hall. As he left, he signaled for a page to follow. The young man fell into step behind him.

James hurried toward the tapestry room and found it empty. He quickly moved on to the Princess's garden and found a very flushed William standing next to the Princess Paulina, obviously reduced to little more than a near babbling fool as the girl held tightly to his arm, chatting about the flowers.

"Ahem," said James.

The relief on William's face was abundantly clear as James bowed to the Princess. "Highness, this page will escort you to your quarters. Your father and brother have turned in for the night."

"But it's early," said the girl with a pout.

"If you prefer, he'll escort you back to the gala. But Cadet William's presence is required elsewhere." She seemed about to object, but James said, "By the Prince's orders."

She frowned, then forced herself to smile as she turned and

said to William, "Thank you for being my guide. It is a pity things ended prematurely. Perhaps we'll have time to continue later during our visit?"

"M-m'lady," William stuttered.

James was seized by a rush of desire as the girl passed close to him while he bowed. As she retreated, the feeling faded.

James turned to find William blinking, obviously confused, and asked, "Are you all right, Willy?"

"I don't know," he replied, still blinking. "While we were together, I . . . I don't know how to explain what I felt. But now that she's gone . . ."

"Magic," said James.

"Magic?"

"She employs magic, according to her brother," said James. "To heighten her charms."

"I find that difficult to believe," said William.

"What an odd thing for someone raised on an island of magicians to say," observed James as William blushed. "Believe it." He put his hand on the young soldier's arm. "I've got to take care of some business for Arutha, and you look like you could use a drink."

"I think I could," said William, "but I have to return to the Cadets' Quarters."

"Not if you come with me," said James.

"How does Arutha's business involve me getting an ale?"

James grinned. "I have to poke around a few places, and the cover story of being out with a friend jumping from tavern to inn is just the thing."

Sighing in resignation and trying hard not to imagine Sword-master McWirth's reaction to whatever plan James had in mind, William fell in beside his friend and they left the garden.

# FOUR

# SURPRISES

ILLIAM kept his eyes forward.

He knew his every movement was being closely scrutinized by Swordmaster McWirth. The old soldier had always paid slightly more attention to William's progress over the last year than with the other cadets, but with his commission set for the end of this week, it seemed lately that every single gesture and word was being evaluated.

William tried to attribute it to his having been an exceptional student, perhaps the best swordsman with the long two-handed sword in the garrison, as well as a proficient student of tactics and strategy. He also considered that his odd situation of being a royal cousin by adoption might have contributed to his being a "special project" of the swordmaster's. But no matter how he tried to please the old teacher these last few days, there was always something lacking in his efforts. Either a thrust was a hair's breadth too low during sword practice, or his decision to reinforce a position in field training was a bit premature. William wondered briefly if the swordmaster had something against him personally, but then pushed aside the thought as

McWirth came to stand before him. In a friendly tone, the old soldier said, "Late night, cadet?"

William still felt sand in his eyes from too little sleep, but he tried to will aside any shred of fatigue that clung to his bones. "Sir! Late enough, swordmaster!" he said as briskly as he could.

"Tired, cadet?"

"No, swordmaster!"

"Good," said McWirth, raising his voice so that the company of cadets could hear him, "because today we're going on an exercise. Some very bad men have surrounded the village of Tratadon and we must ride very fast and rescue the daughters of Tratadon from the clutches of these evil men." Again, he looked at William and added, "Of course these particular bad men are garrison regulars who would love to embarrass a bunch of fuzzy-cheeked cadets, so just make sure they're disappointed."

As one, the cadets shouted, "Yes, swordmaster!"

"Swords and saddles in fifteen minutes!" cried the swordmaster.

William was off at a run with his companions and stole a quick glance up to the palace wing where he suspected his friend James was still sleeping. He was on the verge of a silent curse when he remembered that James hadn't forced him to stay at the Rainbow Parrot, and that the girl, Talia, was very attractive. He really liked the way she smiled at him.

The thought was fleeting; for once he reached the armory to collect his armor and weapons, he got too busy to think of anything but the coming exercise.

James glanced down at the courtyard where the cadets were scurrying toward the armory to be fitted out for the day's exercise. He had forced himself to remain awake while reading the day's schedule and knew that William and the others had a grueling day ahead of them. Tratadon was a ten-hour forced march and the squad sent out to play the part of bandits the night before would be well and firmly dug in. McWirth was making sure his lads knew exactly the sort of trouble they were most likely to encounter in their work.

"Squire?" came a soft voice, gently preventing James's reverie from slipping into a fatigued doze.

"Yes?" James replied to the young page, forcing himself to wakefulness.

"His Highness waits in his private office."

James nodded, forcing aside the warm fatigue that made him feel like sleeping every time he stopped moving. As they reached the side door to Arutha's office, another page opened the door so that James could march in without slowing his pace.

Arutha sat at his desk. He indicated two mugs and a large pot and said, "Please."

James poured and was greeted by the aroma of dark, Keshian coffee. As he added a single spoonful of honey to the Prince's mug, he said, "To think I couldn't stand coffee a few years ago. Now I wonder how one gets through the morning without it."

Arutha nodded as he took the offered mug. "Or chocha."

James shrugged at mention of the Tsurani morning beverage. "Never developed a taste for it. Too bitter and spicy."

Arutha waved James to a chair and said, "I've got court in fifteen minutes, but you're not attending today. I need you to do two things, one trivial, one not so."

James nodded but said nothing.

Arutha continued. "Duke Radswil and his family wish to

hunt. You will instruct our huntmaster to ready a party to accompany the Prince of Olasko to the mountains for a day's hunting the day after tomorrow."

"That's the trivial," suggested James.

Arutha nodded. "Find your missing agents if possible, and see if you can discover the source of all this mayhem in our city. That will involve a rather delicate sort of diplomacy on your part, for you must first begin at the city jail with a social call on Sheriff Means."

"Now do I get to find out why he was waiting for us when we got back to Krondor?"

Arutha regarded his young friend with an appraising look. "You haven't ferreted out that gossip by now?"

James stifled a yawn. "I've been too busy."

Arutha drained his mug and stood. James stood as well. "We have some problems between the City Watch and the sheriff's men. The sheriff was here complaining in part about Guard Captain Guruth's soldiers, especially the squad over in the poor quarter."

"Ah," said James. "A jurisdictional dispute."

"Something like that. Traditionally the City Guard concerns itself with keeping the security of the city, while the constables of the sheriff's office are more concerned with crimes, but lately the two have been clashing over trivial issues. There's always been a little rivalry, but now it's getting out of hand."

"What would you like me to do, Highness?"

As Arutha moved toward the door opening into the great hall, he said, "I want it stopped before it turns into open brawling between constables and guardsmen. See if you can devise a way in which both sides turn their attention to the murders in Krondor and stop this wrangling." Arutha left his private office for morning court, and James standing alone.

James lingered for a moment, savoring the last gulp of warm coffee, then turned and headed for the outside hallway. He had a lot to do, and as usual, not much time in which to do it.

Krondor early in the morning was James's favorite place and time. As he left the palace he was once more struck by the vibrancy of the Prince's city. The sun had risen in the east an hour earlier and already the city was teeming with activity. Wagons were rolling toward the gates to meet arriving or departing caravans, or toward the docks to pick up cargo delivered by ships in the harbor. The stream of workmen already about their jobs was increased by merchants on their way to open shops, customers heading toward those shops, and a thousand other citizens and visitors.

A breeze off the harbor carried the salt tang of the ocean and James breathed deeply, feeling revived. By noon the day's warmth would reveal every decaying fruit rind, meat scrap, discarded bone, and less savory by-product of human occupation. James had been city born and bred, and the stench of a warm day near the tanneries and dyers, or the pungency of the cattle pens and poultry yards, was taken for granted, fading into the background so that it went mostly unnoticed. But the absence of such stench was certainly appreciated.

He took another deep breath in gratitude as an ox cart trundled past, and at that moment, one of the oxen displayed his kind's tendency for flatulence, relieving himself with an heroic discharge. James's nose wrinkled and he hurried away from the spot, knowing that the gods' sense of humor was mean-spirited, and demonstrated thousands of times a day in minor human misery and inconvenience. Had it happened to someone else, he would judge the moment highly comic.

James hurried through the Royal Market, which wasn't truly a royal venue, but named such because it was the market closest to the palace. The hawkers already had their wares on display and shoppers were making their way around the stalls, inspecting the goods offered for sale.

He moved down High Street, avoiding the jam of wagons and carts at several intersections. Idly he thought that one good use of the constables would be to stand at the intersections sorting out the traffic mess in the morning. By mid-day things would have died down a bit, but right now there were at least half a dozen fights brewing as teamsters, farmers, and delivery men all shouted insults at each other.

James ducked through the heavy press of citizens and travelers and reached the next corner to find that a fight had erupted. Two wagons had obviously become tangled when a cart had overturned, causing a horse to shy, back up, then flip over its wagon. Two city constables were hurrying across and just as James reached the scene, someone shoved him aside shouting, "Make way!"

James staggered into a young woman who was carrying a basket of grain, which was dumped in the street when she fell. She shrieked angry demands for repayment. He obliged with a muttered apology, and turned to defend himself from the next stupid thug.

It turned out to be Captain Guruth, commander of the City Guard. He was a burly man with a black beard, dark eyes, and a deep voice with a naturally threatening tone, which was used effectively as he roared, "What is going on?"

Instantly the onlookers quietened, but the two combatants

continued their fisticuffs. Two guardsmen hurried past their captain and set to with spear butts just as the constables arrived to lend a hand. Quickly the two struggling men were subdued and the captain turned once, surveying the crowd. "Everyone! Get about your business or we'll find a place for you in the palace dungeon!"

Quickly the crowd dispersed and Guruth turned to James. "Squire?" he said, his tone indicating he expected an explanation for James's presence at the scene of this altercation.

James was feeling set-upon, what with being shoved aside by the guardsmen, and being addressed in that particular tone, as if he were an intruder in the city of his birth. "I'm on the Prince's business," he said, dusting himself off.

The captain offered a gruff laugh, deep and short, then said, "Well, then, you'd best be about it, while I sort out this mess."

"Actually, my mission concerns yourself and the sheriff. If you'd be so kind as to accompany me to his office," said James, walking away without seeing if the captain followed.

James heard the captain issue orders for his men to let the constables take care of the matter and to fall in. The sound of boots on stone in regular rhythm told James that the captain and his men were close behind. He picked up the pace slightly, ensuring that the captain and his men would have to step lively to keep up with him. The sheriff's office was not too far from the scene of the altercation, near the Old Market Square.

The office served as the entrance into the city jail, which was below ground, a large basement divided by bars and doors, making eight cells, two large ones, and six cells used to isolate prisoners from the general jail population. At almost any time of the day or night, half a dozen drunks, petty thieves, brawlers, and other troublemakers would be found locked up, waiting the pleasure of the Prince's magistrate.

The two floors above were occupied with living quarters for the deputies who did not have families in the city. Sheriff Wilfred Means looked up from a table he used as a desk and said, "Captain, squire," with a polite nod of his head. "To what do I owe the pleasure?" The expression on his face showed it was anything but a pleasure. The conflicts between the City Watch and the City Guard had created enough friction between the sheriff and the captain to keep things chilly between them, and Means had absolutely no use for James.

That attitude went back to James's boyhood, when Jimmy the Hand was a thorn in the side of the city's constables. No matter what rank James achieved, he was certain the sheriff would always consider him a thief at heart, and as such, suspect.

James quickly discarded several different approaches to reconciling the conflict. Arutha had told him what to do, but left how to do it up to James. One thing about both the captain and sheriff, James conceded to himself: both were honorable men, so he decided it was best to approach them directly.

"We have a problem, gentlemen," said James.

The captain and sheriff exchanged glances and each made it clear to the other neither knew what was coming next. "Problem?" asked the captain.

"Because you both have overlapping, but different areas of authority in the city, each of you may lack certain information the other possesses. But I'm sure you know that lately there has been an unusually high number of murders in the city."

The sheriff snorted. "The very reason I came to meet the Prince when he returned, squire," he said with a note of derision.

James let the tone go by. "His Highness," he said, "is concerned that there is more to this spate of murders than may at first be apparent."

Captain Guruth said, "That hardly seems likely. The body count is high, but there seems no apparent connection."

The sheriff again let his feelings show. "You're a soldier, Guruth. Your lads are fine in a donnybrook, but none of them has the knack for sniffing around and finding out things. That's what the City Watch does best."

James barely contained an explosive laugh. There were snitches in the employ of the City Watch, but they were often paid by the Mockers to give false information, and anyone who was truly in their pay was likely to turn up floating in the bay.

James said, "I do not know what His Highness has said to each of you regarding his most recent activities in confronting the Brotherhood of the Dark Path and the Nighthawks."

"Nighthawks!" Guruth shouted. He swore an oath, then said, "They're like weeds in a garden. I thought we had destroyed them ten years ago when we burned down the House of Willows!"

James realized then something he had forgotten. Guruth had been a young soldier, probably a sergeant or lieutenant when Arutha and James had led a squad of soldiers that had destroyed the Nighthawks' headquarters in Krondor, the basement below one of the finest brothels in the city. There they had found a moredhel, and there they had witnessed the power of the dark elves' wizard-king, Murmandamus, for every Nighthawk who had been slain had risen from the dead to fight anew.

Those who had struggled in the cellar below the House of Willows that night and survived would never forget that fight.

Many of those who had entered the sewers below the city to seek out that nest had died in the flames of that battle.

Guruth looked at James and said, "You know what I mean, squire."

James nodded. "Yes, I remember." Sighing, James said, "But as we learned on the road to Armengar, and again at Kenting Rush, the Nighthawks are numerous and as soon as you destroy one nest, another springs up somewhere else."

The sheriff said, "So we've assassins loose in the city, then?" He had not been in that struggle ten years before, but he had heard enough details to regard James and Guruth with a modicum of respect.

James said, "It appears likely, though no one who's reported a murder has specifically stated seeing a Nighthawk."

"No surprise there," admitted the sheriff. "They don't usually want to be seen. Lots of folks think they use magic."

"Not far from the truth," said James. "At least when they were in league with Murmandamus they had those Black Slayers with them at times, and *they* were certainly using dark powers." The Black Slayers had been magical guards of Murmandamus. What James remembered most about them was that they were very difficult to kill. James shrugged. "But the lot we disposed of over in Kenting Rush last month had no magicians in league with them from what we found. And they all died like mortal men."

Guruth gave James a half-smile and said, "But you burned the bodies anyway."

James returned the smile and said, "We did, indeed. No point taking chances."

"What does the Prince require of us?" asked the sheriff, now convinced there were dire matters at hand.

James had no specific instructions, but now that he had the captain and the sheriff considering a common enemy, he decided it would serve to make peace between them. "His Highness is concerned about the possibility of these Nighthawks being agents of a foreign power." James looked at the captain. "It would do well for you to remove your men from inside the city and concentrate on the gates and step up patrols in the neighboring villages and in the foulbourgh. Double the guards at the city gates and inspect any wagon, cart or pack animal if it looks suspicious. And any man or group of men who can't properly identify themselves and their reason for coming to Krondor should be held and interrogated." To the sheriff, he said, "With all the captain's men outside the wall, you'll have to step up your patrols inside the city. And you need to send half a dozen men to help the customs office inspect cargo and passengers coming into the city by sea."

In less than a minute, James had created enough work to have every constable and guardsman in the city cursing the day he was born. But James knew that, as busy as both companies would be, they'd have little time to wrangle over who had jurisdiction over every altercation they encountered.

James made a mental note to stop at the Customs Office and let the staff know there were six constables coming to help them inspect cargo and passengers. He said, "More instructions will be sent to you as the Prince sees fit."

The captain asked, "Anything else, squire?"

"No, captain, but I do need to speak to the sheriff alone for a moment."

"Then I'll be on my way. I need to post a new duty roster and instruct the guards they'll be operating outside the city for the time being." He gave James and the sheriff a casual salute, and left the office.

The sheriff looked at James expectantly. "Squire?" he asked after the captain left.

"You mentioned to the captain that your constables were able to sniff around, so I'm wondering: is one of your lads particularly talented when it comes to getting information on what's going on in the city?"

Means leaned back, stroking a mustache that was no longer ginger, but gray streaked with white. His hair still had some brown in it, but it too was mostly gray and white. Yet the sheriff's eyes showed he had lost nothing where it counted: he could still lay a trap for a thief and he was still a dangerous man with either sword or bludgeon. Finally he said, "There's young Jonathan. He's about as good at getting a snitch to talk as I've seen."

James said, "No disrespect, sheriff, but can you trust him? History being what it is, and all that."

The sheriff said, "No offense, squire. I understand what you mean." The Nighthawks had proven adept at infiltrating the army and even the palace in the past. "You can trust the lad. He's my youngest son."

"Well, then," said James with a grin, "I guess I can. Is he here?"

"No, he's off duty until dusk. Shall I have him come find you at the palace?"

"Please. I should be back before the changing of the guard at sundown. Have him come to the Knight-Marshal's office. If I'm not there, I'll leave word where he can find me."

"May I ask what you need one of my constables for, squire?"

James grinned. "Our past differences have kept us from

working together, sheriff. I intend to remedy that." Then the grin faded. "I've seen enough black murder in my days to last a hundred lifetimes. I'd like to find out what's behind all these seemingly random deaths and put an end to them."

The sheriff nodded and made a noncommittal grunt. "If you say so, squire."

James bid the sheriff good day and left. He took his time wandering the city, and tried to look inconspicuous as he kept an eye out for his missing agents. He paid a visit to the Customs Office at the dock and told the senior clerk that half a dozen constables would be arriving soon to lend a hand in inspecting cargo and passengers. He made it clear he was less concerned with the cargo than he was the passengers; smuggling, while a serious crime, was little more than a nuisance when compared to murder. The senior customs agent nodded absently, and James was certain that he would have to return in a day or two to see if the required changes had been made. Of all the things he had imagined as a boy—riches, power, and fame—he had not for an instant imagined the bureaucracy that came with such things.

James continued his tour of the city, poking around here and there, trying discreetly to uncover the whereabouts of his agents if they still lived. One or two of them might be lying low, he knew, but three missing and one murdered meant almost certainly most of them, if not all, were now dead. The implications of that possibility, that someone knew who they were, and by extension that they were working for the Prince's squire, was a possibility he chose not to dwell on.

As night approached, clouds rolled in off the Bitter Sea, and Krondor was quickly plunged into darkness. *Feels more like fog than rain*, James thought vaguely as he hurried back toward the palace. *And a nasty fog at that.*

If morning was his favorite time of the day, late afternoon and early evening were his least. The streets were crowded with tired citizens and visitors, people who had labored all day were now hurrying to shops to make purchases before closing time. Those inclined toward heavy drinking were already swaggering loudly down the thoroughfares, and the less savory populace of the city was now emerging as darkness fell.

Once he had numbered among those now venturing out of their daytime hideouts, the denizens of the night who preyed on the honest and hardworking, when they weren't preying upon one another. If he had a writ from the Nightmaster of the Mockers, none in that ragged brotherhood would trouble him, and even those who were not part of the Guild of Thieves left him alone, as the protection of the Mockers was not something to be brushed aside lightly.

Now he was the Prince's man, and while that provided him with a different kind of protection, he knew it shielded him not at all with those who once counted themselves his brethren. James had betrayed his oath to the Mockers in order to warn the Prince of the Nighthawks' attempt on his life, and in doing so he had committed treason against the Guild. James was vague on the details, but somehow Arutha had purchased or bartered for his life, and had taken him into the royal household. Despite that miracle, James was under no illusions. While still being on good terms with many individual Mockers, he knew the Guild itself had the death mark on him. As a means of avoiding conflict with the Prince, the Mockers ignored the mark, and viewed James with polite tolerance, no more. He still came and went in the sewers and upon the rooftops when need be, but should he be seen as a threat to the Mockers, they would exercise the death mark in an instant.

James grew tired of trying to navigate the press of people in the central city, and decided to take a shortcut through some backstreets to the palace. If he was quick, he would reach the palace in time to cadge a bite to eat from the kitchen staff, then get to the Knight-Marshal's office before Jonathan Means arrived. The absence of any agents in the city had James concerned more than he cared to let on and if Jonathan's snitches knew anything, he might be able to ferret it out using the sheriff's son.

James ducked between two buildings, through a space too narrow to be rightly called an alley, and hurried to the next street over. Wending his way through the press of the crowd, he reached the other side of the street and entered a proper alley.

The buildings on both sides were two stories tall, so it was as if he had entered a dark crevasse. It was a long, filthy passage, but one which would empty out on to a street only a block from the harbor. That would lead him on a quick route paralleling the waterfront, and take him to the harbor gate into the royal compound outside the palace.

He turned onto Chandler Row, the name for this section of the road that would take him back to the palace, when he suddenly knew he was being followed. Someone had come out of the alley behind him.

James knew better than to look back, but he itched to get a glimpse of his pursuer. He paused for a brief instant to glance into a shop window and heard his pursuer stop as well. In the distorted reflection of the glass, he couldn't make out who might be following him. The few people who passed by were fisherfolk, net-menders, dock workers, and the other types one would expect to see near the docks, and James prayed he might catch sigh of a constable before he went too much farther.

James had just passed his last opportunity to cut across to another street. He moved quickly, then suddenly slowed his pace, listening to whoever followed him.

There were two of them, he felt certain. There were enough gaps of relative silence as they moved along that he could pick out his pursuers from amongst those who passed in the other direction.

James spied an ale-house, The Wounded Leopard. He broke into a jogging run, as if he was late meeting someone, and headed straight for the door.

Once inside, he blinked at the smoke-filled room. The chimney flue hadn't been cleaned in a while, and several of the patrons were smoking pipes or tabac cigars. James had never developed a taste for the habit and wondered how anyone did.

He hurried to the bar and pushed himself between two sailors, who both muttered, but moved to give him room. The one on James's right was a mole-faced fellow whose dark eyes hinted at danger, while the one on the left was a huge brute, easily as large as Knight-Marshal Gardan. James looked forward. "Ale, please!" he demanded of the barkeep.

The man had a face like a well-worn shoe, and the bags beneath his eyes made him look as if he was on the verge of sleeping on his feet. He nodded as he filled a stoneware mug and set it on the bar before James. James paid him and took a sip. It was too warm and too bitter, but he made a pretense of drinking it.

The door opened and James knew at least one of his pursuers was entering. He chanced a quick glimpse of two men, both dressed in common workers' garb, as they stood blinking in the smoky air, trying to find James.

"I did not," James said loudly to the large sailor who stood on his left.

The man turned and looked down at James and said, "What?" It was obvious he was drunk and ill tempered.

"I wasn't the one who said it," James replied.

"Said what?" asked the man, now interested.

"He said it." James pointed toward the door. "Him and his friend."

"Said what?" demanded the drunk, now irritated by a conversation he was having difficulty following.

"I didn't say you were the drunken son of a poxy Keshian whore."

The man grabbed James by the tunic and said, "What did you call me?"

"I didn't call you a drunken son of a poxy Keshian whore," insisted James. Pointing at the door, he said, "They did."

With a bellow the sailor was off, heading right at the two men who had been following James. James turned to the dangerous-looking man on his right and said, "You should have heard what they said about you."

The man just grinned and said, "If you want me to keep those two off your neck, squire, it'll cost you."

James sighed. "You know me?"

"I've been around, young Jimmy the Hand."

"How much?"

"For you, fifty golden sovereigns."

"For that much I'd want you to take them on a long journey. How much for ten minutes?"

"Ten."

"Done," said James as a shout and crash came from behind. Men were now moving away from the combatants and a chair went flying across the bar, smashing several bottles behind the barkeep.

Despite his sleepy appearance, the barman was spry enough to vault the bar with one hand, a truncheon clutched tightly in the other. "We'll have none of that here!" he shouted.

James dug ten gold coins from his purse and laid them on the bar. The slight man scooped them up and pulled out a dagger, turning to face whoever might come his way.

James didn't hesitate. He took his lead from the barkeep and vaulted the bar in the other direction. He hurried to a rear door and ducked into a storeroom. Years of living in the city provided James with a reliable map of Krondor in his head. He knew there would be no alley at the back, rather a yard with a gate opening onto the harborside.

He hurried through the storage area, past a door which opened to the kitchen, and through a door into the ale-house's rear yard. Twenty feet away a large double gate beckoned. James sprinted to it and lifted a large wooden bar from the two iron brackets that supported it, letting it drop near his feet. He stepped over it, pushed open the gate, and was met by a gloved fist which struck him hard across the jaw.

James's eyes rolled up into his head as he fell to the cobblestones.

FIVE

# SECRETS

AMES stirred.

His left temple throbbed—he must have struck the cobbles when he fell—as did the right side of his face. He tried to move and his head pounded. His wrists were bound behind him, and he was blindfolded.

A deep voice said, "Ah, the lad stirs."

Rough hands propped him upright on the floor and the deep voice asked, "A drink?"

James's voice sounded oddly high-pitched in his own ears as he said, "Yes, please."

Someone else in the room laughed, saying, "Polite one, ain't he?" and was shushed into silence.

The original speaker said, "Get him some water."

James waited a moment, until someone pressed a water cup against his lips. He sipped slowly, wetting his throat and buying seconds to gather his wits. The fog in James's head slowly lifted.

"Feeling better?" asked the deep voice.

James took a deep breath and said, "Yes, Walter. Though you could have gotten my attention in a gentler manner than smacking me in the head."

102

The deep voice chuckled. "I told you he'd tumble to this, you twits. Let's get the blindfold off him."

James blinked as his vision returned, and he saw three men standing over him in what could only be a basement. Large barrels and crates were stacked against the windowless wall, and several large piles of goods were covered with dusty canvas. The man with the deep voice said, "How you been, Jimmy?"

"Fair enough, Walter, until about . . . what? An hour ago?"

Walter picked James up by the shoulders and turned him. He pulled off the ties that had restricted his hands and said, "Sorry about that, but you were getting difficult to keep up with."

"If you wanted to talk, Walter, there are other ways."

The man named Walter glanced at his companions. "Things aren't the way they once was, Jimmy. Lots of troubles in the city." Walter Blont was one of the Mockers' more effective bashers, trained by Ethan Graves. He was normally a man of even temper who went about his work in a journeyman fashion, without anger or spite. He had a plain round face, and a thatch of black hair now shot through with gray.

James took a moment and looked at Blont's companions. Both looked the part of Guild bashers: thick necks, heavy shoulders and legs like tree trunks. Either one would probably be able to break a man's skull with a bare fist. Neither man looked particularly bright, but James knew looks could be deceptive. Both men were unfamiliar to him, but he was certain that these were not the two men who were following him when he went into the ale-house. "Those weren't your men who were tailing me?"

"No," said Walter. "They were so fixed on following you, they didn't notice *we* were following *them*." He grinned, his crooked yellow teeth making him look even more menacing than when he didn't smile. "There are all sorts of new gangs in Krondor these days. Bashers and strong-arms arrive every week by ship and caravan. Someone's building up a serious army."

James sat down on a crate and said, "Start at the beginning, Walter."

Walter sat down on another crate and rubbed his chin, thinking. "Mostly, it started a few months ago. You heard of this bloke they call the Crawler?"

James nodded, then wished he hadn't as his head throbbed.

"Well, we've been running up against his men on and off for months now. At first they were just pesky. Then things got nasty."

Walter glanced at his companions. "We're about all that's left of the bashers. A few nights ago, someone broke into Mother's—"

"Someone got to Mother's without being stopped?" interrupted James in amazement.

"Took out each of the sentries as they came, hard and fast and no time for dawdling. Me and Josh and Henry here was out and about, and we got jumped in the sewers. We got the best of the four lads who tried to take us out." He waved to the man on his left. "Josh got a dagger scraped across his ribs for his troubles, and Henry had to sew up my shoulder with a sailmaker's needle and some thread. We found Mother's in ruins and have been lying low since then."

The man named Henry added, "It's a war out there, squire. The sewers are worse than any battlefield I've seen."

"Soldier?" asked James.

"Once," said Henry. "Long time back."

James nodded again, and winced. "I've got to stop doing that."

"Sorry about the bash, but you're such a slippery lad, it was the only way I knew to get you here," said Walter.

James grimaced. His head was going to hurt for a while. "You could have sent me a note."

"Hardly; and besides, we're not traveling too much by the usual routes, what with the cut-throats and assassins haunting the sewers."

"Assassins?" asked James. "Nighthawks?"

"Maybe. Didn't see no black outfits like they was wearing before," said Walter, "but these boys was mean and didn't play at killing."

"They's very serious on the subject," said Henry.

Walter nodded. "We've dodged them because almost no one knows of this place. It was a bit of a gamble going up after you, but one of the beggar lads who's been smuggling us food saw you out and about today and said you were coming this way, so we took a chance. Time was you could have traveled the entire city and have no one catch sight of you."

James grinned ruefully, "I still can, but these days I have little reason to hide. I work for the Prince, remember?"

"That's to the heart of it, then. We need help."

"Who, the Mockers?"

"What's left of them," Walter said grimly.

"What's the Upright Man propose?" James knew that Walter would never presume to speak for the Mockers without the leader's permission. Walter must be his messenger of last resort.

The three men exchanged glances, and Walter said, "You haven't heard, then?"

"Heard what?"

"Rumor is the Upright Man is dead."

James sat back and let out a slow breath. "That puts paid to a lot of things, doesn't it?"

Walter shrugged. "You don't get where he did without making lots of enemies. Someone's hoisting a tankard in celebration if it's true, that's a fact."

"Who's running the Mockers?"

"No one," said Walter. "We're probably all that's left of the bashers. Maybe there are one or two other lads lying low like us. Most of them died when Mother's was hit. They killed everyone, Jimmy. They killed the pickpockets and the beggars, the whores and the street boys."

"They murdered the street boys?" James said in disbelief.

"I think I saw young Limm and two or three others dodging down a culvert later that night but I can't be sure it was them. I didn't investigate because they was on the run from half a dozen men. Maybe they got away, but anyone who wasn't fast enough to dodge out of there, or lucky enough to have been somewhere else when they hit, was killed. Word spread fast and those that could got out of the city or went to ground."

Henry added, "These weren't dock-brawlers did this, squire, or even bashers like us. These were killers, who didn't even give you a moment to think or speak or ask what was what. They were cutting throats and dropping everyone—men, women, children—on one side of the building before those on the other side even knew there was a fight. It's been a fair couple of nights of hunt or be hunted in the sewers, I can tell you. We've been hiding here since then."

James glanced around. "This is the smugglers' hideout?"

"You've been here before?" asked Walter.

"A couple of times, when we were working with Trevor Hull and his gang. Back when Bas-Tyra was regent."

"I remember," said Walter. "Even most of the Mockers don't know how to find it, and since the spot above where the old mill burned down's been paved over with that new road, it's impossible to find from above."

"Anything in those crates to eat?"

"If there is, it's long since turned," answered the man named Josh.

"This place hasn't been used since Hull turned Prince's man and started sailing for the Crown."

James looked around. "How many others do you think know of this place?"

Walter shrugged. "Not many. Assuming any of them lived after the raid. Hull's men did most of the slippin' in and out, and just a few of us in the bashers."

"Then let's keep this our little secret." James stood and his knees wobbled. Putting his hand on the wall, he steadied himself and said, "What of the clock?"

"An hour after sundown, or thereabouts," answered Henry.

"Damn," said James. "I have to get back to the palace, and you've put me twice the distance I was when I started."

"Best get up to the watch station two streets over, and get some guards to go back with you to the palace."

"That will take too long," said James. "Besides, I know a way that will get me within a block of the palace without anyone seeing me."

Walter smiled, for the first time. "Well, there was always that about you, wasn't there? You could find ways around no one else could. That's why you were always able to take those extra little jobs without the Nightmaster's writ."

James returned the smile. "Me, work without permission from the Nightmaster?" he said with mock gravity. "What, and risk you and your lads finding me and roughing me up? I would never do that."

"Well, it's good to see you've kept your humor," said Henry, as he looked from Josh to Walter. Then he looked at James. "What are we to do?"

"Stay here. I'll try to be back before the morning with some food and drink for you."

"Why would you do that?" asked Josh.

"Because you asked," answered James. "And, as of now, you're working for me."

"But our oath to the Mockers—" began Josh.

"—is only valid if there are Mockers," finished James. He started walking to the wall farthest from the sewer entrance. "If, by some miracle of fate, the Upright Man returns, you'll not be bound by me. I know what it is to break oath with him. Few survive. But if he doesn't turn up, well, I've got something you can do to earn your keep and stay on the good side of the law."

"Good side of the law?" asked Josh.

"Fancy that," remarked Henry.

James pointed his finger at each man in turn. "You need all the friends you can get, and right now I may be the only one you have."

Walter nodded once. "You've got the right of that, Jimmy."

"It's Squire James, from now on."

"Yes, squire. I see," answered Walter.

James felt along the wall until he found what he was looking for. He tripped a latch and a door, fashioned to look like a random cluster of stones in the wall, creaked open.

"I didn't know that was there!" said Walter.

"Few do," James replied. As he was about to enter, he added, "Look, if I'm not back in a couple of days, assume the worst and you're on your own. In that case, I suggest you find the sheriff and tell him what you know. Means is a tough boot, but he's fair."

"Don't know about the fair part, but I'll grant you tough," said Walter. "We'll think about that if we have to."

James nodded, and went through the door. He pulled it closed behind him and felt along in the utter darkness. He knew it was only one hundred steps up an inclined passage to a trap that had been laid into the floor of what had once been a root cellar in the house next to the burned-out mill. Fortunately for James, that part of the house hadn't been paved over, and was shielded from curious eyes by heavy weeds and brush.

Once he was above ground, he moved through the darkness, avoiding the larger thoroughfares as he made his way toward the palace district. He reached the city gate just north of the palace itself, and hurried through, passing a surprised-looking guard who recognized him and who appeared about to ask a question, though James didn't linger to hear it.

James reached the small square, which served to separate the palace proper from the city, and hurried toward the gate. The two guardsmen on duty seemed about to order him to halt when they recognized him. One said, "Squire James? Is there trouble?"

"Always," answered James, signaling for the gate to be opened. One of the soldiers hurried to accommodate him, and James swept past him without another comment.

James reached the top of the steps to the palace and waved over the first page he spied. "Carry word to the Prince that I have returned and will join him as soon as I can make myself presentable."

The page wrinkled his nose at the sewer aroma that trailed James like a palpable miasma, then remembered his court training. "Squire!" he acknowledged, and hurried off as quickly as he could.

James almost ran to his room, stripping off his clothing. He'd take a complete bath later, but for the time being the best he could manage was a quick wash with a cloth dipped in the water basin.

Ten minutes later, James emerged from his quarters, to find the same page had return from the Prince. "Squire!" said the young boy. "His Highness says he will await you in his offices."

James hurried to Arutha's offices, knocked, and entered when bidden. Inside, James found a very uncomfortable-looking young man in a city constable's uniform standing near the door, while the Prince sat behind his desk.

"This young fellow was looking for you," said Arutha, indicating the constable with a nod of his head. "When no one could find you, Gardan sent him to me. The constable said you were due to meet him on some matter the sheriff and you deemed important. He was somewhat distressed you were not where you agreed to be."

James smiled and said, "As well he might, for I was being held against my will."

Arutha's face remained impassive but there was a slight hint of amusement in his voice as he said, "It appears you saved me the difficulty of ordering out the guard to rescue you."

"My captors and I came to an agreement."

Arutha indicated he should sit. Before he did, James looked at the young man and said, "You're Jonathan Means?"

"Yes, squire," answered the young constable. He was perhaps the same age as William, yet there was already evident about him a toughness that James knew well from years of dodging city constables. In the presence of the Prince he might appear to be an awkward boy, but in a brawl Jonathan Means could hold his own, James was certain.

Arutha said, "I'll listen to your tale of escape later. What I need to know is, what is going on in my city?"

James said, "Nothing good. As Jonathan and the other constables can no doubt testify, there's been a rash of killings lately that appear to make no sense. As you observed, these killings seem random, but I think the pattern is there. We're just not seeing it."

"You have some sense of things, though, right?" asked Arutha.

James nodded. "The Crawler. It appears he has made another bid to dislodge the Mockers, and from what I saw and heard, he may have accomplished that goal."

Arutha mused aloud. "Does it matter if one band of thugs and pickpockets supplants another? People will still be bullied and robbed."

"Setting aside my familiarity with the Mockers and friendship for many of them, still, there is a difference. The Mockers are thieves. They come in a variety of forms, from those who will deftly cut your purse from your belt without disturbing your ruminations on which silk scarf to buy in the market, to those who will simply bang you over the head as you stagger home after too much ale. They number beggars, street boys, whores, and those who, like myself once, are adept at entering homes and stealing whatever has value without awakening the occupants. But they're not killers."

"I've heard otherwise," said Arutha.

"Oh, from time to time a basher will hit someone too hard, or someone will awake and find a thief in the home. A struggle will ensue and someone gets stuck with a dagger, but the intent is never to kill. The Upright Man was very specific in that; murder brings down far more attention than he wanted for the Mockers."

Arutha considered his one long-ago contact with the man he suspected was the Upright Man. His instinct told him James was right. "What about this Crawler and his men?"

James considered his words a moment, then said to Jonathan, "Did the sheriff tell you why I asked you to the palace?"

"No, he just said you'd requested a constable come to the palace and I was the one."

"I asked him for someone who had a knack for getting information out of folks without having to hold their feet to the fire."

For the first time since entering the office, the young man ventured a slight smile. "I've a snitch or two who trust me."

James regarded the young man for a long moment, then came to a decision. "I'm going to need help, Highness. I've got Jonathan's father and Captain Guruth sorted out for a while on who is in charge of which area of the city."

"Good," said Arutha.

James went on to describe what he had seen as he had explored the city, and went into some detail about the two men who had followed him before Walter had snared him, and then into Walter's description of the men who had raided Mother's. "So if I'm going to do Your Highness any good out there, I'm going to need more men like Jonathan and Walter and his mates. I'm going to need my own company of men."

"A company?" Arutha's expression darkened slightly. "Squires hardly ever command companies, James."

James grinned. "Well, if you remember, it was just a few weeks back I was commanding the entire garrison at North Warden."

Arutha returned James's grin with his own half-smile. "Well, I can't argue with that."

"Perhaps company is the wrong word. That would be too many men, in any event, but I do need men like Jonathan here, men who won't be out of place when they're seen here and there, but who are working for me."

"Is that all right?" Jonathan asked of the Prince. "Your Highness?" he added quickly.

Arutha said, "It's all right, if I say it is. Your father doesn't need to know the specifics of any work you do for the Crown, just that occasionally you'll be called away from your usual duties to help out on some security issues."

James said, "I think maybe a dozen men or so, perhaps even a woman or two if they're the right kind."

"What kind is that?" asked Arutha.

"Smart, tough, able to take care of themselves, and loyal."

Arutha said, "Loyal to you?"

James was silent for a long time before he answered. "Some of the people I'm going to need don't put much stock in loyalty to the Crown, Highness. Personal loyalty and personal oaths are more tangible to them. There are men who would swear to serve me, whom I could trust with my life, but whom I wouldn't trust to stand fast if they were only bound by an oath to the nation. It may not be ideal, but that's the way it is."

Arutha nodded. "You know I've been toying with the idea of an intelligence service to match wits with the Keshians. More than once the king and I have discussed the difficulties of relying on paid informants and rumor-mongers. No matter what their ambassador says before our court, Kesh is always casting her eyes northward, dreaming of retaking the ancient province of Bosania as well as the Vale of Dreams."

James smiled. "And whatever else they can get their hands on."

Arutha nodded. "What concerns me most, at this moment, is the report of the destruction of the Mockers, for if we link that to your confrontation with the Crawler's agents in Silden, and the apparent link between the Crawler and the Nighthawks at Kenting Rush, I can only come to one conclusion."

"What's that?"

"There's something very big underway. And we've only glimpsed small portions of that something."

James nodded. "I am afraid it might be something along those lines. I had thought we'd finished at last with the Nighthawks after killing their leader at Cavell Keep."

"I suspect we'll find he was but one of many leaders, James," said Arutha absently. "In all the years since we first faced the Nighthawks, one thing has nagged at me and until this moment I didn't realize what it was."

"What is it?" asked James, exchanging a glance with Jonathan.

Arutha said, "There are too many assassins."

James didn't follow. His brow furrowed and he cocked his head slightly. "Too many?"

Arutha stood and James did as well. The Prince occasionally

paced when he spoke and James wouldn't presume to be informal with Jonathan in the room.

"Assassins are employed for a variety of purposes," began Arutha. "The first is extortion: they send a note demanding a fee for not killing you and if you fail to comply, they murder you. The second is that they are employed to remove someone as an act of revenge, profit, or for political advantage."

"You've forgotten a third reason," said James.

Arutha waved his hand in dismissal. "No I haven't. I'm ruling out religious fanaticism because the Temple of Lims-Kragma disavowed themselves from any contact with these Nighthawks years ago, and the Temple of Guis-Wa have their own particular brand of murders, and these murders have none of the earmarks of a ritual Blood Hunt."

James flushed slightly. Arutha was rarely not completely prepared in any discourse. "I stand corrected."

Arutha said, "If profit were the motive, then we'd have been alerted to at least one or two threats by concerned citizens. So we'll rule that out. That leaves murder for gain."

"But whose gain?"

"Exactly. Why kill random citizens and attempt to obliterate the Mockers?"

James paused because he realized the question wasn't rhetorical. Arutha wanted his opinion. After a moment, he said, "I have no theory on the random citizens who, as we already suspect, are probably not as random as they appear. As to the latter, the only reason to obliterate the Mockers is either to displace them or keep them from observing something."

Arutha pointed at James. "Exactly. Which is more likely?"

James sighed with fatigue. "Displacing them, I guess. If secrecy were the goal, you'd hardly go about it by murdering

115

dozens of thieves, whores, urchins, and thugs. You'd just go somewhere very quiet and see that it stays quiet. There are dozens of places in the woods and mountains nearby you could use as a base, within a few days' ride of the city where no one would notice even a large company of men. No, for them to want the Mockers out of the sewers, they want to take over control of crime in the city."

"I agree," said Arutha. "Now, how do you reconcile this business with what we've seen of the Nighthawks so far?"

James fought off a yawn. "I don't. It seems they work for the Crawler, yet it appears they have their own purpose."

Arutha nodded. "Remember those false Nighthawks Locklear found in the sewers when he brought Gorath to the palace?"

James said, "I heard the story."

"Did we ever establish who they were working for?"

James shrugged. "They were dead, so Locky didn't think to ask them, and at the time I assumed they were working for those who were trying to keep Gorath from reaching the palace. Now I'm more of a mind that they were trying to get you to send your army into the sewers."

"Either way, they wanted the Nighthawks to get the blame," said Arutha. "I have a theory. Suppose the Nighthawks may have worked for the Crawler when it suited their purpose, perhaps to further some agenda of their own, or simply to underwrite their own needs? After all, keeping men fed and armed in hideouts around the Kingdom isn't done cheaply. Suppose the Crawler became fearful of them for some reason? Then it would make perfect sense that he would attempt to attach blame to them for much of what he and his band of cut-throats were attempting in Krondor."

James said, "So we can sum up by saying that there's more than one band of murderers running around the city? These Nighthawks and another band of killers-for-hire?"

"Apparently," replied Arutha. "But it's more like a small army of mercenaries if the numbers we've encountered so far are any indication." Arutha sat again. "I want you to take Jonathan here under your wing and start setting up an information gathering network. I will not tell you how to do it, but I will caution you to pick only people who are smart enough not to be caught out working for you and loyal enough not to sell you out for a pouch of gold. I will underwrite the costs and you only have to report direct to me."

To Jonathan, Arutha said, "Tell your father you'll be working for me from time to time, but not the specifics, and tell him that if you leave your post or do not show up for your assigned watch, it's at my order."

"Sire," said the young man, nodding. He ventured a slight smile. "He won't like it, but he'll do as ordered by Your Highness."

Looking at James, Arutha said, "You have your company of men, squire."

James grinned. "Now can I get something to eat and a night's sleep?"

"Yes, but in the morning I want you about your business."

As he moved toward the door, James said, "How are our guests from Olasko doing?"

Arutha said, "I'm sending the duke and his brood on a hunting trip up to the mountains. We'll be shed of them for a week or so, then we'll have one more gala and wave good-bye to them as they sail off to Durbin."

James bowed. "Highness."

As he reached the door, Arutha said, "Before I forget, be here early tomorrow. We're commissioning the cadet officers and it will be a formal morning court."

James kept his grin frozen in place, but inwardly he groaned. By the time he finished eating and bathing, that would leave less than five hours before he had to be up again.

Jonathan bowed to the Prince and followed the squire from the office. As James stood aside for a page to close the door, he said to Jonathan, "Come to the kitchen and we'll eat together. That way we can talk and I can steal an extra half-hour's sleep."

With a small smile, the young constable fell in beside James, and they hurried toward the kitchen.

# SIX

# CONFUSION

RUMPETS sounded in the courtyard.

Arutha led his court officials to the balcony overlooking the marshaling yard. As he took his place at the very edge, Swordmaster McWirth saluted and turned to order the cadets to attention.

Arutha paused, then said, "Today you young men are being awarded your offices and spurs. You will be privileged to add the title 'knight' to whatever rank you gain. It is an ancient title, its origins lost in the mists of history and lore. It is held that the original band of knights were companions to one of the Kingdom's earliest rulers, a small company of those pledged to defend the crown with their lives.

"So it is with you, today. Unlike soldiers sworn to the service of their liege lord, your oath is to the crown. You are obliged to show deference to any noble of this land, and if possible to aid him when called upon, but foremost your duty lies to the King in the east, and to my office in the west."

James smiled slightly. As long as he had known Arutha, he had never known the Prince to claim personally what he felt was rightly due the office he held. Other men would have said, "To me in the west," but not Arutha.

The Prince continued. "Today, some of you will be dispatched to garrisons along the frontier, or to join households of nobles who are in need of young officers to serve until their own sons are of an age to command. A few of you may rise to the rank of swordmaster in those households, or return to Krondor when those sons are grown. Others of you will be assigned to the castles of the border lords, and some of you will remain in Krondor. But where you serve is of secondary importance.

"What you have chosen to do is serve the nation, and her people, no matter where you are. Never lose sight of that. You may gain rank and privileges over your life, but that rank and those privileges are not rewards. They are, rather, the means by which you may further serve the Kingdom." Arutha paused, then said, "In the war with the Tsurani, what has become known as the Riftwar, we faced a foe with whom we are now at peace. But the struggle was terrible and long, for those that faced us on the battlefield were men with honor, dedicated to service. We met them with the same dedication, and that was the salvation of our nation."

Arutha paused, then said, "I am pleased to welcome you to the service of the Kingdom, young officers."

He nodded to McWirth who said, "At the sound of your name, come forward and accept your spurs." He then called the first name, and the first cadet stepped forward. Two pages stood close by to quickly affix the spurs to the boots of each cadet. Eleven young officers were quickly sworn to service and given their ranks. William was the last of these.

To Arutha's right stood Knight-Marshal Gardan, in his last

official act before resigning his office. He started issuing orders. Four of the cadets were heading north, to the border barons. Five were being dispatched to various garrisons and households in the west. Two were to remain in Krondor. William was one of those.

James caught a slight frown from William when this was announced, and wondered at the displeasure. Krondor was the best duty station in the Western Realm, both for amenities and political advancement. It might be different in the Eastern Realm, where constant battles with pesky neighbors close to the nation's capital could bring one favor from the crown, but in the west all advancement and political favors started and ended in Krondor.

Arutha turned to James and said, "You have business in the city, I believe?"

James nodded. "Ample business. When shall I return?"

As he headed back inside to his offices, Arutha said, "When you have something important to tell me. You're no longer senior squire."

James almost stumbled. "Highness?"

Arutha turned from the courtyard and gave James a slight smile. He left the balcony and entered the palace as James followed. "No reflection on you, squire, but I've had you running around the countryside so much of late, Master de Lacy and Jerome both complain bitterly they have to make up for those tasks you're not present to undertake. So, while you're to remain my personal squire, we'll elevate someone else to the rank of senior. Besides, spending your days overseeing a squad of boys might seem a little tame after commanding a garrison."

James smiled. "Annoying is the better choice of words."

Arutha laughed, one of his rare displays of mirth. "Annoying it is. One last task, though, before you dash off. The Duke of

Olasko's party leaves at first light tomorrow for their hunt. For reasons I don't understand, they've requested that Lieutenant William be assigned to the guard."

James's brow furrowed. "Paulina?"

Arutha reached his desk and sat. He waved across the room to de Lacy that he should open the door and admit those waiting upon the Prince to conduct the day's business. "The Princess, yes. She is to accompany her father and the Princes on the hunt. Why?"

"She's looking for a rich or powerful husband."

"The son of a duke, in other words."

James nodded. "Though I don't think anyone has told her that the Duke Pug is a bit of an . . . odd duke by most people's standards."

"But well-connected," added Arutha.

James grinned. "Well, there is that. Still, I think I'd better spend a little time today preparing William for his duties."

Arutha looked from James to the door as the first group of supplicants was escorted in by Master de Lacy. "I don't want to know," the Prince said to James. "You know what must be done, so go do it."

"Yes, sire," said James as he left the Prince's offices. He hurried to the marshaling yard, intent on catching McWirth and William before the newly commissioned Lieutenant was assigned a patrol down to the Vale of Dreams or through the bandit-infested scrub grass and woodlands between Krondor and Land's End. Then he would go hunt up young Jonathan Means and start building his network of agents.

James found William in the Cadets' Quarters, clearing out his gear from the small footlocker that had been the repository of his entire wardrobe and other personal belongings for the last six months. McWirth was overseeing the departure of the newly named knights, and his manner was changed. He looked upon the young men as a father would upon his children, thought James. Then he realized that in a few weeks another company of noble sons, ranking Kingdom officers and a few promising young soldiers would come to Krondor and once again the old soldier would be a tyrant who could never be pleased.

William looked up and before James could speak, he said, "Krondor! Why?"

James said, "I have no idea, but any other man in your position would be doing handsprings of joy. Here's where careers are made, Will."

William looked as if he was about to say something, but he held silent for a moment. "I have to move this over to the armory."

James knew that's where young bachelor officers had small, private quarters. "I'll give you a hand."

William nodded, his expression still dark. It would have taken him only two trips to carry all his personal belongings to the armory, but he welcomed the help. William strapped on his sword, which was the only item used in training he would take with him, and picked up a bundle of clothing, which he handed to James. He then picked up a second bundle with two pair of boots, a great cloak, and two books, and nodded to James to lead on.

James turned and walked to the door, passing Swordmaster McWirth. As William reached the door he paused and said, "Swordmaster?"

McWirth said, "Yes, lieutenant?" His voice was calm and even.

James turned and saw William's surprised expression and realized that it hadn't sunk in yet that he was now an officer and McWirth wasn't going to be yelling at him any more. William hesitated and then said, "I just wished to thank you for all you've taught me. I hope I'll not disappoint you in the future."

McWirth smiled and said, "Son, if there had been the slimmest chance of you disappointing me in the future, you never would have been awarded those spurs." He pointed to William's boots where two new silver spurs adorned his heels. "You'll do fine. Now, hurry up and get your things over to the armory before the other lieutenants see you hauling your own kit in and start giving you grief over not having one of the pages or soldiers carry it over for you."

James stood motionless for a moment, then laughed. Suddenly William realized that as a knight-lieutenant in the garrison, he could have ordered a page or one of the soldiers to fetch his kit for him. Then McWirth turned to James and said, "Or you, squire, about being William's dog-robber. Get along now, the two of you."

"Yes, swordmaster," said James.

William hurried along. "Where did that term come from?"

"From what I hear, in ancient times knights weren't so prosperous and their squires had to be clever in where they got their next meal for their masters."

William grinned. "Should I make you my squire, squire?"

James returned the grin with a mock frown. "I'd pay a gold sovereign to see you accomplish that trick, *sire*," he said, sarcastically. "If you're certain you wish a personal squire, I can see if one of the less gifted pages would consider a career with almost no opportunity for advancement. And I'd be interested to see where you get the funds to pay him."

They reached the armory and hurried through the large doors, past racks of swords, shields, pole arms, and other weapons. In the rear of the armory they could hear the noises from the smith as he repaired weapons blunted by soldiers in practice. They reached the stairs at the rear of the building and climbed them to the upper floor. William put down his clothing on the floor and looked around. "That room looks unoccupied," he said, pointing to an open door.

James said, "I'll save you a drubbing. You're supposed to wait for the most senior bachelor knight to assign you a room." He pointed to the apparently empty room. "That room is almost certain to belong to Captain Treggar."

William grimaced. Captain Treggar was a humorless young man who according to gossip must have been an exceptional soldier to have hung on to his post despite being a bully and prone to petty rages. He also was considered to be unusually clever to have lasted as long as he had at the garrison with Gardan in charge of the military.

A few minutes later newly appointed Knight-Lieutenant Gordon O'Donald, youngest son of the Earl of Mallow Haven, topped the stairs, carrying his bundle. "Free room?" he asked.

William said, "We wait for Treggar."

Gordon dumped his kit right where he stood. "And isn't that the end to a perfect day." His voice carried a hint of the lilt common to the Kennararch people from the foothills of the Peaks of Tranquility. He was a broad-shouldered young man, slightly taller than William and James, with sandy blond hair and blue eyes. His complexion was fair, so he was constantly sunburned and freckled.

James said, "You both seem a little sour for having just received the best post in the west."

"The west," echoed Gordon. "My father, I'm betting, asked the Prince to keep me here and out of trouble. My brothers were both killed in war, Malcolm at the fight with the Tsurani at the end of the Riftwar, the one up in the Gray Tower Mountains, and Patrick at Sethanon. I'm the youngest, and Father is trying to keep me alive until I inherit."

"Staying alive is a worthy undertaking," said James with mock gravity.

"Well and good for those of you born here, squire, but a man gets little chance for promotion in the west."

James frowned. "Correct me if I'm wrong, but you're going to be an earl some day. Why would you worry about promotion?"

Gordon said, "We're a little earldom at Mallow Haven, and battlefield honors count for much in the east. You've got your goblins and Brothers of the Dark Path and all out here, but in the east we're constantly bagging away at the Eastern Kingdoms or Kesh. Advancement is fast, and you need all the advantages you can when arranging state marriages."

James and William looked at each other and grinned. In unison they said, "It's a girl!"

James said to Gordon, "Who is she?"

Gordon's sunburned face couldn't hide the blush as he said, "My Lord of Deep Taunton's daughter, Rebecca. She's the daughter of a duke, and if I have a prayer of winning her, I must return home with enough glory around my shoulders to blind the king."

James shrugged. "Well, it may have been once true that you

127

couldn't find a decent war in the west, but that's not been true since I've been in Krondor."

William said, "At least you're in the best place in the west for advancement."

Footsteps could be heard from below as a dozen pair of heavy boots walked toward the door. "Pick up your gear," suggested James.

A moment later a dark head appeared, followed by a broad pair of shoulders as Knight-Captain Treggar plodded up the stairs. He was followed by the other unmarried knights. When he saw the two new lieutenants waiting for him, he frowned. When he saw James, his expression turned to one of open distaste. "What's this, then?" he asked.

William said, "Waiting to be assigned rooms, captain."

The other lieutenants continued to come up the stairs until the hall was full. Several whispered and a couple shrugged. James recognized they were waiting for Treggar to act. The expected hazing of the newly-appointed knights wasn't proceeding as planned.

Treggar was about to speak, when James said, "The Prince is anxious to get Knight-Lieutenant William settled in, as he has a special mission for him."

Whatever Treggar was about to say went unsaid. Instead he pointed and said, "End of the hall. We're short of rooms, so you two will have to double up until someone marries or is reassigned."

"Yes, captain," said Gordon, moving through the press of officers.

William said, "Thank you, captain," and followed.

James said, "I'll wait for you here, lieutenant."

"Off your usual beaten path, aren't you squire? I hear that

you're far more often found in the sewers than the palace," observed Treggar.

James stared at the captain for a moment. He had deep, dark eyes, and there was nothing but anger and contempt in his gaze. His heavy brow always seemed knit in concentration except when he was on public display before the Knight-Marshal or the Prince. It was rumored that more than one younger officer and dozens of the palace garrison had been invited out to a beating after nightfall for displeasing Treggar. At last, in a pleasant voice, James said, "I go wherever my Prince requires." He was tempted to challenge Treggar, but years of dealing with bullies as a boy told James this wasn't a fight he could win. Embarrassing the captain in front of the other young officers would turn dislike into hatred, and whatever else he might be, Treggar was an important member of the palace garrison. Besides, he would most likely take out any slight, imagined or otherwise, on Gordon and William.

Seeing that whatever fun planned for the new officers was not going to happen, the other officers drifted off to their own rooms or down the stairs to their duty stations. After a moment, Gordon and William appeared.

William looked at James. "What's the mission, James?"

Treggar turned and snarled, "When you address a member of the court, lieutenant, you will use his title." He paused, then added, "No matter who he might be."

William said, "Yes, captain." To James he said, "What's the mission, squire?"

James said, "You're to take an escort of a dozen men and accompany His Highness's guests on a hunting trip. Report to the huntmaster with the escort an hour before dawn."

"Yes, squire."

Looking at Treggar, James said, "Come see me before you retire tonight, lieutenant. I may have some last-minute instructions for you."

William said, "Yes, squire."

James turned and departed quickly. He knew nothing would be gained by lingering, save to contribute to Treggar's foul mood. He would likely find something for William to do before nightfall that would either embarrass or somehow punish the young man for robbing Treggar of his fun. James knew bullies. Eventually William and Gordon would have to come to their own terms with Treggar.

Crossing the courtyard, James considered that William was a tough enough lad. He could handle himself. James suspected that Gordon might turn out to be as tough in his own way, too. Besides, Treggar had been a bachelor officer a long time and knew precisely what he could and couldn't get away with in the bachelor officers' mess. Being Head of Mess had privileges, but it had responsibilities as well, and had Treggar been truly abusive Gardan would have removed him a long time ago. One thing James knew about Arutha and his knight-marshal: there was no detail so trivial that it escaped their notice for too long. Problems were quickly uncovered and dealt with.

Passing through the gate, James considered his first stop as a guard waved a casual salute to him. Then James stopped. He had left by the western gate of the palace, once the main entrance, but now used mostly for ceremonial arrivals, processions from the city, holy day rites, and the like, while most of the commerce of the palace now was conducted via the harbor gate and the eastern gate.

A great house sat on the opposite side of the square that marked the western boundary of the palace grounds. Between the house and the gate stood a fountain, modest in size, but ancient and considered something of a landmark, for it had been the first in the city constructed by the order of one of the early princes. James studied the house. It was a large building, the massive exterior promising many interior rooms. And to the best of his knowledge, it had been abandoned for years. James corrected himself; it wasn't abandoned, but unoccupied. From time to time some activity could be detected around the building, a fresh coat of paint on wood trim or the iron gate, or repairs to stones in the outer wall. But now it was clear someone was preparing the building to be occupied.

"What's going on?" he asked a guard at the gate, nodding toward the house.

"Don't know. Been wagons coming and going since yesterday, squire."

"That house has been closed up as long as I can remember," said the guard standing on the other side of the gate. "Don't know even who owns it."

James said, "It's owned by the Temple of Ishap."

Both cast him a glance, but neither asked how he knew. James made a habit of knowing things about the city and neither guard doubted his word.

"They usually keep to themselves," James half muttered. "I wonder what this is about?"

Both guards knew the question was rhetorical and kept silent, as James turned his attention from the new arrival across the street to an old problem: the Nighthawks.

James emerged from between two buildings, his clothing far less fashionable than what he had worn when he had left the palace. He had several stashes around the city where he had secreted clothing, weapons, and money, against a multitude of possible needs. Blending into the common rabble was common necessity for the Prince's squire.

James moved through the midday press in the merchants' section of the city, near where it unofficially turned into the Poor Quarter. No one could point to any map or charter that defined the city's districts in such a fashion, but all who lived in Krondor knew where the market section ended and the dockside began, where Harborside became Fishtown and how the other unofficial precincts were arrayed. And knowing where one district ended and another began was vital to one's health and safety, James knew.

He crossed the nondescript street that separated the merchants' and Poor quarters, and as he entered the latter, the streets seemed to shrink, to narrow, to confine. Buildings rose up on both sides, leaving barely enough room for a cart to pass between, keeping them in gloom except when the sun was at its zenith.

James's posture and walk didn't change as he moved into his old haunts, but his awareness did. The streets of the poor quarter in the daytime were almost as busy as the other sections of the city, but they were far more dangerous. The dangers were less obvious than at night, but they were potentially more lethal for their subtlety. Within moments James sensed the disquiet that permeated the district. Glances were more furtive than usual, people moved just a bit more hurriedly than was the norm. Voice were hushed and strangers were watched closely. The killings were making a suspicious population even less trusting.

James turned into an even narrower path, an alley with an occasional door or a wooden stairway to a second story entrance above. Near the end of the alley he saw a hunched-over figure securing items to a two-wheeled pony cart. The door that had been his intended destination was open.

James drew his dagger and held it so it was hidden behind his wrist. A quick flip would bring it into play if needed.

Reaching striking distance to the figure he stopped and said, "Sophia?"

The figure turned and drew herself to her full height and James relaxed. The woman was gray-haired with just enough dark brown to show the original color of her youth. She held one hand in what James knew was a warding position. A moment later, she relaxed and said, "Jimmy. You just about scared what few years I have left out of me."

James walked over to the pony cart and then glanced at the open door. "Leaving?"

"As soon as I tie down this last bundle."

"Where are you bound?"

"I don't know, and I'm not sure I want anyone in Krondor knowing where I land, Jimmy."

James studied the woman's face. Never a pretty woman— her features had rightly been called horsey in her youth— Sophia possessed a strength in her bearing and a strong body that made her striking, and had won her a fair share of lovers over the years, men of wealth as often as not. But Sophia's trade in spells, charms and magic potions had gained her a life that was ultimately solitary, save for a few trusted friends, like James.

James nodded at her remark. "If you want to vanish, I understand, but I would like to know why if I may?"

"You've heard of the killings; I don't have to ask. You wouldn't be the Prince's man and not know."

"You're fearful of joining that departed company?"

She nodded. Adjusting her blue dress and fetching a black shawl off the top of the cart, she moved to close the door to her small room. "What may not have caught your attention is that most of those who are not members of the Mockers, removed for reasons you're no doubt more familiar with than I, were practitioners of the art."

"Magicians?" asked James, suddenly keenly interested in what the woman had to say.

"Five to the best of my knowledge. Most of their names would be unknown to you, for they practiced in private. We're not as public a bunch as those down in Stardock, Jimmy. Some of us prefer a quiet livelihood."

"And others?"

"Practice crafts which might not be looked upon with favor by those in power."

"Black arts?"

"Nothing so sinister, but let's say a merchant wants a competitor's cargo of grain to rot before shipment, or a gambler needs an edge in a big game. There are those who practice such arts as will provide what is needed."

"For a price," observed James.

Sophia nodded. "Someone is eliminating magicians in Krondor, James."

James glanced around. "How many others are there?"

Sophia said, "Help me turn this around. I should have pointed it that way before I loaded it."

James helped the woman turn the cart around, and watched as she knelt between the twin stalls of the wagon and picked them up. He knew better than to offer to help; Sophia was as independent-minded a woman as he had ever encountered, and he had known several. "You ought to get a small horse or pony to pull that thing."

"I can't afford one," she answered as she started to pull all her worldly possessions out of the alley.

"I can . . . loan you the funds for a horse, Sophia. You were always kind to a rude street boy."

She smiled and years fell away from her face. "You were never rude. Obnoxious, yes, but never rude." Then her smile vanished. "I'd just have to feed the beast, but thanks for the offer."

As they reached the corner Sophia halted and said, "But I should be asking you what brought you to my door."

James laughed. "Actually, it was a minor magical problem." He explained about the Princess Paulina's amulet and its effect, and finished by saying, "If my young friend is to be spending time in her company, I think it would be to his benefit if he had some means of resisting her charms."

Sophia chuckled at the play on words. "Charms. I like that. Well, I have something that may help your friend." She put down the stalls and went to the rear of the cart. She pulled up the tie-down cover she had just fastened and said, "Wish you said something before I did this," and reached in. She pulled out a small bag and rummaged through it. "I have an effective potion, but that will only last for a few hours." She held up a small ring. "But *this* might do." It was simply fashioned, of a gray-silver metal and was adorned with a single dull red semiprecious stone.

She handed it to James. "It protects the wearer from a variety of minor enchantments and spells. Likely the sort of thing the young lady employs. It's useless against anything of sub-

135

stance, but at the least it will keep the girl's effects confined to what nature gave her."

James took the ring. "Thanks. What do I owe you?"

"For you," she said, "nothing." She refastened her tie-downs.

James said, "Why the sudden generosity?"

"You've done me a favor or two in the past, Jimmy. Let's call it a parting gift." She picked up the stalls again and pulled her cart out of the alley and into the street that would eventually lead them out of the Poor Quarter.

James dodged aside as two boys hurried past. For a moment he wondered if it had been a slash and grab, with one cutting his purse and the other trying to grab it, then he realized they were just city boys running for the pure joy of it.

James patted his purse to ensure it was indeed where he had left it, and then he untied it from his belt. Tucking the bag under the cover on the wagon, he said, "Then let me return a parting gift. You'll need some coins to set yourself up wherever you land."

She smiled, her blue eyes bright. "You're a friend, Jimmy."

"When you think it's safe, let me know where you've landed, Sophia."

She said, "I will," and, leaving him, took the major road that led to the eastern gate.

James watched her vanish into the press of the city and then turned back toward the palace. Whatever else he did this afternoon, he needed to return for a short chat with the Prince.

He still had little idea what was behind the seemingly random murders of citizens in Krondor, but the fact that many of them were practitioners of magic was too important not to bring to Arutha's attention at once. The afternoon sun burned hot, yet James felt a chill creeping into his bones.

SEVEN

# AMBUSH

T HE horses whinnied.

William glanced around. He was already tense from having the responsibility of his first command, even though he was accompanied by a well-seasoned sergeant and twenty veteran soldiers. Captain Treggar, even though a bully in the young officers' mess, had taken William aside and said, "If you want to look stupid in front of the men, give orders. If you want to look like you know what you're doing, just tell Sergeant Matthews what you want."

Despite his dislike for the man, William had taken the advice to heart and so far had looked like he knew what he was doing. The sun was near the mid-heaven, so William said, "Sergeant!"

"Sir!" came the prompt reply.

"Find us a likely place to take the midday meal."

They were traveling along a road that was wending its way up into the forested foothills north of Krondor. William was alert, but not overly worried, as this area was considered relatively pacified. An occasional gang of robbers might harass travelers, but no group of sufficient size to attack a score of

138

mounted soldiers had been reported in the region for months. There were areas farther up the coast that were difficult to keep under control, but this area had been selected as much for the safety of the Prince's guests as for the abundance of game.

The sergeant, a weatherbeaten old veteran named Matthews with surprisingly vivid blue eyes and nearly white hair, said, "There's an inn around that bend, sir. I wouldn't suggest nobility spend the night in such a place, but for a midday meal, it should do."

"Send word ahead we're coming," said William.

"Aye, sir."

A soldier spurred his horse on Matthews' command and by the time the procession reached the inn, all was ready for them. It was a modest two-story building with a chimney producing a healthy amount of smoke. The sign over the door showed a large tree under which slept a man with a travel bag. Matthews turned to William and said, "It's called The Tree and Traveler, sir."

The innkeeper was waiting for them. The soldier had obviously told the man that visitors of rank were approaching, for without knowing who they were, the man was bowing and scraping to everyone as they stopped before his door.

The Duke of Olasko dismounted from his horse and a servant quickly had his hand out to help Princess Paulina dismount from her horse. She had insisted on wearing breeches and riding astride, and she ignored the helping hand, jumping nimbly to the ground. "I'm starving!" she announced to everyone. To the innkeeper she said, "What is today's fare?"

The man bowed, "Milady, we have a side of venison on the spit, cooked to a turn. I have game hens roasting and they will be finished within the half-hour. I have a hard cheese and fresh

139

bread, apples and other fresh fruits, as well as dried. I have freshly-caught fish in the kitchen, but it is not yet cooked. If you wish, I can have it—"

The duke interrupted. "The venison will do, as will the hens. But first, ale. I am thirsty as well as famished."

William gave orders for the soldiers to secure the baggage horses, and instructed Matthews to have the men water the horses, before taking their own ease. As he turned to join the guests inside, he said, "I'll have some fresh fruit and ale sent out for the men."

Matthews nodded. "Thank you, lieutenant."

William knew the men had eaten well enough that morning and this was far from a campaign march supplied with dried meats and hardtack, but it was a gesture that would be appreciated. He followed the nobles into the inn. It was a simple establishment, with two large rectangular tables in the center of the room, two small round tables in the corners on the right, a flight of stairs along the left wall leading to the second story, and a modest bar along the back wall, next to what was obviously a kitchen door. A large hearth dominated the right wall. Most of the cooking was done there, it appeared, since a woman came hurrying from the kitchen to add something to the large kettle that sat simmering near the fire. A side of venison was being turned by a boy who sat in wide-eyed amazement at the rare sight of the nobles.

William glanced around the room and saw two men sitting at one of the round tables. Neither appeared armed, so William's first judgment was that they were no threat. One was an older man, his hair nearly gone from his pate, leaving him with a long fringe of gray hair that hung to his shoulders. His nose was a huge hawk's beak, but it was hardly noticeable because of his eyes. There was something compelling about them. William thought his clothing to be of fine weave, if less than fashionable. His companion wore a simple gray robe, with a hood thrown back. He was either a monk, priest, or a magician of some kind, William thought. Most people would not come to that conclusion, but then most people hadn't spent their boyhood growing up on an island full of magicians. He decided he needed to re-evaluate their threat potential.

He looked over to see the innkeeper fawning over the duke and his party, so rather than take his seat at the foot of the table, William crossed to the two men and said, "Your business here?"

The robed man glanced up and seeing that it was an officer of the Prince's guard who spoke, simply said, "We're just travelers, sir."

William sensed something pass between the men and for a moment suspected mindspeech. William could speak with animals, a talent he had possessed since birth, though he found it of marginal use. Only Fantus, his father's pet firedrake, had the intelligence to discuss anything beyond food and other basic concepts. When it came to human magic, William was an observer, but he had observed enough to be sensitive to it. "My prince has important guests in the realm, and it is my duty to see to their well-being. From where are you traveling and what is your destination?"

The man with the compelling eyes said, "I am traveling to the coast, a village called Halden Head. I am coming from the east."

The other man said, "I am bound to Krondor, sir. I come from Eggley."

"So you just happened to decide to share a meal?"

The robed man said, "A chance meeting. We are exchanging gossip about the places to which each of us is bound."

"Your names?"

"I am Jaquin Medosa," answered the man William thought might be a magician.

"My name is Sidi," said the other.

William looked at him for a long moment. There was something vaguely troubling about him. Yet the two men were eating peacefully and bothering no one. "Thank you for your cooperation," he said. Without further comment he returned to the duke's table.

Food and ale were being placed before the guests, and William signaled the innkeeper and asked that ale and fresh fruit be sent out to the soldiers. When that was done, he set about enjoying his own lunch. But throughout the meal he couldn't help but glance from time to time to the corner table, where the two men sat lost in deep conversation. He was sure that on at least two occasions the man called Sidi had glanced his way.

The Princess asked William a question and he turned to answer. After a little banter, he said a silent thanks to James for providing him with his ring, for he found the girl mildly attractive and occasionally irritating now, as opposed to the overwhelming desire he had felt upon first meeting her. Paulina appeared to be unaware of his lack of ardor and she continued to chatter as if he was under her spell. When he had finished answering her question, William looked in the corner and saw that the two men were gone.

It was near evening when they arrived at the camp. Trackers from Krondor had gone ahead and had scouted the area for a likely campsite as well as the location of nearby game. The servants quickly unloaded the baggage train and erected tents for the duke and his family.

William and his men would sleep under the sky, with small

service tents available should the weather turn inclement. As the sun sank in the west, servants hurriedly prepared the evening meal while William sent the trackers out for a quick sweep of the area and posted sentries. There was little danger in this area, but even a newly commissioned knight-lieutenant wouldn't risk the lives of visiting dignitaries by not taking every precaution.

Matthews oversaw the watches and made sure those not standing watch ate and tended their equipment. In the field it was the rule that each man was responsible for his mount, so even though lackeys had accompanied the hunting expedition, each soldier inspected his own horse before turning in.

William joined the duke's family in his quarters—more a pavilion than a tent—in which a table large enough to accommodate six people had been set out with food and wine. The duke invited him to join them for supper with a wave of his hand.

"What have the trackers found?" he asked.

William replied, "Game signs to the northeast, Your Grace. Elk and deer, and a sow bear with a cub."

The duke finished chewing on a quarter hen, and tossed the bones aside. William was thankful the man had no hounds with him. The habit of feeding dogs at the table had been one his mother had never allowed, and as a result William had also grown up with an aversion to having dogs under the table. The servants would remove the bones before the duke retired. "Won't take a sow bear until the cub is weaned. Depletes the game population if you don't let the little ones get out on their own. What else?"

"Maybe a big cat," answered William.

At that the duke seemed pleased. "Can your trackers tell what kind?"

William said, "Not sure, m'lord. Usually we have cougars.

They're bold and think nothing of coming into villages at night to make free with sheep or chickens."

"I know the cat," interrupted the duke. "Wily, but other than that, not much of a challenge once you have them treed. What else?"

"Some true lions occasionally wander up from the southeast, though we almost always get word long before we see them. Young males without a pride, usually."

"Good trophy animal."

"And once in a great while we get leopards."

"Now there's worthy game," said the duke. "If one's in a tree above you, that's where he wants to be."

"Perhaps by morning I'll have new intelligence."

The balance of the meal went by slowly, as the duke and his son spoke of past hunts, reliving each triumph. Paulina spent her time staring absently into the distance or attempting to flirt with William, who responded politely to her banter. Prince Vladic seemed content to stay silently lost in his own thoughts.

When the dishes had been removed by the servants, William excused himself from the duke's presence, citing his need to oversee the disposition of the camp. The duke nodded and waved him away.

William found Sergeant Matthews and asked, "How stand things?"

"Quiet, sir," answered the sergeant.

"I'm turning in. Wake me for the last watch."

"You're taking a watch, sir?" asked Matthews in a neutral voice.

William knew that many officers left the management of the watches to their sergeants. "I prefer my sergeants get a halfway decent night's sleep on the march," he answered, as if this wasn't his first command. "Turn in after the second watch and have the senior guardsman wake me."

"Sir," said Matthews as William moved toward the spot set aside for his groundcloth and covers. He knew the sergeant was just as likely to ignore the command and continue to ensure each watch-change went without a hitch. Still, as with sending out fruit and ale for the trail-weary soldiers, the gesture would be appreciated.

William turned in, and for once was glad for his training under McWirth, for he had slept enough upon the ground atop a thin quilted mat, with a heavy woolen blanket over him, that once he lay down he was quickly asleep.

William's eyes opened and he was awake without hesitation and halfway standing before he realized what had wakened him. It was no sound, no alarm nor shout, but rather a feeling. Then he knew what it was. The horses were disturbed to the point at which his mind was hearing them as if they were shouting. In another moment they would be whinnying. He hurried to where the horses where staked out. They were all standing quietly, heads erect, ears twitching, nostrils flared as they tested the air.

William never liked talking with horses. Their minds were odd, divided.

*What is it?* William said with his mind to the nearest horse.

*Hunter!* came the answer, with an image of something moving silently through the forest nearby. *Smell hunter!*

William glanced upwind in the direction from which a scent would come. *Man?* he asked.

The response was confusing. Some of the horses seemed to agree while others sent impressions of a cat-like creature.

145

"Something wrong, sir?" asked Matthews at William's shoulder.

"I don't know," he answered quietly. "Something's got the horses spooked."

"Maybe a wolfpack hunting?"

Rather than share his unusual ability with the sergeant, William just nodded. "Maybe, but there's something close enough that the horses are—"

Before he could finish the thought, the horses started whinnying and trying to pull up the stakes.

Matthews cried out, "Alarm! 'Ware the camp!"

William had his sword out as something big and dark seemed to fly by, close to the ground, but it was past him before he realized it was not a bird of any sort, but a swift four-legged creature. It bounded into darkness next to trees on the edge of the camp, then appeared again in silhouette against the campfire for a brief instant, before vanishing into the night.

"Damn me!" said Matthews. "It's a black leopard!"

Men were scrambling for weapons and the Duke of Olasko and his son came from their tents, weapons at the ready. By the time William reached them, word of the big cat had already reached the duke.

"That's a bold kitty, what?" said the duke with a grin. "Nice of him to let us know he's in the woods." He glanced around and asked, "What of the clock?"

William glanced at the sergeant, who answered, "Three hours to sunrise, Your Grace."

"Good," said the duke. "Let's eat and then at dawn let's track that big bastard."

William said, "Yes, Your Grace."

The duke returned to his tent and William instructed the

sergeant to order the morning meal prepared early. He had no doubt that by the time the sun crested the eastern peaks they would be at least an hour along the trail of that cat.

As the camp turned to the day's preparation, William watched the edge of the woods, trying to peer into the gloom. As the bustle in the camp grew in volume, he couldn't help the feeling that, somewhere nearby, that leopard watched.

The duke returned a few minutes later, rubbing his hands in anticipation. "Let's eat, to strengthen us for the day to come, lieutenant."

"Yes, Your Grace," said William, tearing his eyes away from the murky woods.

As they walked toward the duke's tent, he said, "Damned accommodating of that beast to let us know he's nearby, what? You'd soon as think he was daring us to come after him."

William said nothing, but his thoughts matched the duke's, and he was nowhere near as enthralled by the notion.

Mist rolled through the trees as the duke, his nephew, son and daughter moved silently through the woods. They were followed at a discreet distance by William and his squad of six soldiers. Bringing up the rear were bearers and servants. William was impressed by the Olaskan nobility; their hunting skills were very evident. They moved with such stealth that in comparison the experienced soldiers sounded noisy and untrained to William's ear.

A tracker from the garrison of Pathfinders at Krondor led the way, indicating leopard signs. William used his mental gifts to search out any hint of the cat's whereabouts, but he kept coming up blank. He sensed the small animals nearby, the red squirrels and chipmunks hiding out of sight, even caught an impression or two of the curious rodents' thoughts. *Big hunters!* they seemed to say. *Danger!*

The quiet of the woods was unnerving. Some animal sounds would usually be heard in the distance, but those sounds were absent. The only noise was an occasional plop as moisture gathered on the branches above and fell to the ground below, or the faint movement of the other men nearby.

With each step, William's apprehension grew. Another twenty yards into the woods and he whispered to the men behind, "I'm moving up with the duke. Close up behind the servants."

"Sir," whispered the soldier.

William picked up the pace and quickly overtook the servants. He noticed the servants who carried the duke's ferocious arsenal of hunting weapons and his other equipment looked uneasy. He closed up behind the Princess, who walked a few paces behind her brother. In the gloom ahead, William could see the duke as a faint form in the haze, Prince Vladic half a dozen paces behind, Kazamir an equal interval after him. William saw that the gloom was deepening, and his internal alarm sounded. The Pathfinder at the side of the duke was looking around, as if he could no longer see the animal's spoor.

Just as the duke held up his arm for a halt, William was moving forward, pulling out his sword. The duke had his bow at the ready, and was peering ahead into the gloom, as if trying to see into it by will alone. Suddenly a movement high above the duke's head alerted William and he shouted, "It's a trap! Above you."

The duke acted without hesitation, dodging to one side as a large black shape pounced from above, launching itself from a heavy branch a few feet above the duke's head. Prince Vladic let fly with one arrow, which split the space occupied an instant before by the big cat. The leopard hit the ground and spun, lashing out with one huge paw, raking the duke across the shoulder as he fell away.

The cat gathered itself to spring as William reached Kazamir's side. The duke's son let fly with an arrow which barely missed his cousin's back as it sped past Vladic and struck at the cat's feet.

William leapt to defend the duke as the leopard launched itself. His blade cut the air, and he felt it rake the cat's side as it sprang. The animal screamed, and rather than attack the duke it bounded into the woods, as more arrows flew at it.

William bent over the duke, who pushed away a helping hand. "After it!" he shouted.

"Your Grace, no!"

The duke yelled, "Get out of the way, boy!" and shoved William aside.

William grabbed the duke's arm, swinging him around in a half circle. The duke's eyes widened and he said, "You dare!"

"Sir, you're wounded," shouted William. "That creature will smell you coming a mile away."

"I've been hunting cats since before your birth, boy! Let go of my arm!"

But William held tight as the duke's son, daughter and nephew reached them, with the servants and soldiers closing quickly. "Your Grace, that was no cat."

"What?" said the duke.

"It was not a leopard."

"I saw it!" said the duke, struggling with William.

"It may have looked like a leopard, Your Grace, but it was not."

149

"What was it then?" asked Prince Vladic.

"A magician," said William, releasing the duke's arm. "A lesser path magician." He put up his sword.

"A magician?" asked Paulina. "How can you be sure?"

William said, "As you know cats, milady, I know magicians. Trust me."

"A shapeshifter?" asked Kazamir.

William nodded. "Leopard totem. And a powerful one to be able to shape himself like that."

"He did come into camp as if he knew what he was doing, Father," observed Paulina.

"He wanted you to go after him," said William. "He was hunting you." He pointed to the Pathfinder who stood a short distance away. "He was first on the trail, but the magician let him pass and tried to break your back."

"Break my back?"

"He leapt so as to land high on your back. It would have crushed your spine. The fact you moved when I shouted saved Your Grace from a painful death."

The Pathfinder said, "It's truth, Your Grace. Had he landed on you, you'd be dead."

"The claws as he departed were his way of making sure you followed," said William.

"Then I shall oblige him. I'll hunt him in turn," said the duke, ignoring the blood that was dripping from the cuts in his shoulder.

"No, Your Grace," said William. He motioned to Sergeant Matthews. "Your pleasure is hunting, but when it comes to hunting criminals, that's my duty." To Matthews he said, "Escort the duke back to his tent and see to his wounds. I want a dozen men up here, armed and ready." To the Pathfinder he said, "See if you can pick up his trail, but be wary. Remember, this is a man you're hunting, not an animal."

The Pathfinder gave a nod and headed up the forest track.

The duke seemed on the verge of starting a second argument when Prince Vladic said, "Come, Uncle. Let's tend to those wounds, then we'll see about this hunting of magicians."

William saw the duke study the trail, then give William a long, appraising look. With a nod of agreement, he turned and started the slow return to the camp. A short time later, a dozen men, armed and ready, appeared, and William signaled the way. Softly he said, "We look for an ambush, either from a man or a cat, and we won't know which until he strikes. Keep your interval on the trail."

William led the way, each man waiting a moment before following the man in front of him. One by one they moved off into the misty woods.

High above the sun shone, but deep in the woods there was nothing but gloom. "It's queer," whispered the Pathfinder. "It shouldn't be this dark."

William nodded. "It's as if . . ." He paused. He knew what this spell was, but had no name for it. Despite having grown up on the Isle of Stardock, William had had no interest in the study of magic—a fact which had driven a wedge between William and his father, Pug—but some knowledge had stuck to the young man. "It's a darkness spell, to make things gloomy so the caster can work his way past . . ." Suddenly he stood erect and shouted, "Back to the camp!"

"He's circled us?"

"It's the duke he wants!" shouted William, turning to run

past the soldier behind him. The others quickly followed. "At the double!"

The men set off at a quick trot. With no need for silence, they made quick time of the distance back to the point of the first attack. William held up his hand and they paused to catch their breath for a minute, then they were off again.

For slow passing minutes, the only sound William heard was heavy boots pounding on the soil of the forest floor, the clanking of armor and weapons, and the labored breathing of the men. No one spoke as if they were conserving their energy, knowing a fight might await them at the end of their run.

William was the first to hear the struggle. As they approached the camp the sounds of battle rang out. He had a dozen men with him, so eight soldiers and Sergeant Matthews had remained in camp with the servants and bearers. Kazamir and the Prince would mean eleven able-bodied fighters, and William was certain the duke could still give a good account of himself despite his wounds. William cursed his own stupidity. He had broken a cardinal rule of warfare: in the presence of an enemy, never split your forces unless by doing so you gain a clear and obvious advantage.

He had thought he faced one magician. He was obviously wrong.

Snarls and cat-screams sounded among the clash of weapons and William caught sight of the first cat as they came into camp. It was a large leopard, but spotted, not black like the magician in his cat form. As William ran at it, he sent his thoughts toward it, *Run! Bad! Danger!* But his mind hit a barrier, a mystic wall which kept his thoughts from reaching the cat's mind, and prevented him from hearing the cat's thoughts. Instead, the leopard snarled in rage and leapt at him.

William's two-handed sword came up and he took the creature in the chest, letting its own momentum carry it past him,
then turned and let the creature fall off the point of his sword.
The animal howled and flailed with its claws at the air, then
lay twitching until it died.

There were men in the camp as well as animals. Three men
stood near the center of the camp, each wearing a robe and
carrying a large staff. Two seemed to be in a trance, and William was certain they were directing the half-dozen large
leopards he could see—and however many others he couldn't—
while the third robed man stood guard over them. William
made straight for the alert magician.

Refusing to be diverted from his purpose, William didn't
see those men trapped in pairs and threes facing snarling animals who were working in concert with one another, fierce
hunters now gifted with human-aided intelligence as they tried
to pull down any soldier whose attentions wavered for an
instant.

The magician saw William coming at a run and raised his
staff, pointing it at the young officer. William prepared to
dodge to the side, but without knowing what spell was coming
he had no means to judge his timing.

Pain suddenly struck him in waves, and behind him he could
hear the soldiers scream. William staggered a step, then realized
that while he hurt from his toenails to his hair, he could still
move. The magician who pointed his staff at him regarded him
with alarm when he didn't fall. Eyes wide, the magician dropped
his staff and pulled a dagger from his belt, leaping toward the
staggering young lieutenant with an animal-like snarl of anger.

William had only to raise his sword, and as he had with
the leopard, the point took the attacker in the chest. But rather

than swing to one side, William pushed with all his strength and the magician practically ran upon the blade. His eyes bulged and he dropped his dagger, then his eyes rolled up into his skull and he died.

William let him fall and yanked his blade free. He turned and saw his companions lying on the ground, twitching in agony.

Around him snarling animals and screaming men told William he had little time. He raised his sword and struck the nearest standing magician, the one he had met in the inn, who had named himself Jaquin Medosa. When his blade struck, it was like hitting an oak tree, and the man staggered but didn't fall. William was not amazed, for he had seen what magic could accomplish all his life, and he knew his foe was empowered by more than mere sinew and bone. Some magicians who looked frail could muster the strength to lift a horse, or resist sword blows and arrow points.

For an instant, the man's concentration turned to William, but before he could marshal his resources against William, the young officer struck another blow with his sword, severing the man's arm from his body. He screamed and fell over, blood spurting from his shoulder. Without mercy, William ended his life with the point of his blade in the man's throat.

The last magician also died quickly, and suddenly the tone of combat changed around him. The animals' sounds of rage now turned to those of terror. Even with the spell broken, the cats would continue to fight. "Back away from the leopards!" William shouted. They were no less dangerous for being free of the enchantment, and William knew men might suffer more if he couldn't quickly drive the cats off.

He closed his eyes and conjured an image, an enraged male

lion, and imagined a roar of challenge, defying the leopard to enter its territory. No normal leopard would challenge an adult male lion if given a chance to flee.

Instantly leopards began to flee the scene. Men shouted and while some sounds of struggle continued for a few moments longer, soon the camp was quiet.

William shouted, "Sergeant Matthews!"

"Sir," came the weak reply. The sergeant hove into view, his left arm shredded from claw-wounds and pouring blood.

"Get yourself seen to, then report," said William.

Duke Radswil and his son emerged from their tent, both covered in blood. "Are you all right, Your Grace?"

The duke nodded, looking around. "All these damned cats. It doesn't make sense. Leopards are solitary hunters—"

Kazamir went pale and said, "Look!"

William looked at the three magicians he had killed and saw that their bodies were transforming. He and the others were witnessing what few mortals ever saw: a magician returning to its totem form. The second magician William had killed, the one who had been surprisingly powerful, was a huge black leopard. William inspected it and said, "This was the one that raked you, Your Grace."

"How can you tell?" asked the duke, as pale as his son.

"This is where I wounded it before," said William, pointing to a mark on its left side. He then showed the severed arm. "And this is where I cut off his arm. This was the man at the inn yesterday, Jaquin Medosa."

Prince Vladic, with considerably fewer wounds than his uncle and cousin, stepped from behind and said, "I recognized him, also."

"You survived," said William with obvious relief.

Vladic said, "My uncle and cousin are heroes. They over-turned the table and we fought from behind it. I fear they took serious wounds protecting me."

"The Princess?" asked William.

"She was behind me," said Vladic. "She's recovering in the tent."

William surveyed the damage. "How many cats?"

"At least a dozen," said a soldier. "Maybe more, sir."

William shook his head. "Summon Totem. It's a rare and powerful magic. Those who tried to kill you, Your Grace, em-ploy men of great prowess. Only a few can do what these three did."

The duke said, "You flatter me, lieutenant. These men didn't come here to kill me."

William said, "Sir?"

Vladic said, "They came here to kill me. They could have killed my uncle easily but they ignored him to come straight at me."

William didn't understand.

The duke, wincing from his wounds said, "I think I can explain: had you not sent me back to camp, I would have been on the trail with you and your men when the leopards struck this camp. Almost certainly everyone here would have died. I can explain at greater length after I get these wounds dressed, but the short answer is that someone wants the Crown Prince of Olasko dead. And they want him dead on your prince's doorstep."

William felt a cold chill in the pit of his stomach. Someone was not trying to kill a noble from a neighboring kingdom; someone was trying to start a war.

EIGHT

# ATTACK

ERVANTS rushed forward.

William signaled to Matthews to sweep the perimeter around the inn before darkness, while the servants hurried inside with the duke and his family. Following the magicians' attack, William had quickly taken stock of the situation, come to several realizations, and made a decision.

The first realization was that two or three very powerful magicians had orchestrated an assault that had been planned and executed with painstaking care. Which meant they had known the duke was coming. With a sinking feeling, William wondered if there was a spy in the palace, or if it had simply been a case of someone observing the party leaving the city and sending word ahead by magical means. He wished James was here, for that sort of plotting was more his province. William just didn't have the temperament to consider every possible turn and twist of a plot. His forte was battle: tactics and strategy, logistics and resupply, defense and assault.

The other realization was that he had lost seven of his twenty men, along with half the servants. By all accounts at least two dozen large cats had struck simultaneously, the result being a dozen men dead before they recognized the attack for what it was. Only Prince Vladic's quick wits had saved the duke, Paulina and Kazamir. He had overturned the table, ordered the others to crouch behind it, and killed everything that tried to come over the top.

Other details were confused. Some of the servants reported seeing men among the cats, dressed in black, while others made no mention of it. Duke Radswil, Kazamir, Paulina and Prince Vladic all reported they had seen no black-clad men.

William had decided the duke was too injured to ride all the way back to Krondor, so he decided to send riders to the city, while waiting at the inn for relief. He asked for a healer to be dispatched with additional guardsmen. Sergeant Matthews had managed to staunch the blood flow from the duke's shoulder wound with a well-fashioned field bandage, but it was still seeping, and the duke was weakening.

Princess Paulina seemed in need of some sort of help, but William was at a loss as to what to do. She sat silently, wide-eyed, looking more like a frightened child than a young seductress.

Night was upon them, and William hurriedly inspected the men and horses. They were well provisioned and armed, but of the eleven remaining soldiers—he had sent three to the city—three were wounded. With the two Princes, he had a dozen able-bodied men to defend the inn should another attack be mounted. He couldn't depend on the innkeeper and his family. Non-combatants could be more of a hindrance than a help in this situation.

William's mind was racing when he finished with the inspection and started back toward the inn. All he knew of magic was what he had grown up exposed to at Stardock: an organized society of magic users who agreed in principle to study and share knowledge.

But he had heard stories, often from young students, which he had taken as wild tales of imagination, stories of dark practices and secret rites, conducted by those serving evil powers. For every magician who had come to Stardock to be part of something great and wonderful, others had stayed away because of their own distrust, but some had remained apart because of their own dark ambitions.

Some of the stories told of magicians who sold dark potions and evil talismans to those needing dark arts, and others who served mad gods. Many of the rites whispered about were bloody and vile, and until this afternoon, William had discounted those stories as being of the same cloth as tales told around the campfire to scare children.

But now he had no doubt some of them must be true

He found himself inside the inn, lost in thoughts of magic. Bringing himself back to the present, he realized two of his soldiers held the man named Sidi under guard. William asked, "Why are you still here?"

The hawk-beaked older man said, "The innkeeper said a well-known trader is due in tomorrow. I thought it safer to travel north with him under the protection of his guards rather than risk the road alone." Glancing at the marks of battle and the servants tending the wounded, he added, "It seems my instincts were correct."

William felt a hot flush of suspicion and said, "That man you dined with yesterday, the one who called himself Jaquin Medosa, attacked us."

If the man knew of the attack he feigned surprise with conviction. "He was a bandit?"

"No, a magician. And he had friends."

Sidi said, "I thought as much. He spoke in passing of some sort of power he served, but I thought he was trying to impress me so I might volunteer to pay for his meal." Shaking his head, Sidi said, "He hardly looked the part of a bandit."

William concluded he had no reason to suspect this man of having a hand in the attack. Had he, it was unlikely he would be sitting idly around the inn.

Sidi said, "You were fortunate, lieutenant. I know a little about magic from my travels and without wards and other protections, even a little magic can be very deadly."

William held up his hand, showing the ring James had given him. "This saved my life. I wore it for a completely different reason, but it warded a spell cast at me just enough to permit me to kill the magicians."

He studied Sidi's face for a reaction to the news of the magicians' death, but all Sidi said was, "Magicians? More than one?"

William nodded, but only said, "They all died."

"Very fortunate, indeed."

A servant came down the stairs and said, "Lieutenant, the duke's wound is worsening."

William started for the stairs, but found Sidi's restraining hand on his arm. "Allow me to come with you. I have some modest healing skills."

William hesitated, then nodded.

"I have some medicines in my travel bag, in my room."

William motioned for a soldier to accompany Sidi and then hurried to the duke's room.

161

It was the largest room in the inn, but still small by any standard. The duke lay in a bed, his face pale and covered in perspiration. Sidi entered a moment later with a big leather satchel. Kazamir and Vladic watched as people shuffled around the room to make enough space for the man to reach the duke's side. Sidi set the bag on the bed next to the duke. He examined the wound and said, "This is turning morbid. There is something working here that is not natural."

William said in a low voice, "That which wounded him was not a natural animal."

Sidi paused as if considering and said, "In my travels I have seen magic wounds that would not heal. Assassins use daggers with potions on them, and certain creatures also can rend flesh that will not heal afterwards. My knowledge of such things is scant, but I have a powder that may slow the damage until you can get him to a temple."

"Talk to me, man. I'm not dead yet," said the duke.

"I apologize, sir," said Sidi. "I know from seeing you yesterday to be a man of some rank. I fear I am too timid in addressing such an august person."

"My Lord, Duke Radswil of Olasko, this man is named Sidi, and he says he may help."

"Do what you can," said the duke, now looking paler by the minute. Then he added, "Please."

Sidi opened his bag and took out a pouch. "This will hurt, my lord."

"Do what you must."

The flesh around the wound was now white and puffy, and the wound itself seeped blood mixed with a thin whitish fluid. It stank of mortification. Sidi opened the pouch and liberally sprinkled a green powder over the wound. The duke sucked his breath between clenched teeth. Kazamir reached past William and took his father's hand, and the duke gripped tight, tears forming in his eyes and running down his face.

After a moment he said weakly, "By the gods! That burns like a cauterizing iron!"

Sidi nodded. "It is much the same, my lord. The powder burns away infection. It does not always work, but in the past it has helped."

The duke lay back and said, "I think I'll sleep now."

The room quickly emptied save for Kazamir who stayed with his father. Vladic took William aside as the others moved down the hall and stairs to the floor below. "Lieutenant, what is the situation?"

William decided that holding nothing back would be the best course. "We have a dozen swords, and this inn is defensible. Relief should arrive at mid-morning tomorrow, and I've asked for a healer to be sent with the soldiers, so your uncle will most likely survive."

"Assuming we're alive when relief gets here." He looked at William and said, "You expect another attack?"

William took a deep breath and let it out slowly. "I don't know what to expect, so I'm preparing for the worst."

"Tell me about the attack. You said earlier you know of magic. What do you know?"

William said, "My father is the Duke of Stardock, and that is where I was raised. I've seen a lot and heard more. Those three who attacked us numbered at least one, probably two very powerful magicians of the Lesser Path. The one who lured your uncle . . ." William paused, then added, "Some magicians swear to a totem creature, in exchange for certain abilities. One of those is the ability to take the creature's shape. The longer

163

the magician is in the animal guise the more he thinks like that animal, so this is a dangerous thing to undertake. But the more powerful the magicians, the more powerful the animal. That great black leopard totem tells us the man calling himself Jaquin Medosa was a very powerful practitioner of magic. I think there are those at Stardock, perhaps my father, who might know this man by another name, for a magician of the Leopard Totem who is that adept will have been heard of."

"Why would powerful magicians seek my death?"

William said, "The reasons to kill a Prince are as numerous as there are ambitious men in your nation, Your Highness. Any of those reasons could be the motive."

"An assassin?"

"I think so; it is the best explanation I can come up with, unless you have enemies with close ties to magicians. There are others in Prince Arutha's court who will be better informed on that topic than myself. All I can give you is speculation, and that is of little worth."

The Prince had a distant look. "You've given me a great deal, already, lieutenant." Then he looked William in the eyes. "But tonight?"

"If there were but three of them, we are safe. Even had they survived, they would be too exhausted to hunt us. Summoning that many animals of the totem is a feat that requires days of recovery. That is why there were two of them. The third was there to protect those controlling the animals."

Vladic nodded. "How is it that you resisted his magic?"

William held up his hand. "This ring protected me."

"A favorable talisman. But why do you wear it?"

William couldn't avoid blushing. "Ah, actually, a friend gave it to me so I might better resist your cousin's charms, and keep my mind on my duty."

Vladic gave William a half-smile and said, "You'll go far, lieutenant." He looked down the stairs and then said, "We need to eat. I doubt we'll have a quiet night."

"Why, Highness?" asked William as he followed.

"For those who undertook this elaborate ambush not to have a contingency plan in case the first attack failed would be too much to hope for; we just can't be that lucky."

William said, "I agree," and walked down the steps, his mind churning with various different defense plans.

William had stationed men at every possible entrance to the building. He had removed two men who had tended the horses, assuming that any in the barn would be among the most vulnerable. There were two soldiers at the kitchen door, two at the main door. Both doors were barred with a stout oak timber, though from the look of the iron fasteners on each side of the main door, they would only stop a casual passer-by trying to open the door; the iron was heavily rusted and one good shove would pop the rivets that held them into the wood. There were men at both the downstairs windows. Sergeant Matthews was upstairs standing guard outside the duke's door, with another man at the window at the end of the hall, overlooking the stabling area behind the inn.

The remaining six men slept under tables in the common room, in their armor with weapons beside them. William had managed to sleep in armor a time or two during training, but reckoned he would never get the knack of it, or have to be a great deal more tired than he had been when he last tried it.

He sat at the table where they had dined the day before,

too keyed up even to contemplate sleeping. He lost track of time, turning over the day's events in his mind a hundred times. He knew he could not have handled things better, yet felt as if he had somehow failed in his duty. A noble of a neighboring nation lay abed upstairs at grave risk, men had died, and he had barely avoided losing everything. He was certain Captain Treggar would have something to say to him.

His mind wandered and he started to doze where he sat when a movement beside him caused him to start awake. It was the man Sidi, who said, "I didn't mean to disturb you, lieutenant."

"That's all right. I need to stay alert."

"If they come, it will be soon. Dawn is but two hours away."

The stranger was correct. Just before dawn was when men were the most sluggish and most commanders took advantage of that knowledge when they could.

William studied the strange man in the gloom, the room's darkness cut by only one small candle. "What do you do, if I may ask?"

"I live in a small village inland from the town of Halden Head, up near Widow's Point."

William knew of the area, though he had only traveled through there once. "Rough country."

"It can be, but it suits my needs."

"And they would be?"

The man shrugged. "I trade. Items, gems, rare minerals, sometimes knowledge. There are men and other creatures, goblins and trolls, who are willing to sell me things in exchange for other goods I have."

William said sharply, "You wouldn't be running weapons, would you?"

Sidi said, "I have other items trolls and goblins value. One does not have to deal in contraband to trade with them."

William sighed. "I'm sorry to be so distrustful, but under the circumstances . . ."

"I understand. I was eating with the man who attacked your party. I do dabble in trade that many would look upon with suspicion."

William stared at the door as if expecting someone to break in any instant. "Are they coming?" he asked absently.

Sidi said, "We shall know shortly."

They waited in silence.

Minutes dragged by, then one of the sentries said, "Lieutenant!"

"What?" asked William, standing up and drawing his sword.

"Movement, outside," said the guard.

William listened. For moments he couldn't hear any sounds out of the ordinary, then he heard it. Someone or something was creeping around the inn, probably inspecting the windows.

Abruptly, the sound of running feet came from outside, then the door exploded inward with a loud crash. There was no need to shout alarm, as men rolled out from under the tables beneath which they had slept, weapons in hand.

Four men had used a large log as a ram, and dropped it as they surged forward. Weaponless, they hurled themselves at William, Sidi and two other sentries, allowing four armed men behind them to enter the room.

William kicked an attacker in the groin and cut the man behind him as he turned toward Sidi. Sidi brandished a dagger and was facing down a man who was in the process of drawing out a curved sword.

Noise from upstairs told William that Matthews was securing the duke's room and getting ready for the two who were now rushing up the stairs.

The armed men proved to be far more difficult foes than the four who had first come through the door. William's men had disposed of the latter quickly, but the armed men were advancing warily.

Each attacker was attired in black, with a loose head-covering that left only the eyes exposed. They wore baggy pants that were gathered at the ankle, tucked into low black boots. Their black shirts were tightly fastened at the neck and wrists, and their weapons had all been blackened. William shouted, "Clear the door in case there are archers outside!"

The man facing William lashed out with his curved blade, and William took it on his own two-handed sword. The clang of metal upon metal rang out all over the room. His attacker slashed from the other side and William realized he was being measured. William intentionally let his guard lower, anticipating that when the third testing blow came, it would be followed by a furious slash that was intended to cut above his blade and take him across the chest.

Instead the man's eyes widened in shock as William's swordpoint took him in the chest. Early on in his training William had realized that most swordsmen consider the longsword a slashing weapon and don't anticipate the danger from the point. He had developed that skill as much as possible, often using the sword as other men used the broadsword or rapier. As more than one instructor had said, the slash wounds, but the thrust kills.

The fallen man had barely hit the floor when William saw two men in black hurrying up the stairs. He sped after them, and found them struggling with Matthews and two guardsmen.

William felled one from behind, while the other killed the soldier next to Matthews.

Matthews managed to cut the attacker, who ignored any pain and spun to push the sergeant into William. Tangled for a moment, they saw the man hurl himself against the door to the duke's room.

The door crashed inward, causing splinters to fly through the air like tiny missiles. A scream sounded from the room next to the duke's.

"The Princess!" William shouted to Matthews as he half-pushed, half-pointed the sergeant toward the duke's room. William raised his foot and kicked hard against the door to Paulina's room. The shock ran straight up his leg to his hip, but the door gave way, swinging inward.

Paulina sat cowering in the corner, her fists before her face as the wooden shutters of her window splintered and fell away. Another black-clad warrior was entering from outside. William raced forward, holding his sword with both hands, leveled like a lance.

The man died soundlessly.

William knelt next to the Princess, who looked at him in horror. "Are you all right?" he shouted, as if his loud voice might reach past the fear.

She stared at him and shook her head slightly. He took that to mean she was unhurt. Without any idea how things fared in the rest of the inn, he could only say, "Don't move. Stay right here until someone comes to fetch you."

He hurried next door to find Vladic, Kazamir and Matthews standing over two dead assassins. The duke lay half-conscious, staring up at his son and nephew, as if confused as to who they were.

Seeing no immediate danger, William said, "Sergeant, come with me."

They hurried down the stairs and found three guardsmen lying dead on the floor, with five black-clad warriors stretched out beside them. Sounds of struggle came from the kitchen and William said, "Sergeant, guard the stairs," and he raced into the kitchen.

Dead bodies littered the floor, among them the innkeeper, his wife, and the serving girl. Two soldiers, obviously wounded, had one last invader cornered. He stood with his back to the wall, a curved sword in his right hand, a dagger in his left. "Keep him alive!" shouted William.

Seeing no escape, the man reached up with the dagger and with one quick motion cut his own throat.

The two soldiers and William stepped back, astonished at the act. William hesitated, then knelt next to the man. His eyes were staring upward, and what life in them fled in moments as the blood gushed from his neck.

"Fanatics!" said one of the soldiers, holding his sword in his left hand while his right hung limply.

William sat back on his heels. "Yes, fanatics," he said.

The other solder, holding his bleeding side with a bleeding hand said, "Lieutenant, what were they? Nighthawks?"

"I don't think so," said William. He had an idea what they were, but thought better of saying anything to the men. He stood and said, "Let's get this place as secure as we can."

The two men nodded and one tried a salute, but William waved it off. "Get yourself bandaged."

William inspected the kitchen. Besides the bodies of the innkeeper, his wife and the serving-girl, three more assassins lay dead, as did the two guardsmen he had stationed there originally.

William stuck his head out of the door that opened onto

the stabling yard and saw the sky to the east was lightening. He heard the horses snort in the stable and counted himself fortunate that he hadn't put men needlessly in the stable. Two or three less men in the inn and they might not have survived.

William returned to the common room and looked around. "Someone's missing," he said to Matthews. "Where's Sidi?"

"Vanished during the fight," said one of the soldiers. "Faced one of the killers with a dagger and when I killed the man trying to kill him, he runs off into the night without so much as a thank you."

William nodded. "Given the circumstances, I don't blame him. Maybe he'll come back." William doubted it. From what he had said, the man skated along the edge of the law and with this many dead, there was bound to be too much royal scrutiny for him to welcome it. William looked at Matthews. "How do we stand?"

"There are five men still living, and you and I, sir."

"Sun's coming up. I think we're safe until reinforcements arrive."

"I'll see to the men, sir. You could use some rest."

William nodded, then stood. "We all could use some rest." He started to pull bodies out of the inn and then said, "Sergeant, I want these assassins searched." He was almost certain they'd find nothing but swords and daggers, no personal items, jewelry, or anything else that might reveal who they were.

As Matthews set about tending the men, William went to the first attacker outside. He knelt next to the body and removed the head covering. He then pried open the mouth and saw the man's tongue had been cut.

William sat back on his heels and shook his head. Looking toward the south, he said to himself, "What are Keshian assassins doing trying to kill a Prince of Olasko?"

NINE

# DECISIONS

RUTHA frowned.

He stood to one side of the Duke of Olasko's bed and watched as a priest of the Order of Prandur examined the duke.

The priest was new to Arutha's service, having been selected by his order to serve for a year as Arutha's spiritual advisor. The position rotated through the various major temples in the city, each sending an advisor for a year's term—though some chose not to—and this year it was Father Belson.

The slender, black-bearded cleric stood up, his purple and scarlet robes shimmering with reflected torchlight, and turned to the Prince. "There is infection and something else, a magical element that keeps the wound from healing properly." Then, looking at William, the priest said, "The powder you saw sprinkled upon the wound was green, you say?"

"Yes, Father," William replied.

He had returned to the palace less than an hour ago, bone-tired and filthy. When relief under Captain Treggar had arrived at the inn at dawn, the healer who had accompanied the relief column had pronounced the duke's condition beyond his ability

174

to improve, and urged Captain Treggar to return the duke to Krondor as quickly as possible. The captain had utilized a wagon out behind the inn to carry the duke and his family, and while the inn's wagon was being made ready, William had made his report. Treggar had said nothing to him after that, save direct orders regarding the return to Krondor.

William waited silently while the priest again examined the duke. "I have magic that will burn out the contamination," he said to Kazamir who stood at his father's bedside. "But like most magic practiced by my temple, there is little in it that is gentle."

"Will it work?" asked the young Prince, obviously worried but trying to hide it.

"Yes, but it will leave a scar."

"My father has many scars. Do what you must to save his life."

Belson nodded. "Highness, I will need a brazier and a clean blade that I may heat."

Arutha called for the required items, and nodded at James.

James motioned to William and said, "Come with me."

William followed James from the duke's bedchamber and when they were outside, James said, "You did well, Willy."

William looked at James in open-mouthed astonishment. "Well? According to whom?"

James grinned. "According to Captain Treggar. He says the fact you managed to keep half your company alive and, more importantly, kept the duke's family alive, was commendable."

William sighed. "I thought I was going to be cashiered right out of the army. It doesn't feel like I did much commendable. All I can think about is the men who died."

James said, "I don't want to sound like the old veteran, but I've seen enough warfare in my life to know that you'll probably never get past that. Just keep in mind that you're a soldier and your line of work isn't known to have a long life-expectancy. Now, come along."

"Where are we going?"

"The Prince's office."

"Like this?" asked William, indicating his dirty appearance.

James smiled. "Remember, I've crawled through sewers with His Highness. Right now, expedience outweighs fastidiousness."

They reached the entrance to the Prince's private chambers, and one of the pages flanking the portal opened it. James led William into the Prince's receiving room.

Princess Anita and the twins were waiting. "Cousin Willie!" shouted Borric, followed an instant later by Erland. The boys jumped up from where they had been sitting as their mother read a story to them, and hurried over to inspect the young soldier.

"You've been in a battle!" shouted Erland. "Outstanding!"

William gave the nine-year-old a frown. "Not if you'd been there. We lost some good men."

That calmed the twins down a little. "Did you kill anyone?" asked Borric.

William nodded, looking regretful. "I did."

Anita rose and said, "James, you and William refresh yourselves until Arutha gets here." She indicated a washbasin that had been placed on a table in the corner. "I'll deposit these two thugs elsewhere."

"Aw, mother," began Erland.

Anita held up a finger to her lips for silence. "Business of the court. You can annoy James and William at supper." Looking at the two young men she said, "You will come?"

James nodded. "Unless your husband has other plans for us, of course."

William hurried to the washbasin and attempted to clean himself as much as possible. A page appeared with a clean tabard, and he stripped off his blood-covered one. He washed his face, hands, and the back of his neck, not wishing to sit at the royal table looking as if he had just come from a slaughter-house. He was toweling off his face and hands when Prince Arutha walked in. "The duke will live," he said without preamble. With a wave of his hand he indicated that the two young men should sit on the divan vacated by his wife and sons.

They sat and Arutha said, "From everything that has occurred in the last two weeks, I can see that we face as big a danger to the sovereignty of our realm as we did from the moredhel recently.

"We have unchecked murders in our streets, a war between criminal factions, someone methodically killing magicians in our city, magicians attempting to assassinate visiting nobility, and a band of Keshian Izmalis operating far north of our border with Great Kesh." Arutha sat back. "In sum, we have as out-of-control a situation as I can remember."

James said nothing, and when William looked at him, gave the young man a slight shake of the head, indicating that the Prince was not to be questioned or interrupted.

After a moment of silence, Arutha said, "James, I have a commission for you."

James smiled. "Another?"

"No, the same, only more clearly defined."

William sat motionless, expecting to be dismissed at any moment.

Arutha noticed the posture and said, "I assume my wife has invited you to sup with us?"

William nodded.

"Good, because you're to play a part in this as well."

"Me?" asked William.

Arutha gave his adopted cousin a faint smile. "You feel as if you've been derelict in your duty?"

William nodded again.

Arutha said, "Losing men under your command is never easy. On your first mission, it can be devastating."

William felt tears threatening, and blinked them back as relief flooded over him. "Thank you, sire," he said softly.

Arutha paused for another long moment, then said, "What is said here, now, stays in this room."

Both young men nodded.

"James, for two years you've been flirting with the idea of setting up an intelligence corps."

James said nothing.

"I want you to stop flirting and start building in earnest. Young William here will help you."

"Me, Highness?"

Arutha looked at William. "The longer you stay in Krondor, the more you will come to understand that trust is a rare commodity to the throne. There are those, of course, who swear loyalty with every fiber of their being, but their own natures make them untrustworthy, since they harbor mental reservations even they are unaware of until the moment of crisis comes. You have shown your mettle over the last two days, and besides, you're Pug's son."

William's expression darkened a bit despite his attempt to keep a neutral façade. "Sire?" he asked, tentatively.

"I know you've had difficulties with your father, about taking service with me. You can be certain he and I had words over this several times. My point is, Pug has a particular loyalty to this family and nation. He has experienced things you and I can only imagine, yet he works for a greater good. Had you been a man I could not trust, I would have learned of that long before you came to Krondor.

"Besides," finished Arutha, "as one of the younger officers, you will be last among those suspected of any special rank within this court."

James said, "And I?"

Arutha looked at James. "Publicly, you will continue for a while with the rank of squire, but we both know you abuse that limit on your authority with regularity and invoke my name whenever you feel that will make a difference."

James just grinned.

"Eventually, if you and Locklear manage to live, I'll promote both of you to baronets, but while you probably have earned that rank half a dozen times over in the last few years, that promotion would only serve to call more attention to you should I award it now. Those men who tried to apprehend you a few days ago have me concerned."

James nodded. "As they do me. And given that some of my informants were among the dead, I shall have to give some thought to how I recruit their replacements."

"Young Deputy Means can help. What you must do is to recruit a few—no more than five—people who know you by name and face. Those must be the ones who work to bring in informants and agents. I shall also have to send you to every

179

city in the Kingdom, and eventually, abroad, so that a true network can be established. It will take years." He rose and the two young men followed suit. "But for the time being, let's see if you can set up a bit of an intelligence service here in Krondor without getting yourself killed."

"I've avoided it so far," James said with confidence.

"Which is why you get the task, my young future duke."

James grinned at the old joke between them. "Are you going to name me Duke of Krondor some day?"

"Perhaps. If I don't hang you first," Arutha said, leading them to the dining area. "Though if we get this network to the state I wish, one that will counter Kesh's, then I suspect you'll end up in Rillanon. The east is where we need intelligence, in many ways, more than we need it here." Ignoring protocol, Arutha pushed open the doors himself.

Seeing the door open from the other side, the two pages inside the dining room hurried to pull out the Prince's chair. William took his place at the foot of the table, next to James. He glanced over to see how James was taking all of this and saw the young squire was already lost in thought about the task before him.

Arutha said, "We'll continue this discussion later." He turned his attention to his wife and children.

Princess Elena seemed content to sing quietly to her doll, which had been propped up next to her dinner plate, and occasionally she informed James and William that the doll was not enjoying supper, mostly because she didn't like the behavior of the two boys next to her.

James nodded to William, and whispered, "Even money says the doll is abducted before the meal is over."

Sizing up the mischievous Princes Borric and Erland, William said, "No wager." Supper passed quietly and pleasantly, with Anita asking William questions that led him to tell of his mission without vivid details that might disturb the children.

After supper, Arutha rose and motioned to the two young men to follow him back to his office. As they left the dining area, and again passed through the private chamber, from behind them came an outraged screech from the Princess, followed by, "Mummy! Borric's got my dolly!"

James shrugged and said, "So I was off, she made it through the meal."

William smiled. "Barely."

When they reached Arutha's office door, James opened it for him.

The Prince swept through the door and William followed when James motioned him ahead. James closed the door and joined William before the desk.

Arutha waved for them to sit and said, "I've given this a lot of thought, James, and as much as I know you'd love to be given a free rein on this, I want you to report to me on every proposed agent you want to recruit."

James nodded. "That will slow us down, Highness."

"I know, but I'd rather not lose agents down the road for haste at the outset. I would prefer you to be circumspect and find us reliable people."

James said, "I've been thinking about this as well, Highness. What if we set up two sets of agents?"

"What's your meaning?"

"What if I line up some snitches and a couple of dock-workers, the sort of blokes I employed before, as if I were replacing those who were killed or fled, while at the same time I was quietly setting up a real ring of agents?"

181

"Sounds plausible, but you realize those you recruit more openly are likely to be punished for the deeds of your real agents, don't you?"

James said, "I know. But this isn't a game, Highness. People are dying right now, and those who willingly take the Crown's gold for being involved in such business should know the risks involved. I don't want to set up anyone to be a decoy, and if I'm just fumble-fingered enough in setting up my snitches and bully-boys, and they're just inept enough to make our enemies think them harmless, perhaps they won't be asked to pay the price for our other work."

Arutha said, "I don't like it, but there are many things associated with this crown I don't like."

William sat silently, and Arutha looked at him. "Do you understand?"

"Sir?"

"I mean, do you understand about doing distasteful things, even repulsive things, in the name of duty?"

William was silent for a long moment, then he answered. "Sire, I've learned a lot in the last year about what it means to bear arms. Training was half of it. Killing men was most of the other half. But watching comrades, men whose safety had been entrusted to me . . . I think I understand."

"Good, because you're the only junior officer I can trust fully, beyond even the normal oath of loyalty to the Crown. Your father never traded on his adoption into the family—he never needed to—but it was a most solemn gift by my father to honor a boy he thought dead, whom he had come to regard as worthy of bearing our family name.

"The children call you Cousin Willie, with affection, but it's more than a simple courtesy: you are a conDoin. If the responsibility that comes with that name hasn't dawned upon you yet, now is the time for it to do so."

William sat back, comprehension dawning on him. "It hadn't, Highness. But I think it's beginning to."

"Good," said Arutha with a half-smile. "I have no doubt James will accelerate your understanding if he doesn't get you killed first."

"What should I do, Highness?" asked William.

"Study, learn, listen, train, do your job. But from time to time James will pull you from your regular duties and you'll aid him in whatever task he requires. As your time here passes, William, I want you to get to know every man in the command, and in your mind mark those who you think can be trusted with special duties. The Household Guard has been a ceremonial command of late. It's time to change that. I will eventually make it clear that my personal guards are the élite of this command, but not quite yet. To do so at this time would send a signal to whoever is behind all the mayhem in my city."

Arutha sat back, formed a tent with his fingers and flexed them for a moment, the only nervous gesture James had ever seen him make. After a moment of reflection, he said, "We have ample proof of agencies in our realm doing mischief. We do not know if we face one or many foes. The Nighthawks? Are they related to those Izmalis? Why would they mount so frantic an attack? Had they moved with more precision, I suspect you would not be here, William."

William nodded in agreement.

"And of course," Arutha continued, "why kill magicians?"

James said, "It would be nice if either Pug or Kulgan was here."

Arutha nodded absently. "Pug wants to send me a new court

magician. After that affair with Makala and the Tsurani Great Ones, and now this business of shape-changers and murdering magicians . . ." He sighed. "I think Pug is correct and I will send him word to have this Keshian girl sent here."

William's eyes widened. "Jazhara!"

Arutha said, "Yes."

"But she's—"

Arutha interrupted. "I know. She's the great niece of Lord Hazara-Khan." Glancing at James. "Who is, I suspect, your opposite in the Court of Great Kesh."

James said, "You flatter me. It will take me a decade to put together agents as cleverly as he has."

To William, Arutha said, "You object to her coming here?"

"No . . . it's just that I'm . . . surprised, Highness."

"Why?"

William's eyes shifted a moment, then he said, "Well, she's a Keshian, and connected to the most influential family in the north of the empire. And . . . she's young."

Arutha had to laugh. "And you and James are ancient veterans?"

William blushed. "No . . . it's just that all my life I've been surrounded by magicians, many of whom are elderly men of great experience. I'm just . . ."

"Just what?" asked the Prince.

"Surprised that she's my father's choice, that's all."

Arutha reflected on that. "Why?"

"There are older, more experienced magicians at Stardock."

"Who?"

"Who?" echoed William.

"Who," repeated Arutha, "would you suggest is a more appropriate choice?"

William said, "I . . . well . . . there are several." His mind raced and he did a quick inventory of the magicians at Stardock who might serve as an advisor to the Prince of Krondor. He quickly realized that most were either too caught up in their own area of study to perform the required duties with any dedication, or they lacked the social skills necessary to be a harmonious addition to the court. After a moment, he said, "Actually, I can't think of anyone. Korsh and Watoom are also Keshians, and they are too involved with the conduct of the Academy. Zolan Husbar and Kulgan are too old. There are some others, but Jazhara has both the knowledge of court politics and a firm grasp of the mystic arts."

"Do you fear treachery?"

"No," William said without hesitation. "Never that. If she swears an oath of fealty to your crown, Highness, she will serve with her life if need be."

"I thought as much." Arutha regarded William for a moment. "There's something else you're not telling me, but I'll let that pass for now." To James he said, "I'll set up a special account for you to draw upon for whatever you need in establishing this new network of agents. I want a weekly report, even if the report is 'nothing happened this week.' And I won't like hearing that."

James nodded. "There are three things we must deal with as quickly as possible. First, what is the relationship between the Nighthawks and the Crawler? Second, what is the purpose behind all the seemingly random deaths? And third, what is the significance of magicians being killed?"

Arutha rose, and the young men quickly followed suit. "I must pay a visit to the Duke of Olasko and his family. You can add to that list why a visiting lord of a friendly nation was set upon so far from home."

"Four things," said James.

Arutha didn't wait for James to open the door, but just opened it himself as he said, "Be in court tomorrow morning, both of you."

After the Prince had set off down the corridor, William turned to James and said, "Did I make a total fool of myself in there?"

"Not total," replied James with a smile. "What's between this girl and you?"

William looked down at the ground and said, "It's a long story."

"We have time, so tell me."

"Time? I have to report in."

"You already did," said James. "Treggar and the other officers will have been told you were with Arutha. From now on, when you're with me or the Prince, the others in the garrison will simply know you're on special duty. That's all."

William sighed. "When I came here, I really thought I'd train and then head off to some frontier outpost."

James laughed. "You're the Prince's cousin, even if only by adoption. You didn't imagine they'd let any member of the family conDoin rot away at Highcastle or Iron Pass, did you?"

"Well, I just never thought of myself as a royal, that's all."

"Living on that island out in the middle of that huge lake, I can see why you wouldn't."

William yawned. "Well, even if I don't have to report in, I could use some sleep."

"Not yet," said James, throwing his arm around William's shoulder. "We have some business to conduct."

"Business? Now?"

"Yes," said James. "And besides, I want to hear all about you and this Jazhara."

William said nothing, but he rolled his eyes heavenward and silently said, *Why me?*

James opened the door into the noisy inn. William had been telling him the story of his relationship with the magician summoned from the island.

"So, you see, it was really a silly boy thing, and she was very kind about it, but it was very embarrassing to say the least. I'll hardly know what to say when she arrives."

"How old were you?"

"Sixteen."

James glanced around the inn. "I think I understand. You'll appreciate my view of such things is different. By that age I was very . . . familiar with women, in both the good and bad sense of 'familiar'." He motioned across the room. "There's a table."

William and James had to maneuver their way past several groups of men standing drinking at tall tables along the wall, and between larger round dining tables. Food could be seen here and there, but most of the crowd seemed to be intent on drinking ale, or the occasional goblet of wine.

As the two of them sat down, William said, "Why are we here?"

James waved his hand around. "Partially, to see what we can see." William frowned, not having any idea of what James was talking about. "And partially, sitting in your tiny room with that other young lieutenant . . ."

"Gordon," supplied William.

"Yes, Gordon . . . would probably do nothing to keep you from some black despair or another over your handling of the mission—which was quite good, no matter how you feel. And lastly . . ." James waved his hand ". . . I promised Talia I'd bring you back here."

"You what—" he started to say, as Talia reached them.

"James, William, how lovely to see you. What is your pleasure?"

"Two ales, please," said James.

She turned and gave William an extra little smile as she left to fetch their drinks.

"See," said James.

"See what?"

"She likes you."

William turned to watch her move through the press of bodies in the room. "You think?"

"I know." James leaned across the table and gave William's arm a brotherly squeeze, then sat back. "Trust me. She thinks you're a Prince."

"What?" said William, now confused. "You told her I was a Prince?"

James laughed. "No, you stone-crowned idiot. A 'Prince of a fellow.' A nice young man."

"Oh," said William, sitting back. Then he looked at James. "So you really think she likes me?"

James could barely contain himself as Talia returned with two flagons. Setting them down, William admired the pretty girl for a brief instant, then looked away as she said to him, "You've not been avoiding me, have you, Will?"

William glanced at her and saw that she was smiling, and

he returned the smile. "No, I was just on a . . . mission for the Prince."

"That's fine," she said cheerfully, scooping up the coins James put on the table for the ale and walking away.

William sipped his ale, then glanced at James. Before William could speak, James said, "She likes you."

"Oh," William replied, turning his attention back to the ale.

James chuckled. They sat in silence for a few minutes, James appearing to be watching the crowd absently, but William noticed that his eyes were going from one man to the next, as if memorizing them or looking for something in those faces.

At last, James said, "We need to leave. Drink up."

"Why?"

James drained his ale and stood. "Now."

William took another sip, stood and followed James. As they edged through the crowd, Talia saw them leaving and called to them, "Don't be strangers!"

William waved, but James just hurried through the door.

Outside the inn, James held up his hand and said, "Wait."

"For what?"

"For that fellow there," James said, pointing to a man nearing a distant corner, "to turn."

The man turned the corner, and James said, "Now. Hurry."

"We're following him?"

"Brilliant."

"I mean, why?"

James said, "Because a few days back he and a few of his friends were following me. And I need to find out why."

William said nothing, but reflexively his hand fell to the hilt of his sword.

189

# TEN

# REVELATION

J AMES glanced around the corner.

The man he had seen leave The Rainbow Parrot was just ducking around the far corner of the road. James held up his hand for William to wait. As the squire expected, a moment later the man reappeared for a brief instant, peeping around the corner to see if he was being followed.

"It's a trap," said James.

William drew his sword. "Do we walk away, or do we spring it?"

"Neither," said James. "They know there are two of us, so they'll be ready for you and that oversized cleaver of yours." He glanced upward. "How're your climbing skills?"

"What?" said William glancing upward. "Here?"

"Where else?" replied James as he followed the roof-line with his eye. "Follow me," he instructed, heading back the way they had come.

Half a block away was an alley. "We don't have much time," James said. "They'll wait another two minutes, then they'll figure we've tumbled to the trap."

James found what he was looking for, a wooden stairway to an upper floor door. He hurried up the steps, trying not to make any more noise than necessary, and William followed close behind. To William the noise of his own heavy boots on the wooden steps was certainly loud enough to wake those inside and warn whoever waited half a block away. Yet James seemed untroubled by it. He reached the door at the top of the stairs and pointed up toward the overhanging roof.

"Give me a boost," James whispered.

William made a stirrup with his hands and lifted James easily upward so he was quickly sitting on the roof. James turned and reached over to help William up. "Hurry!" he whispered.

William grabbed James's hand and came up easily. An instant later both were moving, crouched low, toward the far edge. James again lay down and peered over the edge. He held up his hand and showed four fingers, without taking his eyes off the men below.

William didn't risk looking over as James retreated.

"Ever jump off a roof before?"

"What, twenty feet?"

"Something like that."

"With something to break my fall, yes."

James grinned. "There are four possibilities down there."

He pulled out his sword and sat down on the edge of the roof. He slid until he could grab the eaves with his left hand. He held himself there for an instant, cutting the distance from his feet to the ground by nearly half, then pushed away and landed feet-first on the shoulders of the rearmost man. The ambusher smashed into the ground, either dead or unconscious, as James tucked and rolled across the hard cobbles of the street.

193

William didn't consider the bruises that move would leave, or the splinters he would collect, as he attempted to duplicate James's feat.

His hand missed the roof, so rather than slowing down, William fell hard upon the next man below, crushing his spine as they slammed into the street. William's head swam for an instant, but while he gathered his wits, training and reflex took over. He was sitting on a corpse; without thought he got off and rolled over into a fighter's crouch.

As his faculties returned, William found himself with his sword out, point leveled at a frightened-looking man, who had his own sword at the ready. James was engaged with another man who was either trying to circle him to escape, or get into a better position to fight. The man James had landed on lay groaning on the cobbles.

William's opponent, a stocky fellow with the muscles of a dockworker, lunged with his sword. William, even though still slightly dazed from his fall, easily deflected the lunge and parried. He let the man slide up on him, then threw his shoulder into him, knocking him back.

The man staggered but recovered before William could close. William blinked, trying to clear his vision, and when things cleared, he saw his opponent dropping his sword and putting up his hands, palms outward. James was standing behind him, his sword firmly pressing against the man's spine. "That's the lad," said James. "No sense dying along with the others, is there?"

The man said nothing. He made a small step forward as if he was trying to escape, then threw himself backward with all his weight, impaling himself on James's sword.

William watched in shock. "What?"

James yanked loose his sword and caught the man as he fell. He looked into the man's eyes, and said, "Dead."

"Why?"

He reached inside the man's tunic and pulled out an amulet. It was a dark metal, with a relief hawk inscribed upon it.

"Nighthawks," James said. "Again." He looked around. "Wait here."

William said nothing as James scurried off into the night. Time passed slowly and William wondered what James could be doing. He held his sword ready and waited. Just as he began to wonder if he should leave and find the city guards, James reappeared with a pair of city constables. "Here," he said, pointing to the bodies. "I want one of you to guard them and another to hurry and get a wagon. Bring them to the palace."

"Yes, squire," said a constable. He glanced at his companion, who nodded, and turned and hurried off into the darkness.

"What now?" asked William.

"Back to the palace, as soon as the wagon gets here."

William watched, suddenly overwhelmed by numbing fatigue, as the constable studied the fallen assassins. James was content to remain silent, and William also felt no need to speak. But deep inside, beneath the uncertainty about his handling of the duke's safety, and the enormity of what they were about to undertake, he wondered if he was equal to the tasks being set before him. Taking a deep breath, he resolved that, ready or not, he would do his best, and leave it to the gods to judge his efforts worthy or not.

Arutha stood in the dark cellar as the four dead men were stripped and examined closely by a pair of soldiers. James and William waited nearby, watching.

Every article of clothing, weapon and personal item was examined for a hint of where these men came from. As expected, the search turned up little. Each man had an identical hawk amulet on a chain. Other than weapons, a simple ring on one man, and a small pouch of gold coins on another, the men were anonymous. Nothing hinted at their origins.

Arutha pointed to one of the shirts and said, "Give that to me."

A soldier brought it over and Arutha looked at it closely. "I wish I had my wife's eye for garments, but I think this is a Keshian weave."

James said, "The boots!"

Arutha waved and all the dead men's boots were brought over. Arutha, James and William inspected them and found several bootmakers' marks.

"I don't recognize these," said Arutha. "So they're not Krondorian, I'm certain."

James said, "I'll get pen and paper and copy these. By noon tomorrow I'll know who these makers are."

Arutha nodded and James sent a page scurrying off. In less than five minutes he was back and he said, "Squire, I've just been told they've been looking for you all evening."

Arutha glanced over and said, "Who are 'they'?"

"Jailer Morgon, sire, and his men."

Arutha indulged himself in a slight smile and said, "Why is the jailer looking for you, James?"

James said, "I'll go find out." He handed the pen and paper to William and said, "Do your best."

James left the examination of the dead men to the Prince and hurried along after the page. They parted company when the page headed upstairs to the main floor of the palace, while

James turned and headed down deeper into the dungeon. He reached the door to the jailer's small apartment and knocked.

"Who is it?" came the voice from the other side.

"Squire James. You sent for me?"

"Oh, yes," said the voice. The door opened and Morgon the Chief Jailer looked out. He was dressed for bed in a gray flannel nightshirt. "Just turning in, squire. I sent that boy to find you hours ago."

"I was out of the palace until a while ago. What can I do for you?"

The jailer said, "Nothing for me, but there's a bloke down in the lock-up claims he needs to talk to you." Morgon was a narrow-faced man of advancing years, but his hair had stayed almost uniformly black in all the time James had lived at the palace. He cut it straight across the forehead and down before the ears, so he looked as if he was wearing a black hat with ear flaps. "Bit odd, if you ask me. He's been in lock-up for almost three weeks now, and hasn't said a thing to anybody. But his trial's tomorrow so suddenly he's shouting for you."

"Do you know his name?"

"Didn't ask," said Morgon, fighting off a yawn. "Should I have?"

"I'll go see who it is. Who's on duty?"

"Sikes. He'll take you to him."

"Good night, Morgon."

"Night, squire," said the jailer, closing the door.

James hurried down the small passage that led to the stairs down into the deeper dungeon. The dungeon had two levels. The upper level was excavated so that narrow windows in the cells let in light, and through which courtyard hangings could be watched by those in the death-cells.

The lower level was pitch black. Here the palace dungeon was really a vast gallery with four large metal cages in it, the bars running from floor to ceiling. A cross formed by two paths divided the cells from one another. A torch at the foot of the stairs at the end of one of the walkways was the only source of light for the entire vast dungeon. A solider stood beneath the torch and turned as James came down the steps.

"Squire," he said in greeting.

"Someone looking for me down here?" asked James.

"Bloke in the far cell. I'll take you there."

James followed as the soldier took the torch from its wall holder and led him past the first two cells, both of which were empty. The two far cells were full of men, mostly sleeping, and a few women huddled together for mutual protection in the corners. These were the brawlers, drunks and troublemakers who were guilty of enough chronic lawbreaking as to be facing the Prince's justice. Some of the prisoners called out questions, which James ignored.

The soldier led James to the far end of the cell and James saw the large man waiting with his hands on the bars.

When he stopped before him, James heard the man say, "Glad to see you, Jimmy."

James said, "Ethan. I thought you long gone."

The former Abbot of Ishap, former basher in the Mockers, said, "As did I, but the gods have other plans for us."

"Us?"

With his chin he motioned over his shoulder. "I've got Kat and Limm with me."

"When's your trial?"

"Tomorrow."

"What's the charge?"

"Charges. Unlawful flight, resisting arrest, battery, rioting, and probably treason as well."

James turned to the guard and said, "Get them out of there and bring them to my quarters."

"Squire?"

"I said get them out of there and bring them to my quarters. Put men outside my door until I send them back to you."

The guard still seemed uncertain.

"Would you like me to run up to annoy the Prince for his personal signed order?"

The guard, like almost everyone else in the garrison, knew the squire could get the Prince's warrant if he needed to, so he thought better of delaying the inevitable and said, "I'll get some of the boys to bring them to you."

"See you upstairs, Ethan," James said and left.

A short time later there was a knock at the door of James's room. Graves, Kat and Limm stood before him, shackled and cuffed in irons. "Remove the irons and wait outside," ordered James.

"Yes, squire," answered the senior guard.

After the irons were off and the door closed, James indicated a tray he had sent in before they got there, upon which was a pitcher of ale, cheese, bread and cold beef. Limm dug in without hesitation. Graves loaded up a platter for himself and Kat while she filled two flagons.

"Last I saw you, Ethan, you were going to get Kat and head for Kesh."

Graves nodded. "That was the plan."

"What happened?"

Graves said, "It took me almost a week to find Kat, and then set up the move to Durbin. We were lying low, had a nice little place in the poor quarter, waiting for the day our ship was heading out. Then the murders started." He looked at Limm and indicated the boy should continue the story.

Limm said, "We've been banging up against this Crawler and his men for a while now, squire. You remember last month when Old Donk turned up dead?"

James nodded, even though he was vague as to who Old Donk had been and when he had died.

"Then you must have heard how some bashers were killed out at the docks?"

James nodded, assuming that was related to what Walter Blont had told him about the battle between his group and the Crawler's men.

"Well then, when the Crawler's men hit Mother's we all scattered. I'd been fetchin' for Kat and Graves while they was hiding out, getting ready to go to Kesh, and then the Nightmaster is killed. They find him floatin' in the bay. The Daymaster got together with Mick Giffen, Reg deVrise, and Phil the Fingers and they went somewhere, come back saying the Upright Man is dead, and next thing you know a war's on in the sewer. Most of the boys are dead and all the bashers are too." Limm paused to catch his breath, then carried on. "Graves and Kat and me were heading out to Kesh, playing the part of a proper family, when we got caught up in a riot at the docks. You know the rest."

James said, "There's just been a little too much killing around here for my taste of late." He filled them in on as much as he felt like sharing, leaving out those details of recent events that he felt might compromise Kingdom security.

When James finished, Graves said, "Those Izmali assassins don't surprise me. I spied a couple of rough-looking Keshians down in the sewers, while we were trying for the docks, before we came up and got ourselves tossed into jail. Needless to say, I didn't confront them to find out what they were doing there."

Limm chimed in, "And some of those who were killing the street boys were Keshians."

James silently weighed up how much he was comfortable sharing with his former compatriots. Finally he asked, "Why would they be killing magicians?"

Graves stopped chewing for a moment. Eyes wide, he swallowed, and said, "The only reason I can think of has something to do with the Temple of Ishap. I may be a renegade of that order, but there are secrets I will not reveal. This has nothing to do with my duty to the temple, but it does with my duty to the gods."

James said, "Would it have anything to do with the occupation of a house across from the western gate of the palace?"

Graves said nothing, but there was a slight flicker in his eyes.

"Never mind," said James. "Despite my years, I've seen enough of priests and oaths to last several lifetimes. I won't press. But any insight you can provide about this murdering of magicians would be deeply appreciated."

"By you?"

James grinned. "By the Crown."

"Enough to get us out of that cell and on our way to Great Kesh?"

"This very night if the Prince likes what he hears."

"Then take me to the Prince," said Graves.

James nodded. To Kat and Limm he said, "Wait here." Then he opened the door and told the soldier outside to continue standing guard. He led Graves back to where Arutha and Wil-

201

liam were inspecting the four slain men, presented Graves and finished by saying, "He may have some pieces of this puzzle."

Arutha said, "And they would be?"

"Safe passage?" asked Graves of James.

"Safe passage?" Arutha raised an eyebrow.

James said, "A minor matter of civil disorder which was scheduled to be resolved tomorrow morning."

"This morning, you mean," said Arutha. "The sun is but three hours away." To Graves, Arutha said, "If you provide intelligence of suitable worth, I think we can overlook the matter of a minor brawl."

James said, "More like a small riot, but that's neither here nor there."

Graves said, "Then know you, Highness, that I was the man once named Abbot of the Temple of Ishap at Malac's Cross. I betrayed my oaths and I betrayed my brothers and now I am consigned to the punishment of the gods."

Arutha said, "The required value of your information just went up a great deal, Abbot Graves. I know that name, and by rights I should bind you over to the temple for its justice."

Graves said, "Here is what I may say: there are forces about the land, dark agencies which mean you harm in ways you cannot fathom, Highness. They move in shadows and employ those who may not even realize they are in the service of these powers.

"A matter of great import will occur soon. I think you know what it is and why I may not speak more of it."

The Prince nodded. "Go on."

"There are those who would benefit if things went awry with that matter. It is not important to those dark agencies that they succeed, only that the temples fail."

"Are you asking me to warn the temples?" asked Arutha.

Graves smiled. "Highness, nothing I have said to you is unknown to anyone of rank in the Temple of Ishap, or among the prelates of the other orders. I'm trying to illustrate a point: your enemies may appear to be acting in a random, even chaotic fashion, because they have no goal, other than to create difficulties for you."

Arutha said, "So far I've heard nothing new."

"Then this is the part you don't know. There is an organization overseen by a man you know as the Crawler. He is attempting to displace the Mockers in Krondor, as well as take over criminal activities in other cities. His goals seem simple: wealth and power. But to achieve these ends, he has allied himself with others: the Nighthawks." Graves paused to gauge the Prince's reaction.

"Continue," said Arutha.

"It's an uneasy alliance, for the Nighthawks appear to have their own agendas, including working for those dark agencies I spoke of before. The Crawler's men were those driving the Mockers out of the city. The Nighthawks have been killing magicians."

"Do you know anything of the assault upon the Duke of Olasko?"

"One hears rumors, even in your dungeon. It is the result of a plot by one or the other, the Crawler or the Nighthawks. If it's the Crawler, it is because the duke is seen as an impediment to his plans. If it is the Nighthawks, it is because the duke's death serves those dark forces I speak of."

"Do magicians work for the Nighthawks?" asked James.

"Not that I've heard of, but then they do not work for the Crawler, either. Thieves have little trust of those who practice magic arts, as you know well, Jimmy the Hand," answered Graves.

Arutha smiled at the mention of that name. "James also knows how to ask questions to ferret out the truth.

"So if we were to tell you that those who attempted to take the duke's life were magicians, and their target wasn't truly the duke, but the Crown Prince, what say you then?"

Graves said, "Then a third agency must be involved. Perhaps those dark forces are sending additional agents to insure their ends, regardless of what the Nighthawks and the Crawler achieve."

Arutha sighed in frustration. "Damn me, but at times like these I wish for an enemy in plain sight."

"Highness," said Graves, "I think I can give you at least one."

"What?" asked Arutha.

Graves walked over to the nearest corpse. "A man in death doesn't always resemble the man he was in life, but I know this one. His name, or at least how I knew him, was Jendi. He was a raider from the Jal-Pur, and a man with whom the Upright Man has done business in the past. He is a murderer, a slaver, and a robber." He looked at the Prince. "How did he come here?"

James answered. "He was trying to arrange a conversation with me, against my wishes."

Graves smiled. "Any chat he had in mind was you telling him everything you have ever known and him listening until he decided to kill you."

Arutha said, "So you know this man. Whom do you think he was working for?"

"It is rumored that while Jendi was a common thug, he

worked from time to time with more dangerous people: like the Nighthawks."

"How could that be?" asked Arutha. "I thought the Nighthawks kept to themselves."

"Oh, they do, but they need contact with the outside world, and so they use those they bribe or terrorize to loyalty. Someone has to negotiate on their behalf when it comes to killing for profit."

"I thought if you wanted an assassin's services, you just left the name of the victim somewhere and they contacted you and named a price," said James.

Graves said, "Yes, but someone has to pick up that name and deliver the price. They don't do it themselves."

Arutha said, "Do you know if there are Keshians among the Nighthawks?"

Graves said, "They are a brotherhood without nation, Highness. Bands of assassins in the Kingdom count Izmali clans in the south as kin."

Arutha said, "At least that puts the Keshian assassins in the same place as the Nighthawks."

"Literally," said Graves.

"What does that mean?"

"It means you are almost certain to find your Nighthawks, both Kingdom and Keshian, at a place within a week's ride of here."

"Where?" asked Arutha. "Tell me and your crimes are pardoned and your safe passage guaranteed."

Graves said, "To the south of Shandon Bay lies an old caravan trail, no longer used. Further south of that trail lies a range of hills, upon which once rested an ancient Keshian fortress. I only know of it because that man—" he pointed at the corpse "—spoke of it once in a drunken ramble. Some ancient map or another may have its location. But know this, the upper breastworks and towers have long since fallen, and all that remains are the underground tunnels."

James said, "Sounds a lot like what they were using up at Cavell Keep."

Graves continued. "They have water there; an ancient spring, and they can trade for food at Land's End or Shamata with anonymity. It's close enough to Krondor to strike at will, and unless you know what you're looking for, you could ride past it and never know you'd passed an enclave of murderers."

Arutha turned to William, who had been listening quietly, and said, "Hurry to my quarters. Take as many men as you need, but I want you to go through every ancient map we have and look for any hint of that Keshian fortress."

Graves said, "Can you read Keshian, boy?"

William nodded. "I can."

Graves said, "Then look for a place called 'Valley of Lost Men.' From there trace your finger to the east. If that fortress is on the map, it might be called 'The Tomb of the Hopeless.'"

"I imagine it wasn't considered a choice duty station," James quipped.

Graves said, "I don't know about that, but I do know that's what that drunken murderer called it. Said the garrison had been left to die defending it or some such legend. It's said to be haunted by the spirits of soldiers, and blood drinkers and other such nonsense."

James said, "If you'd seen some of the things we have concerning the Nighthawks, Ethan, you'd change your tune. It's very disconcerting to kill one and then have to kill him all over again a few minutes later."

Graves made a sign. "I said you were confronting dark agencies, Highness, and I mean of the blackest sort."

Arutha said, "We'll forgo your trial in the morning, Graves, but you'll remain my guest a while longer. If this tale of yours turns out to have truth in it, we'll get you on a ship for Durbin or Queg or to wherever it is you wish to travel. James, take him back to his cell."

James saluted. "Sire."

He led Graves out of the room and said, "That went well."

Graves said, "If you say so, Jimmy."

"He didn't turn you over to the Ishapians, and he didn't order you hung, did he?"

Graves smiled. "Well, there is that."

They walked back to James's quarters, where they would fetch Limm and Kat and return to the dungeon below. Far from comfortable, it was still one of the safest places in Krondor. If any place in Krondor could be considered safe these days, James thought to himself.

ELEVEN

# STEALTH

HE Rainbow Parrot was empty.

At this hour of the morning, no one was drinking. James yelled out, "Lucas!"

William glanced around and was rewarded a moment later when Talia entered from the kitchen. "William!" she said with obvious pleasure. "James," she added, her smile fading only slightly. "Father is hauling refuse down to the river for dumping. He'll be back any moment if you'd like to wait."

William smiled and said, "Thank you."

James grabbed William's elbow and stopped him from sitting. "If I don't miss my guess, Talia needs to shop in the market this morning, don't you, Talia?"

Her smile brightened as she said, "Why, yes, as a matter of fact. I was going to leave as soon as Father returns."

"Why don't you escort her to the market, William, as I have some private matters to discuss with her father?"

William almost fell over a chair getting around James to offer his arm to Talia. "If you have no objection?" he asked.

She slipped her arm through his gracefully and said, "No,

I'm pleased to have the company." Looking at James, she said, "You don't mind being left alone, squire?"

James said, "No, a few minutes of peace will be welcome." Her expression turned quizzical and he added quickly, "Things at the palace have been very frantic of late, what with visiting nobles and all."

Her smile broadened. "Oh, yes. I heard an eastern noble was staying at the palace." Turning her back on James as she gazed up at William, she said, "You must tell me all about it."

From behind Talia, James shook his head slightly, indicating that William most certainly should *not* tell her all about it. He said, "I'm sure William can remember what the ladies of the eastern courts were wearing, Talia."

William allowed himself to be led outside, and James sat down to wait for Lucas. He didn't wait long, for as good as Talia's promise, Lucas appeared a few minutes later, entering the inn from the rear door. "Talia!" he shouted; then he saw James sitting alone.

"Where's my girl?"

"She's gone to market with William. I told her I'd watch the place until you returned."

Lucas fixed James with a baleful look, and said, "You're up to something, Jimmy. I've known you too many years not to know that. What is it?"

James rose and came to lean on the bar beside Lucas. "Something awkward, Lucas. I wish to ask you a question, but I can't until I've sworn you to secrecy."

Lucas was silent for a moment, rubbing his chin as he considered his answer. "Can't rightly do that, until I know what's what. I've got obligations, as I'm sure you well know."

James knew well indeed. Lucas was one of few successful

innkeepers in Krondor who didn't have the patronage of a powerful noble, a guild, or the Mockers. Over the years he had
managed to make several useful alliances, including friendships
with several highly-placed nobles in the Kingdom. James he
knew from his dealings with the Mockers, yet Lucas had somehow resisted becoming their tool, or coming under their domi-
nation. There was something very stubborn in the old man's
nature, and it was known without saying that as soon as anyone
tried to control him, Lucas could call upon other resources.
Ultimately, it was easier to work with Lucas than to try to
coerce him.

James had rehearsed his speech several times, and after taking a deep breath, he began. "We both know the Mockers are
no longer a major force. And we both know that someone
else—this Crawler—is trying to tie up all the dodges and capers
in Krondor."

Lucas nodded.

"We also know that, as far as anyone can judge, the Upright
Man is dead."

Lucas smiled. "Don't be so quick. He's a cagey one. Maybe
the Upright Man's dead or maybe he's just lying low."

James said, "Perhaps, but if he's lying low he's as good as
dead, because he's let the Mockers come to a messy end."

"Maybe, or maybe it just seems that way."

James grinned. "Anyone ever tell you you're a pain to talk
to?"

"Yup," said Lucas. "Not too many, though."

"Look, I need . . . well-placed friends."

Lucas laughed. "Well, start with the Prince of Krondor, boy.
I can't imagine anyone better placed than him."

"I mean well-placed *within* Krondor. People who are in a position to hear things."

Lucas was silent as he weighed James's words carefully, then he spoke: "Over the years I've made it a business to be very hard of hearing most of the time, Jimmy. It's why lots of people are comfortable doing business with me. There are them that wants to move cargo without having to deal with the Prince's customs men or the Mockers' fences, and I know the occasional caravan driver heading inland.

"There are those that need to speak to others who want to kill them on sight, and I can sometimes get them together without bloodshed. Things like that.

"But all that goes to naught if anyone thinks I've turned snitch."

James said, "I'm not looking for snitches, Lucas. I've got enough of those on every street corner. I need something more, someone I trust. I need good information, not rumors or lies fashioned to earn some coppers. Moreover, I need someone, after all is said and done, who is my man, no matter what he's telling other people." He looked at Lucas and said, "I think you understand what I'm saying."

Lucas was thoughtful for a moment. Then he sighed and said, "Sorry, but I could never be no man's spy, Jimmy. That's too dodgy a path, even for the likes of me." He moved away and went behind the bar. "But I'll tell you this. I'll never work against the Crown. I was once a soldier and my boys died for the Kingdom. So, you have my word on that. And if I catch a hint of anything like that, well, let's say I'll make sure you find out quick. How's that?"

James said, "It'll have to do."

"Would you like an ale?"

James laughed. "It's still a little early for that. I'll just take my leave. When Talia and William return, tell Will to return to the garrison and report in, will you?"

Lucas said, "About that young fellow . . ."

"Yes?"

"He's a good sort, right?"

James said, "Yes, he's a good sort."

Lucas nodded, then picked up a rag and started polishing his bar. "Just that . . . well, like I told you, Talia's all I've got left. Want to see she's done right by, if you see what I mean."

"I see what you mean," said James, grinning. "If any one will do right by her, William will."

Lucas glanced up. "Father's a duke, you said?"

James laughed and departed, waving good-bye to Lucas.

William felt flushed and a little giddy, and couldn't quite decide if he was in love or just overtired. He'd had numerous conversations with his parents on the subject of men and women and their relationships, as well as hearing plenty of opinions from the academy students at Stardock as he grew up. In many ways he was far more acquainted with the theory of romance than many young men his age, but far less practiced than most.

As Talia chattered on about the current gossip, he tried to keep interested, but his mind wandered. He had known girls all his life, starting with his adopted sister Gamina. But while he had had many female friends as a boy, he had only thought himself in love once before.

He tried to push the image of Jazhara aside, and the more he tried, the more vivid she became in his mind. Four years older than William, she had come to study at Stardock when he was eleven years old. That had been half a lifetime ago, he realized.

She had been aloof at first, a Keshian of noble birth who had eventually put up with his childhood infatuation with good grace and even, occasionally, flattered amusement. Then the year before he left for Krondor, things had changed. He was no longer an awkward boy, but a strong and intelligent young man and for a brief time his interest in her was returned. Their affair had been stormy, intense, and ultimately painful for William.

It had ended badly, and he was still unclear as to what had made their relationship so rocky, and until he had learned that she was being sent to Krondor he had thought he might never discover the reasons why she had pushed him away. Now he considered the prospect of meeting her again with dread and some excitement.

"You're not listening." Talia's voice penetrated his reverie.

"Sorry," he said with a smile. "I haven't had much sleep the past couple of nights." When she frowned, he quickly added, "Business of the Crown."

She smiled and held onto his arm as they approached the market. "Well, enjoy the sunshine and we'll just pretend the Prince and his business are very far away. And promise me you'll get a good night's sleep, all right?"

"I'll see what I can do," William replied. He looked at the young woman's profile as she stopped to inspect produce that had come into the city that morning.

She pointed to a pile of large golden onions and said, "I'll take six of those."

While she and the seller haggled a little, William found his thoughts returning to the differences between Talia and Jazhara.

Jazhara was Keshian, from desert stock, and darkly exotic by Kingdom standards. She was a magician of some skill and great potential, and as fit as any fighter he had ever known. He knew from first-hand experience that she could crack your skull with a quarterstaff as quickly as conjure up a spell, and she was better educated than any woman he had met—she spoke a dozen languages and dialects, knew the history both of her own homeland and the Kingdom, and could discourse on sciences, the course of the stars, and the mysteries of the gods.

Talia by contrast was a sunny, open person, full of humor and grace. She turned to catch William staring at her and said, "What?"

He smiled back. "Just thinking that you are as pretty a girl as I've ever seen."

She blushed. "Flatterer."

He felt suddenly embarrassed by the comment and said, "Tell me about . . . where you grew up. You said you were raised by an order of . . . ?"

She smiled as she handed over four coins to the seller and put the onions in her shopping basket. "I was raised by an order of the Sisters of Kahooli."

William almost let his mouth fall open. Then: "Kahooli!" he exclaimed.

Several shoppers nearby turned to see who had invoked the name of the God of Vengeance.

She patted his arm. "I get that reaction."

"I thought you were sent off to an abbey of a . . ."

"More feminine order?" she finished.

"Something like that."

She said, "Women serve the Seeker After Vengeance. And Father decided if I was to be raised outside the city, it would be by someone who could teach me to defend myself." She reached out and touched his sword hilt with her right index finger. "That's a bit big for my tastes, but I could probably do some serious harm with it."

"No doubt," he said. The orders of Kahooli were primarily dedicated to seeking out wrongdoers and visiting justice upon them. At their most benign, they acted as aides to local constables and sheriffs, locating malefactors and either capturing them or pointing out their whereabouts. At their more malignant, they were avengers who ignored local laws and the King's Justice, and hunted down and executed wrongdoers. And at their worst, they refused to consider any claims of innocence by their prey. An often-stated joke about those who served Kahooli had it that their credo was "Kill them all and let Kahooli part the innocent from the guilty." Often they created more problems than they solved.

Talia smiled. "I know what you're thinking."

William blushed. "What?"

"Do I run now, or wait until her back is turned?"

He laughed. "Nothing like that. Just . . ."

"Don't do me any wrong, William, and you'll have nothing to fear."

Her smile was so open and bright he had to laugh. "I won't. You have my vow."

"Good," she said, playfully hitting him in the arm. "Then I won't have to hunt you down and hurt you."

"You're joking, right?"

Now she laughed. "I was *educated* by the Order of Kahooli, William. I never took any vows in his service."

William realized she was joking, and laughed. "You had me there for a moment."

She slipped her arm back into his as they moved along, inspecting the other produce on display. "I think I have you for more than a moment," she said under her breath.

William chose not to hear the remark. Right now, he didn't know what to think. He enjoyed the warm, slightly apprehensive feeling he got when he looked at her. He admired her dark hair, fair skin, erect posture and youthful energy that seemed to impart itself to everything she touched. All he wanted to do was to keep her at his side from moment to moment, and not think about anything unpleasant ever again.

"Lieutenant!" came a familiar and about as unpleasant a voice as he could imagine.

He turned and saw Captain Treggar approaching with two guardsmen.

"Sir!" he said, coming to attention.

With a tone approaching a growl, Treggar said, "I have been *sent* to fetch you, lieutenant, and Squire James." His gaze was hostile and his manner combative, but he added, "By His Highness," and William could tell he kept some unspoken rage in check because of that admission. Glancing at Talia, Treggar said, "I realize you're *busy*, and haven't had time to stand your watch in the officers' rotation at the palace, but His Highness felt it important enough to have you join him that he sent me personally to find you and the squire."

William said, "Ah . . . I believe Squire James is back at The Rainbow Parrot."

"No, he's here," came another voice.

William turned to discover James striding toward them. James said, "What is it, captain?"

"Orders, squire. You and the lieutenant are to return with me to the palace at once."

William glanced at James, who said, "Very well." He looked at Talia and said, "Pardon us, but we must be going."

To William, Talia said, "I've enjoyed our time together, William. I hope you'll call again, soon."

William said, "Certainly." Glancing at Treggar, he added, "As soon as duty permits."

Talia turned away and continued her perusal of the market's offerings, glancing over her shoulder to direct one last smile at William.

Treggar said, "Squire, if you're ready?"

James nodded and led the way back to the palace.

William followed a step behind Treggar, followed in turn by the two soldiers. There was a growing tension between himself and the captain and he would soon have to deal with it, otherwise he would make an enemy for as long as he was in the army.

Arutha looked around the room. Captain Treggar and the two soldiers who had been sent to find James and William stood off to one side. Four Krondorian Pathfinders—a separate élite command, with trackers and trailbreakers responsible to their own captain—watched as the Prince said, "Here." He pointed to a spot on the map, indicating a location south of Shandon Bay. "If our information is correct, that's where they are hiding."

James stood next to the Prince, and his eyes followed the line from the faint scratching on the map that read, "Valley of Lost Men" in tiny letters under an older inscription in a Keshian alphabet he couldn't read. "That still looks like a fair amount of territory to explore, Highness."

With a gesture, Arutha indicated the four Pathfinders. "They leave within the hour."

"We have committed the map to memory, Highness," said one of them.

Arutha nodded. "These men will follow you within a day. Look for them—" his finger stabbed at a point some miles to the east of the general search area "—here. One of you should make contact each night."

"Yes, Highness," said the leader of the Pathfinders as he saluted. With a gesture he indicated to his companions they should leave.

After the four scouts had departed, Arutha said, "Captain, draw up a battle plan. Tell everyone who will listen that we conduct maneuvers to the southwest and northeast. Then I want you to select two hundred of our best men, ignoring any man who has not been in service for at least five years." James nodded agreement. There had been three Nighthawks posing as soldiers at the garrison at Northwarden. "Make the selection seem random, but at the end of the first day I will lead those two hundred men south. Captain Leland will take the rest to the northeast, so come up with a plausible problem that explains the splitting of my command."

Captain Treggar nodded. "Sire. If I may ask . . . ?"

Arutha nodded.

"Wouldn't it serve better to have the Knight-Marshal draw up the problem?"

"Knight-Marshal Gardan is retiring, captain. We have a parade and farewell tomorrow at noon. He is then leaving on the evening tide to return home to Crydee."

James grinned. "A farewell party, tonight?"

Arutha looked at his squire. "Yes, but you won't be attending."

James sighed theatrically. "I feel slighted, sire."

Treggar said, "I will have the problem here before the parade, Highness."

Arutha said, "No, you will have it back here before sundown tonight. An hour after sundown, you five—" he indicated the captain, two soldiers, William and James "—are leaving with a caravan heading to Kesh. At the cut-off near Shandon Bay you will turn west and find this old caravan route." He pointed to a faint trail marked on the ancient map. "You're leaving half a day behind the Pathfinders, and you'll be moving slowly." Again his finger struck the map. "You should reach this point three days after the Pathfinders. That should give them time to locate our prey."

"And you'll be half a day behind us when they do," said James.

"Yes," said Arutha. He looked around the room. "If you get word, go as fast as you can to where the Pathfinders indicate the Nighthawks' nest is located. Leave clear signs along the way. You and the Pathfinders are to eliminate any sentries and open any barriers, because this time I intend to ride in with my best soldiers and crush these murderous vermin."

James looked at Arutha and said nothing. He knew that at that moment the Prince was thinking of his Princess, in his arms, on their wedding day with an assassin's bolt in her back, hovering near death while Arutha was helpless to do anything.

James said, "We'll make ready, Highness."

He led the others out of the room, and the captain said, "Squire, why me? The Prince has never assigned this sort of duty to me before."

James shrugged. "You were sent to find us, so you three already know that William and I are needed for something special. Sending you with us keeps those who know about our

221

real purpose to a minimum. Nighthawks have the irritating habit of showing up unexpectedly in unlikely places, so keeping the number of people who know of this mission to a minimum is vital." Something flickered in the captain's expression, and James added, "And His Highness certainly wouldn't have picked you if he didn't think you up to the task." Glancing around he said, "We'll have time on the trail to fill you in, captain. But for now, you need to create a convincing battle problem for the garrison, and I need to make arrangements."

"Arrangements?" asked William.

James said, "It will be hard enough for us to sneak up on a band of assassins, lieutenant. Doubly so if we ride up in full armor with battle pennons flying. We'll need disguises." He glanced out the window and said, "It's almost noon now. If we're to leave at sundown, I have scant time."

Captain Treggar nodded. "Squire." To James he said, "Lieutenant, you come with me."

William said, "Sir," and fell in behind the captain as he led the two soldiers away.

James headed off in a different direction, back toward his favorite exit, the servants' gate, where he could slip out of the palace with the least amount of notice. There were some people he needed to see before he left: the sheriff's son, and three thugs hiding in the sewer; then he had to buy quite a bit in a short time.

Sand and dust blew across the plateau, as a small band of travelers, two donkeys, a camel, and a tiny herd of goats huddled around an overburdened cart. Nomads, perhaps, to the casual eye, or a family on their way to a distant village, avoiding tolls and border guards on the patrolled highways.

William hunkered down in his desert-style robes, the hood pulled forward to keep the stinging sand out of his eyes, ears, nose and mouth as much as possible. Over the noise of the wind he shouted, "Captain, are we being watched?"

Captain Treggar shouted back, "If they're out there, we're being watched!"

Three days earlier they had left a camp near the southern end of Shandon Bay. Prince Arutha followed behind by two days, leading two hundred mounted soldiers. Out there somewhere in the blowing sands of the plateau country was a handful of Pathfinders, seeking the ruins of the ancient Keshian fortress.

James said to William, "You look lovely, dear."

"What?"

James raised his voice over the wind. "I said, 'You look lovely, dear.' "

Being the shortest man in the company, William was dressed in the robe of a Beni-Shazda woman. The other two soldiers, also dressed as women, laughed at William's checked irritation at James's remark. The squire had been joking at William's expense on and off since the young lieutenant had been handed women's robes on the first day of the journey. William had made the mistake of voicing his complaint, while the more experienced soldiers had simply put on the robes without comment, and James had shown him no mercy since.

William had now come to realize the futility of complaint, and shook his head as he sat back on his haunches. "Just a few days ago I was strolling through the market with the prettiest girl in Krondor on my arm, gold in my purse, and a bright future ahead of me. And now I have . . . you scruffy bastards. Of course, I also have all this lovely scenery." He waved his hand around him at the barren landscape.

Treggar said, "I'm going to hit you. Fall down and crawl away when I do."

Suddenly his hand lashed out, glancing off William's shoulder. William fell over as Treggar rose up over him. "They can't hear us, I think!" shouted Treggar. "Just the sound of my voice, but not the words."

James remained seated. "Where are they?"

"On the second ridge to the west, squire. Slightly to the north of the trail. I caught a glimpse of movement against the wind. Then I caught it again."

James said, "Everyone, you know your parts."

The other two soldiers hurried around, as if ensuring everything in the camp was secured against the wind. Treggar yelled, "Crawl away, bow toward me on your knees, then get to your feet and see to the goats!" William did as he was instructed. Treggar walked over to the cart, one arm holding a voluminous sleeve as a shield against the wind. He reached the cart and took down what from a distance would appear to be a full wineskin and made a show of drinking from it. He then sat with his back to one of the wheels, in the wagon's lee.

"Now come over here and look as if you're begging forgiveness, and while you're doing that, look up on that ridge and see if you can catch a glimpse."

William did so, bowing and lifting his hands in a gesture of conciliation. "I don't see anything, captain."

"Bow again!"

William did so, and James sneaked around to a position at the edge of the wagon, and while he appeared to be getting something out of the wagon he studied the ridge. After a moment he saw it, a faint movement that was out of rhythm with the wind. "They're watching," said James.

Treggar said, "You can stop bowing, lieutenant."

William did so and said, "I'll get some food and pass it around."

"Make sure you give it to me and the squire first, then the other 'wives'."

The soldiers didn't laugh as they scanned the ridges to the west while they went through the motions of working.

"Tonight one of the Pathfinders should find us, and if we're lucky, we'll find out exactly where those bastards are hiding out."

Throughout the rest of the evening they played the part of a small family of travelers. The wind died out an hour after sundown, and they built a fire and cooked a modest meal. Then they turned in and waited.

At first light the next morning, the Pathfinder still hadn't come.

# TWELVE

# IMPROVISATION

CREGGAR stood up and shook the dust off of his robe.

The eastern sky had lightened and the dawn was fast approaching. As the others stirred, the captain gestured toward the rising sun. He then turned north and made another gesture.

"What are you doing?" James asked.

"Looking for our friends," the captain answered as he turned to the west. "I hope this looks like some sort of morning ritual." He finished with a gesture to the south, and said, "Go get the 'women' working."

James feigned a kick at William and said, "Stoke the fire and start cooking. They'll expect us to be on the move by the time the sun's cleared the horizon."

William cowered for a moment, he hoped convincingly, then hurried to obey. He fed dried dung into the flames and soon it was hot enough to cook over.

The other "women" prepared food and seemed intent on their chores, but their eyes were constantly searching for any sign they were being watched. James sat crosslegged, plate upon his lap, eating. As he chewed he said, "If they're up there, I can't see them."

Treggar said, "They're up there. At least one, anyway, until they're convinced we're what we seem to be. If they had found the Pathfinders and thought we were involved, we'd be dead."

"What do you think happened to the Pathfinders?" asked William as he leaned over Treggar's shoulder to fill his cup from a waterskin.

"I think they ran into something they couldn't avoid," said Treggar. "Either they're dead or lying low. Maybe they're circling back toward Prince Arutha, avoiding us altogether because we're being watched." He drank his water, then stood. "I don't know. But I do know that we must get moving." To the two soldiers he said, "While we get ready, I want each of you to go down into that gully and relieve yourselves." He looked around, as if giving instructions, pointing at the goats. "Lieutenant, go over and look at the goats as if you're ensuring they're sound. While you're doing that, look as if you might be leaving a mark or message."

William looked slightly confused at the order, but complied. James said, "What's the plan?"

"I think our friends up on the ridge went home last night, but they left one man to watch us. I think as soon as we're safely on the way, he's going to come poking around here to see if we are what we seem to be. I want him down in the rocks where the boys are pissing or searching through goat shit, looking for a message while I leave a simple sign that the Prince's scouts can follow."

James nodded, stood up and started fastening the tie-downs over the wagon's cargo.

Treggar went to the wagon, removed the waterskin, and

poured it over the fire. As the steam hissed and white smoke rose into the sky, he kicked sand over the fire, dislodging embers and moving the stones around the fire pit.

James came over and pointed at the goats, as if speaking about them, and said, "That's a message?"

Treggar said, "Yes. Old army trick. Different messages depending on which quarter of the circle is broken. North means 'wait here.' West would mean 'come fast.' East would mean 'go back.' South means 'bring help.' As soon as we're out of sight, we're leaving the cart and animals and heading back up into those rocks to the southwest to see what we can find."

James sighed. "I was afraid of that." He glanced at the fire circle and saw the south side was broken.

Treggar said, "Squire, by all reports you're an adventurous lad who is no stranger to risk."

James said, "Yes, but somehow it seems less dangerous and stupid when I'm the one who thinks these things up."

Treggar gave out a sharp laugh, then said, "Let's get moving!"

Soon, the unseen onlooker saw a ragged band of Keshian travelers continuing their journey toward the west.

It took them most of the day to be certain they were no longer being watched. Treggar called a halt half an hour before sundown and said, "Let's double back to that wadi we passed a half-mile back and leave the wagon and the animals."

James said, "At least we've discovered the location of their hideout."

Treggar said, "How do you reckon that, squire?"

James knelt and drew in the dust. "Here—" he made a point with his finger "—is about where I judge they picked us up, about an hour before we made camp." He drew a line a few inches to the left and made another point. "Here is where we camped last night." He drew another point and said, "Here is where our unseen friend stopped following us."

"And?" prompted the captain.

James said, "Remember the map?"

Treggar said, "Yes."

"At midday we were due north of a large plateau, one that gives a commanding view of this entire area for miles in every direction.

"That wadi you want to leave the animals in runs up into the hills to the south. A half-mile from the trail we're on, it swings to the southeast as it rises up to . . . ?"

"The plateau!" William finished.

"And the ancient fortress!" said Treggar. "Yes, it's a natural sally-port! Only one way in or out."

"It's the only possible location around here."

"So what next?" asked William.

Treggar said, "Squire, care to state the obvious so it seems less dangerous and stupid than it would if I did?"

James winced, then said, "We scout the wadi. If Prince Arutha comes riding through here and sees signs we've gone that way, he could be riding into a trap. We have to make sure that doesn't happen."

"Sir?" asked one of the soldiers.

"Yes?" answered Treggar.

"If that wadi is the way in, what do we do with the wagon and the animals?"

Treggar looked at James. "We can't leave them around here where they might be found."

William said, "We three will stay then?"

James nodded. "One man will have to drive the cart, and

we can tie the camel to the back of it. The other will have to herd the goats along."

Treggar gave that order to the two soldiers. "Keep moving until an hour past sundown," he finished, "and stay in camp for three days. If someone doesn't make contact, return to Krondor the best way you can. Try for the outpost on the southern shore of Shandon Bay, or get to Land's End. Report what we've found here. But get back to Krondor."

The soldiers saluted, and their grim expressions showed how likely they judged that outcome.

Stripping off his heavy robe, Treggar looked like a common mercenary, wearing a tunic and leather jerkin, a sword at his side, and no helm or shield.

James was likewise dressed except that his baldric held a rapier. William's choice of weapon was a heavy hand-and-a-half sword, carried on his back.

Treggar looked around and said, "We stay close to the south side of the trail, hugging the rocks just in case we're not alone."

The shadows were getting longer by the moment, and James said, "We should be able to stay out of sight if we don't stir up too much dust. I'll lead the way."

Treggar didn't object, and as James moved eastward, the captain cast his gaze over his shoulder at the disappearing cart and his two soldiers.

William didn't know the men, but he knew what the captain was thinking: Would those two make it safely home again? As he turned his attention to the rocks above, William wondered if *any* of them would make it safely home again.

Bats flew overhead, seeking out the insects that somehow thrived in this arid land. James knelt in the darkness, trying to see in the gloom what his mind told him must be there, an ambush or trap. So far, nothing. If anyone was aware of the three men's approach, they were not revealing that fact.

James held up his hand, and turned as Treggar and William neared. He whispered, "I don't like this. We're walking up to their front door."

Treggar said, "What do you propose?"

"Have you ever seen any fortification without a back door?"

Treggar said, "A few, actually, but nothing on this scale. To control this large an area, even in ancient times, the Keshians would have had to garrison at least a hundred men here, more likely two or three hundred. That makes it a prime target if there's a war. Which means you need a way to slip men in and out."

"But where?" asked James in frustration. "On the other side of the fortress?"

William whispered. "If the fortress was still standing, maybe we could have gleaned its location, but with all the above-ground structure missing . . ." He left the thought unfinished.

James said, "Let's go a little further, then if nothing pans out I suggest we move back down to the trail and start again from the eastern side of the plateau."

William said nothing, but he knew that would mean climbing the rock face. While they moved, he prayed silently they wouldn't have to do that. He had no love of heights.

They moved slowly through the night, and then a thought touched William's mind.

"Wait," he whispered.

"What?" asked Treggar.

"Something . . ." William held up his hand and then closed

his eyes. His mind reached out and he detected the thoughts of a rodent scurrying through the rocks. *Wait!* he sent to it, gently.

The rat's thoughts were primitive and difficult to understand. It hesitated as it considered flight. The three large creatures were a potential threat, and there was nothing of interest nearby.

As a child, William had spoken to rodents, mainly squirrels and rats. He knew they had a limited attention span and little ability to communicate. But he also knew they had a firm grasp of routes in and out of their lairs.

He tried to send a question, asking if something large had a lair nearby. The creature quickly flashed back an impression of a large tunnel, long enough for William to get a sense of location. Then the rat fled.

"What is it?" repeated Treggar.

"I think I know where the back entrance is."

"How?" asked the captain.

"You wouldn't believe me if I told you," said William. "This way." He pointed up the wall against which they crouched. "We're going to have to do some climbing to reach it."

Treggar nodded and said, "Show us."

William looked around and pointed upward. "It should be above this rock wall."

James said, "Follow me." He felt for a handhold in the darkness, and reached up, running his hand along the rock face. When he found a good grip he pulled and raised his right leg, finding a toehold after experimenting a little. Step by painfully slow step, he moved upward.

William turned to Treggar and asked, "Captain, does climbing this rock face in the dark fit the obviously dangerous and stupid category?"

Treggar said, "Almost certainly, lieutenant."

William reached up to follow James's lead. "Just wanted to be certain."

Treggar waited until William was on his way, then followed silently.

Middle Moon rose while they climbed, and before long James found a cut in the rocks which was large enough for all three of them to crouch in. When Treggar reached them, William asked, "How high?"

James said, "Not far. A hundred feet or so."

William shook his head in disbelief. "I thought at least twice that." He pushed aside an almost uncontrollable urge to refuse to move from the ledge. He had made the climb so far by sheer will power, ignoring the terror which every second threatened to rise up and consume him. It had been a seemingly endless struggle of reaching up blindly and feeling for cracks and ledges, testing them, pulling up a few inches, moving a foot, trying not to give in to terror when rock crumbled beneath his toes or broke off in his hand.

"Feels like it, doesn't it?" asked the captain.

"Look," said James, pointing upward. Above they could see the night sky lit by the moon and stars, and it was clear that the top of the ridge they had climbed was no more than twenty feet above.

To William it looked like two hundred. He glanced down and saw darkness. He decided that not being able to see how far he had come made things worse. He decided not to look down again.

James said, "Well, no good comes from waiting." He started climbing again.

"Go slowly," cautioned Treggar.

William started to climb and said, "Trust me; I'm in no hurry."

Slowly William went up the crevasse, using one foot on each side of the gap to push himself to the top. As he neared the top, he felt James's hand reaching down to help him. He let the squire pull him up, then lay on his stomach, reaching down to help Treggar up. When all three were safe, James looked right, then left across the relatively flat ridge and said quietly, "We can walk from here."

"Where now?" asked the captain.

William looked around. The impression of the tunnel he had got from the rat was difficult to associate with these surroundings. Even if he had been sitting there in broad daylight, he would have had problems: the scale of the tunnel from the rat's perspective was of an immense cavern, and William suspected it was really a narrow bolt-hole that could accommodate just one or two men at a time.

"I think that way," said William, as he scurried along. There would be two moons tonight, Middle and Small, and by the time Middle Moon had reached the zenith, the smaller moon would have caught up with it, bathing the entire countryside in enough light for them to be seen by any watchful sentry.

James looked from side to side, while Treggar periodically glanced over his shoulder. The ridge they followed was rocky and broken, large upthrust fingers of rock worn smooth by centuries of wind-blown sand. At times they had to step carefully around needles of rock that provided scant room for them to pass.

After nearly an hour of this, William said, "If friend rat

knew what he was talking about, the entrance should be somewhere below us."

"Friend rat?" asked Treggar.

"I'll tell you later," said James. "Right now we need to find
a way down."

William looked around then caught a glimpse of light.
"What's that?"

James looked in the direction in which his companion
pointed and said, "Moonlight reflecting off something."

"How far do you judge?"

"Twenty feet," answered James, years of running across the
rooftops of Krondor having taught him to judge distances
accurately.

"How do we get down there?" asked Treggar.

"Hang and drop," said James.

"Even hanging by your fingers means a fall long enough for
you to break your legs," said the captain. "You don't know
what's down there."

James glanced at the rising moon. "Wait a few minutes."

As the moon climbed higher in the sky, the deep shadows
cleared. After a few minutes, Treggar said, "It's a pathway!"

Below them, between two walls of stone, a narrow passage
to the ancient fortress ran alongside the larger pathway they
had left.

James said, "William, lie down and lower me, then I'll drop.
I'll catch you two."

Quickly the three men made their way down to the narrow
pathway, and Treggar said, "I hope we don't have to retreat in
a hurry."

"Retreat?" asked William.

"No room to fight, lieutenant," answered the older soldier.

William realized he was correct. Even with daggers, all a man could do in this narrow confine would be to hold an opponent at bay. The rocks on either side rose twelve feet above his head and he had scant inches of clearance to left or right.

"This way," said William, who found himself in the lead. Even if they had wanted a different order, there was no room, save to climb over one another. No one suggested it.

When the two moons were directly overhead, William whispered, "Look at the walls!"

James stopped and examined the rocks. "This is new work. You can see the chisel marks."

Treggar said, "Our friends, I guess."

James said, "That means the old entrance is almost certainly trapped." He was silent, then he said, "No horse could get through here, so they must either have a third way in or out, or they have a stable and forage hidden away close by."

"The latter, almost certainly," suggested Treggar.

As they moved along the pathway, it widened a little, until they reached what appeared to be a dead end. As William raised his hand toward the stone wall, James said, "Don't touch anything."

William withdrew his hand and James said, "Move back and let me squeeze by."

They did so and James stood motionless for a time, looking closely at the rock surface. He whispered, "I wish we could risk a light."

"We can't," answered Treggar.

"Quiet," instructed James.

He reached out to the wall on his right, then moved his

fingers forward until they reached the junction with the wall in front of him. He touched the surface lightly, barely putting any pressure on it, then quickly withdrew his hand.

He repeated the examination with his other hand, starting from the left wall to the wall in front of him, and again quickly withdrew his fingers. Turning, he said, "It's trapped."

"How do you know?" asked Treggar.

James said, "I know."

"What kind of trap?" asked William.

"A very nasty one, I wager," said James, as he knelt. He examined the ground before the wall, again inspecting the intersection where they joined. "Stand back," he instructed.

They retreated a few feet. "If you want to know how I know, captain, spend half your life negotiating traps and you develop a sense for them. This one is pretty fair, but no natural rock formation has a continuous seam on both sides, from top to bottom, of almost exactly the same dimension. Someone cut this rock in front of us and put it here." James reached down and pushed slightly. The entire wall effortlessly tilted toward him for an instant, then swung back. He put his fingers under the lower edge of the hidden doorway and lifted up. Silently and without effort it rose until it was parallel to the ground, suspended on two hidden pivots. Looking over his shoulder he said, "They cut this door to match very closely the other rock around here, but it's not an exact match. Now, don't touch anything but the ground. In particular, don't touch the door as you crawl under it." Then he vanished into the darkness below the suspended door.

William and the captain followed.

The tunnel was pitch-dark, and James whispered, "Don't move."

A few painfully slow moments passed, then a light flickered into existence, a tiny speck of flame ignited by James.

"How did you do that?" asked Treggar.

"I'll show you later," said James. He handed a tiny burning taper to William. "Move down the tunnel a little."

He then carefully put the door back as it had been, and turned, holding out his hand. William gave him back the taper. The tiny light did a remarkable job of illuminating the area around them, just enough for them to see where to step, but not casting light very far down the tunnel. They would be almost upon anyone before their light was detected.

Whispering, James said, "Now we must use all our senses. Be wary."

He set off. The tunnel inclined downward, leading them deeper into the earth.

After a long, silent walk, a light appeared in the distance. James extinguished the burning taper and put it away. Just before reaching the source of the light, they encountered a tunnel which crossed the one they were in. James turned right, away from the light, and motioned for William and Treggar to follow. When they were once again in the darkness, he relit the taper.

They moved down the corridor. It was clearly a manmade passage, with close-fitted stone on both sides, and large paving stones beneath their feet.

William said softly, "I think this is the way the rat indicated."

"What rat?" asked Treggar.

"Probably means the kitchen or food storage isn't far from here," replied James, ignoring the question.

They heard the sound of someone moving a few yards ahead. James quickly extinguished the taper again. Moments later, they saw a light appear, as two men crossed before them, from right to left along a perpendicular tunnel. Neither spoke, and it was hard to tell what they wore, save their clothing was dark.

"What now?" whispered William.

"We follow," said James.

Treggar said, "Remember our way back. One of us has to reach the Prince and tell him of this place."

Neither James or William answered.

They moved carefully to the intersection, then turned to the left to follow the two men.

A hundred yards down the corridor, they could hear voices murmuring. As they neared the light, they saw men standing before the entrance to a large, well-lit gallery. Their backs were to the three invaders.

James glanced around and then pointed to a portal with stairs leading upward. He moved quickly up the stairs and the others followed.

They found themselves in a circular chamber, up in what might have been a small servants' sleeping area, overlooking what must originally have been an armory. Ancient forges lay unused against the far wall.

Clearly they had found the location of the ancient Keshian fortress, and were in basements that had been hollowed out of the rock upon which it had once stood. The murmur of voices from below masked James's words as he whispered, "Those servants who worked in the armory must have slept up in this loft."

"What's going on down there?" asked William softly.

James hazarded a peep over the edge then quickly pulled back.

Even in the indirect light from the chamber below, William and Treggar could see James go pale. "Take a breath before you look," he whispered.

William peered over and saw at least a hundred men, all wearing black robes or cloaks, all watching a ceremony directly across from where the three of them hid. The ancient armory was now a temple, and the brown stains upon the wall clearly showed it was a temple dedicated to dark powers.

Four men who were obviously priests were in the midst of a sacrifice, and that sacrifice lay bent backwards across a large stone, hands and feet held tightly by four black-robed men.

Upon the wall behind the priests was a mask, larger than a tall man, a hideous creature from a demented nightmare. Roughly the same shape as a horse's head, the creature's snout was pointed, like a fox's, but two long tusks protruded downward. Twisted horns, like a goat's, rose from behind pointed ears. And where the eyes should be, two flames burned.

The lead priest began to chant and the assembled men responded as one.

"What language is that?" asked Treggar.

"Sounds Keshian," said William, "but no dialect I'm familiar with."

Suddenly a drum boomed and a horn blew, and the men below shouted a name. James felt a chill pass through him.

The priests' chanting grew louder and one opened a large tome, then moved to the side of the victim. Another priest retrieved a golden bowl from a man standing nearby. He moved to the victim's head and knelt beside him.

The chanting never stopped.

The three standing priests picked up the pace of the incantation, and the witnesses answered. The assembled voices rose and the chanting grew louder, more insistent.

With a flourish, the chief priest revealed a black knife, which he held before the eyes of the victim. The man was naked save for a loincloth, and unable to move, but his eyes widened at the sight of the knife.

Then with a deft move, the blade sliced the man's neck, and blood fountained from the wound. The bowl was lifted to receive the blood, and as the first drops were caught, James felt a deeper cold pass through him.

William spoke softly, though his voice wouldn't be heard over the chanting by the men below. "Did you feel that chill?"

"I did," said Treggar.

William said, "Magic. And it's big."

Suddenly the room seemed to darken, though the torches in the wall-sconces burned no less brightly. A black cloud coalesced and took shape behind the altar upon which lay the now-twitching victim.

"Back!" said William as the black cloud grew more solid by the second, and the voices of the priests rose in unison.

Retreating to the back of the small servants' loft, James said, "What was that?"

"A demon," said William. "I'm almost certain. Keep low. The priests might not notice us in the shadows, but that demon might." They ran along in a crouch, and started back down the stairs.

Screams sounded from the makeshift temple and Treggar said, "What was *that*?"

"The blood was only used to bring the thing here," suggested William. "Now it's feeding from among the faithful."

243

Treggar's battle-hardened expression couldn't hide the fact that the blood had drained from his face. Through tight lips he said, "They willingly stand and die?"

"Fanatics," said James. "We've seen them before, captain. Murmandamus?"

Treggar nodded. "The Black Slayers."

"We must warn Arutha," said William. "He's got the men to crush this company, but not if they have a demon serving them. The Prince has no magicians or priests in his company."

Remembering an attack upon the Prince at the Abbey of Sarth, James said, "It won't be the first time Arutha's faced a demon."

More screams sounded. "Come on," said Treggar. "We have to start back. They're distracted now, but for how long?"

James nodded and led the way.

Quickly they made their way down the steps and retraced their way up the corridor, heading toward the secret entrance. The entire way the sounds of men dying followed them. More than once they thought the murders had stopped, but just as quiet descended it was shattered by another scream.

When they re-entered the darkened portion of the tunnels, James relit his taper.

William said, "That man on the stone never cried out."

Treggar said, "He wouldn't. That was one of our Pathfinders."

James said nothing.

They reached the exit and James motioned for them to halt and handed the light to William.

After a long moment of inspection, James put his hand against the hidden door and pushed to open it.

Nothing happened.

THIRTEEN

# CONCEALMENT

AMES pushed again.

Nothing happened, again.

"What's wrong?" asked Treggar.

"It won't open," said James. He ran his fingers around the edge of the door, then up and down the wall on the right side.

"Why won't it open?" asked William.

"If I knew that, I could open it," snapped James.

Treggar said, "If it slipped your notice, squire, we are at the end of a very long hall with no place to hide. If you can't open that door in the next minute, we will have to return to one of the corridors we passed and seek another way out of here."

James was focused, but there was urgency in his movement. "I don't know . . ."

He quickly moved to the left side of the door and continued his inspection. After a moment, he said, "Let's go."

He headed back down the hall and turned left at the first corridor. "Where are we going?" asked William.

James said, "I don't know, but I know in a fortress this big there are almost certainly some empty places where we can lie low."

"Why this way?" asked Treggar.

"Because it's in the opposite direction from where we were."

Treggar said nothing, content with the answer.

They left the sparsely-lit corridor and turned into one that was pitch dark, and again James lit his taper.

"How do you do that?" asked William.

James said, "If we find a place to hole up, I'll show you."

They moved along in silence for a while, turning a couple of times as James sought to move as far as he possibly could from the temple. Suddenly he stopped. He held the taper down close to the floor and said, "Dust. Not a lot of traffic through here in a few years." He straightened up and they moved forward again.

Before long they came to what appeared to be a room once used for storage. The door frame was rotting and the hinges had fallen off. Whatever had become of the door would remain a mystery.

James entered the room and held the taper aloft. The flickering light illuminated the space: roughly twenty feet wide and half again as deep, the actual dimensions hidden by a fall of rock.

James said, "Come over here," and motioned for them to sit in a corner, as far from the door as possible. "No one may have come this way in a while, but Ruthia—" the Goddess of Luck "—is a fickle woman at times and I don't want some passer-by to notice a light in an unused room."

Treggar looked at the fall of rocks and said, "It's unused because it's unsafe. Look at those timbers."

James moved his light a little closer to a fallen lintel and said, "Dry as paper." He pushed aside a few pieces that had fallen so he could sit on a large rock.

"I thought old wood got harder," said William.

"Sometimes," said Treggar. "I've seen old buildings where the timbers are as hard as steel." He picked up a small piece and crumbled it between his fingers. "Sometimes it just gets old."

"What do you judge the clock to be?" asked James.

Treggar said, "Near dawn."

"I wager our friends over there are likely to sleep during the day. Their trade is usually conducted at night. I'm going to slip out and look around. If I can't find another way out, I'll look at that door again. We can't stay here long."

"See if you can find some water," said William. "I'm parched."

James nodded. It had been hours since they had left their equipment and found the newly-carved entrance to this ancient place. "I'll see what I can do."

"Before you leave: what is that trick with the light?" asked William.

James handed over the lit taper and said, "Watch." He reached into his belt-pouch and pulled out another long taper; it looked like a thick punk of slow-burning wood, the kind used to light fires and torches. "These have a substance rubbed into them." He then produced a small vial of liquid and poured a drop onto the punk. For a brief instant nothing happened, then a flame burst out on the tip. "I bought these from a street magician in Krondor a while back. Very handy and you don't have to strike sparks with flint and steel—even works in high winds."

William grinned. "I thought maybe old Kulgan taught you that finger-fire trick of his."

"Hardly," said James. "I'd leave these with you, but I may

248

need light more than you do. Sit tight." James stood up, stepped through the doorway and was gone.

William held the burning taper James had left behind, until Captain Treggar said, "Better put that out, lieutenant."

William obeyed and plunged the room into darkness. "If you don't mind, I'm getting flint, steel and tinder out, just in case."

"I don't mind at all."

William could hear him moving in the dark, then Treggar said, "Here's some of that wood. If you need to make a torch in a hurry, it should catch quickly."

"Thank you, captain."

A long silence followed.

Treggar spoke. "That squire is an unusual fellow, ain't he?"

William said, "From everything I've ever heard. I've only spent time with him occasionally when my father brought me to Krondor on visits. You've been in Krondor for years. I would have thought you knew him better than I do."

"Hardly," said Treggar. Another long silence followed, then he said, "He's the Prince's squire. 'Pet Squire,' a few call him, but not to his face. Lots of special privileges."

"From what I know, he's earned them."

"Seems that way, don't it?"

William said, "Captain?"

"What?"

"Just want to say I plan on pulling my duty. Not being around the first week . . . well, it wasn't my idea."

"I'm getting that impression."

Again silence.

William said, "Well, I really didn't want duty in Krondor, actually."

"Really? Why not?"

"I'm not really related to the Prince. My father was adopted into his house by Lord Boric, years ago."

"Makes you a member of the royal house, boy."

"So I've been told. But I just want to soldier, captain. I want to earn my way."

"Soldiering is a hard life," said Treggar after a moment. "Lots of noble boys come to the palace and train with the swordmaster and then take their commissions and go home to their families. They show up on state occasions, in shining armor, riding a horse the like of which I'll never sit on in my life, and they get . . ." He fell into silence.

"And you feel overlooked?"

"You could say that. I started off as a soldier, enlisted during the first years of the Riftwar. I was with Dulanic's garrison and got run up to the front in Yabon when Duke Guy came to the city."

William had been a baby when that had occurred, but he had heard the story before.

"Your Squire James was a brat thief in those days, and I was a scared soldier, holding a pike and standing next to other scared soldiers watching those Tsurani maniacs charging us with no fear in their eyes."

William said nothing.

"Anyway, it was a long war and a lot of lads didn't make it. By the second winter up there in the mountains I was a sergeant. By the third I was a lieutenant, and because I was in the Prince of Krondor's garrison, that made me a 'knight-lieutenant.' He was silent for a moment, then said, "Talking about myself. I don't do that much."

"I'm glad for the sound of your voice, captain. It makes the darkness less oppressive."

"I'm the oldest bachelor officer in the garrison, Will."

William took note of the use of his given name. It was the first time Treggar hadn't addressed him by rank. "That must be hard, captain."

"I'm the officer who doesn't get invited to the dances, to meet the young girls. I'm the officer who isn't connected by birth to anyone. My father was a dockman."

Suddenly William realized the captain was afraid. Revealing that there was something beneath the mask of bully was his way of sharing that fear. William didn't know what to say, save, "My father started off as a kitchen boy."

Treggar laughed. "But he didn't stay one, did he?"

William chuckled. "That's the truth. If you had your choice, what would you do?"

"I'd like to meet a woman. She doesn't have to be someone of rank. Just a nice woman. I'd like a post where I'm in charge. Where I'm not always looking over my shoulder to see if the swordmaster or knight-marshal, or a duke or anyone else, is watching to see if I'm going to lose my temper and beat some young cadet over the head. I just want to do my job. Even somewhere like that little outpost we refit near Shandon Bay. Fifty men, a sergeant, chasing smugglers, thumping bandits, home for dinner."

William laughed. "If we get out of here, I'll be happy to go with you and just be left to do my job. I just found out last week the Prince expects things from me."

"That's a burden. Being royal family, I mean."

"So they tell me."

They lapsed into silence.

Finally, William said, "I wonder what James is doing?"

*   *   *

251

James was crawling on his stomach, as silently as he could. He had found one route past the perimeter of the closest population of assassins, but he knew William and Treggar would never be able to win past it undetected; it had taxed his considerable skills to avoid being seen. Now he was trying to find another route, and a broken sewer pipe was providing the way, as long as it got no smaller.

The structure was ancient. Kesh had abandoned the fortress centuries ago, for reasons lost in history. A revolt in the interior of the Empire, or down in the subject nations of the Keshian Confederacy. Perhaps a power struggle in the heart of the Empire itself.

In the scant light from the taper he lit from time to time, James had seen enough to wish he had more leisure time in which to investigate fully. He had found a room full of ancient bones, many obviously dumped there recently. James assumed the present occupants of the fortress had moved them there.

He had also found stones from above, weathered and sun-bleached, piled in several larger rooms—one he judged an officer's mess, and three barracks rooms—which surprised him. He deduced that the assassins had found some remaining structure from the ancient fortress above ground and had labored to remove traces of their lair.

James saw light ahead and moved even more cautiously. He inched his way until he was directly under the light. The upper portion of the pipe was broken below a large hole in the floor. James was below the level of the floor, lying on his stomach. He slowly turned over and then sat up even more slowly.

The room was empty. He got up.

He was in a guardroom of some sort, with cell doors in three walls. The guardroom door let out into another long dark

hall. James peered into the nearest cell through a small barred
opening in an iron door. A solitary man sat against the far wall,
wearing only a white linen breechcloth. "Hey!" James
whispered.

The man's head came up and he blinked as he tried to make
out the features of the man whose head blocked the small
window. "Who are you?" he whispered in the King's Tongue.

"James, squire of Krondor."

The man scrambled to his feet and came to the window,
where James could see his features. "I'm Edwin of the
Pathfinders."

James nodded. "I saw them sacrifice your companion a few
hours ago."

"That was Benito," he said. "They killed Arawan the night
before. I'm next unless you get me out of here."

"Patience," said James. "If I let you out now and they come
and check on you, they'll know we're in the stronghold."

"How many of you are there?"

"Three. Myself and two officers. We're waiting for the
Prince to arrive."

"So are the assassins," said Edwin. "I don't know what they're
planning, but I understand enough of their speech to have some
sense they know His Highness is on his way and are preparing
a welcome for him."

"The demon," said James.

"A demon?" whispered Edwin. "I knew it was some sort of
dark magic . . ."

"I'll be back," said James. "If they plan on sacrificing you
tonight, that gives me the better part of a day to find a way
out of here."

"I know a way out! They caught me at the eastern edge of

their fortress. They've opened an ancient gate, probably a sally-port. Horsemen could ride through it two abreast."

"We found another way, a footpath cut deep into the rock next to the ancient main gate. But I can't figure out how to open it from inside."

"I can't help you, squire. What do you plan to do?"

"Tell me first about the entrance you found."

"There's an underground stable where they keep their animals, next to an armory. From there a short but large hall leads to a drop-gate across a small dry moat. There are look-out positions, cleverly disguised, along the eastern face of this escarpment, and anyone approaching that way will be seen long before he reaches the gate."

James considered. The overall layout of the place was coming into focus. "I'll be back to get you. How long before the sacrifice will they come for you?"

"An hour. They feed us—me—once a day. That should be in a couple of hours."

"Eat. You'll need your strength. We're leaving before they realize you're missing."

With bitter humor, the Pathfinder said, "I'll be here, squire."

James hurried to the far corridor. He moved quickly along one wall until he came to an intersection, then he vanished into the gloom.

William and Treggar both drew their daggers at the sound of movement. They had been lost in thought, after talking on and off for a time, when the approaching noise startled them.

"Easy," came James's soft voice in the darkness. A moment later, he lit one of his tapers and said, "We have a problem."

"Only one?" asked Treggar.

"Big one. The last of our Pathfinders is going to be sacrificed at midnight if we don't get him out first."

"Can we get him out?" asked William.

"Yes."

"Then we get him out," said Treggar.

"It's not going to be easy. We have no food, water, or horses, and it'll be at least two days before Arutha gets here— if he even knows where to find us. I'm not sure how many assassins are holing up here, but I'd hazard a guess of at least three hundred, maybe more." James handed the taper to William. "Hold this."

He drew with his finger in the dust on the floor. "This is where we are," he said, "and directly to the east of us is the main center for the Nighthawks, or whoever they really are. To the north are some abandoned rooms, storage mostly. I spent a little time crawling around in the sewer—"

Treggar said, "You don't smell like it."

James shook his head. "That part of the sewer hasn't been used for centuries." He drew a rough rectangle around the areas he had outlined. "We're in the southwestern corner of the old dungeon. We saw the armory, which they're using as a temple. The barracks seem to have become their commons, probably because the old below-ground kitchens are there. To the north are some empty rooms. To the east is their stable and there's an old sally-port there they use as their main access."

"What about the way we came in?" asked William.

"I checked it again on my way back here. It's a bolt-hole, but one with a hidden trigger. I suspect it was originally installed that way to keep less faithful members of the Guild of Assassins from departing unexpectedly. The triggering mechanism is located behind a false rock at the last intersection you come to before reaching the door. It's a tricky one; if you open it from the outside incorrectly, you spring a trap."

"What kind?" asked Treggar.

"I don't know, and I wasn't willing to experiment, but there were cogs and wires connected to the pivots. It's even rigged to go off if you push the door in the wrong fashion. You push on the bottom, and you're in trouble."

"I thought the way you opened it looked pretty awkward," William observed.

"By design. The least comfortable way is the correct way."

"How did you know?" asked William.

"Old thieves don't get that way by being stupid. Smart young thieves listen to them when they reminisce about how brilliant they were at springing traps. I was not a stupid young thief. I listened." He chuckled. "The door has pivots on both sides, instead of hinges, so it wasn't designed to be opened like a normal door. After that, I assumed the way you would most wish to open it would be the way most likely to get you killed."

"What about the original western entrance?" asked Treggar.

James said, "I couldn't find a direct route. But I think I found a way up." He pointed to the rubble clogging the western wall of the storage room.

"That's the way up?" asked William.

"Maybe," answered James. "The main entrance would be a marshaling yard and bailey around a keep, I'm guessing. So the wall and gate would have stood right above us. There would have been a couple of quick routes from the armory back there—" he pointed down the corridor "—to the yard above us."

Treggar stood and inspected the fall. Most of the rocks were manageable, with large boulders clogging the bottom of the room. He picked one and tried to move it. After a few moments' effort, he got it to move a little. He gave up.

James said, "I thought of that. The timbers here are weak. Pull the wrong rock and the ceiling comes down on us. There is another corridor leading to a room even more filled with even more rocks to the north of here. So, unless there's another way up, farther east, the only way out is through the way we came, or the east gate."

"Which?"

James said, "The way we came in is easiest, but as soon as they see Edwin the Pathfinder gone, they'll comb the hills around here. If we take horses from their stable we might be able to steal a march on them. If we reach Arutha before they do . . ." He shrugged.

"Have you even seen the stable?" asked Treggar. "Do we know how to open the gate? Is it a windlass and ropes? Is there a portcullis? Counterweights? Is it a drop-bridge over a moat or just flat rock on the other side of the doors?"

"Your point is taken, captain," said James.

"Besides," said William. "If we escape and carry word to the Prince, will they still be here when the army arrives? Wouldn't it be easier for them to scatter and just set up somewhere else?"

James looked at William and then said, "Yes, probably." He sat back. "I need to think."

He extinguished the light and William and Treggar could hear him settle down, his back to the wall. For over an hour the three of them sat in silence.

Then James's voice cut the darkness. "I have an idea!"

*     *     *

James lay motionless in the broken sewer pipe, listening.

When he was sure there was no movement, he climbed up into the guardroom next to Edwin's cell.

He looked in.

Edwin glanced up and said, "Now?"

"Now," said James, examining the lock. It was a simple mechanism, very old, and he could have opened it while blind-folded. He reached into his belt-pouch, pulled out a long metal probe and inserted it into the lock. A moment later he heard a satisfying "click" and turned the probe. The lock opened.

The Pathfinder came through the door immediately and followed James back into the sewer pipe. As they crawled through the darkness, Edwin said, "They'll start searching when they find me missing."

James spoke softly as he pulled himself along. "I'm counting on it."

They reached the end of the pipe and James flipped for-ward, gripping the lip of the pipe with both hands and landed easily on the floor below. "I'm below you," said James in a whisper. "Hang from the pipe and drop. It's only three feet."

The Pathfinder dropped silently to the stones. James put his hand on his shoulder and whispered, "From here, silence. Keep your hand on my shoulder, for we move in darkness."

James was relieved to discover Edwin was calm and sure-footed in this awkward situation. He neither hesitated nor hur-ried but followed at even pace, so James was slowed only a little.

Several times James halted and waited to hear if anyone else was moving nearby. He was pleased that not once did Edwin ask why.

When they reached Treggar and William, Edwin finally spoke.

"Thank you, James."

James lit a flame. "I've only got four more of these things, so we have to make them last."

Treggar said, "How did they catch you?"

Edwin shrugged. "They know the land better than we. I took precautions, but there are large areas out there where any movement will be noticed by someone looking for it. Arawan and Benito and I were all caught within a day of one another."

Treggar said, "I thought the Prince sent four of you south."

Edwin smiled. "Bruno. He's still out there."

"Can you find him?" asked James.

Edwin nodded. "I can find him."

James said, "Good. I think I know a way I can get you out, after I steal us some food and water. You wait here." Without another word, James put out the light and vanished.

"I hate it when he does that," muttered William.

Treggar just laughed softly.


James hugged the wall around the corner from the cook's sleeping pallet. He had known he was hungry and thirsty, especially the latter, but it had hit him like a sledgehammer as he approached the kitchen. The rest of the garrison would be sleeping through the day, but the cooking staff would be up any minute to prepare the first meal of the new day.

James peered around the corner and saw the sleeping cook roll over, snoring. Two boys lay a few yards away, dressed in rags. Probably they were slaves purchased in Durbin or stolen from a caravan in the desert. James saw a large waterskin hanging from a peg on the wall nearest what was obviously a well—

a circular brick structure four feet high and an equal size in diameter. It made sense that a garrison of this size would have its own well. Looking up, James saw a hole over the well, and realized that this must be the old shaft up to the central keep courtyard.

James amended his plan. He hadn't known about the shaft, and that might make things easier for him. He hurried silently to the well and, jumping up onto its edge, leaned over and put his hand on the opposite wall. He looked up. A hundred feet above was a tiny circle of light. The well still opened to the plateau above!

The ancient well superstructure had been torn down, with the rest of the fortress, but no one had filled in the shaft.

Glancing down, James saw a hook with a rope around it, which descended into darkness.

James took the waterskin. It was full. He saw a pile of empty skins lying next to the well. He hung one of them where the full one had been. One of the boys would likely receive a beating for not having filled it, but that wouldn't matter much longer.

In a day or two the boys would either be dead or free.

James moved silently through the kitchen, lifting bread, cheese and dried fruit. He hurried off, and once he was a short distance down the tunnel, he put everything on the floor. He hurried back to the kitchen and stood again on the edge of the well.

He climbed up onto the waist-high wall, then flexed his knees and leapt into the overhanging shaft, slapping his hands hard against the walls. It was a tight fit and he had to struggle not to slip into the well below as he drew his knees up quickly and jammed himself into the narrow shaft. He wiggled upward, knees and elbows getting rubbed bloody, and dislodged a heroic amount of dirt along the way. The cook would have to be blind not to see it around the well.

He let himself down as best he could and then let go.

He fell toward the well below. As he passed the top of the well, he seized the edge. The noise was, in his ears, considerable, but the cook snored on. The jerk on his shoulders felt as if his arms were being yanked from their shoulder-sockets, but he endured the pain and shock. He remembered the last time he had tried something like this, and realized it had been the first time he had faced a Nighthawk, on the rooftops of Krondor the night he had saved Prince Arutha from the assassin's crossbow. Somehow the experience didn't get better with time.

James took a deep breath, then pulled himself out of the well. He avoided dislodging any of the dust he had so generously deposited around the well mouth. He jumped silently beyond the dust, then turned and inspected the mess. He could clearly see where his hands had gripped the top of the bricks. He quickly spread the dust around, hoping no one would take a close look at those spots.

Wasting no more time, he hurried out of the kitchen, retrieved the food and water, and hurried back to where the others waited. Along the way he rubbed each shoulder and decided to avoid trying that trick again.

As they ate, James said, "One of two things will happen first. Either the cook will notice the mess around the well, or the guards will check on you before the sacrifice and the alarm will sound. I'm hoping for the first."

"Why?" asked William as he finished his portion of bread.

Treggar said, "Because if they find him missing first, then they're going to search every room in the place, or at least until they see the mess in the kitchen. If they see the mess first, they'll investigate, find the prisoner missing, and head outside straight away, thinking he shimmied up the old well."

Edwin said, "So then, how do we get out?"

James said, "We don't. You do. Arutha is coming this way with two hundred men-at-arms. But there are at least three hundred here, waiting for him to show up. Someone's got to warn him and you stand the best chance once you're free of this fortress."

"How do you plan on getting him out?" asked Treggar.

"Through the eastern gate," said James. He reached into a bundle he had carried in with the food and took out a black tunic. "Try this on." He then produced pants and a black head-cover. "Just another Izmali fanatic out looking for the escaped prisoner."

"What are you going to do after I'm gone?" asked Edwin.

James said, "Someone's got to be here to open the gate for Arutha. If there are three of us here, that's three times the chance of someone surviving long enough to do it."

"Have you even seen the gate?" asked Treggar.

"From across the hall, while I was hiding in a hayloft."

"And?"

"Two large wooden doors, iron-banded, opening inward. Broad enough to ride out two abreast."

"How do we keep it open?" asked William.

"We don't," said James. "We keep it closed, until we want it open."

"I don't understand," admitted Treggar.

James said, "How many men would you send after the Path-finder, captain?"

"Every man I could spare. They caught the Pathfinders be-cause they were heading toward this location. On the loose out there, trying to hide, that's a different story."

Edwin said, "If I can escape and put a mile between me and my pursuers, they'll never find me."

"What now?" asked William.

"We wait," said James.

They didn't have to wait for long. Within an hour the murmur of activity could be heard. James said, "Wait here," and went to investigate.

He came back shortly and said, "It's a hornets' nest out there. The cook must have awakened to find the mess I left, and they think Edwin's climbed up to the surface." To William and Treggar he said, "You wait. If I'm not back in an hour, assume I'm dead and do what you think is best." To Edwin, he said, "Come with me."

Left alone in the dark again, William said, "Captain?"

"Yes?"

"Does it bother you to take orders from a squire?"

Treggar laughed. "If you'd asked me a week ago, I'd have said I never would. But James is not like any other squire I've met." Then his voice dropped and he said, "Besides, he's got the Prince's authority, and I would never argue with that. Does it bother you?"

"Sometimes," William admitted. "But that's mostly because he's so damn cocksure."

Again Treggar laughed. "That he is." After a moment, he continued, "But being cocksure, or at least looking that way, isn't a bad thing in a leader. Always remember that. When you're a general or duke, and your men are looking at you, make sure they see a man who's certain of what he's doing. That counts for a lot."

"I'll remember that."

They fell into silence as the sounds of alarm spread throughout the fortification.

James and Edwin moved cautiously. The noise of running men had died down. James had exhausted unused routes, and now they were working their way through a series of former storage rooms that were being used by the assassins. Two rooms and a connecting hall remained between their present location and the stabling area and the east gate.

Edwin clutched a short sword James had liberated in the previous room. He wore the stolen robes and looked like an Izmali assassin.

Movement ahead caused James to halt. He didn't have to tell the Pathfinder to do likewise. *He might not be a thief,* James thought, *but he knows how to move with stealth.*

Two men were coming toward them. James quickly pushed Edwin in front of him, and tried to keep close to the wall, so at first glance the assassins might judge them two more of their own number.

The ruse worked for a moment, but as they got close, one of the men's eyes widened. That was all the alarm Edwin needed, and he took two quick steps and threw himself at the first man.

The second man was drawing his sword when James's dagger took him in the chest. Edwin sat atop the first assassin, and quickly cut his throat.

"We've got to move these bodies out of the way," said Edwin.

"Over in that room," said James, dragging one by the arms. Inside the room they found an empty weapons trunk, and put the bodies inside.

They took one quick look to make sure they hadn't been spotted, then hurried to the stabling area.

When they got there, they found it still in a state of frenzy, though it was clear the last squads of riders were being dispatched. All but half a dozen of the forty stalls were empty and the two large corrals were vacant. James whispered, "They've got nearly a hundred riders out looking for you."

"Good," whispered Edwin. "That much confusion will make tracking easy."

A band of men stood in the center of the large underground stable, conferring. They wore dark robes, but they looked more like the ritual robes of priests than the assassins' garb worn by the others.

Finally the priest turned and moved toward an exit in the western wall of the stable.

When they had vanished, the stable was almost empty save for a pair of guards at the gate and a couple of men still saddling horses. James suspected they would be used as gallopers, to recall those out on the search should the fugitive be caught.

James motioned toward the two men readying their horses. Then he and Edwin moved in stages, from stall to stall, hugging the shadows, toward the unsuspecting men.

When they got next to the two stalls where the riders were preparing their mounts, James signaled and Edwin moved out, passing the first rider, who glanced up for a moment, then seeing one of his fellow assassins passing, returned his attention to tightening the girth on his saddle. He looked up when an unexpected movement caught his eye and he saw the newly-arrived assassin had stepped behind the rider in the next stall and now that rider was slumping to the ground.

He never knew James was behind him until a dagger struck deep in to his lower back.

James nodded and both men led the horses out of the stalls, mounted, and started riding toward the guards.

One guard looked at them and it took him a moment to realize one of the riders wasn't wearing black garb. He shouted, and his companion looked over, unaware of what had triggered his comrade's warning.

Edwin leapt out of the saddle, taking the first guard down to the stone floor. The second guard pulled out a curved scimitar as James threw his dagger. The man ducked to one side and instead of a killing blow, the blade glanced off the man's shoulder.

"Damn," said James, leaping from the saddle and drawing his blade. "I hate it when they don't stand still."

Edwin wrestled with his opponent and got his own sword across the man's throat. With a sudden downward jerk, he crushed the man's windpipe.

James almost walked into the point of the scimitar, dancing backward from an unexpected thrust. "Now I'm really mad!" he shouted, smashing the blade aside with a violent blow, then slashing sideways toward the man's neck.

The man pulled back, blinking in shock at the speed of the move, the point of James's sword narrowly missing his throat.

He leapt backward two steps, then crouched, sword at the ready. James marched forward, swinging his sword in the opposite direction. The man lunged, and James hesitated, letting the sword-blow pass. As the man fell back, James pressed again, at the same pace as before.

Three more times the man swung, James hesitated, then pressed forward. The fourth time, as the assassin began his swing, James suddenly stepped forward and impaled him with the point of his sword.

Looking toward Edwin, James said, "Never fall into a rhythm. It'll get you killed."

The Pathfinder nodded once, and silently leapt on the back of the closest horse. With a slight wave of one hand for a goodbye, he kicked hard at the horse's flanks. The horse was two steps off into a gallop.

James hurried to close the gates before anyone appeared. He muscled the two bars into place, a feat that drenched him in perspiration.

He dragged the two bodies into the nearest stalls and covered them with hay, then did the same with the first two assassins they'd killed.

Abandoning stealth for speed, he ran from the stabling area and into the two rooms that led him toward the abandoned portion of the fortress.

He was nearly out of breath by the time he reached William and Treggar. He sat down and lit his last taper. Between gasps, he said, "Edwin's away. With luck, Arutha will know what's happening and where we are within a day."

"With luck," said the captain.

"What do we do now?" asked William.

James caught his breath, then he asked, "Have you eaten?"

"Yes," said Treggar. "We finished off our portions. We left a bit for you. Just in case."

"Thanks, but I'll eat later, if I can." He looked at his two companions. "Arutha has two hundred men with him. If he comes straight here, he may find some of the searchers still out looking for Edwin.

"I've killed my share of Nighthawks. In an open fight they're just like other men. Their strength is reputation, stealth, surprise, and fear. If Arutha catches any number of them outside, he'll crush them."

"What about those still here?"

James said, "If he finds this place, and arrives at the eastern gate, he's going to find himself looking at a bare stone wall with two large wooden doors in it. There are loopholes dug through the wall above the door so he's going to lose men breaking in the door. Once the door is down, he'll be facing superior numbers in room-to-room action."

Treggar said, "He could be defeated."

William said, "What do we do?"

Treggar and James drew their swords. "We make sure none of the assassins leave before Arutha gets here, and while we're waiting, we lower the odds."

William looked from James to Treggar, then he, too, drew his sword.

FOURTEEN

# MURDERS

AMES held up his hand.

He signaled to Treggar and William that three men were waiting in the next room. Treggar walked forward in a crouch, sword out.

William stood behind him, his two-handed blade at the ready. A fearsome weapon, it was hard to wield at close quarters and all agreed he should be the last into the room, lest his presence hinder his companions.

James took a deep breath, saying a silent prayer to any gods who might be listening. He exhaled, stepped into the room and threw his dagger at the closest man. He then stepped forward as the dying man's companions hesitated and calmly began to pull out his sword.

Treggar was past James and attacking even as James unsheathed his sword. The captain was a brutally effective swordsman, without scruple when it came to combat. Any dirty trick that would defeat an opponent was employed, something that James had come to appreciate. The captain faked a high lunge and when the assassin's sword came up to block, Treggar kicked him between the legs.

James winced in sympathy as the man started to fold, but he appreciated the efficiency of the tactic. Before the assassin could will himself to keep his guard up, the captain struck him on the side of the head with his sword hilt, and as the assassin went over backward, Treggar thrust home with the point.

James quickly disposed of his opponent, and then William entered the room. "That's sixteen, counting the four you killed in the stables," said the young lieutenant.

"That leaves a hundred and thirty-four or so," said James, retrieving his dagger from the first man he had killed. "Things are still frantic around here, but soon they'll start finding corpses and then they'll start looking for us."

Captain Treggar said, "Someone's coming!"

"No time to hide the bodies," said James. "That way!" He pointed down a side corridor. They ran.

They were moving through a series of chambers used by the assassins, with torches burning in the wall-sconces. In the third room, they burst in on a single man who looked up with surprise. He died before he realized these were enemies, Treggar barely breaking stride as his sword lashed out.

They reached a "T" intersection, with torches visible off to the right, and darkness on the left. "This way," said James, pointing to the left.

They rushed into the dark corridor. After a short run, the darkness forced them to a slow walk. The sounds of pursuit followed them.

"Put your hand on the left wall," said James. "There's a nasty break in the floor ahead on the right. If you hug the wall when I tell you, you'll avoid it."

"How did you find it?" asked William.

"The hard way." He didn't provide further details.

William still almost lost his balance when his right foot didn't meet resistance a few steps further. He was glad of the warning, as an updraft gave him the impression the hole was a deep one.

They reached a series of small rooms, and James said, "I think these might have been cells or storage, but all the doors are missing."

"I can't see a thing," said Treggar.

"Neither can I," responded James, "but in my former line of work it paid to remember where you'd been, even if you were fumbling around in the dark. Keep your hand to the walls."

"Where are we going?" asked William.

"A place I think we'll be safe for a while."

"Think?" asked Treggar.

James said, "We're not in what passes for ideal surroundings, captain. There are no rooftops and only a short run of abandoned sewer to hide in. This is solid stone and brickwork, and we're fifty feet below ground. Our choices of hiding places are limited."

They moved around the corridor and James said, "Step to the right wall and put your hand on it. Then follow me."

They did as he instructed, and continued on into the new corridor. "But I have found one place."

"What?" asked William. "A bolt-hole?"

"No," said James. "We're here."

"Where?"

"I had a torch the last time I came through here. Directly above us is a crack in the ceiling, a flaw in the stones of this place. It looks big enough for us to hide up there for a short time."

"Looks?" said William.

"I had no way to go up and see," said James. "Boost me up."
William said, "In the dark?"

"Do you have another light?" asked James.

"No."

"I thought not. Now boost me up, please."

William sheathed his sword, then reached out until he touched James on the shoulder. "Hands, or shoulders?"

"Kneel down, so I can step on your shoulders, then when I tell you, stand up."

"If you say so." William knelt.

James stepped on William's shoulders, balancing like an acrobat. "Now," said James, and William stood, holding James's ankles.

"Let go," instructed James and William felt the weight vanish from his shoulders. After a moment, James said, "Just reach straight up with your hands outstretched now and I'll pull you up."

William had to leap three times before James caught his wrists and pulled him up. Treggar followed. When all three were sitting, stooped over, in a low and shallow space above the rock ceiling, William said, "What is this place?"

"I don't know," said James. "Sometimes stone has flaws. Water leaches holes."

"Water would have to come from somewhere, and last time I looked, there wasn't a lot of water in this region," said Treggar.

James spoke: "We're below the surface, and maybe the water level in the well was higher years ago. I don't know. But at some time in the past the ceiling here gave way, and here we are."

William said, "There's close to fifty feet of rock between this level and the surface. There might be some upper chambers."

"But you said you didn't find any stairs," said Treggar to James.

"There are those two rooms we found at the west end of this place, with the rockfall. Maybe those hid stairs?"

"What now?" asked William.

"We wait," said Treggar.

A few moments later, they heard footfalls pounding through the hall, and light could be seen. Men hurried along beneath them, weapons ready, holding torches. All were wearing black armor, save one who brought up the rear, who wore the robes of a priest.

When they had passed, the three fugitives could hear them searching nearby rooms. No one said anything until the sounds of the searches grew faint.

James said, "I saw some loose stones above us when those torches passed by."

William asked, "You were looking up?"

"Old habits," said James. "When you're running around in the sewers or up on the roof at night, if a light suddenly appears you look away, to avoid being blinded."

James ran his hands along the surface above him. "These are man-made," he said. "They're each a foot and a half square."

"Sounds like we're under a floor," said Treggar.

"Help me push this," said James, as he experimented with one of the stones above him.

Treggar duck-walked two steps and sidled up to James. He reached up and they pushed. Mortar and dust rained down as the stone moved upward with a crack. James stuck his hand experimentally through the hole. "It's a room," he said.

The other stones were set far more solidly so it took some work, but they got two more up and moved, allowing them enough room to climb through. James said, "Step this way. I don't think those stones directly above where we hid would support our weight."

The air was musty and stale. The darkness was total.

James added, "Don't move until I've had a chance to scout a little and see how big this chamber is."

William and Treggar stood still, while James stepped cautiously away, moving slowly through the darkness. His tread was light, but in the silence of the room they could tell roughly where he moved. "I've found a wall," he said after a few moments, his voice coming from about twenty feet away. They then could hear him moving along the wall, measuring as he went. "The floor feels solid, except where we broke through," he said absently.

William said, "Let us know if you find a light. This darkness is tedious."

James said vaguely, "You get used to it. Ah!"

"What?" asked Treggar.

"A door. Wooden. Closed."

A few seconds later, a spark was struck. "We have light," James said, igniting an old torch he had found in the wall-sconce. Putting away his flint and steel, he said, "Let's see what we have here."

The room was forty feet square and the walls were lined with empty weapons racks. Two racks stood in the middle of the room, empty of the long spears that had once waited there for a call to action.

"If the armory is below . . ." mused James aloud.

"Then this is where they kept spare arms close to hand," finished Treggar.

James returned the torch to the wall-sconce, and went to the door. "This should lead to the marshaling yard above."

He tried the door. "It's jammed." Examining it, he said, "Let's try the hinges."

William and Treggar pulled out their daggers and worked at the ancient iron hinges. "If we had some oil," said William, "maybe."

James said, "I'll get some."

"Where?" asked Treggar.

"Down there," said James, moving back toward the hole in the floor.

"You're mad," said Treggar.

"Probably," answered James as he ducked out of sight.

After he had left, William and Treggar looked at one another and sat down to wait.

Time passed slowly, then suddenly James's voice sounded in the dark. "Give me a hand." William hurried over and lay down, lowering his hand through the hole. After a couple of misses in the darkness, James seized it and came up.

"Here," James said, handing a jar to William. "Oil."

William said, "I didn't even hear you until you spoke."

James replied softly. "You weren't supposed to. A couple of disagreeable men were trying to find me, and once I shook them I didn't want them hearing me climbing up here."

"What's it like down there?" asked Treggar.

"They're into their second sweep. They probably have someone above at the top of the old well, and since no one came up, then they figure we must still be in here somewhere. They probably think it's your Pathfinder Edwin loose down here, killing their men. But sooner or later one of those bright lads is going to suspect there may be a passage up to this level and then they're going to start inspecting every inch of ceiling."

"Eventually they'll find us," said William.

"Almost certainly," said James. "Being caught was never my first worry."

"If that wasn't, what was?" asked Treggar.

James pulled out a heavy crowbar, two feet in length, and said, "Oil." He nodded toward the hinges. As William poured oil on the upper hinge, James continued. "Getting caught before word got to Arutha. As long as we're running around in here, those down below are going to be too concerned about catching us to prepare well for Arutha's arrival. If everything works out, those coming back will have Krondorian soldiers hard on their heels, and will run right into a barred door, with those inside slow in getting it open for them."

"That's your plan?" asked Treggar.

"It's the old plan," said James. "If this door leads where I think it does, I have an even better plan."

With the oil and crowbar, they got the pins out of the hinges. Treggar inserted the bar between the door and jamb and pulled hard. A dull scrape sounded as the door moved a fraction, then stopped.

"Whatever's jamming it is holding it tight," observed the soldier.

"Captain, may I?" asked William.

The captain relinquished the bar to the broad-shouldered younger man.

William looked at the door, then moved the bar to a position slightly above his shoulders. He pulled hard, and downward, and the door moved. William yanked hard again, and the door moved again, and he fell backwards with the release of the bar.

James and Treggar leapt away as the door seemed to fly off the jamb, spinning as it fell with a loud crash to the stone floor. Clouds of fine dust filled the room, as thick as smoke, and the three men came up coughing.

"Look," said William.

The original room had been excavated just below the surface of the ancient fortress's marshaling yard. Behind the doorway, a ramp led up to the surface, and at the top of the ramp, parallel to the floor, was a barred trapdoor. The release bar for the trap was set across it in such a fashion that it could be pulled free by two ropes or chains. The iron eyelets were still intact, but any ropes had long since rotted to dust. James inspected the trapdoor. "Clever," he said at last. "It's hinged here and there—" he pointed to the far end "—so that when it falls open it lands atop the ramp."

Treggar said, "Old Keshian trick. I've never seen it, but the old Knight-Marshal, Dulanic, once told us of a fight here in the desert where they took a fortification. As they crested the walls, it seemed the defenders were all dead. They got inside and set up camp, and that night the Keshians seemed to come out of nowhere." He glanced around the room. "He mentioned we should always inspect for hiding holes like this if we found ourselves in a similar situation."

Treggar climbed the ramp next to James and put his hands up to examine the door. "There's probably a piece of canvas and some dirt spread out over this old wood. Enough so that if you're walking across it you'd have to be listening for the hollow sound to know that ramp is there."

"Add to that a few centuries of dust," muttered James, testing the weight of the door on the bar. "This isn't moving unless we can tie a pair of ropes to it."

"We'd need horses to pull that bar out with all the weight on it," said Treggar.

James sat down. "Maybe." He inspected the bar again and finally said, "Unless we can loosen those brackets."

William held up the crowbar and said, "I can give it a try."

He set to with purpose, and after a minute said, "This wood is very dry. It's splintering easily." He worked at it until the first of the two brackets fell away, striking the stone ramp with a loud clatter. He then turned to the second bracket and shortly had it free. The bar followed, crashing to the floor and bouncing down the ramp, causing James to have to leap over it. William sprawled on his back, and Treggar leapt to the side.

William lay motionless for a moment, expecting the doors to swing down upon him, but instead nothing happened. He rolled and crawled a little way, came to his feet and then stepped to the bottom of the ramp.

"Shouldn't those doors have swung down?" asked William.

"Supposedly," answered Treggar.

He started to move back up the ramp, but James's hand restrained him. "I wouldn't. It could give way at any moment."

Treggar shook off the squire's hand, saying, "I don't think so." He moved to what would be the closest edge of the opening where the door jamb met the door itself and inspected it. He then pulled out his dagger and stuck it between the door and the jamb, and pried something out.

He returned to his companions holding out a sliver of something brown.

"Mud."

"Mud?" asked William. "Here?"

"It doesn't rain much in this region," said Treggar, "but it does rain. And over the years dust has settled upon that door, then gotten rained upon, and then the heat returns."

"Brick," said James, taking the sliver from Treggar. "The door is covered by a slab of this stuff, maybe two or three inches thick."

"But what's holding the door in place?" asked William.

"Suction," said James. "I've had to pull more than one heavy object out of the mud and if you don't break the suction first, you're doing it the hard way."

"So we're stuck?" asked William.

James looked around and said, "Not necessarily." He moved to one of the large racks and said, "Help me lug this over to the bottom of the ramp."

They did so, and after it was where James wanted it, he said, "Now move that bar over here." Quickly he had the bar jammed in to the bottom of the trapdoor, braced against the heavy rack. "This won't prevent the trap from falling on top of me, but it should slow it enough for me to get out of the way if it starts to go."

"What are you doing?" asked Treggar.

"I'm going to cut away some of this mud, enough so that any weight above it should release the door."

"You're mad," said Treggar.

James said, "You're only coming to that conclusion now?"

He moved up the ramp and said, "Stand back. If this goes, I want a clear path down that ramp."

He worked diligently and carefully, and after a while William turned his attention to the hole in the floor, watching and waiting for them to be discovered.

After an hour, James said, "That should be enough."

William glanced at James. "For what?"

James smiled. "For it to give quickly when I want it to."

"Another plan?" asked Treggar.

"Always," said James with a grin. "Now, do either of you have a good guess as to what time of the clock it is?"

Treggar said, "I put it near midnight, give or take a quarter of an hour."

"Good," said James, sitting. "Then we wait."

"For what?" William asked.

"For the half a dozen men set to watching the well above to get bored and sleepy."

James hugged the wall between two large sets of shelves, trying by force of will to become one with the slight shadow between them. A single guard was stationed near the well, absently cutting the skin from an apple as he glanced around from time to time.

James weighed his options. He could chance a dagger throw, but the odds of it being a killing blow were slight. He could rush the man, but suspected there were others close by who would appear within moments of any outcry.

James had moved into the kitchen a few moments before the guard appeared and had ducked into the only cover at hand. He now remained motionless, hoping the assassin wouldn't notice the shape in the shadows on the stone wall.

The man looked away and James reacted without further thought. He stepped across one of the shelves and walked around a large butcher's block that stood between the shelves and the well.

The man glanced over as James moved casually toward him.

281

James smiled. "Hello," he said, the only word he knew in the Keshian desert dialect.

The man blinked for a moment, then replied, "Hello?" Then he asked a question in the language they had heard the assassins using.

James had a dagger palmed behind his wrist, and as the man repeated the question, James slashed him across the throat.

With a gurgling sound, the man gripped his throat and fell backward, into the well.

Voices coming from somewhere close by spurred James and he leapt on top of the well. He repeated his earlier feat of jumping up into the shaft and pulling his legs up, jamming his knees and shoulders into the walls of the ancient stone-lined tube. A slight gasp of pain escaped his lips as he discovered how bruised his shoulders and knees were from the last time he had pulled this stunt.

He shimmied up the well, feeling every inch of the ascent, until he was just below the lip. He knew he couldn't stay there long, and the sky above was lightening, so he started up the last few feet.

James listened for voices and heard none. He peered cautiously over the lip of the well and found six sentries nearby, four of them obviously sleeping and the other two involved in a quiet conversation, their attention on one another, not the well.

James judged them to be ten feet or closer and knew that if he tried to climb out one of the two was almost certain to see him. He decided on a dangerous course.

He turned his back to the two men, and started slowly to snake his way over the lip of the well. Should either glance in his direction, in the dim pre-dawn light, they might miss the distorted form on the edge of the well. If they paused to look in his direction, they would certainly see him. He prayed they were convinced no one was coming up this way after all these fruitless hours of guarding it.

James got his shoulders over the edge of the well and let his own weight carry him slowly down behind the bricks. If fate was kind, Edwin should have found either the other Path-finder or Arutha's advanced scouts by now. If so, Arutha would be coming within the next day, two at the most. If not, James didn't want to consider the chances of getting out of the area alive.

He put his hands on the ground and gently let himself down. With as silent a movement as he could manage, he turned, sitting with his back to the well. He drew his sword and took a breath, ignoring the pain in his back and knees, then he leaped up.

It took a moment for his presence to register on the two men who were talking and they both stood slowly, as James took off at a run.

One of them shouted and the others came awake, slowly, asking questions in sleepy voices. James ran straight to where he judged the trapdoor to be, listening for a hollow sound.

This proved futile, since the yelling from behind drowned out any sound from below, but he did feel the ground give slightly at one point. He stopped, turned and jumped backward a few inches.

The soil below his feet felt as if it had given slightly. He ran backwards for a few feet, then crouched as if waiting for the men who raced toward him. They began to slow, and he realized with alarm they were on the verge of fanning out to surround him.

He turned and ran as if suddenly in a panic, and he heard orders shouted from behind.

Then a loud crack and a crash followed and James turned to see all six men falling through the trapdoor. He raced as fast as he could toward them. While holding the advantage for a moment, James and his companions were outnumbered two to one.

He reached the near end of the trapdoor and leapt, turning in mid-air so that he landed facing down the ramp.

The caked mud had prevented the left side of the door from falling fully into the ramp. The twisting ramp caused the men to fall, one atop the other. James found himself staring down into the darker interior of the ambush chamber, lit by only the one torch, as William and Treggar battled two guards.

Suddenly James felt his heels slip, and his feet went out from under him. He landed with a bone-jarring crash on the wooden ramp and slid a few feet, bowling over two assassins who were trying to rise.

James kept sliding, and saw that one of the enemy was trying to climb past him rather than fight. James slashed with his sword but missed as the man vaulted up the ramp past him.

James couldn't lavish any more attention on the fugitive, as another assassin sat up next to him, cutting at him with a backhanded blow from his scimitar. His only option was to throw himself backward on to the ramp, striking his head hard, as the blade cut through the air. Lying prone, James lunged with his sword, killing the man sitting next to him.

He sat up and found a black-clad back turned to him. Without hesitation, James struck it. His head pounded and he felt dizzy from the concussion he had just taken.

Treggar stood over one dead assassin, while dueling with another.

William struck one man while he kicked out and backed off a second.

James leapt on the closer of the two facing William and knocked him to the ground, wrestling him down, while William killed the one he faced.

James shouted, "One's getting away!"

William shouted back, "I'll get him!" He leapt over the dying man and raced up the ramp.

Reaching the top of the ramp, William saw the man more than a hundred yards ahead of him dashing down an incline leading to a gap in the rocks.

William started running.

James and Treggar killed the last assassin and appeared at the top of the steps in time to see William vanish down the eastern access. James said, "Go after him, and if he kills that man, then take him with you."

"Where?"

"To find Arutha," said James. "My original plan was to get back into the stable and hold the door while Arutha killed those trapped outside the door, then open the door and let him come inside to kill the rest."

"And we three were going to hold the door alone?"

"That's why I was trying to cut down the odds, captain."

"Now what?"

James said, "Get Arutha to send two dozen men through this room, down that hole and come into the fortress from the east. Have him use a ram to batter down the eastern doors. They'll be so intent on holding those doors they won't notice those you lead in through here."

"What are you going to do?"

James said, "Distract them. If they find this way to the surface, we lose a big advantage."

Treggar looked as if he was about to say something, then just nodded. He turned and ran after William.

James took a deep breath of fresh air as the late afternoon sun set behind the eastern peaks. Then he turned and climbed back down into the ancient fortress.

William had never been the fastest runner among the children on Stardock, or the fastest cadet at Krondor, but he had always had endurance. He knew he would have to call upon that endurance to overtake the assassin, who was clearly faster. William suddenly realized the assassin had made a mistake and had chosen to run down the ancient wadi, to the passage along the west that William and his companions had used to enter the fortress. Had he run the other way, he might have found allies outside the eastern gate, or pounded on it to get attention and quickly bring help. Now, William had a chance.

He saw the assassin ahead of him when the wadi widened out as it began a long gentle turn to the north. Running downhill, William could see the man had slowed slightly. Excitement or fear had lent speed to the man's first burst, but now he was slowing into a more conservative pace, a long loping stride.

William wasn't certain if the man even knew he was being chased, since he had not looked back at any time when he had been in his sight. William's heart pounded and his eyes stung. He blinked perspiration out of them. He breathed evenly, but his throat was dry and he could feel his body aching. Lack of sleep, water and food was taking its toll.

Putting everything out of his mind but his duty, he forced

himself to pick up the pace, and slowly he could see he was gaining on the assassin. William had no sense of where he was, and no idea how much farther he would have to run before reaching the trail that passed north of the wadi's entrance. He could imagine it being scant yards ahead of the assassin, or another mile. He didn't know which.

He saw he had halved the distance between himself and the man; he had closed to barely a hundred yards when the assassin looked over his shoulder. Either he had sensed William behind him or he had heard him, but regardless of the cause, he now knew he was being chased.

The man picked up the pace and William fought off a moment of resignation. Whatever James's plan was, it was clear the squire didn't want the assassins to know of a way into the fortress through the plateau.

William bore down, ignoring the burning in his legs and a heart that seemed ready to burst from his chest. This assassin must be tired as well, William thought. And then he thought of why he must not fail. The Prince needed to know of this place, how to get in, and the demon. He thought of his duty and those he was protecting: the royal family, the common people of the city, the servants in the palace; and then he thought of Talia. He remembered the demon that had appeared at the bloody rites, and he vowed he would die before allowing such a horror to be visited upon her.

Slowly he closed the gap with the assassin. The realization that he was gaining filled him with an elation that soon caused the fatigue to fade. It was clear the assassin was tiring and would soon have to face him.

The wadi broadened and now William could see the trail

where they had bidden farewell to the two soldiers who had left with the goats and cart.

Reaching the trail, the assassin hesitated on which way to turn, and in that moment he had sealed his own fate. He had to turn to fight.

The man did so, pulling out a scimitar, and readied himself. He obviously expected William to slow and draw his own weapon, but rather than do as expected, William pulled his bastard-sword on the run and managed to let lose with a war-cry as he lifted the long blade over his head.

The assassin leapt aside, startled by the rush, but not losing his wits. He parried William's blow, spinning to face him as William slid to a stop in the dirt and also turned.

The two men crouched, facing one another. The assassin drew a dagger from his belt with his left hand and held it as if using it to parry, which William knew would be foolish against his long blade. He stayed wary, for the assassin would surely not hesitate to throw the blade if he saw an opportunity. He had no doubt the man could fight with either hand.

The assassin was shorter than William, presenting a compact target as he stood with knees bent, waiting to see what William would do next.

William circled to his left, looking for an opening. When rested, William was as fast with his long blade as many other men were with a broadsword, but he was far from rested. He knew he had only two or three blows left before he would be at the other man's mercy.

William leapt forward, turning his blade as he moved, so that he could level a backhand slash at the man's right-hand side. He hoped to force the assassin to parry with the scimitar. William prayed the scimitar would snap when he struck it.

Apparently sensing the risk to his blade, the assassin jumped back, rather than parrying, and William seized the moment to press forward. He jerked his blade up short rather than let it carry around, leaving the point just to the right of the assassin's dagger hand.

The assassin let fly with the dagger, the blade aimed straight for William's throat, or where it would have been had he followed through with his blow.

Instead of striking him in the throat, the blade glanced off William's shoulder at its juncture with the neck, slicing the muscle just above the chain mail he wore over his tunic. "Damn!" William said as his eyes teared from the pain.

He didn't have time to consider the ill-luck of it not having struck one inch to the right, where it would probably have bounced off his chain, for the assassin followed his throw with a headlong rush.

William barely managed to get his sword up to block the man's scimitar. His breath burst from his lungs as the assassin drove his shoulder into William's chest, taking them both to the ground in a heap.

William ignored the fiery pain in his shoulder, rolled away from the assassin, and tried to come to his feet. Pain exploded in his face as the assassin kicked him, causing him to fall backward, his vision swimming as the sky turned yellow and red.

Fighting to remain conscious, William was abruptly aware of having lost his grip on his sword. As he tried to sit up, another blow struck him, and his head rang from the pain. Half-conscious, he was barely aware of the weight which landed on his chest.

Blinking hard, trying to force his senses to obey him, William looked up to see death upon him. The assassin was standing over him, one boot firm on William's chest, his scimitar poised to deliver the killing blow.

In the split second between the recognition of his plight and the thought that he must somehow act—grab the assassin's boot and knock him off balance—and the knowledge that he would be too slow to do it, William saw the assassin freeze for an instant, then fall away.

A figure in chain mail not unlike his own stood above William. It took a few moments for him to recognize Captain Treggar.

The captain put his sword away and knelt over William. "Can you hear me?"

William blinked and then managed to croak, "Yes."

"Can you stand?"

"I don't know," whispered William. "Help me to my feet and we'll find out."

Treggar got a hand under William's arm and helped him to stand. "Let me see that," said the captain, looking at William's wound. After a moment, he said, "You'll live."

William's head still rang and his legs were rubbery, but he said, "That's good news."

"But that cut's going to burn like hell for a while until we can dress it."

The captain tore off a piece of his tunic and jammed it hard against the wound. William's knees threatened to buckle and Treggar held him up. "We don't have time for you to faint, lieutenant."

"No, sir," said William weakly.

"We're going to find the Prince, and if I have to leave you behind, I will."

"Understood, sir," said William, forcing himself to take deep breaths. "I'll do my best."

"I know, Will," said Treggar. "Come on, and let's hope we find the Prince before those assassins find us."

William looked around. "Where's James?"

"He went back inside. Said he was going to make them spend time looking for him rather than us."

William said nothing, but inside he was wondering if he possessed that sort of courage. James would be lucky to survive the time it would take to find the Prince and return with him.

They set off toward the east, moving slowly at first, then picking up the pace as William regained his senses.

James glanced around. He had taken a few minutes to move the rocks that had fallen when he and William had moved the flagstone above the crack in the ceiling. There was little he could do about the dust but he still tried to move some of it around with his feet.

Unsatisfied, but resigned to that being his best effort, he hurried toward the route he judged most likely to get him to where he wanted to be without being set upon by an army of angry men in black with large arsenals of weapons at their disposal.

"Ruthia," he said quietly, invoking the name of the Goddess of Luck. "I know I've abused our relationship at times, and I'm far overdue in visiting your shrine, but if you could see your way clear to granting me just a little more of your favor, this time, I swear I will be far more rigorous in my devotions."

He turned the corner and stepped into a large room, and an instant too late realized that there were men who had been standing motionless upon each side of the door. He spun to be confronted by two swords pointing at him, just as another half-dozen assassins suddenly burst into the room from three other doors.

Glancing around, he saw it was hopeless to fight, so he held up his hands and let his sword drop from limp fingers. Under his breath, he muttered, "Ruthia, you didn't have to be so emphatic in saying no!"

One of the assassins stepped forward and struck James across the face with the back of his hand. James fell hard to the flagstones and the man kicked him brutally in the ribs.

Vomiting the scant contents of his stomach, James coughed and said, "Ruthia, you can be such a bitch." Then the man kicked him in the head and James lost consciousness.

FIFTEEN

# DESPERATION

AMES awoke slowly.

The cell was dark, the only light a torch in the antechamber which filtered through the tiny window. He recognized it as the same cell Edwin had occupied.

He was lying on a pallet of stale straw. The air was fouler than he remembered from his last visit, but then, he thought, he hadn't been inside the cell.

He sat up and his whole body ached. His head still rang from the beating he had taken and he doubted he had more than a few square inches of skin that weren't bruised.

James took a deep breath and looked around. No food or water, and he doubted his captors had given a second's thought to his comfort. He expected the general thesis was that he wouldn't be around long enough for comfort to be an issue.

The fact that he was alive led him to believe one of two things was about to happen. Either he would be questioned, to determine how many people knew of this hideout and how soon enemy forces could be expected to attack, or he was to be the guest of honor at the next demon summoning.

If the former, he thought, he might stall for time. He could pretend the beating had befuddled his senses and that he needed some rest before it would all come back to him. If the latter, he had only until midnight for Arutha and his army to arrive and get him out alive. Jimmy shook his head again, trying to force himself into alertness. He stood up slowly, quietly, and wobbled to the opening in the door.

Looking through the tiny window, he saw they had placed guards in the room, against the chance of another of James's companions being loose within the fortress. James stepped back quickly, lest a guard notice he was awake. If they are going to question me, he thought, the longer they wait to begin, the better the chances of the Prince getting here.

He sat down quietly and tried to rest. The stones were not cold, but this deep below the surface they were hardly warm. The straw was as much an irritant as a comfort, yet he dozed off after a few minutes.

Some time later, he came awake with the sound of the door opening. Without a word, two guards strode through the door and grabbed him under the arms. He was dragged through the door and frog-marched through the fortress.

They took him to the one portion of the underground labyrinth he had failed to explore, which he assumed was the quarters of the leaders, the priests of the demon worshipers. He was soon to discover, with no satisfaction at all, that his surmise was correct.

Cast to the stone floor at the feet of a man in black robes, he waited.

"Stand up, so I may look at you," said the man standing above him. His voice was dry, like the rustling of aged parchment.

James looked up and saw a man with an ancient face looking down at him. Slowly, on unsteady feet, James rose until he looked into the old man's eyes. There was power there, a dark, dangerous power. The face looked impossibly old, barely more than blotched and discolored skin stretched taut across a skull. What little hair remained as a fringe around the sides and back hung like white spider-silk. The old man looked closely at James, and suddenly James realized the creature before him wasn't breathing, save when he needed to speak. Hair rose up on the back of James's neck when he realized he was looking into the eyes of a dead man, somehow still animated.

"Who are you?" the old man asked.

Seeing no benefit from an outright lie, James said, "My name is James."

"You come to spy, from the Kingdom?"

James said, "More or less."

"Those with you, they are but the tip of the wedge, yes?"

"I believe more of my countrymen will be arriving shortly, yes."

"It does not matter." With a grin exposing crooked yellow teeth, the creature took another breath and said, "We here serve to the death and beyond. We fear not the lances of your Kingdom soldiers. We know what is to come, and by the grace given to us by our master, we do not fear it. Tonight is our final conjuration, and our master will send us a tool, a demon to destroy your Kingdom!"

He gazed into James's eyes a moment, then said to the assassins standing nearby, "Take him to the chamber. The hour is nearly upon us."

James was speechless. He had expected a dozen questions, possibly a beating or two, and the opportunity to delay and equivocate. Instead he was being dragged off to have his throat cut at a demonic rite.

They took him to a room next to the former armory and roughly stripped his tunic, boots and trousers from him, leaving him only his small-clothes. Two men grabbed him firmly by his arms and held him motionless.

Another black-robed priest entered the room and started an incantation. He carried a small bowl fashioned from a human skull, from which he pulled a bone covered in a dark, viscous liquid. He waved the bone in the air and James's skin grew cold. Bumps appeared on his arms and the hair on the back of his neck rose. When he touched James on the forehead, his skin felt burned.

A third priest appeared, with another bowl holding a viscous white fluid. He held the bowl up to James's face and said, "Drink."

James clamped his jaws shut. He didn't know specifically what was being offered to him, but he suspected it was to make him more tractable.

A black-clad assassin came from behind the man on James's right. He gripped James's jaws with powerful hands, attempting to pry them apart. He got his hand bitten. James clamped down hard enough to draw blood, and received a staggering blow for his troubles.

"Very well," said the old priest. "Let him feel every exquisite moment of pain as his life runs from him and his soul feeds our master. But hold him tightly, lest he disrupt the ceremony. Our master does not suffer error."

He turned and led the way, with the other priests following. James was taken then by the two men who held him, with two other guards following behind.

Every fiber of his body hurt, and the likelihood of his survival seemed close to non-existent, but James found he felt no
fear. Somehow he had always avoided imagining his own de-
mise. He knew, abstractly, that some day he would die, just as
every mortal being eventually succumbed at the end of their
days, but at no time had James dwelled on that simple fact. As
his old friend Amos Trask had once said, "No one gets out of
life alive."

But despite the high probability of it, James could not accept the reality of his own death. Part of his mind was astonished at this; he knew he should be mewling like a baby,
pleading for his life.

Then he realized that, to the core of his being, he *knew* it
was not his time to die. Instead of fear, his mind turned to
how he was going to get out of this mess.

They moved into the armory, where James could see the
ceremony was already underway. The hundred-odd assassins
knelt as the old priest entered. They were chanting and already
the place felt fey with dark magic.

Torches flickered around the room, and James used every
skill of observation he possessed to notice details he had missed
the last time he had witnessed the sacrifice. The ancient bellows
over the forge was still intact, though they had not been used
in over a hundred years; the chains used to lift and move the
cauldrons once used to pour molten metal for fashioning armor
and weapons were rusty, but looked serviceable. His mind's
eyes measured the distances between the dais and two large
stone repair tables, and the forges, and how close to those
tables the chains hung. James realized that it was unlikely he
was going to run through this throng, so every other possible
means of escape had to be evaluated, and quickly.

The assassins faced the dais upon which he was to be killed, gazing upon the visage of the demon painted upon the wall. The two who flanked James continued to hold him, while the two who had followed joined the others on the floor of the makeshift temple.

As he was marched up the steps to the base of the stone over which he would be stretched, James looked down to see an intricate design chalked upon the floor, a five-pointed star with a large wax candle burning at each point. He observed that the priests took great care to avoid those points or stepping over the lines of the pentagram. He racked his memory; something about the marks on the floor was disturbingly familiar.

As they moved him toward the stone altar, James felt his pulse increase. He still felt no fear, but instead a strange sense of urgency. Whatever he was going to do, he needed to do it in the next few moments and he still didn't have any idea what it was.

Suddenly, he went limp, crying out, "No! No! Anything but this!"

The high priest turned for a brief instant to see what the commotion was, but the sight of a victim begging for his life was nothing new, and he went back to the spell casting.

One priest opened a large book and held it aloft before the high priest so he could read from it. The old man read in silence for a moment, then cried out in a language harsh and alien to James's ear. The room seemed to darken, as if something was absorbing the torchlight, and a vague shape formed in the center of the pentagram.

James knew that as soon as blood was spilled, the creature would solidify and enter this realm. He felt the two assassins lift him, dragging him the last few steps to the stone.

James took a deep breath, for he knew this must be the moment. If he was bent back over that stone, held hand and foot, he would die.

He feigned a convulsion, sobbing and screaming as he collapsed to his knees, pulling the two men over slightly. Then suddenly he planted his feet and stood up, throwing the two assassins off balance. Ignoring every ache and protesting joint, he pressed upward with his hands, causing the two men to instinctively change their grip on his wrists. At that instant, he pulled free.

With his right hand, he pulled a dagger from the belt of the man to his right, and threw his shoulder into him, knocking him back into the sacrifice stone. Then he kicked out with his left leg, knocking the man on that side backwards.

The man on the right reached for his belt and found his scabbard empty. James said, "Looking for this?" He lashed out with the blade, catching the assassin across the neck, opening his artery so it sprayed blood across the stone and onto the floor. "If you're so anxious to make this horror appear, use your own blood to do it!"

The high priest shouted, "No! It is not time!"

As soon as blood hit the altar, the figure in the pentagram coalesced, even more horrible than James remembered. It was nearly nine feet in height. The face was as he remembered it, vulpine, with flaming eyes, and curving goat's horns. And now the lower half of the body was visible; the demon stood on goat's legs.

"No!" cried the high priest, again.

The creature glanced at him. In a deep and terrifying voice it asked him something in the same language the assassins used. The priest seemed at a loss for a reply, and instead grabbed the ancient tome that had fallen to the floor and attempted to read something.

James kept moving. The man with the slashed throat twitched atop the stone, while the other guard tried to regain his balance. James helped him out, by reaching out and grabbing the front of his tunic, pulling him forward. He moved out of the way and swung him around in the direction of the high priest.

Then James lifted his right leg and planted his foot against the chest of the uninjured assassin and pushed. The man fell backwards with a startled expression and crashed into the high priest and the one hurrying to get the bowl into which James's blood was to have flowed.

The ancient book flew from the high priest's old hands, and instinctively he reached after it, howling, "No!"

Those near the dais were starting to rise, unsure of what was happening in those furious moments, but those at the back were still upon their knees.

Trying to retrieve the book, the high priest reached across the lines of the pentagram. The demon shrieked in rage. It reached down with two powerful, clawed hands and seized the old man.

Realizing his blunder, the high priest screamed in terror; then babbled incoherently as he witnessed his approaching death. The demon's great maw opened, revealing jagged teeth as long as a man's finger, dripping saliva that smoked faintly. With a sudden snap of its jaws, it ripped the face from the skull of the priest, splattering those nearby with gore.

For a brief instant, all eyes in the room were upon the grisly sight, and James again took advantage. He grabbed the remaining priest by the shoulder and belt and gave him a shove—what he had heard tavern-keepers call "the bum's rush"—toward the pentagram.

The wounded man and the priest with the bowl both stumbled into the pentagram. The priest knocked over one of the candles, and chaos erupted.

The creature bellowed. It snatched the head off the second priest, then ripped the arm off the wounded assassin. Pieces of bodies were torn and devoured and blood ran down the monster's chin.

The other candles went out and cries of fear filled the chamber.

Some members of the assembled band of assassins chanted, rocking back and forth, while others rose, looking for an escape route. Two drew scimitars, to defend themselves against the demon, but others simply sat in mute amazement.

James judged it the perfect moment for his escape. He leaped on top of the sacrificial stone and glanced at the demon. The demon looked back at him, and with terrifying certainty he realized the creature was no longer confined.

James leapt toward one of the chains hanging overhead, just as the demon reached for him. James pulled up his legs, then shot them forward, swinging clear of the black talons. He arched away from the slaughter, and let go of the chains. He landed upon an old work table, next to kneeling assassins, who regarded him in amazement.

Then all attention was returned to the demon who was stepping down from the dais and starting to feed in earnest.

James jumped a few feet to another table, and from there to the floor between two fleeing assassins. They ignored him, for whatever religious fervor they might feel at the sight of another dying, it was clear they were less devout when their own lives were in the balance.

Most of the fleeing assassins were heading toward the stables, and James did not wish to risk going that way. He ducked into a side corridor and ran back towards the break in the ceiling where he had found the ambush room. He was astonished at how fast he reached it when running, compared to creeping around in the dark.

He glanced up and cursed. There was no way he could reach the crack overhead by himself. Hurrying to the closest room, he found a weapons trunk. This he emptied, then dragged it to the spot below the crack.

If he had been able to ignore his wounds before, they were now clearly evident to him. Sweat dripped from his hair and off the end of his nose, and the salt of it stung every abrasion and cut. His bruised muscles threatened to cramp as he dragged the heavy trunk along.

He shoved the trunk upright and for a brief moment his vision swam and he felt light-headed. Breathing slowly, he calmed himself then climbed up on the truck. He reached the opening in the ceiling and with great difficulty pulled himself through, despite almost losing his grip and falling. He held on by force of will, for he knew he could not muster the strength to try again. Then he climbed up over the flagstone floor of the ambush room and saw the ramp opening to the night sky.

From below came screams and an inhuman roar, and James knew that eventually whoever was still down there would be dead. And then the demon would start looking for a way out. Half-walking, half-staggering, James made his way toward the ramp. He took three steps before he fell face-first into the dirt, unconscious.

303

\*　　\*　　\*

James came awake with someone pouring water over his face. He blinked and saw William holding his head upright, while someone else held the waterskin to his mouth. He drank greedily.

When the skin was withdrawn, he saw that the other man was a soldier from Krondor. The sound of footfalls echoed in the room and James sat up and saw men moving toward the hole in the floor. He said, "Wait!" His voice was a dry croak.

"What?" asked William.

"Demon. It's loose down there."

William grabbed the tunic of the nearest soldier and said, "Urgent message for His Highness. Squire James reports there's a demon loose down in the fortress."

To the soldiers in the room William said, "You lot stay here, but I don't want anyone going into that hole until you get orders." To James, he said, "You come with me. The Prince will want to hear this from you."

He put his arm around James's waist and helped him to his feet, then half-carried him up the ramp. As they neared the top, William said, "Is there a good story attached to why you were face-down in the dust wearing only your smalls?"

James winced from the movement. "Not really."

William got them to the top of the ramp and asked, "Can you ride?"

"Do I have a choice?"

"You'll double with me," said William. He signaled for a horse. A soldier responsible for the mounts led one to them, and held its head while William got James up into the saddle. William swung up behind James and took the reins. He set off, shouting, "Hang on!"

James groaned but held on. They cantered down the wadi as the sun rose in the eastern sky. Cradled against William's chest, James asked, "Where's Arutha?"

"Before the eastern gate!" said William. "Edwin got to the Prince and he ordered a forced march. Treggar and I found them fighting a band of assassins, and led them here."

"I hope to the gods he hasn't led a charge into that stable," said James.

They rode hard to the base of the wadi, and turned east. After one of the most painful rides in James's life, they reached Arutha's position.

No camp was set up; rather the Prince and his officers had gathered atop a nearby outcropping of stone, watching as the soldiers were deployed before the open gates. Arutha looked over as William rode up and reined in. Captain Treggar sat next to the Prince and two other officers, around a camp table upon which a map lay.

"You going to live?" the Prince asked James.

James half-slid, half-fell to the ground, staying upright by hanging on to the stirrup of William's horse. "Not if I can help it," he replied.

Arutha indicated that someone should put a cloak around the near-naked squire. A soldier quickly complied. To James, Arutha said, "What is going on in there? We chased a bunch of assassins inside after thrashing them five miles from here, and most of them came running right back out again, glad enough for a fight. We were forced back for a bit."

"Demon," said James. "Those fools conjured one up."

Arutha nodded. "Orders," he said to a runner nearby. "Tell Lieutenant Gordon to hold his position." Looking back to James, he said, "Well, squire, what can you tell me?"

James winced and motioned to William for the waterskin. "Not much, Highness. I'm not an expert, but I suspect that creature won't come out until nightfall. Once he does, I don't know how you're going to keep him here."

Arutha looked at the open doors of the stable and said, "We must go in and finish him inside."

James said, "Wait a minute—"

"Yes, squire?" interrupted the Prince.

"Forgive me, Highness, but I've seen that thing. We need a plan."

Arutha indulged himself in one of his infrequent laughs. "From you: a plan? Squire, that's rare."

"Well, I've seen that thing up close, Highness, and it's got the power to rip a man's arm from his shoulder with a single yank. We need a priest to banish it to its own realm, or a magician to destroy it."

"We have neither," said Arutha. "And from what I remember from my study of demonic lore, unless this is some higher power we face, it can be killed. If it doesn't care for sunlight or cold steel, we have the means."

The Prince turned to William. "Lieutenant, you and the captain ride back to the other entrance. Take a squad of archers with you. Drive that thing to this door before the sun sets."

Treggar and William saluted and rode off, leaving James holding on to Arutha's stirrup for support. "What if it doesn't want to be driven, Highness?" asked James.

"Then we'll have to go in after it," said the Prince. He then looked down at James and said, "And 'we' doesn't include you, squire. You've looked better." He motioned to one of his aides and said, "Take the squire somewhere and see he eats and drinks water. I don't think you'll have a struggle getting him to rest."

James allowed the soldier to lead him to a rocky outcrop where he sat in the shade, eating hard rations and drinking tepid water from a skin barely cooled by evaporation. He knew this meant that the baggage train was miles behind the column and this was probably as good fare as any man, including the Prince, had eaten in days.

James had to fight to stay awake between bites. He only half-remembered someone bringing him a fresh tunic and trousers. He knew his boots were down there in the room behind the armory, where he had been stripped for sacrifice, and vowed that when this was over he was going to get them.

That was his last waking thought.

William and Treggar mustered their men and the captain said, "Lieutenant."

"Sir?"

"I'm going down with the first six men. Wait a bit, then send the sergeant and next six, and you lead the last six a bit after that. The archers will stay here."

"Yes, sir."

Treggar said, "The first squad will move straight to the east. I want the second squad to move to the south. It's a fairly obvious route that will eventually turn east." To William he said, "You get the tough one, Will. Move to the north and head to the armory."

"Sir," said William.

"Whoever makes contact with the demon, sit tight and send for the other two squads. Defend yourselves if you must, but don't attack until we get organized. I want to try to use the archers to drive the thing toward the Prince's men."

Ropes were tied to the base of the two heavy ready racks

and were lowered so that two men at a time could descend or climb back if need be.

When they were secure, Treggar led the first squad down into the darkness.

William watched as Treggar and his six men vanished, then the second squad under the command of a sergeant, then he led in his own six. Twenty-one soldiers, thought William, to drive a demon out into the sun. He hoped it was enough. Never a magician, he had lived among them all his life, and nothing he had ever heard about demons over those years was good.

Putting aside his misgivings, he motioned for the last company to move out.

William took the lead, refusing to let one of the soldiers go first. He justified the order by claiming he had been this way before, then realized that he needn't justify anything to these men; he just needed to give the order.

They were slowly working their way through a series of rooms that had been turned into one big abattoir. Blood splattered the walls and recognizable body parts were strewn around with chaotic abandon.

The one fact William noted was that all the heads had been split or bitten open, and the brains eaten. William glanced at the faces of his men and saw battle-hardened men to pale. He swallowed hard to keep from retching and felt less self-conscious.

A noise in the distance alerted William to the demon's position. He motioned for the others to wait while he quietly went ahead to reconnoiter. He moved in a crouch, slowly working his way down a hall. Before him was a large barracks room, if his memory served.

He glanced through the door in front of him and could see nothing, so he moved slowly, stopping every few feet to observe the expanded angle of view. As he neared the door, he had a terrible feeling the demon was sitting in one of the two corners beside the door, meaning that William would have to actually look into the room to get a view of the creature.

Right or left side? he asked himself.

The demon saved him the decision by moving, the noise coming from the left.

William put himself hard against the right wall, moving as slowly as he could, crouching low. The creature's legs came into view first, and William realized that it was sitting on the floor, legs extended, as if waiting.

Waiting for what? William asked himself silently.

Then it registered: it was waiting for the sun to go down. William was torn between retreating now and calling for the archers, or glancing around the corner to get a better look at the thing. He judged the risk worth the reward.

He moved slowly, afraid that any sudden motion might catch the demon's eye. He saw the creature looking away from the door, several wounds visible upon its body.

He pulled back. Slowly, every step a painful exercise in self-control, he moved away from the room. When he was near the point where his own men could be seen, he held up a finger to his lips, then motioned for the men to move back.

William had the men fall back to the last intersection they had passed. When he was certain they were far enough back to not be heard, he whispered, "The demon's in that room ahead. Looks like some of the assassins gave as good as they got. The thing's bleeding a fair bit."

"Good," whispered one of the men.

William said to him, "Loop around to the south and find Captain Treggar and the others."

The soldier ran off.

To another man, William said, "Go fetch the archers, on the double."

The man hurried off.

William turned to the others and said, "Be ready, but no man is to speak or make a move until they hear an order from me."

The men nodded and waited, silently.

SIXTEEN

# DISCOVERY

THE archers arrived.

The six bowmen lined up silently behind William. A little while later, Captain Treggar and his six men joined them.

"How lie things, Will?" asked Treggar.

William outlined the situation, drawing in the dust on the floor, to show where the demon waited. Treggar swore. "It will cost us to ferret him out. The first lads through that door are almost certainly dead."

William said, "Not if they don't stop."

"What do you have in mind?" asked Treggar.

"Hare and hound?"

Treggar smiled. "If the demon will follow them, the hare can lead him to the stable. Then we can drive him out to the Prince."

William began to strip off his armor. "Not they, me."

"You?"

"I know the way. No one else here does but you, captain, and, with respect, I'd wager I'm faster than you are."

Treggar said, "I remember catching up to you yesterday."

William smiled. "For which I'll be eternally grateful, assuming I live an eternity." He handed his scabbard to one of the soldiers, but held on to the sword. He now wore only tunic, trousers and boots. He motioned for a torch, and was given one by a soldier near the back. "No time like the present," William observed.

William ran down the hall, not pausing as he entered the room in which the demon rested. He made it to the center of the room before glancing backward and was horrified to discover the demon was already after him, a specter of terror, bellowing in anger.

William still hurt from the struggle the day before and the hard ride with Arutha, but right now his body answered a basic demand: fleeing for his life.

He ran without hesitation and hoped his instincts would keep him from going the wrong way. Down a long stone corridor, through a large empty room, then into another tunnel he ran, the demon staying with him every step of the way.

William almost died when he burst into the stable and barely avoided running headlong into a forge. He bounced off the stonework and ducked his head under the metal hood that led to the stonework chimney. Had he struck it and fallen, he knew the demon would have overtaken him.

He was gratified to discover the demon wasn't quite as nimble, since a few seconds later he heard the crash of a heavy body against the forge and hood, followed by a scream of frustration.

William saw the sunlight at the far end of the stable and started the final sprint. It was only a hundred feet or so, but it seemed to take forever to cross that paltry distance.

He raced into the sunlight, half-blinded by it. Shading his

eyes for a moment, he saw Prince Arutha and a company of horsemen directly in front of him. Behind him, the creature had come to a halt at the edge of the sunlight.

The creature might not be particularly bright, thought William, but it wasn't stupid either. It had recognized the ambush and refused to be baited.

William turned, pointing his sword. He took a deep breath, then shouted a challenge.

The demon suddenly bellowed in rage, but it had nothing to do with William's challenge. Rather, it was being attacked from behind by the six bowmen in the stable who were loosing their arrows as rapidly as possible. It spun around, and William could see three shafts protruding from its back and one from its side, and several minor wounds were also visible from arrows that hadn't penetrated.

The creature charged back into the stable and William ran after it. Inside the stable, the demon was standing in the center aisle, while the bowmen kept shooting at it. William saw that only a few shafts that struck square to the creature had gone in. The rest of the arrows glanced off, some shattering against the magically-imbued skin.

William was almost struck by one. He shouted, "Stop shooting! You're going to kill someone on the other side!"

The arrows stopped flying. Then William drew back his sword and attacked.

He swung as hard as he could against the creature's back, but when the blade struck, the shock ran up both his arms as if he had struck the bole of an ancient oak tree. The demon screamed in pain and rage and turned to make a backhand grab. William fell back just in time to avoid being decapitated.

He rolled to his feet and ran, uncertain as to whether the

demon was following, or turning its attention to the other soldiers in the stable, but just as he reached the door and sunlight, a crushing blow to his back informed him of the demon's whereabouts.

William went sprawling forward, scraping his forearms and hands, then scrambled to get to his feet as quickly as possible. A scream from behind alerted him to the fact that someone else was distracting the demon while he made good his escape. With a lunge, William staggered upright in time to see a score of horsemen riding straight at him.

The vibration coming through the solid rock under the earth and the sound of hooves growing louder by the second caused William to glance to either side, seeking escape.

Given the circumstances, he did the only thing he could do: he stood stock-still and prayed that they would ride around him.

The riders drew up their mounts and leapt from their saddles, the closest rider hitting the ground less than a yard from William. Displaying years of drill, one man in each group of five grabbed reins and led mounts to the rear as the other four drew weapons and stood in a line. They waited until Arutha joined them. At his signal, they charged.

William hoisted his own weapon, and charged with them.

The demon had backed the bowmen into the stable, but it turned at the sound of so many new arrivals. The Krondorian soldiers spread out and quickly formed a ring around the demon, using their shields to good effect.

Arutha shouted, "When you see its rear, attack!"

At the sound of Arutha's voice, the demon turned and two men behind it dashed forward and struck as hard as they could.

It whipped around, and as it did so other men struck from behind.

Within a few moments, the demon seemed to be spinning in place, its back a mass of bleeding cuts.

Despite the damage being done, the tactic was not without cost. At least three men had been struck so hard they had been knocked across the room where they now lay dead, and two more were gravely wounded. The demon lashed out to right and left, with no apparent pattern, occasionally slashing a shield or, worse, over a shield into armor or exposed flesh.

Men cursed and bled, and a few more died, but they continued to fight.

William poised himself and delivered a spine-crushing blow with his two-handed sword, and was rewarded by the sight of a deep groove fountaining black, smoking blood. The creature spun, slashing at William, who used his sword to parry. Sparks flew as black talons scraped along the steel blade, but as the creature drew back its other hand to strike, it screamed and turned away, distracted by a blow from the opposite side.

William took a step back, getting ready to deliver another blow when a voice from behind said, "How goes it, lieutenant?"

Recognizing the Prince's voice, William answered: "Bloody work, Highness. The creature bleeds, but seems reluctant to die."

Arutha moved to stand next to William, sword at the ready.

In that instant, there was no doubt in William's mind that his cousin was no mere court ruler, who wore armor only for state occasions, but an undoubted warrior who had seen more conflicts than most men twice his age.

Arutha said nothing, but stepped in front of William, pointing his sword at the creature. A small portion of the demon's side, under the left arm, was exposed, and Arutha struck with such swiftness that William was only aware of the strike when the Prince pulled away.

The demon seemed to freeze for an instant, and then it trembled and screamed louder than before. But rather than rage, the scream was one of terror. The demon faced Arutha, its eyes fixed upon the Prince as if he were the only enemy in the room.

Instantly those soldiers behind the creature closed in, slashing at its already bloodied and tattered back. But the demon's fiery eyes were focused solely upon Arutha and it slashed downward with a raking blow.

Arutha moved back deftly, then slashed with his rapier, and a smoking, dripping groove appeared on the back of the demon's clawed hand. The demon swung a backhand blow, which caused William to leap backwards, while Arutha simply moved aside a half-pace, then stepped in, slicing the creature across the chest.

William shouted, "Your blade! It somehow does more damage!"

Arutha said, "Ask your father about it some time. Right now I'm busy."

The Prince of Krondor was the fastest swordsman William had ever seen, and the demon was not even close to reaching him.

William joined in with the others, worrying the creature's flank as he sought to close with the nimble monarch.

Across the stable floor the bloody dance moved, until the creature was on the verge of entering the light of day. It hesitated, turning to snarl at those on its right, and William took a step back. Then the creature, now clearly weakened, took another step into the light, seeking to close with Arutha.

William's arms and shoulders were starting to knot with fatigue, but still he forced himself to hack away at the creature's flanks. The demon's sides and back were a mass of shredded flesh. The fur upon its goat-legs was thickly matted with blood, and they trembled with every step.

If anything, Arutha appeared to get faster as the demon slowed. His blade flicked in and out, bringing agony to the demon with each thrust.

Finally the demon staggered a step, then fell.

Without hesitation, Arutha stepped forward and drove his sword deep into the creature's neck where it joined the shoulder. He pushed hard, plunging the blade halfway to the crossguard, then pulling it free.

With a moan, the creature thrashed, and after a while went still. Smoking blood dripped from Arutha's blade, and a small flame erupted at the demon's neck wound. The soldiers who were now surrounding the demon stepped back as the flame spread rapidly, a green blaze that filled the air with the stench of decaying flesh and burning sulfur.

Most of the men were coughing and a few were retching, but within moments the demon was gone, leaving only a blackened outline of its form on the ground, and a foul stench hanging in the air.

The Prince's attending page ran up, ready to do his lord's bidding. Arutha opened up the bag on the page's hip and withdrew a wad of bandages. He wiped off the blade, and where the demon's blood touched the fabric, it blackened and smoked. In a conversational tone, Arutha said, "Tell the men to be careful cleaning off the demon's blood, lieutenant."

"Sire!" answered William; but every man present had seen the Prince's actions.

Then Arutha said, "Well, I've seen worse messes, but not many and not by much." He looked around the group of soldiers standing ready and said, "Captain Treggar."

"Sire!" Treggar stepped forward.

"Well done, captain. Now, pass the word. We've got plenty of work ahead of us. I want squads in the hills in all directions looking for any assassins who weren't caught up in this carnage."

"Yes, Highness," said Treggar, turning to give instructions.

"Lieutenant," said Arutha.

"Highness," William answered.

"I can't fault your bravery, but if I ever see you doing something as stupid as running back into that stable again I'll have you standing guard over the Princesses' laundry until you retire. We had dozens of men in full armor, and you were wearing none. Not a very bright thing to do, lieutenant."

Blushing under the grime and blood, William said, "Sorry, Highness."

Arutha gave him a faint smile. "We all make mistakes. We learn from them . . . if we survive them."

Glancing around, William said, "I could do without another such as this."

Arutha put his hand on William's shoulder. "I was not yet a year into my rule of Krondor when I faced my first demon. That victory did not truly prepare me for this fight. Just as this fight will never truly prepare you for the next." Softly, so that William alone could hear, he added, "You're never ready, Will. You just make it up as you go. All your best plans fall apart the moment combat starts. The good general is the one who knows how to improvise and how to keep his men alive." Raising his voice he said, "Do you understand, lieutenant?"

"I think I understand, Highness."

"Good. Now, let's see what we can find inside." As Treggar sent out the horsemen to scour the surrounding hills, Arutha signaled for a dozen men to accompany William and himself as they searched the fortress.

As they walked into the bloody stable, William said, "James should be here. He's the one who explored most of this place."

Arutha smiled. "If I'm any judge, James is sleeping soundly now and he's earned every moment of slumber he can steal."

William nodded. "He was looking ill-used."

"As my old horsemaster at Crydee used to say, 'ridden hard and put away wet.' "

William laughed. "That would be Algon, sire?"

Arutha's eyebrow rose in question.

"Father used to tell us stories of his boyhood in Crydee from time to time, and I've heard more than one quote attributed to his teachers. Kulgan supplied a few of the more humorous ones."

Arutha glanced around. "No doubt." He remembered the acid sense of humor the old magician could employ at precisely the moment guaranteed to cause the subject the most embarrassment.

They entered the old armory and William again felt as though he would lose the contents of his stomach. Several soldiers did vomit at the carnage.

Here the demon had done most of its damage. Arutha whispered, "Black-hearted murderers they were, but no man deserves this."

He didn't avert his gaze, rather he studied the carnage, as if to fix it in his mind. Blood had been splattered over nearly every exposed surface. Bodies had been torn asunder. Every conceivable organ was on display, drawing clouds of flies as the sick-sweet smell of rot began to cloy the air.

"When we are done here, I want this place scourged by fire," said the Prince softly.

William nodded, and turned to two of the men. "Ride and find whatever wood you can." To two others he said, "There are jars of oil in rooms to the south; find them and bring them here."

Arutha spied the large tome the high priest had cast aside at the moment of his death and motioned for it to be brought to him.

A soldier complied and Arutha examined it. "What dark words are written here someone else will have to say."

"Highness, may I?" asked William.

Arutha handed over the book. "I am no practitioner of magic, sire, but I was a student." William gave Arutha a half-smile. "As you know better than most," he added softly, again embarrassed.

William read only a few lines, then he slammed the book shut. "I don't know this language, but even so, these writings speak of power." He said, "It chilled me even to look at the words. This is a matter for a priest, I think. For safety's sake, Highness, don't let anyone read it until wards have been placed around it."

Arutha nodded. He handed the book to a soldier and said, "In the saddle-bag on my horse. Guard it."

The soldier saluted and carried the book away. Looking at William, Arutha said, "This more than anything gives weight to my decision to revive the office of court magician. If our new magician was here, what would she say, do you think?"

A spectrum of emotions passed quickly over William's features as he considered a response to the Prince's question. He fought the impulse to say something acid about Jazhara or to feign ignorance of her competence. But at last, as men spread out to search the area, William said, "I can only guess, Highness. But I know she would be able to tell us much about what has occurred here. She . . ." He hesitated, then said, "She is an exceptional student of the arts and is well-versed in lore."

"Then doubly I wish she were here, today," said Arutha.

They traveled through a hallway to what appeared to be sleeping quarters. Men went quickly through the rooms, emerging with several leather-bound books. Arutha ordered these also be carried back to Krondor.

They reached the last room at the end of a short hallway, wherein two soldiers were rifling a wooden chest. Nearby, another chest sat unopened, and as Arutha entered a soldier said, "There is a seal upon that one, Highness, and I thought it best not to tamper with it."

"You did well," said Arutha. "Bring it to Krondor and we'll have an expert examine it."

From behind them a voice said, "Why go to Krondor when you have an expert here, Highness?"

They turned to find James standing at the door, hand upon the jamb. He held up a fine-looking pair of boots. "I wasn't leaving without them," he said.

"Are you well enough to be here?" asked the Prince.

"I'm here, aren't I?" answered James with a shrug and a weak attempt at bravado. "You didn't expect me to sleep with all that noise the demon was making while you were killing it, did you?"

Arutha smiled and shook his head slightly. "Tell me what you can about that chest."

James dropped to his knees and looked closely at the seal

and lock. After a few moments of inspecting hinges, iron bands and sides, he said, "I can tell you it is a very good idea to take it back to Krondor. After a priest makes sure nothing particularly nasty will happen when that seal is broken, I'll pick the lock. My tools are back in my apartment in the palace, sire."

One of the soldiers who had been searching the open trunk held out a parchment, and said, "Sire, I think you should read this."

Arutha glanced at the document and said, "Do you know what this is?"

The soldier said, "Highness, I speak and read three Keshian tongues as well as the King's Tongue. This writing is akin to a desert tribe's language, yet not close enough that I can read it. But I do recognize a word here, Highness."

William restrained his curiosity, but James presumed to read over the Prince's shoulder. "What is it, sire?"

Softly, Arutha said, "It's a name: Radswil of Olasko." Turning quickly, he added, "William, stay and search every room. Ensure that every document you find here is brought back to the palace. James, you're with me. We leave at once for Krondor."

William snapped out orders and men started running.

Despite his calm demeanor and even pace, no man in the room could miss the urgency radiated by the Prince of Krondor.

William watched as Arutha and James vanished down the hall, and then turned to conduct the final search of this foul nest. Already men were returning with firewood and oil, and when it came time to leave, William was glad he would be the one to put the torch to this place.

Coming out of his momentary reverie, William hurried to begin as thorough a search as if Arutha himself were remaining to oversee it.

SEVENTEEN

# MISDIRECTION

IND whipped the standards.

After leaving the fortress, they had pushed hard and ridden the horses to the edge of exhaustion to reach the closest Kingdom garrison, six days' travel instead of eight. Arutha pointed to the small fortress on the shore of Shandon Bay. Dust blew across the hills and the horses stamped impatiently, sensing that fresh water and food were not too far away.

James said, "Looks like we've got company."

He had slowly recovered while riding, and though he was not as hale as he would have been with bed-rest, most of his injuries were healing. He was still sore in more places than he cared to count, but he had sustained no permanent damage.

Arutha said, "Apparently."

When Arutha had sailed from Krondor to this base at the south end of Shandon Bay, he had ordered the ship to wait for the return voyage. Three other ships now sat at anchor off the tiny wharf.

James laughed. "That's Amos's ship, isn't it?"

"*The Royal Leopard*, yes," answered Arutha. "And *The Royal Adder* and *The Royal Hind*. It's the better part of his squadron."

326

As they rode into the fortification, the local garrison had turned out and was waiting at attention. The captain in charge had prepared a reception, but Arutha had no time. He dismounted and walked over to greet the burly man who stood next to the captain.

"Amos," said Arutha, "by what chance of fate do we find the Admiral of the Western Fleet waiting on our convenience?"

Amos Trask's gray-shot black beard split with a grin. His eyes had a merry glint, one that both Arutha and James knew never left him—even in battle—and he answered in his usual booming voice. "I always make a sweep of this bay when I come south. I find that Keshian smugglers and the odd pirate waiting to ambush traders like to hide in the lees of the north shore if the weather's nasty. I was making my usual rounds of the area when I spied *The Royal Falcon* there—" he pointed to the ship anchored near the wharf "—flying the royal household banner. So I asked myself, 'What's Arutha doing in this forlorn corner of the Kingdom?' and I hove to and waited to find out."

Arutha said, "Well, as you have the faster ship, we'll be transferring my personal belongings to the *Leopard*."

Amos grinned. "Already done."

"How soon can we leave?"

"Within the hour," said Amos. "If you wish to rest a bit, in the morning."

To the captain of the garrison, Arutha said: "Thank you for preparing the welcome, captain, but matters of state require my rapid return to Krondor." To Captain Treggar he said: "Rest the men and horses for a day, then as soon as the baggage train catches up to us—"

"Again," added James under his breath. Arutha had intercepted his own baggage train along the way and had ordered it turned around as he had sped past.

"—board the *Falcon*."

"Understood, Highness," said Treggar.

William and his squad had caught up with Arutha late the second day after leaving the fortress, carrying a large number of documents and a few items believed to have magical properties.

Arutha said, "Lieutenant, bring along what you've found and sail back with me." He turned to Amos. "We leave now."

Amos stepped aside to make way for the Prince. "I anticipated your order, Arutha, so we weigh anchor as soon as you're aboard."

Arutha signaled and his horse was brought over. He retrieved the saddle-bag containing the books and papers taken from the assassins, and handed them to William, who was carrying a similar bag filled with parchments and books. Arutha then led the way to the water's edge where a longboat waited to row them out to the admiral's ship.

Arutha, William, and James boarded, followed by Amos. Sailors and soldiers shoved the boat out into the calm waters of the bay.

Within an hour they were aboard and the three ships were in full sail, departing on the evening tide. Arutha and James took the admiral's cabin; Amos bunked in with the First Officer, William with a junior officer. By the time James had unpacked, a knock on the cabin door announced the arrival of the admiral.

Amos sat down at his own table, and said, "I've sent for a little supper." Glancing at James he added, "Jimmy, me lad, I've seen you battered and bruised before, but this looks like a personal best. Good story?"

James nodded. "Better than most."

Arutha smiled at his old friend. "Glad I am to see you, and for more than the fast voyage."

Another knock came to the door and William appeared. "Highness," he said in greeting. "Admiral."

Amos said, "I know you. You're Pug's son. Haven't seen you in, what? Ten years?"

William blushed a little and said, "Something like that, sir."

"Well pull up a seat and rest yourself. Supper should—" He was interrupted by a knock at the door. "Enter!" he bellowed. The door opened and a pair of sailors appeared with food and drink. After they had served the meal, they departed. Amos took a long pull on a flagon of wine and said, "So, then, what's the story?"

Arutha outlined all that had happened, from the seemingly unconnected murders in Krondor right up to the raid on the Nighthawks' lair.

"So we have this document, in a tongue neither William nor I can read, but the Duke of Olasko's name is on it."

"Let me see it," said the former pirate. "I picked up a number of desert tongues when I . . . sailed along the Keshian coast."

James smiled. Trenchard the pirate had raided Keshian ports as often as Kingdom ports in his youth. Amos read the document twice. "The problem is that not only is this one of the more obscure dialects, the scribe was only semi-literate. Anyway, from what I get out of this, it's a death order. Someone is paying . . . no, I'm assuming. Someone has ordered the assassins to kill the Duke of Olasko."

Arutha said, "But we think that's a false trail."

"Really?" asked Amos. "Tell me more."

"The Crown Prince of Olasko is also in the party and from the reports of the officer in charge of the attack on the duke, it appears it was really him they were after."

Amos sat back. He read the document again and said, "There are some other names here, Vladic and Kazamir, and Paulina."

"Members of the Royal House of Olasko and Roldem," said Arutha.

"Someone wants them dead, too."

Amos studied the document a bit, then shoved it aside. "Well, I'd get another opinion on the translation, Arutha. Have an expert look at it, because I might be wrong." After a moment of reflection, he said, "But, either way it looks like someone wants to start a war between the Kingdom and Olasko."

"Who?" asked William.

Amos looked at William and his eyebrows went up. "Find out *why*, and that will tell you who."

James sat back. Looking out the large sterncastle windows, he saw the little moon rising as he considered what Amos had just said. Softly he wondered aloud, "Why?"

The weather was nearly perfect when they sailed into sight of Krondor. Amos had broken out both his personal banner as Admiral of the King's Fleet in the West and the Prince's royal pennant, and ships cleared the harbor as he headed for the royal docks.

The always-efficient Master of Ceremonies de Lacy had a formal guard waiting on the dock, along with the Princess and the children. Arutha endured the barest minimum of ceremony and spared a moment to kiss his wife and each child. Then he excused himself, James and Amos to a meeting with his staff.

Anita knew her husband well enough to recognize that the matter was urgent, and she took the children back to the royal apartments. Arutha gave orders for his best translators of Keshian desert languages to attend him by the time he had changed into clean clothing.

William bid James good-bye and hurried to the bachelor officers' quarters, where he endured a dozen questions from the other junior officers as he hurried to bathe and don a fresh uniform.

Gordon O'Donald came up the stairs as William was finishing a quick polish of his boots and said, "William! My best friend, how goes it?"

William smiled. "Best friend?"

"I'm giving you credit for getting Treggar out of here for the last few weeks. I can't say it's been heaven, but it's the closest thing to it I've experienced in a while."

William fixed him with a skeptical eye. "I think you judge the captain harshly, Gordon. Take my word: if you're in a fight, he's who you want standing next to you."

Gordon rubbed his chin. "Well, if you say so. Certainly the mess has been a great deal calmer."

William chuckled, then said, "How do I look?"

"Like a freshly-washed lieutenant."

"Good. I have to head back to the Prince's council room."

"Ah, I thought perhaps you were going to visit your little friend over at The Rainbow Parrot."

William had just started down the stairway, and he almost tripped, he turned around so quickly. "Talia?"

O'Donald said, "I checked up on her a few times while you were away."

As William's expression darkened, Gordon quickly said, "As a friend, of course."

With a grim smile, William echoed, "Of course."

Indulging in a theatrical sigh, O'Donald said, "Which is a good thing. That girl would have none of me. Or any other lad, I think. Seems you've got yourself a sweetheart, Will."

William couldn't control his grin. "Really?"

O'Donald gave him a playful shove. "Don't keep the Prince waiting. I'm sure you'll get some free time later to visit Talia."

William was so distracted by Gordon's comment that he almost fell down the stairs, just catching himself on the next step. Laughing, Gordon said, "Go on. You can't keep the Prince waiting."

William hurried through the armory and across the marshaling yard to the palace. By the time he arrived, the others were also arriving at the Prince's council chamber.

William glanced around and James waved him to come sit beside him near the Prince. Between the Prince and James was the chair reserved for the Knight-Marshal of Krondor, empty since Gardan's retirement. Amos had joined the council, which also included Captain Guruth, Sheriff Means, and Captain Issacs who commanded the Royal Household Guard.

Arutha said, "I have a half-dozen of our scribes who are fluent in the more obscure Keshian dialects examining those scrolls. Father Belson of the Temple of Prandur is examining the chest and will be here shortly with his initial impressions." He looked at the two captains and the sheriff, and said, "For those of you who were not with us, let me sum up our situation."

Even after ten years in the Prince's service, James marveled at how Arutha's mind worked. He knew exactly how to impart the necessary information without embellishment, yet with enough detail to drive home the relative weight of the various topics.

As Arutha was finishing his background for the two captains and the sheriff, Father Belson entered the room.

"Highness," began the priest of Prandur, "I have used every

art available to me and as far as I can determine, there is nothing mystic about that seal. It appears to be a simple wax seal designed to show if the chest has been opened or not."

Arutha waved him to an empty chair. "We'll examine it after we adjourn." To the group, he said, "I want the guard doubled on the duke and his family until they depart."

Captain Issacs looked uncomfortable as he said, "Sire, His Grace is recovering from his injuries, and is complaining about the guards we have protecting him now. He's . . . made the acquaintance of a number of ladies who . . . visit him."

Arutha looked caught between irritation and amusement. "Well, the best advice I can offer, captain, is to remind the duke that his wife would certainly want him protected. Perhaps within earshot of those . . . ladies, you mentioned."

James grinned and William had to struggle to keep a straight face. Amos laughed out loud and slapped the table. He started to say something, but Arutha cut him off. "Don't you dare tell me I take the fun out of life, Amos."

Amos's laughter redoubled.

To Captain Guruth and Sheriff Means, Arutha said, "We tore out the heart of the Nighthawks in the area, but we didn't destroy them all."

Amos nodded. "Damn things are like cockroaches. Turn on the light and they're scurrying for the shadows. You don't see them most of the time, but they're there."

James kept grinning, while Arutha showed his displeasure at the interruption. "As I was saying, we didn't destroy them all. If some of them reach the city, and if there are already agents here, they may mount a renewed attack on the duke to discharge their obligations."

The door opened, and a soldier admitted a scribe, who

bowed. "Highness, I've read the text you surmised as being the most important." He was a little man, in a simple blue tunic with gray trousers, and plain black boots. His most noticeable feature was a tendency to squint.

"What can you tell me?" asked Arutha.

"Admiral Trask mentioned to you the possibility the scribe might have been semi-literate," said the clerk. "That is how it might look to the untrained eye, but rather than such being the case, it's actually a clever code."

"Code?"

"Not a cipher, such as the Quegans use—badly I might add—but rather a set of agreed-upon phrases that I believe are substitutions. The names of the duke and his family are quite plain to read, but other pertinent information is cleverly disguised by phrases that are seemingly innocuous.

"Let me cite an example: 'Our lord instructs everyone to be in place by the tide of green fulfillment.' 'Tide of green fulfillment' is obviously a particular time agreed upon in advance by the writer and whoever the message was intended for. Here's another: 'The gift must reach the named one before he departs the feast of crows.'"

Arutha said, "Is there any way to make any sense of this?"

"Had you a captive who knew these keys, and if you could get him to give them to you, then all would be clear. But to guess at what these arbitrary phrases mean is fruitless."

"Read a couple more, please," asked James.

"Ah . . ." began the scribe, "'Word must reach the master at winter's coldest night.'"

James nodded. "I doubt this will help, but there used to be a Keshian gang that ran slaves out of Durbin. Called themselves the Woeful Brothers, or something like that."

"Brotherhood of Woe," supplied Amos. "I ran up against them a couple of times in my . . . raiding days. Bad bunch. Ignored laws in every land, took freeborn as well as prisoners and sold them on the blocks at Durbin."

"They used to come into Krondor from time to time, and the Mockers would run them right back out as soon as we knew they were around," said James. "I heard they used this code in which a place was a person, a person was a time, a time was a place, like that."

"So the 'feast of crows' could be a place, rather than an event?" asked Arutha.

"Yes," said James. "Not that it will help much to know that, but I thought I'd mention it."

Arutha sat back. "It might." Looking at the scribe he said, "Does that help?"

The scribe said, "Perhaps. We have quite a number of such phrases in a large number of documents. Maybe we can learn something by looking for similar or identical phrases."

Arutha waved him from the room, saying, "See to it, and report tomorrow morning on what you have learned."

To Captains Issacs, Guruth, and the sheriff, Arutha said, "Turn over every rock and if you find any of those murderers, bring them here and don't let them speak to anyone."

The three men saluted and departed.

Arutha stood and the others at the table immediately did likewise. "Let's look at that trunk." To the priest, he said, "Father, if you would join us, just in case there's some magic that eluded your inspection?"

The priest of Prandur nodded.

William and James fell in behind the Prince, and Arutha said, "Join us, Amos?"

With a laugh, Amos answered, "As if you could stop me."

They went to a large storage room used by the royal family for a variety of purposes. It was currently half-filled with furniture, trunks of old clothing, toys the royal children had outgrown, and other family items.

James said, "Perhaps we should move this lot down to the lower dungeon before we open it?"

"After you inspect the lock, squire, if you think it's dangerous, we will do so."

James produced a set of tools, rolled up in a leather strip. He untied it, unfolded it, and took out a probe. He examined the lock and after a few moments said, "There is a trap, but it's a very simple needle, almost certainly poisoned." He removed a tool and inserted it in the lock. He experimented a bit, then everyone in the room heard a loud click. At that instant, James swiftly removed the probe, and cut the needle with a tiny pair of metal clippers.

"Just in case," suggested James as he stood up, "everyone stand back."

James lifted the hasp from the lock and opened the trunk.

Instantly the room darkened, as if a cloud had passed over every light in the chamber. A puff of wind came from within the trunk and a dark shape billowed up.

It was man-shaped, but lacked depth, as if a shadow could be cast in air, without a surface upon which to rest. It appeared to look around the room, then stepped out of the trunk and hurried toward the door.

Everyone in the room was rooted to the spot in astonishment, until James shouted, "Stop it!"

Arutha pulled out his sword, as did William and Amos. William was the only one in a position between the entity and the door, and he tried to block its movement by thrusting his sword before it. The creature walked through the sword as if it wasn't there.

"After it!" shouted Arutha. To James he said, "What is this thing?"

"I've never seen anything like it," said Amos.

"Neither have I," said James, "but I've heard about them."

"What is it?" repeated Arutha.

"It's a Shadow Stalker. A magical assassin. The reason the chest was so easy to open is that someone *wanted* it here and easy to open!"

"You'll have a hard time convincing me the assassins let their entire population be slaughtered so that we could bring this chest here," said Arutha, hurrying after the creature as it passed through a closed door into the hall.

They pulled open the door and peered down the hall. There was no sign of the creature. James said, "I don't think that, Highness, but they might have been getting ready to bring that chest to someplace we could find it—there!" He pointed down the hall.

"What?" asked Arutha.

"Movement in the shadows."

"I see nothing," said Amos.

James was running, Arutha a step behind him. James shouted, "You could have looked right at it, admiral. You wouldn't have seen a thing!"

Abruptly a ball of flame came flying overhead, then it came to a halt and hung at the corner where the hallway turned to the right. All shadows seemed to fade in the bright light, except for the man-shaped shadow-assassin who stood revealed in stark relief.

Arutha and the others looked behind and saw Father Belson holding his hand aloft, as if guiding the ball of fire. "Prandur's fire burns true, Highness. I do not know if I can halt the creature, but I can show you where it hides!"

"Keep following, Father!" shouted the Prince.

William said, "Highness, where is it going?"

"Wherever His Grace, the Duke of Olasko, rests," said the Prince.

James said, "It's heading for the guest wing."

Arutha caught up with the creature and slashed at it with his sword. The blade passed through the man-shaped shadow, which hesitated, its head moving as if it was looking around, then it continued on.

"You got its attention," said James, "but it doesn't seem harmed."

Arutha said, "I welcome any suggestion as to how to stop this creature."

"Keep hitting it," said Amos.

Arutha again overtook the moving shape and struck it several times. The shadow flinched and turned this way, then that, then it fled straight up to the ceiling where it looked like a painted human silhouette. It paused for a moment, then resumed its journey.

Then the fireball went out and the creature vanished into the gloom.

James pointed, "There!"

Father Belson said, "If I cast another globe, I may not be able to do much else."

"Have you any spells that might stop this creature, Father?" asked Arutha, hurrying at a fast walk after James.

"Most of my order's spells suited for combat tend to result in extreme damage, Highness."

"I would risk a fire in the palace to stop a war, Father."

"But it might not do any good," said the priest.

William said, "Should I run ahead and make the guards ready?"

Arutha said, "Ready to do what? Their weapons are no bar to that thing."

James was hurrying along, keeping his eyes on the ceiling, lest he lose sight of the entity. Amos shouted, "Clear the way!" as they reached a more heavily trafficked hall.

Servants and guards stationed at the corners looked over at the odd sight of their monarch and several members of his council hurrying along, eyes cast upward to the ceiling. When they glanced up, all they saw was a slight flickering of shadows, but nothing else.

James said, "Now, at least, I know who was killing magicians in Krondor and why."

"So the Prince couldn't send for anyone to stop this thing?" said William.

"Or check the trunk with different magic than used by the good Father," said Amos.

"What else do you know of these creatures?" Arutha asked James.

Keeping his eyes on the moving shadow on the ceiling, James said, "All I know is what one of the old street magicians told me of this conjuration. It's mindless. Once set on its task it does not stop until it's killed its prey or is destroyed."

The cleric said, "There are counter-spells for specific magic, but I have no idea what would be required for this one, and I hardly have time to consult my superiors at the temple, or request help from the other orders."

William said, "I may know something."

"What?" asked Arutha.

"I'm guessing, but I've got an idea."

James said, "Don't be shy, Will. We're nearing the guests' wing."

"It has two possible ways to kill, as I see it. It either solidifies and tries to kill the duke as a man would, with a weapon or by strangling him or—"

"Breaking his neck," supplied Amos. "Yes, we get the idea. Go on."

"Or it has to . . . afflict the duke with a poison, or an illness, or something of that sort."

Arutha said, "Father, if it strikes the duke with an illness or injury of some sort, can you help?"

"I can keep the duke alive," said the priest. "Certainly long enough for you to bring other healers to the palace."

"What if it turns solid?" asked James as he reached the large doors leading into the duke's quarters. "Open the doors!" he shouted to the two soldiers guarding them.

To Arutha, Amos echoed, "What if it turns solid?"

"Then we kill it," answered the Prince.

Running ahead, William ordered guards to open the doors before James lost sight of the flickering shadow on the ceiling. In moments they reached the duke's private quarters. The creature ignored that door and continued on down the hall. It reached another set of doors and paused. Arutha shouted, "Open those doors!"

The guards hesitated for an instant, then complied, but in

that brief moment, the creature seemed to slip between the top of the doors and the jamb.

Vladic, Crown Prince of Olasko sat up in bed, the woman at his side sliding under the covers, as if to hide. "What is the meaning of this?" shouted Vladic.

James looked up at the ceiling and then around the room. "Father, if you please," he said in an insistent, pleading tone.

The priest cast another fireball, and Vladic drew back. "What is this?" he demanded, getting out of bed and grabbing his sword.

"There!" cried James as the creature came into sharp relief again. It crouched on the wall behind Vladic.

William, seeing where James pointed, leapt forward, grabbed Vladic and yanked the Prince away.

At that moment, the shadow stepped down from the wall to the floor. Before everyone's eyes, it swelled, filled out and became solid.

Arutha moved in front of Vladic and said, "Pardon, Your Highness."

Vladic, ignoring his own nudity, stood with his sword at the ready. "What is that?"

"Something that doesn't want you around, apparently," said James, coming to join Arutha. He had his sword out as well.

The shadow-form now appeared fully solid, looking like a man without features, hair, or any visible blemish, painted coal-black. No light reflected from it.

Arutha slashed at it and, as the creature hesitated, the Prince's blade cut through it.

Then it sprang for Prince Vladic.

EIGHTEEN

UNMASKING

ILLIAM leapt.

He knocked Prince Vladic aside as the monster lunged. Soldiers hurried into the room, while Amos and Arutha prepared to attack. Several hurled themselves at the shadow-stalker in an attempt to protect their prince, and the first of them tried to shield-bash the stalker, to knock it off balance. The shield rang as if he had struck a tree bole, and the stalker slashed with his hand. The soldier's throat dissolved into a red fountain as blood sprayed across the room.

James worked his way around behind the creature, as Arutha shouted, "Archers!"

One soldier hurried out of the room to relay the order, while two bearing long pikes attacked. The weapons were decorative, heads gilded and hardwood polished, bearing the royal pennon of Krondor, but they were still fully functional. Both men were well-schooled in their use and approached the stalker, barbs ready to hook and pull, points ready to impale.

The first soldier thrust with all the force he could muster so that the steel point should have impaled the creature, but it

344

slid off harmlessly. The shadow-stalker paused for a moment and caught the pole under one arm, then with a sharp blow struck with the other hand and snapped the pole as if it were kindling.

"That's solid oak!" said Amos.

William was up and pulling Vladic across the bed, past the young woman who was now crouched down on the other side from where the stalker was cornered. Sensing that its prey was leaving, the creature leapt upon the bed, and the young woman screamed and cowered even lower. The shadow-assassin ignored her.

Arutha hurried around and lunged at the creature, the point of his blade sliding off its featureless hide. "Highness!" shouted James. "You're doing no good; please avoid getting yourself killed."

Amos took a more direct approach, grabbing Arutha's shoulder and yanking him back as the monster turned and lashed out at where the Prince had stood a moment before.

"You're irritating it, Arutha," said the former pirate.

Archers entered, bows at the ready, and let fly as William half-dragged Prince Vladic out of the room. The arrows merely glanced off or broke as they struck the stalker's hide.

"This is doing no good!" shouted Arutha. "Fall back, but slow it down!"

Soldiers with shields and swords moved to form a shieldwall and more soldiers with pikes fell in behind. The shield-bearers braced themselves, their shields overlapping like scales. From behind, the pikemen reached over and formed a steel barrier; but the creature ignored it, walking into the points. Strong men braced themselves as the heavy shafts were pushed back.

The stalker raised both arms and smashed downward. One

pike on the left shattered, while another was knocked to the stone floor, flying out of the grip of the soldier holding it. More soldiers hurried to support those who faced the monster, and their sergeant looked to William for instructions.

"Pin it against the wall," said William. "Use shields and be cautious, for it is extremely powerful."

The sergeant shouted, "You heard the lieutenant! Charge!"

The shieldmen and pikemen charged as one, and the creature was borne backward. It resisted but could not get traction on the smooth stone floor.

More men arrived and slowly they pushed the stalker away from Prince Arutha and the others. The stalker sensed its prey escaping, and its struggle intensified. It drew back an arm and lashed out, crushing the face of the closest soldier. He fell, tripping two soldiers behind him, and the mass of soldiers pressing the creature back disintegrated.

Suddenly the stalker was flailing, first with one arm, then the other, smashing back any soldier who hindered it. The blows were pulverizing, breaking arms, smashing shoulders, crushing faces. Tough, experienced veteran soldiers were tossed aside amid cries of agony and fury, as if they were no more than bothersome boys. Injured men were held in place by the press of other soldiers. More than one unconscious man was held upright until the movement of the mass allowed them to fall, threatening them with being trampled.

More soldiers raced in to protect their monarch and his royal guest. Again they pressed the stalker back, pushing it to the floor. The soldiers piled onto the stalker, pinning it to the floor. The groans of the men near the bottom of the heap revealed the price paid for enduring the weight of the men and armor on top of them. Those closest to the creature risked their own lives twice, from the creature's blows and the crushing weight of their own comrades.

The pile of soldiers heaved, as if the stones beneath them shook, once, twice, three times. Then suddenly the heap collapsed, as if on a ball that had suddenly deflated. From within the pile a voice said, "Sire! It's gone!"

James shouted, "No it hasn't!"

A shadow slithered out from under the pile and moved across the room to Arutha and Vladic, where it rose and solidified again.

Arutha attacked.

His sword was a blur as he slashed at the creature. His blade had been given the power of an Ishapian talisman by Macros the Black before Arutha's final confrontation with Murmandamus at the end of the Great Uprising. Since then, only the demon he had killed at the fortress had tested the strength of that magical power.

This shadow-stalker seemed more annoyed than harmed by Arutha's blade. It flinched from Arutha's cuts and it lashed out at him with a powerful blow.

Arutha dodged aside, and James stepped in from the rear, striking as hard as he could with his sword. The blow rang as it bounced off the stalker, and James felt the shock all the way up to his shoulder.

Looking at Father Belson, James shouted, "Is there anything you can do?"

The cleric called back, "I can only think of one thing, but it's very dangerous!"

Arutha was caught in a duel he couldn't win, but he was effective enough in staying between the creature and Prince

Vladic that Vladic was still unharmed. He shouted, "It can't be any more dangerous than this, Father! Do it!"

The priest stepped aside and began an incantation in the mystical language of his order. James again attacked the stalker from behind, and again felt as if he were striking unyielding stone.

The bedroom brightened and grew hot. Father Belson held his hand aloft, and above his head a ring of fire formed, swirling flames that could be felt by everyone nearby. The circling flames moved faster and faster, growing larger and hotter by the second. The priest finished his spell and shouted, "Run!"

No one had to be told twice. Everyone who could turned and sprinted out of the room, save Arutha, who attacked the stalker one last time to buy those around him a few seconds of safety before he, too, backed away, turned and ran.

Wounded men lying on the floor behind the creature crawled away, leaving behind unconscious comrades.

The priest shouted a single word in his order's secret language and the flames coalesced into a form as man-like as the stalker. The intense heat could be felt by those running: Arutha's back felt as if he was standing too close to a forge.

James turned and saw the flame creature interpose itself between the stalker and Vladic, who stood watching with mute fascination.

Father Belson cried out, "O creature of flame, elemental of fire, destroy that darkness!"

The elemental attacked and a wave of heat struck the onlookers, intense enough to make them retreat even farther from the conflict. Only the priest of Prandur seemed unfazed by the searing air near the creature.

The stalker turned from its inexorable pursuit of Vladic and defended itself. The creatures came to grips, silently, and the only sound heard was the crackling of flames.

James left the hallway and moved through an antechamber into a side passage. He ran down it, and crossed through a gallery, returning to the main hall near Arutha and Vladic. He signaled to a nearby guard, saying, "Go through there," pointing to where he had come from. "At the other end of this hall lie injured men. The heat is doing them no good. Call a squad and get them out of there."

"Yes, squire," said the soldier. He motioned for others to follow, and led a half-dozen men the way James had outlined.

Arutha didn't take his eyes off the struggle, but he said, "I should have thought of that."

"You're busy," said James, motioning for one of the remaining guards to remove his cloak. He handed it to Prince Vladic and said, "I know it's warm, but . . ."

Vladic, riveted by the scene before him, covered himself and said, "Thank you."

The two magical creatures were locked together, each gripping the other's arms, staggering first this way, then that, like two drunken wrestlers pushing one another around the arena. Each time the elemental came close to something combustible the item would smoke and char, or burst into flames if the blazing creature lingered long enough. The stalker slammed the elemental against the stone wall in an attempt to shed its grasp, but the elemental's fiery grip held tightly and it endured the blow in silence. Then the elemental spun and slammed the stalker into the wall in return.

Arutha said, "If this doesn't end soon, that thing is going to burn the palace down."

Several decorative tapestries were smoldering and two had

349

started to flame. The stalker pushed the elemental backward, into a decorative table upon which sat a vase of fresh cut flowers. The blooms withered in seconds, and the table burst into flames as the vase shattered from the heat.

"Look," said James. "Something's happening."

Where the elemental gripped the stalker, smoke was starting to rise, black, oily wisps that thickened by the moment. Soon clouds of black smoke reached the ceiling, where they spread out, engulfing the hall in a malodorous dark miasma.

The stalker thrashed wildly, whipping the elemental first one way, then another, but the flaming creature would not release its death-grip.

The hall was now ablaze and Arutha shouted to nearby soldiers, "Clear everyone out of this wing of the palace! Call for water!" A bucket-line would have to be formed quickly, as the heaving bracing timbers which held up the stonework of the hall were beginning to smolder and smoke.

"Look!" shouted James. "They're getting smaller!"

The two mystic figures clung to one another in a revolving struggle, a twisting dance of power, moving faster as they diminished in size. Smoke now billowed off the pair, filling the hall with a choking, greasy cloud that threatened to suffocate everyone.

"Out!" ordered Arutha. "Everyone get out to the garden!"

One of the palace's several carefully-tended gardens was near the guest wing. James reached the large double glass doors that opened from the hall into the garden, and threw them wide. The evening air was cool and fresh after the soaring temperature in the hallway.

People staggered out of the door behind James, coughing,

eyes streaming as they escaped the smoke now filling the corridor with a reek of burning sulfur and rotting garbage.

Voices reverberated from nearby precincts of the palace as the fire alarm was sounded. James turned to look at the conflagration. "Did Father Belson get out?" he asked Amos.

"He was behind us," replied the admiral. "I don't see him."

James hurried back to the door, falling to the floor to get as low under the smoke as he could. Acrid smoke made his eyes water as the pungent stench filled his nose. The ceiling rafters were ablaze and the conflagration flowed along overhead like a river of flame. James blinked hard to clear his eyes of tears and saw a solitary figure at the far end of the hall.

The priest of Prandur stood with arms spread wide above his head, singing a spell of magic. James could barely make him out, a dark outline in the blue-gray haze that filled the hall under the black, billowing clouds of smoke.

The priest's song turned dark and solemn, a funereal keening that struck a note of sadness in James as he listened. Glancing upward, fearful of stones falling, James shouted, "Father Belson! Come away! The fire will consume you!"

Abruptly the flames racing along the hall shuddered, then drew back, as if sucked away from the ceiling and walls by some great intake of a god's breath. The flames and smoke withdrew.

James looked back at the people who waited in the garden and saw them staring in amazement at the sight of the retreating flames and smoke. Then he turned back and saw all the flames and smoke gather in a giant ball above the head of the priest, who stood motionless. The ball quickly contracted into a smaller sphere, which grew brighter as it got smaller. At last it was compacted to the size of a child's ball, though it burned as bright as the sun at noon. James had to turn his eyes away from the glare, and the garden outside the doors was ablaze with light.

Then suddenly the light vanished, and the hall was plunged into darkness. James sat up and returned to the garden, coughing and rubbing his eyes.

"What happened?" asked Arutha.

James said, "I think it's over."

A moment later Father Belson walked out the door. Smoke swirled at his feet and came off his robes in wisps. His face was blackened with soot, but otherwise he appeared unharmed.

"Are you all right?" asked James.

Belson said, "The last thing a priest of Prandur needs to fear is fire, young man." Looking at the Prince of Krondor, he said, "Highness, the damage—" He shrugged as if apologizing.

Prince Vladic, clutching the cloak tightly around him, laughed and said, "For saving my life, I'll rebuild this entire wing, and I'll raise a new temple to Prandur in Olasko, priest!"

Father Belson looked pleased, and said, "That would be nice . . ." before collapsing.

James was the first at his side, kneeling to examine the cleric. "He's fainted," said the squire.

"Carry him to his quarters," Arutha instructed, and four guards were detailed to carry the exhausted cleric to his bed.

A scribe wended his way through the garden, blinking at all the smoke and the crowd around the Prince. "Sire!" he called.

"What is it?" asked Arutha.

"We've . . ." he blinked and tears started to run down his cheeks as he coughed. "Sorry, Highness, but smoke makes me dizzy."

"What is it?" Arutha repeated.

"Sorry, sire. We've deciphered more of the messages. Some

are from agents here in Krondor, as well as other cities. One in particular seemed urgent, so I came as soon as it was pointed out to me."

"What is it?" Arutha demanded finally, his patience clearly at its limit.

The scribe held out a parchment. "This message specifies the need to deliver a sealed chest to the palace. It contains a trap of some sort. I thought it important enough to warn you, should such a chest be delivered here."

Arutha shook his head in amazement. After a long moment, he looked at the members of the court. "Let's get some supper." To the scribe he said, "Return to your work. Let me know what the other scrolls say after we break fast tomorrow morning."

"Sire." The coughing scribe bowed and quickly departed, obviously glad to get away from the smoke.

James said, "Highness, don't be too hard on him."

Arutha nodded. "I won't be. He tried his best. It just wasn't all that . . . timely."

William and Amos both laughed, and Prince Vladic said, "I shall return to my chambers if they're not too befouled with smoke, and don . . . something more appropriate for dining, Highness."

Arutha nodded and motioned for guards to accompany the royal guest. To James, he said, "If we'd known . . ."

"We'd still have opened the trunk," said James. "Only we'd probably have been in the deepest cell in your dungeon with only a dozen guards, and that would have been a disaster."

Arutha cast a long, sideways glance at him. "You always have such a positive view of things, squire. Come, let's eat. I'm sure my wife will want to know why we tried to burn down a significant portion of our palace."

With a wolfish grin, James said, "Just tell her you hope she'll redecorate the suites, and that will make her happy."

Arutha returned a pained expression, and said, "Someday, squire, when you meet the right woman, I pray she takes pity on you, else your days as a husband are certain to be rocky."

"I'll keep that in mind," James replied dryly.

William came up beside the Prince and said, "Highness, do you require my presence?"

Arutha stopped and looked at the young officer. "Why? Have you somewhere more important to be?"

William flushed. "No, sire, just that . . ."

James laughed, and Arutha said, "I'm just having some sport at your expense, William. Go and see your young lady and have some fun."

"Young lady, sire?" William was taken aback by the reference. Glancing at James he said, "Does everyone know?"

James grinned, while Arutha said, "My squire insures that I am aware of all significant situations involving a family member. Now go."

"Sire," said William with enthusiasm, but blushing a little at the joke.

"We shall have a serious talk in the morning, all of us. But until then, a little relaxation is in order."

William turned to go, and James said, "Willy!"

William stopped and looked over his shoulder. "What, James?"

"If I were you, I'd go change first. You look like a chimney sweep."

Noticing that everyone around him was covered in soot, and that therefore he must be as well, William said, "Ah, thanks for that."

"No matter."

James watched as William hurried off towards the armory, and said, "I envy him."

Arutha said, "What, his infatuation?"

"Yes. I expect some day I'll meet someone special, or perhaps not, but either way, I have never had that . . . boyish joy at meeting a young lady."

Arutha laughed. "You were a cynical old man when I met you, Jimmy. What were you, fourteen years old?"

James returned the laughter. "I guess so, Highness. With your permission I'll withdraw and clean up before joining you for supper."

"As shall I," said Amos. "I'm feeling a little cooked myself."

Arutha nodded. "Go, and I'll order in extra wine and ale, and let us have a little revelry." His expression darkened. "Tomorrow, we turn our attention back to bloody works."

James and Amos exchanged glances and then departed. Both knew Arutha well enough to know he expected to find whoever was behind the assassination attempt on the Prince of Olasko and, when he did, to extract a bloody penalty for bringing destruction to his palace.

William worked his way through the crowded inn, and found Talia behind the bar, helping her father to serve ale. The demand for food was minimal, and the inn was filled with working men taking their ease before going home for the night.

He reached the end of the bar and waited until she caught sight of him.

"Will!" she said with a broad smile. "When did you get back?" She hurried over and gave him a kiss on the cheek.

Blushing, he said, "Just this evening. There was some business at the palace, and then the Prince gave me the rest of the night off."

"Have you eaten?"

Suddenly he realized he had last eaten at midday, aboard the admiral's ship. "Why, no."

"I'll fix you something," she said. "Father, look, it's Will!"

Lucas looked up and waved a greeting. "Good evening, lad."

"Sir," said William.

Talia vanished into the kitchen.

Lucas came over. "You've got that look."

"What look, sir?"

"Seen some duty."

"Some," William said, with a nod.

"Rough?"

"Rough enough," William conceded. "We lost some good lads."

Lucas gave William a fatherly pat on the forearm. "Glad to see you back, boy."

"Thank you, sir."

Talia returned with a plate heaped with food. "I'll get you an ale," she said.

She drew a large jack of ale and placed it next to his plate. "I've missed you," she said, her eyes glistening. "I know it's bold of me to say that, but I did."

William face flushed. He glanced down at his ale as he said, "I'm glad you did. I . . . thought about you a lot while I was gone."

She glanced around the room to see if anything needed her attention. Her father waved at her, indicating she should take a few minutes and talk to William.

"So," she said, "tell me what brave things you've done."

He laughed a little. "Stupid is more like it, given the aches and bruises I've picked up."

"You were wounded?" she asked, her eyes widening with concern.

"No," he laughed. "Nothing needing more than cleaning and a dry bandage."

With a feigned look of anger, she said, "That's good. If you were gravely injured, I would have to avenge you."

"You would?" he asked, laughing.

"Of course," she responded. "I was raised by the Sisters of Kahooli, remember."

He said nothing, just smiled, while enjoying the moment, eating his food and gazing at her pretty face.

Arutha had been up all night. It was evident to James the moment he walked into the Prince's private chamber. From the look of him, William had also been up all night, but James suspected the reason was as different from the Prince's as could possibly be; William's inability to keep a smile from creeping over his face every few seconds provided an obvious clue.

Amos looked his usual self: keenly observant and enjoying any excuse for humor.

Arutha waved James to a chair and said, "I trust you're recovering from your many abuses of late?"

"Enough that I feel life is worth living again, sire," answered James, sitting down.

"Good, because there are a few things that need your immediate attention."

Looking around the room, Arutha said, "Amos, I've trusted you with my life more times than I care to remember. William, you are a member of my family. That's why I am telling you this. A while ago I gave James the responsibility of establishing an intelligence corps."

"About bloody time," said Amos with a grin. "He's the sneakiest little bastard I've ever met, even if I do love him like the son I pray I never have."

James looked at Amos and said, "Thank you, I think."

"I wouldn't mind a son," Amos mused aloud. "I might even have one or two out there I've not met yet—" he looked at James and laughed "—but if I do, I'll drown him myself the moment he reminds me of you, Jimmy."

James replied dryly, "If you do have a son, I'll have to remember that and help him escape."

"Enough," said Arutha. The Prince's usual demeanor was replaced this morning by an even deeper edge, and both Amos and James fell silent. Arutha said, "No one outside this room is to know this. I include you two for several reasons. The first is if anything happens to me, you'll be able to inform my successor of James's special status. If Lyam sends someone as regent before Prince Randolph is of age, for example.

"The second is that if anything happens to James, I want people who are in place to whom his successor can report." He glanced around the table. "We three," he said to Amos and William.

"Successor," said James with feigned trepidation. "I hope you mean should I retire."

"I mean if you're dead," said Arutha coldly. "Some time in the next year I expect you to have recruited enough agents that you'll be able to identify one you think almost as canny as yourself."

Amos laughed.

"Do not tell anyone who he is, including we three. We'll

work out a means for that person to identify himself to one of the three of us at the appropriate time. Also, I command you keep your agents as ignorant of one another as possible."

"Yes, Highness," said James. "I've already considered a system that will allow me to have several agents and keep them unaware of each other."

"Good," said Arutha. "And I have some thoughts on the matter as well. Finally, there's one other person who will know you're in this position: Jerome."

James barely held his groan in check. "Jerome! Why, Highness?"

"Master de Lacy will be retiring soon, and Jerome is the logical choice to succeed him as Master of Ceremonies. You will need funding for many of the things you wish to undertake, and the Master of Ceremonies' office has discretionary funds for a variety of reasons. Jerome will provide you with the resources you need, subject to my approval."

James sat back, obviously not happy, but willing to accept the wisdom of the Prince's choice.

"Now, to the matter at hand. The scribes have completed their translations and we now know who was behind the attacks on Prince Vladic."

"Who?" blurted James.

"His uncle, the duke."

William said, "But he and his son were almost killed in the first attempt, sire."

Arutha said, "It may be that the attack went wrong, or someone else has a separate agenda, because we also found a warrant for the death of Duke Radswil and Kazamir, unfortunately."

James asked, "Are there any signatures to these warrants?"

"No," said Arutha. "That would make things too easy, wouldn't it? The warrants all end in more of those cryptic phrases. Perhaps someday we'll deciper them and know who the author of the orders is. But for the time being, we have no clear-cut proof of who's responsible."

"What are you going to do?" asked Amos.

"Put the duke and his son and daughter under guard, call it 'protective custody,' and ship them back to Olasko, with a long letter under my personal seal to the duke's brother. My only concern in this is preventing war between the Kingdom and Olasko. I'll leave Olasko justice to the rule of Olasko; the archduke can decide who's closer: his brother or his son. He can also worry about who put out the order for his brother's and nephew's deaths." Arutha sighed. "I will certainly welcome the moment they leave Kingdom soil."

James said, "What of the Nighthawks? Have we finished them?"

Arutha sat back, a look of futility passing over his features for a moment, then he said, "We've wounded them gravely, but they still have agents out there. I think there is someone above that priesthood, one from whom they took orders."

"The Master," agreed James. He had recounted to Arutha every detail of his experience with the priests before the demon escaped.

"But it may take them years to recover," observed Amos.

"We can hope. Still, I want our new intelligence service looking for clues as to the whereabouts of remaining Night-hawks as well as any agents for Kesh, Queg, or anyone else, for that matter."

"I'll start today," said James.

"How long do you think this will take?" asked Amos playfully. "A week or, maybe, two?"

James said, "Years, Amos, years." Looking at Arutha he said, "And I suppose I'd better change my ambitions from Duke of Krondor to Duke of Rillanon."

Arutha laughed. "Yes, I suppose you had better, if you're going to build a network in the east some day. But not this week, all right?"

James grinned. "Not this week, Highness."

Arutha said, "We have much work ahead of us, but right now I have to go outrage a duke and ruin an otherwise lovely day for a Prince."

"One thing, more, if I may, Highness," requested James.

"Yes?"

"Could you persuade Her Highness to host another of her galas, soon?"

Arutha had been about to rise, and at this request he sat down again. "Why, squire? You take no pains to hide the fact you would rather be crawling through the sewers than attending one of Anita's soirées."

William cleared his throat and said, "Ah, Highness, it's my request, actually. James said he'd ask on my behalf."

"I don't understand," said Arutha, looking from soldier to squire.

James said, "William would like you to confer an award upon Captain Treggar, and then introduce him to some young ladies from good families."

Arutha looked at William and said, "Why?"

William blushed and said, "He's really a good officer, and he acted with great courage and . . . well, he saved my life."

"That does warrant notice," said Arutha, nodding in agreement.

"And maybe an estate," suggested James. "It doesn't have to be a big one, just a little one with a bit of income."

Amos started to chuckle. "Why not a title, too?"

James nodded. "Court squire should be enough."

Arutha said, "What are you plotting, you two?"

Amos's laughter exploded. "Can't you see! They want to get the captain married off!"

"Married?"

William sighed. "It's the other junior officers, sire. They made me promise I'd come up with a way to get Captain Treggar out of the unmarried officers' mess."

Amos's laughter redoubled and James and Arutha joined in, while William sat uncomfortably waiting for an answer.

EPILOGUE

# ENCOUNTERS

SEAGULLS squawked overhead.

The royal dock was busy as James and his three companions hurried to a ship at the far end, making ready to depart. Ships in the harbor were weighing anchor, leaving on the evening tide. Several at the outer break-water were unfurling sails and getting underway; others were being towed away from anchor by longboats, under the direction of the harbormaster and his pilots.

James, Graves, Kat, and Limm reached *The Royal Leopard*, and halted. At the bottom of the gangplank, two guards saluted as the Prince's squire was greeted by Amos.

"Admiral Trask, may I present my companions?" James said formally.

Amos grinned. "As if I didn't know them already." He nodded to Ethan Graves and Limm and came to take Kat's hand. "I understand you have a baby on the way?" he said with a solicitous smile.

"Yes," she said as she blushed slightly.

James smiled and winked at Graves. As long as he had known the female thief, he'd never seen her embarrassed.

"Well, my dear, we have a cabin set aside for you and your husband. The lad can bunk in with the cabin boy." He led her up the gangplank.

James said, "Farewell, Kat!"

She turned and waved, and Ethan said, "We'll be along in a minute."

James said, "Limm, I need to talk to Ethan in private."

The boy-thief said, "I thank you, then, my very good squire. I am in your debt for life, sir."

James tried not to laugh at the ridiculously formal, if heartfelt, wording. "Get along, Limm, and enjoy your fresh start. Remember, Durbin is nothing like Krondor, and it will be very tempting to slip back onto the dodgy path."

"No need to worry, squire, sir. You are my hero and I will pattern my life after yours. If you can rise above thievery and knavery, so can I."

"I'll keep him on the straight and narrow, Jimmy," said Graves with a laugh. "Now get along with you." He gave Limm a playful slap to the back of the head as he ran aboard.

James waited until the boy was up the gangplank, then motioned Graves away from the two guards. He reached into his tunic, held out a pouch and said, "Here."

"I can't take your gold, Jimmy. You've done too much for us already."

"You'll need it to get started. Consider it a down-payment."

Graves nodded. "I understand. Thank you." He took the gold and put it in his tunic.

"Amos says he knows two men in Durbin he trusts with his life. He'll tell you how to get in touch with them. One is a shipfitter, and the other is a supplier of foodstuffs. Both will be able to carry messages to Kingdom ships."

Graves said, "I've broken two oaths already. What makes you think I won't break my oath to you?"

James shrugged. "Nothing, except that I know you, Ethan, and know why you broke those oaths. I could warn you about the Prince's wrath reaching out to find you, even in Durbin, but that's pointless. You're as fearless a man as any I've known . . ." He paused for a moment, then added, ". . . when it comes to his own safety."

Graves glanced up to the deck where Amos was doing his best to charm Kat and Limm. "I understand," he said, his expression darkening and his voice turning cold.

James shook his head. "No threat to them, Ethan. On my oath."

Graves relaxed.

"All I mean is . . . responsibility changes us," said James. "Look at me!" He grinned.

"Some things will never change about you, Jimmy the Hand," said the former basher, returning the grin. "What are you going to do with Walter and the others?"

"Nothing," said James. "I'll drop by their hiding place in the sewers tomorrow and tell them it's safe to come out. They'll think they're working for me, but I know those two like a dog knows ticks. They'd sell me out if they thought they could get a coin or two for doing it." James looked thoughtful. "Besides, I think the Upright Man is about to make an unexpected reappearance and those who will be back in the bosom of the Mockers before Mother's is rebuilt. No, it's men like you I'm going to need, Ethan, and that's going to take a while, for men like you are scarce."

"Thanks again," said Ethan, extending his hand. "It's rare to get a second chance in this life; a third is a miracle."

"Well, maybe Ishap had different plans for you than you'd thought."

Graves nodded. "Evidently."

"When you get to Durbin, start a nice little inn somewhere, perhaps close to the garrison and the governor's palace. The sort of place off-duty soldiers and minor government functionaries drink. Keep your prices reasonable and listen to *everything*."

Graves said, "I'll see what I can do."

"Get aboard, then," said James. "I have some business to finish today."

He watched as Ethan climbed the gangplank, then as Amos ordered the gangplank pulled in and lines cast off. The crew jumped to carry out his orders, as the harbor pilot in the bow called down instructions to the longboat crew to pull *The Royal Leopard* away from the quayside.

James took one last look at his old friend Ethan, then turned away and started back along the royal dock. He had long-term ambitions, and some day he would have agents within the palace of Great Kesh's Empress, but for the moment he was ecstatic that he had won Graves's cooperation in establishing a ring of agents in Durbin. It would be the first test of his model. Graves would have Limm contact the two men Amos had identified, who would then be the conduit for messages traveling via Kingdom ships calling at Port Durbin.

As he left the docks, James saw Jonathan Means waiting for him. The young constable nodded in greeting.

"Did you find him?" asked James.

"Yes, squire. He's got that little shop at the end of the jetty, the sign of an anchor and two crossed oars. He's a chandler."

"Did you talk to him?"

"No," said Jonathan. "I watched from a distance to make sure the shop was open, then came here."

"Good," said James. "Get back to your regular duties. And make sure you thank your father for finding out that this man was back in the city."

Jonathan left and James considered what to do next. Lacking a better choice, he picked the bold one and made his way to the shop Jonathan had described.

As he reached the shop with the sign of the ship's anchor over two crossed oars, James's mind raced as he debated what to say. He hesitated for a moment, then opened the wooden door, causing a tiny bell to ring.

A man of middle years, but with gray hair bordering on white, turned as James entered. He was heavy-set, but not fat. His brow furrowed a little and he said, "I'm about to close, young sir. Can your business wait until morning?"

James said, "Is your name Donald?"

The man nodded, and he leaned upon the counter. Behind him sat items common to any chandler's shop in the Kingdom: barrels of nails, tools, coils of rope, anchors, and other fittings.

"I'm Squire James, of the Prince's court," he said, pausing to see if there was any reaction.

The man displayed none. Finally he said, "I know the royal purchaser, lad. Now, if he didn't send you, tell me why you're here so I can go home and get off my feet."

James smiled. The man wasn't remotely daunted by his mention of the Prince, as James had suspected he wouldn't be. "Actually, my business is more in the area of law enforcement, these days."

Again, no reaction.

"Your name turned up on a list recently."

There was a slight whitening of the man's knuckles upon the counter, but otherwise he was immobile and his expression remained unchanged. "What list?" he asked evenly, his light blue eyes fixed upon James.

"A list of people murdered in the city recently."

"The killings? I heard of them. Well, as you can see, I'm not dead. I don't know how my name got on such a list."

"Where have you been these last five weeks?" asked James.

The man forced a smile. "Visiting family up the coast. I left word with several people. I'm surprised no one told the constables I was away for a month."

"I'm surprised, too," said James. "Perhaps you could tell me who you told?"

The man shrugged. "A couple of lads at the local tavern. I mentioned it to several ships' purchasers. And I told Mark the sailmaker next door the night before I left."

James nodded. He was certain the sailmaker had been told at the last minute, and that the other men he claimed he had also told would turn out to be difficult to name. "Well, then," said the squire, "when you turned up missing among all the murders going on, it was not unreasonable to make the assumption that you were among the dead."

"I suppose so," said the chandler. "Have you stopped the killings?"

James said, "For the most part. There's still some bloody work down in the sewers, thieves and the like, you know how that goes."

"Not a place for honest men," said Donald. "But what about above ground?"

"Things are as they were," said James, "before the murders, more or less."

The man said, "That's good to know. Now, if you have no more questions, squire, I must get home."

James nodded. He said, "We'll talk again, I'm sure."

The man followed James to the door, and as it closed James turned to catch a final glimpse of the man's face. James considered. He was almost certain he had just spoken to the Upright Man.

The Mockers would return, and there would be a continuation of the struggle with the Crawler and his men, but with the Nighthawks deeply wounded, the mayhem in Krondor would subside for a while.

James walked away. One thing Arutha had taught him: from chaos comes opportunity, and while the Upright Man was rebuilding his criminal empire, James stood a good chance of getting an agent or two into the Mockers. With what he knew of the structure of the Guild of Thieves, he was certain he could coach the proper candidate to pass scrutiny. The problem was finding the proper candidate.

But that was a worry for another time, thought the former thief. He had many things to occupy him right now, and Arutha had requested that he return to the palace after seeing Ethan and the others on their way.

There was, for example, the matter of ferreting out information about the Crawler. James was becoming certain the Crawler was not in Krondor, but rather was operating his ring from some other location, perhaps in Queg or Kesh, maybe the Free Cities. He put Kesh at the top of his list, as there seemed to be an inordinately high number of Keshians working for the Crawler.

There was also the problem of untangling the many strands that seemed to bind the Crawler and the Nighthawks. James had come to concur with Arutha's opinion that the Nighthawks had an agenda all their own. The gathering in the desert certainly looked more like a small army than a tiny band of skilled killers.

And the magic. Who was behind that? James wondered.

He reached the palace dock and was saluted by two guards as he passed back through the gate. So many mysteries and other problems. But, he thought, he was alive, young, and still had his wits. It might take years, but eventually he would come to understand who stood behind all the trials visited upon the Kingdom.

The creature had once been a living man, a magician of significant power. It sat now upon a throne of carved stone, deep in a labyrinth of caves. The pounding of surf in the distance could be felt more than heard, for the secret temple rested near the sea, deep below the water level. The cave's rocks constantly sweated moisture, and the air was always damp.

Before the throne rested a huge carved hand, fashioned from rock, which held a giant black pear. Also before the throne stood a magician, dressed as a common man of trade. The creature on the throne turned to face the magician. The hawk-nosed man felt no fear being in the presence of the undead sorcerer—a "liche", *man-like thing*, in the old tongue. The liche's servants were equally malevolent, the animated skeletons of his Death Guards. The magician had no fear of the guards, either.

"You failed," said the liche to the magician. Its voice was as dry as the cave was wet.

Sidi turned, and waved his finger. "No, the Nighthawks failed. We always succeed. People died, the Prince in Krondor searches under every rock for who is responsible, and vainly looks for patterns where none exist."

"But is there enough disruption?"

The slender magician shrugged. "Is there ever enough? Be-

371

sides, too much and the Ishapians might change their plans. As it's taken me twenty years to get to this point, I'd rather not have things change unexpectedly and have to wait another ten or twenty years to try again. The gods may have lifetimes to wait, but we do not."

The creature on the throne laughed, a scratchy, parched sound. The skin on its face was stretched tightly across its skull, and its wrists were no more than bones with tatters of skin hanging from them as it pointed at the magician. "You may not have lifetimes, but I do."

Sidi leaned forward and said, "Be not overly proud of your petty necromancy, Savan. It didn't keep your brother alive when Arutha's pet spy tossed him to the demon."

"I thought giving Neman oversight of the Nighthawks would keep him focused. He was not ready to attempt the summoning. He was mad."

"You all go a little mad when you come back from the dead; it can't be avoided, it seems," said Sidi. "That's why I kept you locked up here for a few years when you returned from the grave, remember?" He waved his hand in an expansive gesture. "Madness has its uses," he said with a nod of his head. "In fact, at times it's extremely useful." He turned with eyes wide and the liche chuckled. "What?" asked Sidi.

"You're as mad as I," said the undead magician.

Sidi laughed. "Perhaps, but I don't care." He cocked his head to one side as if listening. "He's here."

"Who?" asked the liche.

"One who will gain for us what we've sought for the last twenty years, Savan. I do not wish him to enter this chamber; he is not ready to see you and your servants, to know to whom he is swearing fealty. When I have given him the gift, and let it work upon him, perhaps then. I shall go now."

As Sidi walked away, the dead magician said, "Bind him to our service!"

"Soon."

Sidi walked along the tunnel leading to the passage up to the surface. The pirate they called Bear would be putting ashore in a small boat soon, wending his way through the wrecks submerged off the rocky prominence called Widow's Point. Sidi would meet him on the sand below the secret entrance to the Black Pear Temple. Eventually, thought Sidi, if Bear carried out his mission and showed his usefulness, he would enter the temple, to be sworn finally to Sidi's service.

But until that time, Sidi would let him think he was working on a simple commission, as the Nighthawks had for years before they discovered they were serving more than their petty family and clan loyalties. By the time Bear learned the truth it would be too late.

As he neared the secret entrance, Sidi reached into a deep pocket in his robe and pulled out an amulet. Fashioned from burnished bronze, the heavy chain was curiously darkened, a tarnish that no amount of polish could remove. It showed a face, the icon chosen by those who served the Nameless One, the fox-faced demon who provided their liaison with the demon realm.

So many things to do, and such unreliable minions, thought Sidi as he triggered the release to open the sliding door hidden in the rocks of the cliff. He really should find someone reliable one day. But he conceded to himself that the lack of reliable servants was the price one paid for secrets; of all who served Sidi, none knew his true agenda, or more importantly, who really was the source of the magician's dark power. As the door began to slide, Sidi thought it might be nice someday to have someone to take into his confidence, to confide in, to serve as more than a witless pawn. He pushed aside such thoughts as the door came fully open.

The western wind blew spindrift across his face and he raised his hand to shade his eyes against the setting sun, crimson on the horizon as it sank. A ship lay at anchor off the point, a one-time Quegan war-galley taken in a raid, its outline a dark and brooding shape against the sunset.

The longboat made its way between the upthrust masts of ships that had blundered upon the rocks in foul weather, giving this spur of land its name. Few came to Widow's Point willingly, which made it the perfect place from which to strike at a ship. The pirate who approached was familiar with these waters and had raided from them before.

As the longboat entered the surf and was carried forward by the combers, Sidi looked once more at the relief on the amulet. The ruby eyes of the fox-faced demon had begun to glow. It had taken years for Sidi to fashion the artifact that he was about to give to the pirate, but it would protect Bear from the priests' magic and from physical harm. He would be invulnerable while he wore it. Moreover, it would allow the master to whisper in his dreams, bringing Bear to his service.

Despite the setbacks in the desert and the failure to remove the Upright Man in Krondor, Sidi felt almost triumphant, for soon he would possess the single most powerful artifact on this world, and once he had that in his possession, his work on behalf of the true master would really begin.

As the large pirate climbed out of the boat and walked knee-deep through the brine towards Sidi, the magician basked in the knowledge of ultimate victory.

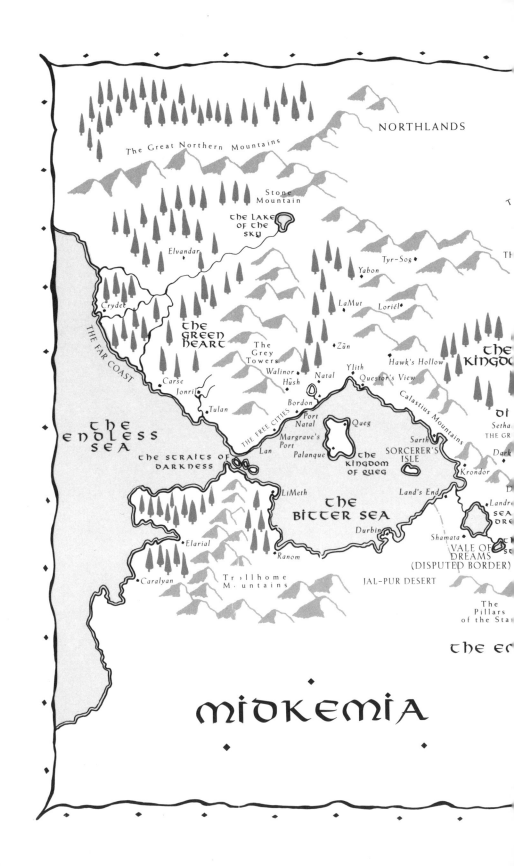